THE GIRL WHO WOULDN'T DIE

JEFF ABUGOV

The Girl Who Wouldn't Die
by Jeff Abugov

J-Stroke Productions
Publication Date: June 2025

Author Website: www.jeffabugov.com

J-Stroke Productions
Los Angeles, California

ISBN: 978-0-9985784-3-9 (EBOOK)
ISBN: 978-0-9985784-4-6 (PRINT)

CONTENTS

PART 1

HER FIRST

CHAPTER ONE

Long Island, New York
November 2016

L IKE SO MANY EPIC TALES, hers began with a death.

It was a beautiful day for a funeral, which was kind of weird. Funerals are almost always gray and rainy and cold—it's a statistical anomaly that it works out that way, but anyone who's been to a few knows it to be true. Yet on this particular day, the soft warmth that shone from the golden sun above, the cool breeze that tempered its heat, and the plush green grass and the luscious trees with their multicolored leaves that enveloped the Locust Valley Cemetery prevented the hundreds in attendance from grieving over Al's death, leaving them to only celebrate his life.

A World War II hero, then a distinguished Toledo, Ohio police detective, Alan Herbert Lang took early retirement from the force at the age of forty-four to study finance at New York University in New York City, New York. With his lovely wife and three of their four children in tow, he took one giant financial step backward in order to soar so many millions of dollars forward.

Al's remaining children, all in their sixties, had stood by their

3

father's side as he battled the pancreatic cancer that destroyed him. They watched as he endured the excruciating pain far longer than most mere mortals ever could or would. It was a testament to the great man's inner strength, and yet they each had secretly hoped that he would give up the ghost to at last be at peace. They would miss him terribly, but they took solace in the fact that he was in a better place.

It was their mother who they now worried about.

Millie Lang was a kind, witty, often funny-as-heck, stubborn ole biddy. She had been a strict mom when they were children—always making sure their homework was done, their teeth brushed, and their TV limited—yet a genuine champion of their choices once adults, always fighting for their right to make any life decision they believed best for themselves, regardless of what she or Al had thought. She had spent almost every waking moment by Al's bed as he fought the fight he'd never win, watching her once big man wither away to nothing, distracting him from his pain with stories of their grandchildren or moments of their life together. She cried only when alone, and offered comfort to all others who shared her soul-crushing sadness.

But her memory was slipping, her kids knew. Her grasp on her surroundings went in and out. She wasn't able to get around like she had only a few years prior, even with her walker. The kids had hired round-the-clock nurses for Al during his final months, paying them a little extra on the side to keep an eye on Mom, and the reports were never good. She'd often forget to turn off the stovetop after making herself a cup of tea, or leave the front door wide open after spending an evening by herself sitting and musing on the rocking chair on the front porch.

It was obvious to everyone who knew her that she should no longer live alone, especially in a house as large as the Lang's, but she refused. "Strangers living in my home, muffing up my affairs, stealing my cutlery? No way, José." And the ninety-three-year-old lady wouldn't even entertain the idea of assisted living. "Sit around and wait to die? Just when I get to be a hot-to-trot single broad again?"

It had fallen on Michael, the middle of the three remaining Lang kids, to re-broach the topic with her, a task to which he wasn't looking forward. As the casket was lowered into the ground, he studied his mom from a distance. The little woman's shoulder-length gray hair was pulled back in a bun. Her conservative black dress was collared to the top of her neck and dropped down to just below her knees, purposely revealing that ugly old three-inch scar on the back of her right calve. No one ever understood why she so refused to cover it up. Michael, his siblings, and even Al sometimes, would try their best to convince her to, but she'd never listen.

"It's a part of me," she'd answer. "It's who I am. And I'm not going to hide who I am just because the likes of you think it's a tad unseemly."

As the casket hit bottom, Michael couldn't help notice that his mother seemed lost, as if she wasn't completely sure where she was or what was going on—she even flashed a smile at one point. At the gathering at his kid sister Caroline's house that followed, Millie was genteel and gracious, welcoming the handful of Al's old retired cop buddies with big warm hugs, thanking them for traveling all that way, and telling them how happy Al will be to see them after all this time.

No, Michael was not looking forward to the conversation at all.

* * *

Long Island's Gold Coast boasted some of the grandest homes in all America, and the Lang estate was, although by far not the largest, one of the most admired. The couple purchased the barren two-acre spread in 1982, shortly after Al was promoted to managing director of global bond trading at Salomon Brothers, whereupon the ex-cop hired the best architects he could find, personally scouring over every detail of construction, firing one architect or builder after another in order to get it perfect.

It had gravitas and style, yet remained utilitarian in nature, true to Al and Millie's humble beginnings. It had an exquisite master bedroom, nice-sized rooms for the kids and grandkids, a den for Al, a sewing room for Millie, and a two-bedroom guesthouse off into the woods. The downstairs was an elegant mix of modern technology and downhome charm with its handcrafted wicker furniture atop Persian rugs atop hickory wood floors, an oak bookshelf lining an entire wall, and a seventy-five-inch LCD television. There were rocking chairs and a swing set on the front porch to offset the grandeur of the opulent entranceway, and they had kept much of the original forest and swimming ponds intact to maintain that country feel, as well as for a serene setting in which to picnic and play with their grandchildren.

Michael's black Mercedes-Maybach cruised slowly along the majestic circular driveway toward the front of the small mansion, while Millie admonished him for driving too fast. He had tried several times during the ride to diplomatically broach the conversation that neither of them wanted, but Millie had consistently succeeded in finding ways to avoid it—talking about what a lovely service it had been or giggling at the awkwardness between Al's retired banker friends and his retired cop buddies. He pulled the car to a gentle stop by the front door and tried once more. "Mom, there's something I'd like to talk to you about."

Millie paused for a moment, then proceeded to open the passenger door as if oblivious to what he had just said—but the door was on auto-lock so the handle did nothing. "Your door's broken," she told him.

"It's not broken, Mom. It's locked."

She tried again to the same result. "You should have someone look at it."

Michael sighed, flipped the switch, and Millie opened her door.

"It's okay now, I fixed it," she told him.

He didn't know if he wanted to laugh or scream.

He got her walker out of the trunk and helped her into the house as he realized that gentle diplomacy would never work on his mother, not on this topic. He would just have to be blunt and firm and let the chips fall where they may.

"Mom, Chantal and I have been talking," he began.

6

"Would you like a martini?" she interrupted. "I'll make us a pitcher."

"No, Mom, thank you. Now listen. The kids are on their own now and doing fine. Why not come live with Chantal and me? You can have Allegra's old room."

"Live with you two? You're old fogies. You should go into assisted living."

"Mom, I'm serious," he said as he took her hands. "Everyone's worried about you. We have to talk about this."

She paused for a moment, sighed. "I know," she conceded. "But not today. It's been a long day today. Truthfully, I just want to be by myself for a little while, enjoy my martini, take a bath, a nap. Please?"

"Okay," he conceded back. What else could he say? "But tomorrow then."

"Yes, tomorrow."

"Promise?"

"Yes. I absolutely promise to disagree with you tomorrow."

He couldn't help but laugh. "Do you need a hand getting up the stairs?"

"No, the escalator-chair's working fine again. I fixed it."

"I'm sure you did, Mom," he smiled. "I love you."

"I love you too, Mikey," she said as she kissed his cheek. "Now, scat."

She patiently watched him off through the large stained-glass window as she leaned on her walker. Only once he and his fancy automobile were completely out of sight did she pull down the chenille drapes.

Time to get to it.

She dragged the walker behind her as she made her way to the grand oak staircase with a lively bounce to her step. She flipped the switch on the escalator-chair to send it chugging upward, then took the stairs two at a time to the second floor where another walker awaited, dragged that one toward the master bedroom, then into the bathroom. She turned on the shower's hot water and got undressed.

Other than her face, hands, calves, and shins, there wasn't a single wrinkle on her.

She buried her face in the shower's wet heat in the hope that it would wash away her grief, but it didn't—only time would, she knew, and she'd have plenty of that. The gray dye dripped down from her hair and along her youthful body, yet it took soap and a brillo pad to scrub out the liver spots on her hands and the varicose veins on her calves. She peeled away the latex wrinkles on her face and legs, then let the soothing warmth bash against her sultry back for several minutes more while she wept for the loss of her true love.

The ninety-three-year-old woman stepped out of the shower, then towel dried her lush, soft blond hair as she stared at her reflection in the mirror—the epitome of a drop-dead gorgeous girl in her mid-to-late-twenties. She sighed nervously, and then forced a phony smile.

"Well," she told her reflection with a trace of dread, "it's show time."

CHAPTER TWO

I T WAS A NICE LITTLE home surrounded by so many other nice little homes in the Perrysburg district of Toledo, Ohio—home to cops and firemen and plumbers and grocers and carpenters and all the other many occupations that made up the American middle-class at the time, even though none of them thought of themselves as being in any economic class at all. It just wasn't how they thought about things.

Millie and her new friend Clara Mueller were putting the final touches on supper—a swell pot roast, creamy mashed potatoes, and succulent roasted green beans—while their husbands sat in the dining area waiting to be served, drinking beers and laughing, Clara's husband laughing far more loudly than Millie's.

Clara was somewhat of a frumpy woman. Thirty years old, not short but on the short side, not fat but on the pudgy side, having yet to fully shed the pregnancy weight after the birth of her baby son two years earlier. On the other hand, Millie, at forty-two, looked almost identical to how we last left her—a drop-dead gorgeous blond in her mid-to-late-twenties, the only difference being her Doris Day hairdo, the subtle mascara, rouge, and lipstick on her eyes, cheeks, and lips, and the Betty Crocker apron she wore over her conservative, green cotton dress.

Millie did not yet know that she was special, only that she had aged well, that she was lucky. But her feelings of good fortune extended far beyond her beauty—in fact, she barely thought about her looks at all, and then, only when others brought it up, and then, she would blush in modesty or embarrassment. The reason she felt so fortunate in life was because she knew that she had married the most wonderful man in the world, she adored her children, and she felt completely fulfilled by her volunteer work at the church and PTA. If women were considered second-class citizens at this time in history, Millie just didn't see it. She was living her dream.

She had only met Clara for the first time earlier that evening and found her to be a very pleasant woman. It had been wholly unnecessary for Clara to help out in the kitchen, and Millie had told her so, but Clara insisted anyway. Millie liked that.

"I'm glad we did this," Clara said as she tended to the roast. "Christoph talks about Al all the time, so it's nice to finally meet the woman behind the hero."

"Oh, that's sweet, I'm glad we met, too," Millie blushed, seemingly due to the compliment, but the truth was that she hadn't heard of Clara or Christoph till a few days prior, and her inability to fully return the courtesy was uncomfortable for her.

"And who do we have here?" Clara asked, referring to a photograph of four teenagers magnetized to the refrigerator, one of them in military uniform.

"Only my pride and joy," Millie beamed as she launched into her all-time favorite topic. "That's Lori. She just got her driver's license, and she's been quite the little helper. This one's Caroline, my youngest, and you can just tell she's going to be turning a few heads someday."

"Just like her mother."

"Oh hush, that's sweet," Millie blushed, then returned to the photo. "That's Mikey, he's fifteen, and quite the handful. I can't even count how many times I've had to wash his mouth out. But he has his father's spirit, and boys will be boys.

"And this is my oldest. Robby," Millie went on, referring to the strapping young soldier. "Doesn't he look heroic? He enlisted last year, right out of high school, we were so proud." She paused. "Then a month later, my baby was shipped away from me. It's funny. I had never even heard of Vietnam at the time, and I was actually happy when I thought they sent him somewhere quiet. Little did I know, huh?"

"I'm sure he's fine."

"I'm sure he is, too. Yes, he's fine. He's fine."

"Wait. You have a nineteen-year-old?" Clara suddenly blurted with a puzzled look. "You can't have a nineteen-year-old. Unless you had him when you were five."

"I was twenty-three."

"Fat chance. That would make you . . . forty-two?"

"Shhh," Millie whispered with a wink and a smile. "Thirty-nine forever."

"More like twenty-nine."

"Oh stop."

* * *

"BULLETS WERE FLYING EVERYWHERE," Christoph boomed. "Americans firing on Germans. Germans firing on Americans. Everyone firing on everyone!"

The bespectacled, fifty-year-old German was seated at the foot of the small faux-wood dining table across from Al at the head, with Millie and Clara on the sides. He was a small man, short and slender, but his presence was so large and his oratory so powerful that anyone present would have sworn he was six-ten and standing tall.

"Of course, we—my compatriots and I, men of science all—didn't know who exactly was out there, hidden as we were in the under-ground bunker. All we could hope and pray for was that it was the Americans who had come to seize us, and not the Russians. The Third Reich was dying from its last breath, everyone knew it, and we

German men of science would likely be tried as war criminals unless one of the Allied governments thought our knowledge and skills useful for the pending Russian conflict to come. Yet we would all have rather died by an American bullet than live one day under the iron thumb of the Soviet Union.

"Suddenly, the door was kicked open from the outside. There stood Alan, his M1 Garand held in his arms, his uniform grimy and torn, a real-life John Wayne—"

"He actually does look a little like John Wayne!" Clara piped in good-naturedly. "Yeah, he really does! Same height and everything."

"Liebchen, please. Now, where was I? Oh yes . . . there stood Alan, his M1 Garand resting in his arms, his uniform grimy and torn, but the bloodstained eagle on his tattered sleeve told us that our prayers had been answered."

"Oh please," Al muttered to himself.

Millie leaned over, playfully slapped her husband on the thigh, and looked at him with admonishing eyes. "Be nice," said the slap. "I'm enjoying the story," cautioned her eyes.

"'Come with me if you want to live,' he told us," Christoph went on. "We leapt to our feet with relief and joy in our hearts, when a squad of German soldiers burst onto the scene, their guns a'blazing.

"Now you have to understand how difficult to fathom this was for me and my compatriots. These soldiers had spent years as our subordinates, serving us, defending us. They had, to some extent, become our trusted friends. But the German High Command had issued very specific orders to not let any of us scientists fall into enemy hands. If they couldn't prevent us from being taken, they were to kill us themselves. And we Germans, if nothing else, are very good at taking orders.

"But not as good as my paratrooper buddy over here! Alan snapped around like a whippoorwill and opened fire. Three more American troopers burst onto the scene, and the bloodbath roared on. One American dead, one German dead, another American dead, another German dead. Both my compatriots were killed. I took a bullet to my thigh, fell to the ground, and cracked my skull open on the concrete floor. By the end, only Alan remained standing, despite the German bullet he had taken to his chest that had ripped through his lung. But when he realized I was still alive, he flung me over his shoulder nonetheless, and . . . "

Al rolled his eyes, glancing at the two women so captivated by the bullshit.

He had never liked Christoph. Christoph was a talker, and Al was anything but. When they had been recuperating together in that army hospital so long ago, their beds side by side, the period Christoph would come to describe as the "beginning of their deep-rooted friendship," the German just wouldn't shut up.

But, in truth, it wasn't the tall tales that bugged Al so much—many of Al's dearest friends were given to hyperbolic fish stories, especially when it came to the ladies. No, it was the actual mission Christoph was describing that had always left a foul taste in the war hero's mouth. For having parachuted into the enemy side of Normandy on D-Day, having spent countless frozen months on the front lines of Bastogne, watching his buddies, his brothers, die by Nazi bullets, being ordered to save one of them just never sat right.

That said, orders were orders, and if his higher-ups felt it vital to secure men like Christoph, who was he to question it? The army knew what they were doing—Al believed that to his bones. "Mine but to do and die," paraphrasing his favorite poem from high school.

So when the German scientist phoned him out of the blue after all those years saying that he was in town for a medical seminar and would love to catch up, Al knew he couldn't say no. Christoph was a fully naturalized American by then, and had been so since shortly after V-E Day. He was a family man with a young American wife of five years and a new baby son, a respected doctor with a thriving Virginia practice, and West Germany was one of America's closest allies in the war against communism. Refusing to see the man would simply be petty and rude, unpatriotic even. Besides, worst case scenario, maybe Millie would get a kick out of the guy.

She did, and that bugged him too.

There was just something about the man he didn't trust.

" . . . and with me hanging over his shoulder," Christoph went on, having never stopped, "blood dripping from his open chest, my knight-in-grimy-fatigues wheezing from his punctured lung, Alan climbed atop the Tiger tank and held the soldiers within at gunpoint as they crawled out. He carried me inside, stealing the tank right from under the Wehrmacht noses, rode us to the countryside when—"

Al couldn't take it anymore. "Enough!" bellowed the buzzed-cut policeman. "I didn't steal a tank," he told the ladies through a laugh. "There was no tank. I was never shot in the chest. My lungs are, and always have been, fine. This is not how any of it happened."

Christoph laughed back. "It's how it happened when I tell it because I make it more interesting, and you make it less."

"I make it true."

"You think you can tell it better than I, my friend? Be my guest."

"Fine. The war was ending, and we were ordered to round up German scientists before the Russians. My CO told us where to go. We snuck in and found Christoph. We got him to the jeep, and some Germans fired. One of my guys took a bullet to the arm, Christoph and me to the leg. None of his compatriots were killed because Christoph was the only one we found, and we all got away. End of story."

"Good grief, Alan, that was terrible," ribbed the German. "You left out all the bloodshed, the carnage, and all your wondrous feats of derring-do." He turned to Millie and added, "Your husband is a true hero, madam."

"I've always thought so," Millie replied proudly.

"But he can't tell a story worth beans."

"I've always thought so," Millie answered playfully.

"Hey, who's side are you on?" joked Al, and they all laughed together.

"At any rate," Christoph began anew, "when my clinic sent me to Toledo for this seminar, I knew that I had to seek out my old savior. But I never expected such a fine meal, nor such astonishingly beautiful company." Then he turned to his host with a smile, "And I'm not referring to you, Alan."

"Thank you, that's sweet," Millie blushed.

"Can you believe she's more than ten years older than me?" Clara asked, then turned to Millie. "Bet you don't have a single blemish or scar on you."

"Actually, she doesn't scar at all," Al boasted.

"What? I was kidding," Clara responded incredulously, then turned to her doctor-husband. "Is that possible?"

"You know, Alan, I vaguely recall you mentioning something like that when we were in that hospital together, when our deep-rooted friendship began." Then, turning to Millie, Christoph added, "Kudos to you, Liebchen."

"This is becoming very embarrassing," Millie blushed. "Can we please change the subject?"

"Of course. Embarrassing you was the furthest from my intent. What would you prefer to discuss?"

"Well, um, golly, I don't know. Um, what kind of science do you do?"

"These days, I am just an ordinary pediatrician. I love children, and I derive much joy to make them feel better. I'm afraid the so-called 'exciting' experimental work I was made to do during the war soured me on research altogether."

"What were you researching?" Millie innocently asked before remembering which side of the war Christoph had actually been on —how uncomfortable for everyone—and she tried to take it back. "Oh, I'm sorry. That was nosy. Forgive me."

"No, it's quite all right. It was very theoretical, and very new, and most likely rather preposterous. But we were examining, in very concrete scientific terms . . . " He paused, took a sip of wine, and then completed his thought.

"Immortality."

CHAPTER THREE

Long Island, New York
December 2016
1 Month Since Al's Funeral

Despite the sound-proofed, brick walls, Al and Millie had often referred to the space as the "batcave" because of the cutting-edge technology within, and also because of its general creepiness. It was eighteen by eighteen feet, with no windows or visible exit other than the trap door in one of the corners that opened to a freight elevator that went down to the tunnel under the basement that led to the mouth of a small mound near the woods a mile-and-a-half away.

On some of the many tables lay ultra-high resolution teraflop computers, logic analyzers, and signal generators, while others were covered with theatrical makeup, hair dye, and wigs of many colors and styles on disembodied Styrofoam heads. In one corner was a small sink, mirror, and counter, upon which was even more makeup. In another was a dentist's chair and an x-ray machine; another, a horizontal freezer. Wardrobe racks abounded—its outfits ranging from the chic and formal to the downright slutty. The reddish-brown walls were littered with paper maps, bulletin boards, shelves with technical manuals, college textbooks, LSAT practice tests, and sexual seduction non-fictions. Giant flat-screen TVs displayed views of every possible entrance to the Lang's Gold Coast mansion, windows included.

There were two, and only two chairs, both on wheels. They were nice chairs.

Millie sat before one of the teraflops, wearing her old lady bathrobe, hair, and makeup, intensely searching for something. It had been weeks since she first hacked into the appropriate databases —not exactly easy, but a snap compared to the many federal intelligence systems she had hacked in the past. Local was always easier.

It was the last task to be accomplished, and the only task that couldn't be started until after Al was gone. Other than that, all the money was sitting neatly laundered in Swiss and Cayman banks, having been siphoned off so gradually over so many years that no one could ever notice. The dummy corporations were firmly established; the phony California hick town discreetly implanted within the satellites above; passports, social security numbers, and birth certificates acquired; social media history entrenched; and college apps submitted. Just this one last thing to do before it would all be over.

Millie sighed. She had looked at everything there was to look at on this day, meticulously checking out every possible candidate that had been logged in the past twenty-four hours, but the prize simply wasn't there yet.

"That's it for today," she groaned, then turned to the cluttered bulletin board next to her on which was tacked an old black & white Polaroid of her and Al. She was wearing a yellow polka dot bikini, he a loud, baggy, flower-patterned swimsuit, and the caption at the bottom boasted, "Miami Beach 1954." It was the year before Caroline was born. Their three kids were staying with her parents, so she and Al were free and young and without a care in the world for a whole entire week, and the giant smiles on their faces showed it.

"We always knew this part of it could take time, Al," she told the photograph. "We always said it might. But it's so hard without you.

So lonely by myself." She paused, and then added with an ironic smile, "You know, three months more, we would've been married seventy-five years. You couldn't hold out three more months, ya big idiot?" She paused again and allowed herself to well up. "Why did you have to die, Al? Why does everyone have to die but me?" She paused once more, remembering what he had told her so many times over so many decades of her training. "I know, I know. Pull it together, Mill, more to be done. I know."

A "ding" sounded from a speaker next to one of the surveillance monitors. She glanced at the screen to see Michael's posh Mercedes pulling up on the mansion driveway, Caroline with him. "You're twenty minutes early, guys," she said to her children, slightly annoyed. "Most punctually-challenged people go the other way."

She put her index and middle finger to her lips, kissed them, then placed them on Al's image. "I miss you so much, my darling."

She stood up, went to the mirror to check her hair and makeup, and then moved to the only section of wall that didn't have anything in front of it. She pushed on that piece of wall so that it pivoted open, creating two small entranceways on either side. She slipped through and stepped into the shower stall of her bedroom's bathroom, then carefully pivoted the piece of wall behind her closed again.

She grabbed her walker and dragged it behind her toward the staircase, flipped the switch on the escalator-chair to send it chugging downward, then took the stairs down the old-fashioned way. The doorbell rang just as she hit bottom. She latched onto her downstairs walker to head to the front door, but then remembered something. She sprinted into the kitchen, turned the gas stovetop on high, and then raced back to her walker once more just as the doorbell rang a second time.

"I'm coming, I'm coming!" she shouted oldly.

CHAPTER FOUR

Toledo, Ohio
November 1965
4 Months Since Dinner With The Muellers

M ILLIE'S EXTRAORDINARY DAY began ordinarily enough—making breakfast, packing lunches, getting the family on their way. She spent the morning at the high school helping at the blood drive, then back home for laundry and light cleaning.

She entered the boys' room to put away Mikey's fresh clothes. As usual, she was blasted with a flash of worry the moment she saw Robby's sports trophies lining the bookshelves, and the bed that she had last made over a year ago. She prayed every night and every morning that her baby was safe. She truly believed the Lord would take care of him, but she worried still. She couldn't help herself.

But her focus on the one son vanished the moment she found a small envelope of reefer in the underwear drawer of her other.

She knew what marijuana was—Al had done a seminar about it at a PTA meeting last year, showing samples to the parents and teachers, explaining how it was spreading through college campuses like a virus, and even seeping into high schools. She remembered empathizing with the poor kids who fell prey . . . but she never thought for an instant that a child of her own would be among those seduced.

Michael arrived home from basketball practice around five, threw Millie a casual "hi-mom-gonna-get-started-on-homework," and headed upstairs. Millie waited but a moment, and then followed. She entered his room without knocking, held up the envelope, and pointedly asked, "Looking for this?"

Michael's face went pale. He looked to the ground in shame when a new thought occurred to him. "Have you been going through my things?!" he shouted. "That's an invasion of my—"

"Don't even try it, mister," she said firmly. "Sit."

He sat. She remained standing, looking down upon him. "First of all," she began. "You are grounded, young man. So very grounded."

"No kiddin'," he seethed.

She didn't care for his attitude, of course, but she had expected an excuse, an explanation, a lie, something. Yes, the punishment was established, but the mystery lingered on, and all she could think to say next was, "Why?"

"Why what?" he seethed again.

"Why, why this? Since when do you take drugs? This isn't who you are."

"Gee, Mom, it's not 'tay-ay-aking dru-uggs.' I just smoke some MaryJane with my friends now and then, and it was my turn to buy it."

"First of all, 'taking drugs' is exactly what it is, by definition. Secondly, what do you mean 'your friends'? I know all your friends. I'm friends with their mothers."

"You don't know any of my friends."

"Of course I do. The boys on the basketball team."

"I hate those idiots. I always have. And I'm not on the basketball team."

"What? What are you talking about?"

"I . . . " Michael began, wanting to tell her the full truth because he knew it would hurt her, yet simultaneously not wanting to tell her anything because the truth would hurt him, too. There was a long pause as his conflicting adolescent emotions of shame, rage, and confusion bashed together. "I wasn't good enough!" he blurted as his eyes welled up. "I didn't make the team, okay?! I'm not good enough!"

"Of course you are."

"I'm not!" he wept.

"Shhh," she said, sitting down next to him. "Maybe you just had a bad week at tryouts. I'll call Coach Murphy and get you another chance. He loved Robby and—"

"I know he loved Robby! Everyone loves Robby! And Coach Murphy gave me tons of chances. It was embarrassing. Finally, I just told him, 'If I'm not good enough, cut me.' So he cut me."

Millie sighed sympathetically. The puzzle was at last solved. She stroked her child's hair to soothe him. "It's okay, sweetie. It's just a game."

"No, it's not. Not to you. Not to Dad. Not to anyone in this stinkin' family."

"Don't get fresh."

"Look around," he began, bouncing from the tears to the rage and back again. "My bedroom's stuffed with my older brother's trophies. My father's den is replete with even more, and a ton of war medals to boot. You, you were like this champion high school swimmer who could hold her breath for like a billion hours. Even Lori is a team captain—granted, it's girls field hockey, which is stupid, but still. In this family, if you don't excel at a sport, you're nothing," and the tears returned.

"Oh sweetie, that's not true at all," she said softly as he wept on her shoulder, continuing to stroke his hair. "I guess that's why you fell in with this reefer crowd."

"No!" he exploded, jumping up, back to rage. "Don't you get it? They're not 'this reefer crowd.' They're my friends! They're good people, and they're smart. I don't have to pretend to be dumb like with the jock idiots. I have to work to keep up, and I like that. They read poetry. They watch movies from France and Italy. They talk about big, lofty things like the meaning of life, is there a God, politics, war—"

"It's rude to talk about religion and politics. You've been raised to know that."

"No, it's not, Mom. You only think so because the powers that be want you to so you won't see their corruption. They want you ignorant, so you stay ignorant."

"Watch your tongue, young man," she said firmly, standing up to face him.

"It's 1965, Mom. The world's changing, and I want to be part of that groovy change. Because fat chance am I going to stay here and end up some loser policeman, and I'm sure as heck not joining the army like my idiot brother."

Millie slapped him. "Your brother is a hero. And so is your father."

"My father is a hero because he risked his life because our country was attacked. My idiot brother is risking his life to impress his parents. So shame on you for being impressed."

She was about to slap him again when the doorbell rang.

Fudge. Now? she thought. Who on earth could that be?

"I've got to see who that is," she told him. "You stay here. We're not finished."

"I'm finished," he belligerently shot back.

"And I'm not! You do not leave this room, young man. Possibly forever."

She slammed the door behind her and headed down the stairs.

My baby on drugs? she pondered. How could I have missed that? Were there signs? I didn't see any signs. What a bad mother I must be for not having seen the signs.

Little did she know that the tumultuous conversation she just had with her son would not be what was ultimately remembered as the eventful part of her day.

She opened the front door to two very large, intimidating men in black suits and dark glasses.

"Mildred Lang?" asked one before she had a chance to say anything at all. They removed badges from their inside jacket pockets as the first man continued. "Agents Samms and Unger, United States Treasury. Please come with us."

THE GIRL WHO WOULDN'T DIE

"Um, what? Why?"

"It will all be explained to you soon enough. Please."

The men gently took her by her elbows and proceeded to escort her toward a black sedan parked on the curb. Despite her many verbal protests, she put up no actual physical resistance. She had been raised to respect authority, particularly male authority, so she simply let herself be led, protesting all the while.

"Wait," she insisted as she walked. "You should talk to my husband. He's with the Toledo Police."

"Detective Lang will be notified in due time, ma'am."

"Wait, I have to tell my children I'm going out. Wait. You need a warrant. Don't you need a warrant? No, I'm not doing this. Where are you taking me? No."

"Watch your head, ma'am," Agent Samms said dutifully as he helped her into the back seat. He got into the passenger seat, and Agent Unger into the driver's.

"I said no," Millie cried. "You can't do this." She tried to open the doors, but there were no handles. "Please. I don't want to do this. Call my husband. Please?"

And off they drove.

* * *

AL KNEW ALL TOO WELL that a person is not considered legally missing until they've been gone for at least twenty-four hours, but the duty-bound stickler-of-rules didn't care. Such protocols don't apply when it comes to his family. Al's police friends—seasoned detectives and young rookie uniforms alike—also knew the rule, but when the colleague you most admire asks for your help, you show up.

The children were upstairs in their bedrooms, presumably doing their homework—it had always been Millie's job to stay on top of such matters. None of the kids thought anything was odd, for it wasn't unlike Millie to spend an evening helping out at the church or PTA or playing canasta with her girlfriends. On such occasions, Al would pick up a pizza pie on his way home, so as far as the kids knew it was just another pie night with dad. Even Michael figured that Millie's lack of return to his room was just her way of punishing him with the torture of suspense.

The twelve cops sat in the Lang's comfy TV room, several cases of beer on the coffee table. Al stood before them and told them what little he knew. Millie would never leave the house without notifying anyone, he explained, especially with the kids home. He had phoned everyone he could think of—her friends, the church and PTA ladies, even the neighborhood grocer, but to no avail. Michael was the last to see her but had no helpful information to offer. Whoever rang the doorbell was the culprit.

But why? Who would want to kidnap Millie? What financial gain is there in taking a policeman's wife hostage? The notion of it being some bad guy Al once put away come to seek his revenge was discussed, but all law enforcement officials know such things are the fantasies of fiction. When someone is released from prison, either they go straight, which is rare, or they return to their life of crime to make a living.

Another idea postured was that the caller was a friendly with whom Millie walked to the curb to get the mail only to be hit by a car, whereupon the friendly took her to the hospital—but no, there would have been signs, blood, skid marks, and the friendly would've certainly told of what had happened. So, no.

Even the notion of Millie being abducted by some sexual deviant was awkwardly suggested. "I'm sorry to have to be the one to say it, buddy," apologized Al's partner and oldest friend Morty, a Jew but a good man nonetheless. "But we live in sick times, and your wife is a beautiful woman."

"I considered that," Al replied. "But if a man she didn't know grabbed her, she would have screamed, and the kids would have heard her from upstairs. If she did know him, thought it was nothing and went with him voluntarily, she would have told the kids she was going out. No matter how you look at it, it doesn't add up."

One unlikely theory after another was bandied about and then tossed aside—but when there is nothing plausible to pursue, the improbable must be explored.

Al assigned two of the detectives the task of checking all the hospitals; two were charged with scouring the records of recently released inmates; Al took it upon himself to canvas the neighbors; then he gave a list of places Millie frequented to the on-duty uniforms so they could patrol the areas in their black & whites.

"Don't worry, ole friend, we'll find her," encouraged Morty.

Al nodded his agreement, and then turned to the others. "Gentlemen. I thank you for your assistance, God bless you all. Now let's get to it. Help yourself to some cold ones for the road. If you'll excuse me, I've got to go tell the kids what's going on."

"Um, I'd hold off on that if I were you, big guy," said fellow detective Bill.

"Why?"

"Maybe it's not as dire as we think. Maybe she'll come waltzing through that door with some goofy explanation we'll laugh about. Why worry the kids if it's nothing? For now, just tell them she's spending the night at Grandma's or a sick aunt."

"I raise my children not to lie," Al explained. "And so I must first teach by example." Then he headed upstairs wondering. Who would want to harm Millie?

* * *

FROM THE OUTSIDE, the building seemed to have no importance at all —just a long, rectangular structure surrounded by a nearly empty parking lot surrounded by trees by a single dirt road—an old abandoned something of no use to anyone.

Inside, Millie awoke groggily, and it took her a moment to get her bearings. She wore a hospital gown, which meant someone had changed her clothes while asleep, which added a whole spoonful of creepiness to her terror. She was in some kind of hospital bedroom, albeit larger than typical. Around her was fancy medical equipment the likes of which she'd never seen; her beloved American flag and a framed portrait of her President; two sinks by the wall; and desks on which lay the kind of computer consoles NASA used, which she had once seen on the TV news.

She could remember being driven to a small airport despite her protests, trying to flee the moment she was out of the car, snatched before she got but a few steps, knocked in the back of the head, and then she remembered nothing at all.

She noticed the wood door across the room. A handsome Hispanic man in his late twenties and sporting a big burly mustache was watching her through the small square window. She raced to the door, tried to open it, but it was locked. "Help me?"

The man looked at her with sad brown eyes, clearly empathizing with her plight, but giving no indication she would receive anything more than his empathy.

"Please?!" she wailed, frantically pulling the door toward her and away, as if fear alone could magically fix her predicament. "Help me! Please!"

The man exhaled a genuine sigh of compassion, then moved off. She pressed her face to the glass to get a better look. He was of average height, wore white, and tended the floor with bucket and mop. The door swung open, and she stepped back.

Agents Unger and Samms entered, followed by three nurses pushing carts with scary-looking medical thingies on them, followed by two men in lab coats—one young and gangly with buck teeth, the other whom she already knew.

"So nice to see you again, Liebchen," said Christoph.

"You?"

"I must apologize, for I may have spoken a few untruths at our dinner. No clinic sent me to Toledo for a seminar. You were the reason I went to Ohio."

"We need you to lie down now, dear," the elderly nurse softly told her, gently taking her by the arm to lead her to the bed.

"No!" Millie shouted as she flung her arm away from the nurse's hand. "Not until I have answers! Christoph, I want to talk to Al, and I want to talk to him now!"

Christoph sighed sadly, then nodded to Agent Unger.

"We need you to lie down, ma'am," Agent Unger said in that horrifyingly calm tone as he led her to the bed, moved her into a lying position, and held her in place as the nurses clanged iron manacles around her wrists, ankles, forehead, and throat, and thick leather straps tightly over her thighs and torso.

"Please, Christoph," she cried. "I want to go home."

The buck-toothed young man next to Christoph pointedly cleared his throat.

"Of course," Christoph said in reply, then turned back to Millie. "Liebchen, I'd like to introduce you to my colleague, Dr. Woodrow Szabo."

"Woody," corrected the scrawny young man as he smiled at Millie. "Ma'am."

"We consider ourselves quite fortunate to have snatched young Woodrow for our team three years ago. At only twenty years old, he had graduated from MIT with a PhD in biology as well as a master's degree in the burgeoning field of genetics."

"Wouldn't have missed this for the world, Doc," Woody said with a slight drawl. "These are exciting times, Miz'iz L. A real privilege to be working with you."

During this exchange, the elderly nurse wrapped a band around Millie's arm to take her blood pressure. The pock-faced nurse opened Millie's gown to tape electrodes to her arms, legs, tummy, and exposed breasts. The Negro nurse flashed photographs of every part of her body, blinding Millie's eyes with each POP, POP, POP.

"Christoph, please?" she begged. "What is going on?"

"Since the dawn of man," the German began as he moved to the sink to wash his hands, "as Dr. Mengele's thesis goes, there have lived amongst us the unsterblich. The immortals. I suppose 'un-aging' is a more precise term, for we don't know if one can die from injury, but 'un-aging' lacks the romance of 'immortal', or 'unsterblich!'"

"Unsterblich!" Woody repeated in awe, also washing his hands.

"The concept is not new," Christoph went on. "Most every ancient culture has some myth or other about some un-aging creature lurking in the shadows, but all rooted in magic and superstition. Herr Dr. Mengele taught us how to apply science.

"Our problem was finding a subject on which to test his theories. It's not as if the unsterblich advertise—and anyone who's lived as long as they would know how to blend in, falsify documents, create new identities. The key was to find them before they learned such tricks, perhaps before they even learned who they were."

He took a towel from the rack to dry his hands. Woody followed suit.

"We thought we had found such a man. An impoverished Slav farmer, if you can imagine. All early experiments seemed to confirm our hopes, but absolute proof requires the test of time. How strong would his heart pump thirty years hence? How well would his liver function in forty? My immediate supervisor, a man of much knowledge yet little sense, sought a quick resolution. Despite my pleas, he cut deep into the Slavic man's brain. The man died, of course, leaving us all to wonder if an unsterblich can indeed perish, or whether the Slav was unsterblich at all.

"No one ever heard from my supervisor again—your typical Nazi response to gross incompetence—and Dr. Mengele honored yours truly as his replacement."

"What's any of that got to do with me?" Millie pleaded.

The activity in the room stopped. The two scientists looked at each other dumbfounded, then Christoph turned back to Millie. "You truly don't know?"

"Know what?"

"We're pretty sure you're one of them, Miz'iz L," Woody answered with a smile, proud for her. "We're pretty sure you're unsterblich."

"That's crazy!"

"That's what we're here to find out, Liebchen," Christoph said as he sat on the stool beside her, Woody following suit on the other side of the bed. "You see, when Alan was ordered to find me, it had nothing to do with you—that was just one of life's many zany coincidences. No, the reason was that the Americans were well aware of Dr. Mengele's findings and wanted his compelling project for their own. Given that he had already fled, I, as his number two, was the next best thing.

"So when Alan mentioned in that army hospital so many years ago that you didn't scar, I was intrigued. Oh, that was my other untruth. I never soured on my research. Also, my pediatric practice is just for a cover, two mornings a week.

"At any rate, at that time—well, it took us some years to establish the program, so say by 1948—you were a woman in her twenties who appeared to be in her twenties. Nothing remarkable about that, and we had other test subjects to study—all of whom turned out to be terrible disappointments."

"I saw the data. Even worked on a few," added Woody. "They really were."

"So seventeen years hence," Christoph continued as he held out his hands for the Negro nurse to place surgical gloves upon them, "we return to the woman who allegedly doesn't scar to find not a line upon her face, not an ounce of new fat, not a single variance to her breasts or derriere—a forty-two-year-old woman identical in every way to her twenty-five-year-old self. A fine specimen indeed."

"What—what are you going to do to me?" Millie trembled.

"Nothing too terrible. We need to excise a small sample of certain vital organs for future reference—the deterioration of organs being a far greater indicator of aging than that of skin alteration or fat cell displacement. We'll begin with your large intestine today—just a small piece, nothing you'll miss."

"Plus, we get to see about this scar business," added Woody.

"Indeed," said the German as the pock-faced nurse swabbed alcohol over Millie's tummy. "Human skin is designed to self-heal. Any child who ever scraped a knee from a bicycle fall knows this. But sometimes the cut is too deep, and a remnant of the injury sustains. But perhaps not in your case, which is our hope."

"So if I scar you'll let me go?" Millie asked through her tears.

"I'm afraid not, Liebchen. All known science points to the fact that you should scar, therefore, if you do, it doesn't prove anything."

"But if you don't," Woody added optimistically, "it proves a ton."

"Christoph, please," she wept. "You're Al's friend! I'm his wife! He saved your life! You owe him! We had you to dinner in our home! Please, let me go home!"

"You're looking at this all wrong, Miz'iz L," Woody said warmly as he took her hand, all friendly-like. "Think about the contribution you'll be making to mankind. If you are who we think you are, and we can figure out the why's and the how's of it, disease and decay will be a thing of the past. You'll be a gosh-darn hero."

Christoph gazed softly into Millie's eyes as the elderly nurse slapped a scalpel into his waiting palm. "Now, I'll be cutting deep into your abdomen. I'm sorry we can't apply anesthesia, for your response to pain is something we must monitor as well. But I assure you that at no point will your life be at risk. I promise. Ready?"

"Please? Don't! Please!"

The pock-faced nurse held Millie's skin tight as Christoph made the incision. There was a barely audible squish as the blade tore through skin and tissue, as her blood gushed, as samples of the organ were removed and placed in test tubes, as the squiggles on the monitors to which she was connected skyrocketed, as the machines beeped and bopped and blurped, and she screamed.

And she screamed.

And she screamed.

CHAPTER FIVE

Long Island, New York
December 2016
15 Minutes Since Michael And Caroline Arrived

"You're going to make me a prisoner?" Millie asked her children in shock.

They were sitting in the formal living room, drinking tea. Millie could tell the moment they arrived that something big was up, but she never expected this. This could muck up the entire plan—although, as she thought about it, she and Al should have seen it coming. Of course the kids would do this. She had overplayed her hand.

Got to stop making mistakes, Millie, she told herself.

Michael and Caroline were taken aback by the word "prisoner." The last thing they wanted was to make their mother drudge up those awful memories of her past.

"You're not going to be a prisoner, Mom," Caroline said sympathetically.

"Isn't that what 'filing for power of attorney' means? That I'll no longer be allowed to make my own choices? How could you do this to your own mother?"

"How could we not?" Michael answered sadly. "Dad's been gone for weeks, and you can't live alone anymore. Swear to God, we didn't want to do it this way. We tried to talk to you about it, but you change the subject, you stall, you obfuscate—"

"Ooh, good word, Mikey. You were always very good at vocabulary."

"Be that as it may, you need someone with you, round the clock," he went on. "Different ladies on different shifts, including overnight. And we need to get started."

"I'm fine," Millie insisted.

"But you're not fine, Mom," said Caroline. "Your stove's been burning on high since Lord knows when. If we hadn't shown, who knows what could've happened?"

"That wasn't me. It turns itself on by itself sometimes. It's broken."

The kids looked at her blankly. She knew she was beat, and she needed a new strategy. "All three of you are in cahoots on this, I suppose?" They nodded. She sniffled. "Will I still be allowed to have my martinis?" she wept. "Your father and I used to have one every afternoon and watch the sunset together. I miss him so."

"Of course, Mom," Michael replied. "Would you like me to make you one?"

"I'll do it!" she snapped. "There are still some things I can do!" She made her way to the wet bar to fix her beverage. "Sometimes we'd have two," she added with a girlish giggle. "Sometimes three. Rarely four, but, you know, after three you kind of lose count." She returned to the couch, balancing her glass over her walker, spilling a third of the gin on the Persian rug—a sad sight not unfamiliar to her children. "All right, fine. But you don't have to put me in front of a judge like I'm some Perry Mason character. You win. You've beaten Mommy into a pulp. I hope you're proud."

"Yeah?" smiled Caroline.

"That's great, Mom," smiled Michael. "That's all we wanted to hear. I already have a list of possibles. I'll get on the phone first thing in the morning."

"But I have to like them. That's the deal. I have to like them."

"Absolutely," said Michael, grasping on to whatever little victory he could get. "You'll have full approval of whoever we hire."

Millie stayed in character, playing up the sadness of her defeat while keeping her giant smile hidden inside. She bought the breathing room she needed. All she had to do now was not like any of the caregivers she was made to interview.

It wasn't a permanent solution, she knew. She just had to get lucky, and fast.

CHAPTER SIX

MILLIE'S DAYS WERE ALMOST always the same. Seven days a week, Christoph would personally bring her morning meal. He'd examine, clean, and photograph her post-surgical wounds, and gloat over the loveliness of her recovery. He was always pleasant and jovial, reminding her how grateful they all were for her participation in the project and how she may go down in history as the savior of the world if her positive results continued—all while seemingly too distracted to hear her pleas for mercy. He'd offer to bring her books or magazines to help her pass her alone time at night. He'd talk openly about his childhood in Hamburg, his education, his work under Josef Mengele, whom he adored, all while craftily avoiding any questions regarding Al or her children. The most she ever got from him on the topic was, "Don't worry about them. They're doing fine. You just focus on your work here."

She knew Al was out there searching for her and he'd never give up, but she had come to wonder if he was simply outmatched. One small-city cop against the awesome power of the United States government? Not exactly a fair fight.

After breakfast, she would be poked and prodded ad infinitum, mostly under Woody's cheerful supervision. Her body was photographed outside and in. Eyes, ears, and throat were examined regularly, reflexes tested, blood and urine extracted, swabs from vagina and rear end seized. A forty-minute lunch break would be followed by further violations, along with x-rays and EKG examinations.

Initially, she tried to resist in any way she could—forcibly pushing the nurses away, flipping carts upside down, throwing gadgets and surgical tools across the room—but the treasury agents would simply overpower her, shackle her to the bed, and the tests would resume. In short order, her tirades seemed pointless.

Tuesday afternoon was surgery day, the only afternoon in which Christoph would make an appearance. The German would cut her open to excise tissue samples from one organ or the other, merrily whistling Beethoven or Wagner over her tortured screams.

Her only hope to see her family again was to prove she wasn't unsterblich—but she was starting to face the fact that she might be. Her incisions were healing like any other cut she ever had, meaning a scar was unlikely. It had never occurred to her that there was anything magical about her healing—she had always just assumed that none of her injuries were ever serious. But thinking back, she couldn't even remember having had a cold.

With no idea how to achieve her goal, she guessed. She'd lick up dust in the corners of her antiseptic room in the hope it would mess up her urine or stool samples. She'd peel off her scabs, then dig her luscious, long fingernails deep inside in the hope that it would force a scar that would stick, or at least cause an infection—another affliction she realized she had never had.

No one ever accused or chastised her for it, no one even mentioned it, and they all remained as polite and respectful to her as always—but she did notice that the Hispanic janitor with the big burly mustache became significantly more diligent while cleaning her room, especially in the corners.

One morning after breakfast, the elderly nurse told her that she had convinced Dr. Szabo to let her give Millie a manicure, smiling sweetly as if that's what all women want always. She removed a pair of little scissors from her cart, clipped Millie's nails to the nub, then buffed what remained down to below the fingertips—cheerfully chitchatting about skin and hair products like it was a day at the salon.

Millie knew that she had to keep trying, had-to-just-had-to prove she wasn't the unsterblich she probably was—she just didn't know how.

One evening after her supper, Woody entered her room, pushing a small cart, smiling chipper as usual—except it wasn't usual because he never visited her at night; no one did. "How we doing tonight, Miz'iz L?"

"Fine," she answered suspiciously.

"No need to be worrisome, ma'am. Just going to do a little test that'll either be plum pleasant for you, or no effect at all. Me, I reckon no effect, but I could be wrong so we've got to do it nighttime—we don't want to lose a whole day of work, do we?"

"Okay," she replied neutrally. She saw that on the top of the cart was a syringe, a small vial of something, a bowl of cotton balls, a bottle of rubbing alcohol, and a rubber band—she just didn't know what that meant.

Woody sat on the stool next to her and rolled up her sleeve. "It's time to see if you respond to pharmaceuticals. Your records say you've never been prescribed nuthin'—which, as far as our goals go, is a real positive sign." He tied the band around her arm. "So we'll be giving you a little shot of morphine, and see what happens."

"What'll it do to me?"

"Like I said, I reckon nuthin'. Otherwise, it'll be nice. May make you a bit drowsy, but the good drowsy, warm and fuzzy-like, like a teddy bear under a Christmas tree." He swabbed her inner arm with the alcohol, tapped on her vein, and made the injection. "There. We'll know what's what in just a moment or two."

This is good, Millie thought. If the drug doesn't affect her—which she knew was what they wanted—it was definitely something she could fake. She didn't know what a morphine state looked like, but it didn't sound much different than being drunk, and she had, over the years, seen plenty of folks who'd had a little too much.

It occurred to her that she herself had never been drunk, not even a little tipsy, but she tucked that thought away for the moment.

"How we feeling, ma'am?"

"Niiiice," she slurred. "Like a teddy bear in a . . . um, um . . . what was the question?"

Woody smiled. "I'm happy for you, Miz'iz L. I mean, it would've been better for the project if you hadn't responded, but still, it's nice to see you smiling."

"Wha-a-at?"

"You have a pretty smile, is all," he said as he eased her into a lying position. He moved to the EKG machine and untangled the wires, returned to her, opened the top of her hospital gown to attach them, and stopped suddenly.

He had seen her naked body many times before, of course, but there had always been other people around so he had forced himself to look away to appear professional. But he was alone now, and there was nothing preventing him from gawking—and the more he gawked, the more tantalized he grew.

Her tummy was so smooth and flat, her belly button so cute and friendly, her curves so curvy, and her bosoms the most glorious sight of all—round and soft and beckoning. It hadn't been his intention to do what he was imagining, but in the moment, he knew he'd be a fool not to. Those nipples, he had to taste them.

He cupped his hands over her breasts and began to fondle, squeeze, kiss. The genius virgin-boy had never felt anything like it.

"What are you doing?" Millie asked faux-groggily, desperately trying to maintain her drugged charade while stopping him at the same time.

"Nothing," he answered as he tongued circles around her areola. "I'm not even here," he moaned in delight. "The morphine is making you imagine these dirty, dirty things," he whispered as he began to suckle.

"Stop it," she told him.

"I'm not here. No one's here."

"Stop it!"

"Shhh," he hushed as he unzipped his fly. "You're hallucinating. Talking to no one." He pulled up her gown, crept on top of her, and—

She clenched her fist, then punched him in the nose. She had no leverage to add power to the blow, but it was enough to draw a little blood and shock the boy up to a kneeling position. She then raised her leg fast and hard, bashing her knee into his groin. He shouted as he clutched his privates and tipped over to the floor.

In a blind frenzy, she leapt off the bed and upon him, pounding her right fist then her left into his head, over and over, a month of bottled rage, shame, torture, and hatred exploding through her hands. "Kidnapper! Nazi! Torturer! Villain!"

Woody cowardly curled himself into a ball, covered his head with one arm for protection, and slid his free hand into his lab coat pocket to press a small red button attached to his key chain. Within moments, two treasury agents burst into the room and peeled Millie off him, while the boy frantically and discreetly re-zipped.

Unlike every other occasion in which Millie had faced an agent, she did not accept her fate gracefully. "I'm not finished!" she howled crazily as she tried to fight and slither her way out of the G-man's grasp. "Let me at him! Let me go, you ape!"

But she was no match. The agent threw her onto the bed, held her kicking and screaming in place, while the other agent manacled her back into submission.

"Are you all right?" the agent asked Woody.

"Yes, fine, thank you," he said as he pressed a hand towel to his bleeding nose. "She just caught me off guard. My mistake."

"Would you like us to stay?"

"Yes!" Millie shouted. "The little bugger tried to rape me! Stay!"

"I'll be okay," Woody said calmly. "She's securely fastened now. You can go."

"Yes sir," said the one agent, and both left.

Woody waited till the door clicked closed, then turned to Millie with a smile. "Looks like I was right after all, huh? You don't respond to drugs."

"Doesn't matter," she seethed. "Once I tell Christoph what you tried to do, you're done here. You're done everywhere. You're done for good."

"Oh, he won't believe you," the virgin said matter-of-factly, studying his nose in the mirror to see that the bleeding had stopped. "He'll just figure you're trying to pit us against each other, divide and conquer. All the test subjects do that."

He moved back toward her as he peeled a piece of white surgical tape off a roll, and then sealed it over her mouth. "My mama always said that if you don't have nuthin' nice to say you shouldn't say nuthin' at all, and I got a feeling you're going to be hollering some pretty nasty stuff." He opened the top of her gown, slid the bottom up, and placed a towel between her legs to catch any damning evidence. He took a step back to ogle her once more, letting the visuals alone harden him. "I really should be mad at you for beating on me like that, ma'am," he smiled. "But I can't stay angry at you, Miz'iz L. You're just too gosh-darn beautiful." With that, he latched onto her breasts, massaging, kissing, suckling. He pulled down his pants and proceeded to straddle her inner thigh, while the president in the portrait next to the flag watched on.

Millie struggled as best she could, but the manacles had her locked in solid, and the iron only managed to chafe at her ankles, wrists, and throat. It was no use. As far as she could tell, this was to be her life for the rest of her very long life.

NEW YORK MEMORIES, PART I

Long Island, New York
February 2017
5 Weeks Since She Agreed To Caregivers

S HE SPENT THE WEE HOURS of the morning in the batcave searching the local databases, but to no success. She brushed up on her hip-hop, rap, and pop, and posted a bunch of whatevers on her social media platforms to keep them current. After breakfast, she and Caroline interviewed another potential caregiver, Millie hating this one because "she smelled funny." She had hated the Puerto Rican lady because her accent was too thick, the Swede because she had no sense of humor, the Russian because of the Cold War, and on and on. In truth, they all seemed like lovely, kind women who would do a fine job tending to the needs of an old lady.

She was running out of excuses, and her kids out of patience. It was just a matter of time before they filed for power of attorney despite her promise to accept a caregiver. A good lawyer could drag it out in the courts for a few weeks more, but her stellar portrayal of the helpless ole biddy made anything longer quite unlikely.

One way or another, she knew it would all be over soon, and she was feeling nostalgic. She took a taxi to the hospital where two of her grandchildren had been born, another to the hospital that gave life to another, and one more to St. Mary's Church in Hell's Kitchen where Caroline had been married.

After the church, she hobbled south to a dumpy building a few blocks away. She struggled with her walker in case anyone was watching as she made her way up the creaky stairs to the third floor. She knocked on a door, and a fat, bald man answered. She told him that she and her family had lived in that unit when they first arrived in New York, and asked if she could look around. She knew he'd say yes—one thing she'd learned over the years was that nobody says no to feeble old ladies.

The place looked so different, yet so the same. She thought back to their first New York Thanksgiving, and how wonderful it had been. They had had so little back then, scraping by on a cop's partial pension, her part-time work at an off-Broadway theatrical make-up shop, and Lori's contribution from her job at a vintage bookstore. Mikey was thrilled to get to complete high school in the Big Apple, "where the action was," as he put it.

Millie smiled as she remembered how close to a fiasco that day almost was. She and Lori were in the kitchen preparing the holiday feast when they heard urgent pleas emanating from the bathroom.

"Mom? Um, it's happening. What do I do, I forget? Daddy, go away! Mom? Mom!"

It was little Caroline's first period. Millie had had many talks with the girl about the life and birth cycle, but there's a big difference between knowing what's to come and having it actually arrive. Lori didn't feel up to the task of preparing the holiday dinner on her own, but offered to tend to little sister so that Mom could keep cooking. The matter was handled without issue, and all was soon well.

Lori.

Millie knew, like all moms know, that a mother is not supposed to have a favorite, yet Lori had secretly been hers anyway. She couldn't help it—her first girl, her baby girl, her big girl. Both in Toledo and those early days of New York, Lori had been Mommy's little helper, utterly devoted to the family, the rock when Al or Millie couldn't be.

"Mommy Junior" they'd affectionately call her. Even Robby, two years her senior, would go to her for counsel or defer to her in disagreements.

It was little more than a year later when the family huddled nervously around the television set—on that dilapidated old couch in that corner over there—watching the first Vietnam draft lottery, praying their prayers, which were not answered. The first date announced was September 14, the day Mikey was born.

Her baby had been drafted.

Mikey's jaw dropped to his chest. His eyes widened to the size of a golf ball, his face turned ashen white, and Caroline wept. The few seconds that passed before Lori turned off the TV felt like hours, and the silence that followed was deafening.

"You'll be okay," Lori said, her lack of conviction transparent. "It'll be fine."

Mikey couldn't speak, could only nod.

"Sure it will," added Al. "I'll take you out tomorrow, show you some pointers."

"I'll join you," added Robby. "Different war, Dad, different tricks."

Robby had completed his service a year earlier. While Al had come home from his war a proud hero, Robby had returned from his a broken one. He moved into the cramped apartment with his parents and siblings, got a job as a mechanic, from which he was fired, another as a waiter, from which he was fired too. "Chin up, little man," the big brother continued. "You're smart, you write well. Maybe you could get assigned to Stars & Stripes."

"Or something else that'll keep you in the rear with the gear," Al added.

Mikey nodded once again, still ashen faced, still unable to speak.

"I have a better idea," Millie finally weighed in. "Mikey, pack your bags. I'm taking you to Canada."

"What?!" blurted Al, far more a statement than a question.

Millie glared at her husband, shooting fireballs from her eyes into his. There was no chance in Hades that she was going to let anyone force her baby into battle. To heck with the awesome power of the United States government! "You heard me," she told him.

It took Al but a moment to play out the forty-five-minute argument he'd ultimately have with her in private, and saw she was right. "I'll tag along," was his warm reply.

"We should all go," Lori announced in a burst of inspiration. "We'll make it a family vacation, returning home minus one."

"Minus two," Millie corrected, teasingly tussling Mikey's hair. "My boy doesn't know how to take care of himself. His mama spoiled him too good for that."

They all laughed, except Mikey, who just looked up at his mother with tears in his eyes and mouthed, "Thank you." She mouthed back, "You're welcome."

It was the ultimate lemons-to-lemonade, best family trip ever. Al rented a beat-up old station wagon for the family to commit their heinous crime, drove north as they sang old campfire songs and cracked cheesy jokes, crammed into a cheap motel room, and eventually found a small, furnished apartment in the Notre Dame de Grace district of Montreal where Millie would stay with her son until he learned the basics of cooking, cleaning, and balancing a check book, ready to live on his own.

Mikey would thrive in Canada. Before completing high school, he received a scholarship to McGill University to study political science, but soon discovered he had a knack and passion for finance, just like his old man. He met Chantal Lefevre, a lovely, quick-witted French-Canadian girl, and they married in 1972. They gave Millie and Al their first grandchild a few years after that, two more in the years that followed, and moved back to New York in the mid-eighties for Michael to cofound Lang Investments with his father.

It was on that same trip that thirteen-year-old Caroline decided to become fluent in French, which came so easy to her that she picked up Spanish, Italian, and Hebrew after that, leading to her career as a UN translator, leading to her meeting her first husband, Sergio Pinazo, an up-and-coming car designer at Ferrari.

It was the trip where Robby at last began to lighten up, the feeling of family and camaraderie helping to fill the hole inside him that Vietnam had torn open. They were all there for Michael, yes, but really, they were all there for each other, hence there for him too. It's not that he didn't know any of this before, he just hadn't felt it. He was even able to laugh along when Lori teased her jock, stud, big brother about being too picky when it came to girls. After returning to New York, Robby got a job stocking shelves at a local grocery store, and this time it stuck. As the store grew into a supermarket, then a regional chain, Robby grew with it. He'd eventually meet Tim Stein, a pleasant, easygoing young man, a fellow vet, and Robby's partner for life.

Yet even without knowing all that future at the time, for Millie, it was the best week of her life. The joy, the laughter, the love—her family so different as individuals yet so united in the single cause of each other. It had all been perfect.

But God doesn't let good memories go untainted, and He doesn't give anything away for free. On the drive home, just a few miles south of Plattsburg, a drunk in a red Plymouth plowed into the station wagon. Al, Robby, and Caroline sustained injuries from which they recovered. Lori was killed.

Lori, her big girl, her secret favorite—the one who had always tended to the needs of everyone else—was suddenly, tragically, randomly, taken from the world.

As far as Millie was concerned, God was thus forever relegated to the same category as the United States government—both real, both crazy powerful, and both with an agenda of their own that had little regard for the happiness of their constituents.

CHAPTER SEVEN

THE DETECTIVES' FLOOR WAS A flurry of activity, as per usual. Detectives and uniforms, witnesses and lawyers, nosy reporters, and newly released prostitutes moved from hither to yon with speed and purpose, creating an aura of orderly chaos. Bill and Ralph, the sleuths assigned to Millie's case, made their way to the captain's office, Al in hot pursuit. They adored Al, but he was driving them batty. They had reminded him on many occasion that department policy prohibits a cop from being involved in the case of a family member. Each time, Al acknowledged his awareness of the policy, complimented its wisdom, and then ignored it.

"I'm just saying that if you tell me where you're at, maybe I can pitch in. If you're stalled, maybe a pair of fresh eyes can shed new light."

"Al, imagine the situation in reverse," Bill offered sympathetically. "Let's say it was your case, my wife was missing, and I told you what you just told me."

"I know," conceded the husband. "But I'm going nuts. I have to do something."

"We're sorry, man," said Ralph. "Just, just hang in there, buddy."

Al sighed. The two detectives trudged into the captain's office, shutting the door behind them, leaving Al alone to wallow in his frustration and despair.

"What?" barked the captain, consumed with his paperwork and without looking up.

"We need some guidance, Cap," said Bill as he and Ralph took their seats across from him. "The Millie case is turning up a big fat donut hole. Here's what we got so far. A couple of women neighbors say they may have heard some arguing while they were making dinner, but by the time they looked there was nothing to see. We got one woman who says she saw a black sedan pull out around five, but couldn't confirm Millie was in it, couldn't see who was in it, didn't get the plates, and couldn't even say what kind of car beyond 'black sedan.' And other than all that nothing, we got nothing."

"If it was your standard kidnapping," added Ralph, "where's the ransom note? If it's some vengeful con trying to send Al a message, why hasn't he made himself known? If she was taken by force, why didn't she scream? If she did, why didn't anyone hear her? Cap, if this is a kidnapping, why?"

"Sounds like you're looking for more than just guidance, boys."

"No, we got a theory. We're just hoping you talk us down from it."

"I'm ears," said the captain.

"Maybe Millie wasn't kidnapped. Housewives these days, many have trouble coping with the pressure, the boredom, the both at the same time. Some take pills. Some have affairs."

"So . . . what if Millie wasn't taken? What if there's some other man, and she left?"

"Millie?" asked the captain. "Come on."

"Like I said, feel free to talk us down."

"No, it kind of makes sense, objectively speaking," the captain sighed. "Who knows what kind of marriage they really had, what goes on behind closed doors, what goes on in a woman's head. But

Millie?" he repeated, paused, then continued. "How would you proceed?"

"Start off by talking to pretty much the same people we already talked to, but with a whole different kettle of questions."

"Yeah," the captain sadly concurred. "If it turns out to be true, at least Al will get some closure. Till then, we keep him in the dark. Mum's the word. If it turns out to be a wild goose, the poor bastard doesn't need to know we ever considered it."

Both detectives agreed, but what none of the three men realized was that Al had remained by the captain's office the whole time, overhearing their ludicrous theory through the shaded glass window. He sighed, and then returned to his desk.

Think, Al, think! he commanded himself. With the department officially off chasing the impossible, it was now unofficially all on him to figure it out.

That's when he noticed the manila envelope on the top of his inbox, the words "Detective Lang" emblazed with colorful letters cut out from various magazines. He looked around to see who could have possibly put it there, but there was no way to know. He opened it to find a note inside with the same colorful cut letters, and it read simply:

```
Dr. Mueller is not your friend.
Pursue government contacts. Trusted
only.
```

* * *

AL DIDN'T LIKE NOT KNOWING who the note was from, but he was grasping at straws and it was the only straw he had. He left the precinct to make his phone calls from his bedroom at home so as not to be overheard by anyone, not even the kids.

Donny Donaldson had been Al's corporal during the war, his right hand, and the two had shared many a foxhole. Unlike Al, Donny had re-enlisted when the war ended to make the military his career. He had risen to the rank of sergeant major and was currently working at the Pentagon—as good a place to start as any.

Al and Donny began with the obligatory catch-up small talk

about wives, kids and sports—Al purposely keeping it casual in case he was probing too deep. When he finally got down to business, he remained vague as to why he was seeking the information he sought, asking only if Donny knew anything about a German scientist they had once captured named Christoph Mueller. Donny told Al that it was the Defense Department that oversaw such matters, then reminded him of one of their Easy Company comrades who currently worked there.

That trusted brother told Al that NASA was the best place to track down German scientists, recommending Al get in touch with another Easy Company vet, who in turn recommended another in another department, who recommended another, who recommended another. It took five days of calls, each one requiring twenty minutes of mind-numbing chitchat, until it was finally suggested that Al contact Lieutenant Henry "Hank" O'Keefe at Treasury.

Lieutenant O'Keefe had been assigned to Easy Company late in the war. He was a terrible officer, but it wasn't entirely his fault. By that point, all the good officers had been promoted or killed. Replacements were brought in with rushed training, weak on tactics, and terrified of the bullets and bombs exploding around them.

What made Hank better than most bad officers was that he was a good man at heart, a smart man low on ego who truly wanted to do well by his men. As a result, he deferred to his senior staff sergeant whenever possible, and Al rose to the occasion. Together, they got their men through horrific battles, and a special camaraderie between them was forged. Al saved Hank's life on numerous occasions, helped get him decorated, and Hank would often jokingly refer to himself as "Al's inferior superior."

In civilian life, Hank joined the Secret Service, a division of Treasury, to protect presidential candidates and diplomats. Although well liked and clever, he wasn't much better a bodyguard than a field commander. He was ultimately transferred to a desk job, a glorified pencil pusher, handing out assignments to the other agents. Turned out he was quite good at it, had finally found his niche, and he knew everything about everything as a result.

Like all the other vets, Hank was thrilled to hear from his ole

Sarge . . . until Al mentioned Christoph. Suddenly, the former lieu-tenant began to hem and haw. "I didn't realize it was your wife," he whispered more to himself than to Al.

"You didn't realize what was my wife?"

"Nothing. Al, you know I'd do anything for you, you know that. But not this. This is too big. You've got to walk away, old friend."

"Walk away from what?"

"I'm sorry, boyle. I can't help you."

"The hell you can't!" Al shouted. "How often have you said you owe me? This is it, the big payback! Right now! Where would you be if I hadn't stepped up for you?"

"Dead, probably," Hank shamefully replied.

"And?!" There was a long pause. "Please, buddy," Al begged. "She's my wife."

There was another long pause, which this time Hank filled. "Okay, but you didn't hear this from me. If you tell anyone you did, I'll say you're a big fat liar. If anything goes south on whatever stupid thing you might try, you're on your own. I can't help you, won't help you, barely remember you."

"On my word."

"It's not my project, I'm not involved, I just know about it. Oh God, do you know how many federal laws I'm violating? Okay. Here it is." Then he told Al everything. Al's knees buckled, and he had to sit down on the bed to hear the rest.

* * *

CARMEN VINCIO WAS A BIG, bad man. A low-level thug in the Toledo mob, he had done time for his numbers ring, and a second stint for assault and battery. He was facing charges for possession of heroin with intent to distribute, as well as resisting arrest because he tried to take a swing at Al during the bust.

He waited alone patiently in the interrogation room when Al walked in, all chipper and giddy-like. "Hey buddy, how goes it?"

"I don't gotta talk to you without my lawyer present," Carmen challenged.

"Maybe, maybe not," Al smiled as he took his seat. "See, I've been a tad out of sorts lately—never mind why—but it's getting so bad that I'm afraid I may wind up misplacing some crucial piece of evidence that would convict you, and you'd end up going free. Still want your lawyer?"

"I'm listening."

"You'll need a dark suit, a car, and a friend. Got any of those?"

NEW YORK MEMORIES, PART II

MANHATTAN, NEW YORK
FEBRUARY 2017
30 MINUTES SINCE SHE LEFT HELL'S KITCHEN

MILLIE AND AL'S SECOND New York apartment was a spacious three-bedroom on the Upper West Side with a stunning view of Central Park across the street. The old doorman—who Millie could remember as the young doorman—was happy to see her, pleasant and cordial as always, but regretted to inform her that the current residents of her old unit were out of town so he couldn't get her in to see it for at least a week. Millie said she'd come back, but was pretty sure that wouldn't happen.

She decided to take a walk through the Park, knowing it to also be filled with reminders of lovely and sad moments from the past. It was starting to get dark, no snow on the ground but a little cold, yet her quest for nostalgia superseded her desire for comfort. As she waited for the light to change, her eyes fell upon the swanky Essex House Hotel down the street, and the memory it stirred caused her to smile coyly and blush.

It was her sixtieth birthday. Al had rented them a suite at the

Essex, told her to meet him there because he had to work late but he had a big surprise for her, and she should come as her "real self," not the made-up-to-look-older version.

"What if someone we know sees us?" Millie asked him, assuming a fancy night on the town to be part of the celebration. "What will they think?"

"That I'm cheating on you," he chuckled. "Then we'll see if they tell you, and you'll know who your real friends are." She laughed along, and he added, "But you won't be leaving the room, so don't worry about it."

Al didn't get romantically mysterious often, but when he did he went all out, and the anticipation was making her crazy. He wouldn't rent a room in the city just to stay in, and he saw her as her "real self" all the time. What could the surprise be?

She arrived as instructed in a stunning, blue chiffon dress. Al was already there, an open bottle of Dom Pérignon waiting on ice. He gave her a whopper of a happy birthday kiss, poured their drinks, and had them sit down on the bed.

"You know I love you, Millie, and that I'd do anything for you."

"Of course I do. I love you too. What's the surprise?"

"And this surprise, this gift, is because I love you."

"You're killing me, ya big idiot. What is it?"

He kissed her on the forehead, crossed the room to open the door, and shouted into the hallway. "You can come in now." He turned back to his beautiful bride with a Cheshire-Cat grin. "Happy birthday, Mill."

A tall, handsome man in his twenties entered. He had short, sandy brown hair, and piercing green eyes. He removed his overcoat to reveal that he wore nothing underneath except a golden Speedo and a red sash with a bow draped across his powerful chest, like gift wrap. Every muscle of his body was defined to perfection, and the teeth behind his sultry lips seemed to sparkle when he smiled. "Happy birthday, Melanie."

"Mel," corrected Al. "She goes by Mel for short."

"Happy birthday, Mel," the man repeated.

It took Millie just a moment to figure out what her present actually was, then she turned to her husband and asked, "Are you out of your flippin' mind?"

"Mel," the beautiful stranger began in a deep, inviting voice, "I think you and I are going to have a very special—"

"Go away!" she shouted at the Adonis.

"Just give us a sec," Al told him. The god put his coat back on and headed out.

"You got me a stripper for my birthday?" Millie asked angrily.

"Well, he's not exactly a stripper," Al replied with a good-natured chuckle.

"What is wrong with you?"

Al took his wife by the hand and knelt down on one knee like when he first proposed. "I love you, Mildred Talbot Lang. I love you so much."

"It's a really sick way to show it."

"But I'm sixty years old—"

"So am I!"

"Chronologically, yes, but not really. Not biologically. And I know I'm not as, let's say, good as I once was. I can't please you as often, and not as well when I do."

"Aw honey, you're fine," she said comfortingly as she put her hands to his face.

"But you deserve better than 'fine,' sweetheart, so much better. And I'm only going to get worse, while you are always going to stay the spectacular same."

"Al, this is crazy."

"It's not, not if you think about it. Given who we are, who you are, it's not."

"So you want me to cheat on you, that it? Happy birthday, go cheat on me?"

"It's not cheating if it's my idea," he giggled. "But if not like this, one day you'll need to, and you'll feel bad so you won't tell me, and *that* will be cheating."

"You've thought this all through, have you?"

"For years. I knew this day would have to come sometime."

"So, what, like, anytime I'm feeling a little frisky, I'm supposed to just go out and hire a boy prostitute?"

"If you want. Although, dollars to donuts, I'm pretty sure you can just sit alone in a bar and some pretty terrific fellows will come to you."

"And you're okay with this? How could you possibly be okay with this?"

"Because I have to be, Mill. Honest to God, I have to be. You know those nights when you go out with your girlfriends to play cards or see a movie? I'll frame it in my mind like that—Millie's out for the evening without me, having a nice time."

"I don't know, Al. This is nuts."

"What'd you think of him?"

"The boy? He's okay I guess."

"No, come on. What did you think of him?"

The truth was, she thought he was gorgeous. Those hypnotic green eyes, those rock-hard pecs, that chiseled jaw, that bulge in his Speedo so ready and waiting for her, and that youth. Oh, that glorious, sexy youth. To be with someone her own age again—he wasn't her age, she knew, but at the same time, he was. She smiled coquettishly, looked at Al, but was too embarrassed to hold her husband's gaze. She looked to the ground, smiled even more coquettishly than before, and blushed.

"Then that's that," Al said, fully understanding his wife without needing her words. He kissed her on the forehead once more, headed to the door, and stopped. "But hey, for the record, I'm not dead yet. Save a little for me every once in awhile."

She smiled. "You got it, ya big idiot."

"You can come back in now," Al shouted into the corridor. The boy returned and Al smiled at him. "Hurt her, and I'll kill you."

"Don't worry, sir, she's in good hands."

And Al was gone.

That was a good memory, thought the ninety-three-year-old Millie as she leaned over her walker hobbling through Central Park, blushing for no one as the rest of that glorious night played itself out in her mind's eye. Funny, she couldn't remember the boy's name—

only the second person in her life with whom she'd ever had sex—yet she could recall all else in perfect, lustful detail.

She continued on her aimless way, different sights prompting different recollections. The tree with the hollowed-out trunk over there that six-year-old Joanie had climbed against her parent's insistence, then fell to break her leg in six places; that water faucet where the twins got into that stupid, bloody fist fight; that bench where Robby had come out to her and Al; and that other bench where he told them that he and Tim had been approved to adopt a little baby girl from China—Millie's eighth, youngest, and most darling grandchild.

Triumphs and tragedies, she reflected, highs and lows, the life of a woman. Anyone who lived as long as she would have similar stories of big ups and downs, but what of all the other, smaller memories? Those seemed hazy. She could fondly remember picnics, walks, duck feedings, days at the beach, but only as generalities because nothing great or terrible had happened, nothing stood out. Same with all the wonderful friendships she had garnered over the years, she realized. She could recall beginnings, ends when there were ends, but no detail beyond. All the laughter, debate, joy, and love, talking about movies, plays, and sporting events over meals or wine or beer or coffee, arguably the most treasured gifts of life, so cherished yet so erased, like a beloved old book with the words on the pages removed.

Is that how memory works? she wondered. Do only the triumphs and tragedies remain, all else relegated to some kind of category that motivates a warm smile, even though the reason for the smile had been obliterated by time or repetition? If so, she asked herself, what will happen to the moments I remember now? Will I remember my children even if I have countless more going forward? Will I remember my precious Lori once the deaths of future offspring become commonplace?

Will I remember asking myself these questions?

So lost in her lonely reflection was she that she didn't notice the large skinhead boy approach her, until he was already hovering over her.

55

He was six-five at least, with a swastika tattoo blazing ugly between his eyes. Despite the cold air, he wore on his torso nothing but a ski jacket vest to flaunt his mammoth, tattooed biceps, each arm wider than Millie's waist. He pointed his six-inch blade at the old lady, and said, "Gimme your purse."

For a brief moment, Millie debated letting him try to kill her just to see what would happen, but she realized that wouldn't be fair to Al. Al had devoted so much of his life to her training that she owed it to him to see what would come next, at least once. "Here you go," she quivered as she held out her Gucci bag.

"And the ring," the skinhead demanded as he snatched the purse.

The wedding ring itself wasn't worth much—two months of a police cadet's salary way back in the day. On many occasions, Al, once rich, had wanted to exchange it for something more opulent, but Millie had always refused, so there was no chance in Hades that she'd give it to this pathetic cretin. "No," was all she said.

"Yes," said the punk, twirling his knife in her face. "I want it."

"You got cash and credit cards, and the purse itself will render a pretty penny to boot. It's a very nice mugging for you, congratulations. But you don't get the ring."

"I do. Even if I have to cut it off your decrepit old finger."

"Try."

The monster-boy lunged, thrusting his blade at her chest. With lightning speed, she parried his arm and snapped it back with a crunch, fracturing several bones in the process. The knife sprang free from the punk's hand, whereupon she thrust her palm heel into his elbow, snapping it hard in the direction that an elbow was not designed to bend. She grabbed his shirt with both hands, jutted out her hip, yanked him toward her, over her, and to the ground. With his shattered arm locked against her knee in hellish agony, and her orthopedic shoe pressed snugly into his larynx, she stared icily into his eyes.

"Don't mess with the seniors, sonny."

CHAPTER EIGHT

LANGLEY, VIRGINIA
FEBRUARY 1966
2 DAYS SINCE AL MADE A DEAL WITH THE HEROIN DEALER

E VER SINCE LITTLE DIETER had learned to crawl, it had been Christoph's policy to leave his lab at 4:30 sharp to play with the kinder before his bedtime, grab a quick bite with Clara, then work well into the night to complete his analysis of the daily data. This day was no different except that he stopped on his way home to buy a new teddy bear because the current one was getting a little straggled, and his son deserved the best. Boy oh boy, did he love his boy!

"*Yoohoo, Daddy's home!*" he sing-songed in German as he entered the house. Receiving no response, and with the playpen in the living room empty, he added, "*Clara? Where are you, Liebchen?*" He put down his briefcase but kept the bear as he headed to the nursery, to find no one still. "Clara! Where are you?" he shouted, this time in English, this time a little peeved.

"In here!" he heard a man call. He followed the voice to his study to see Al sitting reclined on his chair with his feet up on the desk, smoking Christoph's pipe.

"Alan? What are you doing here?"

"You know, this is really good," Al smiled as he puffed. "I've always been more of a cigar man myself, but maybe I ought to switch over."

"Where are my wife and child?"

Al laid the pipe over the ashtray, leaned forward, smile gone, all business. "I want her back, you son of a bitch."

"I—I don't know to what you're referring, Alan."

Al said nothing. He picked up the phone, dialed, and said, "Put her on." He passed the receiver to Christoph.

The German could hear his wife sobbing before he even said hello. "Christoph, what is happening?"

"Shhh, Liebchen. Shh. Where are you?"

"I don't know! These big men in black suits and sunglasses came to the door. They flashed badges at me and said you wanted us to go with them, then they blindfolded me in the car. They say that if you don't do what they say, they'll kill us both. They'll kill little Dieter right before my eyes!"

"Shh, Liebchen, don't worry, I'll—"

"That's enough," said Al as he hung up the phone, adding with a wink, "You got your G-men, I got mine." He then went on to describe the top secret details of Christoph's top secret project, implying all the while that he was some sort of high-level government operative, and that he'd have no qualms killing an innocent woman and baby if he didn't get what he wanted.

Of course, it was all a bluff. Al would never do any such thing. In fact, his goons had been specifically instructed to treat mother and child with the utmost respect and offer them every comfort possible —well, as much as can be offered to hostages. It was the one condition for Al to "misplace" the evidence that would convict Carmen, and he had no doubt that the thug and his cohort would abide.

Al had played "bad cop" before, but he had always had Morty by his side playing "good cop." In those instances, the worst-case scenario was that law enforcement wouldn't get the confession they sought. Here, anything going wrong would be catastrophic. Millie would remain a lab rat forever, and he'd go to prison for a very long time. There was zero margin for error.

"Forgive my perspiration, Alan," said the German. "This is very stressful for me. Do you mind if I get my handkerchief from that drawer?"

"Not at all. Or are you really looking for this?" Al said as he produced Christoph's Luger and twirled it around his finger. "Maybe you have others hidden around the room. Then again, maybe I already took them. Either way, do you want to have a gunfight with me, or talk this out like men?" Christoph mumbled something that Al heard just fine, but he wanted to make it clear who was in charge. "I'm sorry, Chrissy. I didn't catch that."

"Talk it out like men!"

Al raised and lowered his hand, signaling for Christoph to calm down and sit.

Christoph sat. "You know I can have you arrested with a single phone call."

"Can you? I know that you report to Thomas Jennings, undersecretary at Treasury. You know who I report to?" Christoph shook his head. "That's right," Al grinned. "You don't. So do you really want to play chicken over which one of us is higher up with the good ole red, white, and blue? Because I guarantee you this: we both may lose, but Chrissy, you won't win."

Christoph could only look at the man in disbelief. Who was he? Clearly not the run-of-the-mill policeman he had thought him to be. The German knew all too well the intense secrecy within which his project was shrouded, so how could Alan know anything about it, let alone so much? How high in the government did he go? He seemed to be aware of all of Christoph's cards, yet Christoph knew not one of his.

But Millie was the unsterblich for which they'd been searching all these many years, the specimen that would change the world, eradicate disease, possibly even death itself. He himself would be forever immortalized in the annals of history, above Salk and Pasteur, above Mengele. But to challenge this man would clearly cost the life of his wife and child. Was he willing to pay that price?

Of course not. His wife maybe, but certainly not his son.

Yet before accepting defeat, he took one final stab on behalf of science. "Your wife's telomeres don't shorten!" he crowed before realizing that the proclamation would mean nothing to Al. He quickly dumbed himself down and self-corrected, pointing out how Millie doesn't age, doesn't scar, doesn't respond to drugs, detailing the many tests and surgeries performed that provided irrefutable results, listing all the benefits for mankind that the continued study of her could render.

Just hearing about the surgeries made Al's blood boil. He leapt across the desk, lifted Christoph up by the collar, and pinned him against the wall. "She's my wife, you Nazi bastard!"

"I am not, nor have I ever been, a Nazi."

"Do you think I give a damn, you sniveling kraut?"

"No, I suppose you don't," the German sighed. His shoulders slumped. His posture sagged. He got smaller. "All right. You win."

"Good," Al said calmly as he let him go. "You got one hour to get her to my motel room, along with all other documents, files, and journals. All of them! I don't want someone coming back for her a year from now. One hour."

"That I cannot do."

"You think this is a negotiation? You think you have any choice but to do exactly as I say?"

"Alan, please. I'm agreeing to what you ask, for the sake of my family I am. We're in the boat together now. But to release her so randomly will only raise suspicion, in which case, I can promise you that others will come back for her, and I will likely be imprisoned forever. Please. I need at least three days to get her out safely."

It was Al's turn to size up Christoph. Was this a trick? Had his bluff been transparent? Was the mad scientist merely going to phone his higher-ups the moment he was out of the policeman's presence? Al had spent the bulk of his adult life catching liars lying, and

Christoph was showing no signs of it. Plus, what he said seemed to make sense. With nothing tangible to go on but his gut, the detective reluctantly decided to accept the terms—also because he had no other choice.

CHAPTER NINE

MILLIE KNEW THE KIDS needed a sense of progress or they'd file their legal briefs despite her agreement. She also wanted them to feel they did everything they could on their mother's behalf so they wouldn't blame themselves after what came next. If she consented to hire one caregiver once a week, she could buy herself a month-and-a-half, which had to be enough. It was already a mathematical aberration that it was taking this long—she knew this because she and Al had run the numbers.

Rosa seemed a kind woman, as had most of the other applicants. A thirty-something Filipino lady with two children and no husband, she had solid references and a sunny demeanor. Millie agreed to hire her for the eight-to-four weekday shift.

Robby and Tim were floored—thrilled but floored. To them, Millie's agreeing to hire the woman seemed utterly random, for the Filipino hadn't said anything different than any of the other applicants. Tim turned to his husband and quipped, "Guess we're just better at this than your brother and sister."

Millie walked them all to the front porch and watched them drive off. "Ola, Mrs. Millie," interrupted chief landscaper Juan as he approached. "Good time for inside now?" Millie smiled sweetly and told him it was—good as any, she thought. Juan turned to Jorgé, the newest member of the staff, and told him in Spanish to go water the inside plants. Millie understood every word, but no one knew that.

She headed into the house, but with Jorgé the gardener about, she had to hobble oldly for appearance sake, riding the clanky escalator-chair to the second floor, using the upstairs walker to lumber into her bedroom and close the door behind her before she could move safely at a normal speed into the batcave to continue her search.

On the whole, still nothing. She grew excited for a brief moment when she thought she had at last located her prize, but that quickly turned to disappointment. The candidate had known relatives, so was therefore of no use to her. She sighed.

"I got to get laid," she said aloud to no one.

* * *

HER LAST TWO sprees had been high end—a Madison Avenue ad man one night, a real estate tycoon on another—but she felt like going blue collar this time.

She studied herself in the batcave mirror. Her hair was dyed a dark brown and left wavy. She wore a plaid flannel shirt over a black push-up bra, unbuttoned at the top to show just enough cleavage to still maintain a good girl illusion; tight jeans to accentuate legs and ass; and vinyl thigh-high boots to befuddle the good girl illusion. Her makeup was light, her cheap perfume subtle. She grabbed her black velour coat, opened the trap door to the freight elevator, and took it down to the sub-basement.

Three vehicles awaited her, each legally registered to people who didn't exist—a dented old blue Camaro, a spankin' new pink Corvette for upscale outings, and a black Nissan cargo van for hauling, the latter reminding her of the task she had yet to accomplish. She tried not to think about it. Tonight was about fun.

She got in the Camaro, drove through the tunnel to the opening of the small mound near the woods a mile-and-a-half away, instinctively checked the surveillance cameras to make sure the coast was clear, then blasted some indie rock and rode off to the pool hall.

* * *

SHE HADN'T HAD trouble picking up boys since she was sixty. For the most part, she could just sit in a club by herself baring a bit too much skin, and the fellas would come to her. But where's the fun in that? Besides, there was no guarantee she'd lure the ones she actually wanted that way—and tonight she wanted what she wanted.

It was a decent crowd for a Thursday night. Of the twenty or so tables, close to half were in use. She sat at the bar, nursing a beer, scoping the joint for the object of her night's pleasure, and quickly narrowed it down to two. The runner-up was hanging with his buddies at the far end of the bar. A gorgeous young jock of a man, he was tall and buff with jet-black hair and a firm jawline. Nothing wrong with that. She had been with his type on many occasions and they always made for a fine evening, like a high-quality steak not quite spiced to perfection but still pretty good.

Her first choice was more off-menu. He was playing at a table on the other side of the space, clearly hustling another man, but doing so with such warmth and good cheer that the mark kept playing despite his growing frustration. The hustler was, although not classically beautiful, a knockout in his own right—five-nine, fit but not buff, floppy blond hair to his shoulders, happy eyes, a dazzling smile, and a thin nose that slanted slightly to one side as if it had been punched too much.

She called the waitress over and asked her to send the boy a fresh beer. She waited till he received her gift, and for the waitress to point her out. The hustler smiled warmly at her from across the way, and she smiled seductively back. He raised his bottle in a toast to her, she raised hers, and then he returned to his game.

Okay, she thought, so he takes his work seriously. Not necessarily a bad trait.

She headed to his table as the mark proceeded to miss his next shot, but her eyes were all on her prey. "A smokin' hot chick buys you a drink and all she gets is a lousy toast?" she good-naturedly accused.

"You're right," he replied. "That was rude. What would you like instead?"

"A genuine 'thank you' is always appreciated."

He clasped his hands to his chest. "From the deepest recess of my soul, I thank you with all the gratitude my humbled heart can muster."

"Nice."

"Hey, we fucking playing or not?" demanded the mark, a short, stocky, mid-fiftyish man with a comb-over that failed to hide the Florida-shaped birthmark embedded on his scalp. "This is a money game, Barbie doll," he informed Millie. "If you want to watch, watch, but keep your pretty little mouth shut."

"Aw, Pete, don't be like that," said the hustler, then turned to his new lady friend. "You'll have to excuse my buddy. He's had a terrible run of luck all night."

"I'm good," she smiled.

"Hey, wait a sec, do I know you?" Pete the mark asked her out of nowhere.

"I don't think so. But it's nice to meet you now."

"You look familiar."

"I used to do some print modeling back in the day."

"You were a model?" asked the hustler. "That's hot."

"So are you," she responded with a smile.

"Okay, enough," the mark bellowed with a trace of mock nausea, and then turned to his opponent. "Let's go already. Shoot."

"Excuse me but a moment, m'lady," the hustler said as he began to survey the table. "Wow, Pete, you didn't leave me anything. We're shooting five, right? I'm never going to make this. Hmmm, corner or side? I guess corner, but it won't matter 'cause I won't make it anyway. What do you think?" he asked Millie.

"Side."

"Why?"

"Because you said 'corner' and I'm testing your level of obedience."

"Nice. Okay, side it is." He took careful aim and knocked the cue ball into the five but not at the angle it needed to be sunk. "See what I mean? I knew it." The errant five-ball rolled sleepily along the bank to tap into the nine-ball which sleepily plopped into the corner pocket to win the game.

"Oh for crying out loud," moaned the mark.

"Holy hell!" yelled the hustler. "I never get lucky like that! Like never! Swear to God! Like, wow, right? Okay, Pete, rack 'em up."

"I've had enough for one fucking night," Pete said as he flung his cue stick on the table, removed his wallet, and counted out his losses in twenties and hundreds.

"But we had fun, right? Maybe the gods'll be on your side next time."

"Choke on it, asshole," barked Pete as he threw down the cash, started off, but then stopped with a gnawing curiosity and turned back to Millie. "Have you ever been involved in some kind of insurance fraud?"

"You really know how to charm a lady, don't ya?" she playfully answered.

"Hrmph," he grumbled, paying little heed to her response, and moved off.

Millie turned back to the hustler and asked, "So you boys played one little game of nine-ball for all that money?"

"We started at twenty, but then we kept going double or nothing. Poor guy."

"I can handle twenty," she said as she opened her purse. "Play me."

"I don't think so," he smiled.

"You don't want to play with me?" she asked with pretend wide-eyed innocence, her true meaning not lost on the boy.

"I'd kill a man to play with you, m'lady, I just don't want to take your money."

"How do you know I won't take yours?"

"Tell you what. I'll play you for your phone number."

"Gee, I'm not in the habit of giving my number to strange men I don't know."

"I'm Lucas."

"Mel."

"Nice to know you, Mel."

"Hmm, well, yeah, I guess we do know each other now. Okay, rack 'em."

Lucas smiled and set the balls into a tight diamond as Millie chalked up the cue stick that Pete had left behind. Meanwhile, Pete sat at the bar, watching her, trying his best to figure out where he'd seen her before.

"This is going to drive me crazy," he muttered. He took out his cell phone, pointed it at her and snapped a shot. "I'll figure it out. Barman, another brewsky!"

"So let me see if I got this straight," Millie told Lucas as she continued to chalk her stick. "If you win, you get my phone number, and if I win, I get yours."

"That's the wager."

"Doesn't seem fair. I'm not going to use yours."

"You're not going to win either."

"Let's find out." She bent low to table level, her breasts heaving up just a tad as a result, raised her right elbow, and plowed the stick into the cue ball with all the force of her hundred-and-twenty-pound frame behind it. The diamond shattered in all directions. Three balls were sunk, including the nine, for Millie to win the game. She gazed into his eyes. "So what's double or nothing on a phone number?"

Lucas could only laugh.

* * *

SHE WAS on him the moment they entered his sparse one-bedroom. She enjoyed being in control and enjoyed that he enjoyed it. After the initial kissing and groping and tearing off each other's clothes, she shoved him onto his bed and leapt upon him, taking his pulsing thick cock into her mouth as she landed, planting her dripping wet pussy on his face. He knew what to do with it, and he did it very well.

The pillow talk that followed began as a continuation of their catty banter, until Lucas suggested they team up, gleefully describing the many scams they could pull together. Millie was flattered, even entertained the exciting notion for a brief moment, but knew she'd never feel right tricking innocent people out of their hard-earned money. Still, she liked him. He was smart and he was sweet, despite his icky profession. Feeling too good and relaxed to bother to lie, and preferring the conversation to return to the light and frothy, she decided to blow the kid's mind.

"I can't join you in your life of crime, dude. I'm starting law school in the fall."

"No kiddin'?" he chuckled. "So if I ever get in trouble, you can protect me."

"How do you know I won't be the one prosecuting?" she smiled.

"You wouldn't do that to me," he smiled back.

"In a heartbeat," she giggled.

"No you wouldn't," he giggled along, crawling upon her and kissing her neck.

"Oh, absolutely I would," she moaned in delight. "Mmmm. Okay, maybe not."

She let him be the man on that second go and gave herself to him completely. She was impressed with how he could be so forceful and tender at the same time, taking charge of her body with ease and warmth as he maneuvered her from one obscene position to the next, holding himself back to make sure she came twice before exploding inside her—which only served to have her cum again.

He was ready to nod off shortly after that, but Millie wanted more—and she had learned over her decades of youth how to coax a man into performing beyond his own expectations. In the end, Lucas didn't disappoint.

Hours later, he was awoken by the sound of her getting dressed. "Where you going?" he asked. "Let's get a little more shut-eye, and I'll take you to breakfast."

"I like to wake up in my own bed."

"Can I have your number at least?"

"You lost that particular match, remember?"

"Seriously. I want to see you again."

"I'm sorry, Lucas, you can't. But I wish you all the very best in your life." She leaned over and kissed him passionately. "Thank you. You were spectacular."

"Then come back to bed," he said, gently edging her toward him. "It's a long time till September."

"Sorry. Can't."

"I feel so cheap."

"Me too. Pretty cool, in'nt?" And she left.

What a swell night, she beamed.

CHAPTER TEN

Langley, Virginia
February 1966
3 Days Since Al Gave Christoph 3 Days

A L PACED THE CHEAP MOTEL room. Seventy-two hours he had given the German. "You don't get yours until after I get mine," he had said in no uncertain terms, and the German fearfully agreed.

It was seventy-two hours and nineteen minutes—not necessarily a sign of betrayal, but not a good one either. He turned on the TV. He didn't even know what he was watching when he heard a knock at the door six minutes later. He opened it to two large men in dark suits, obviously government agents.

"Detective Lang?" asked one.

Al nodded, not knowing if they came to arrest him, to give him information, or to give him what he wanted. The agents separated like the Red Sea to reveal Millie standing behind them. She ran into her husband's arms, sobbing incoherently.

"It's okay, baby, shhh," he said, holding her tight, then turned to the agents, "Go!" He kicked the door shut, then back to her. "It's all right, honey, shhh."

"The th-th-things they d-d-did to me . . . "

"You're safe now, sweetheart, and you will always be. God as my witness."

* * *

SHE DIDN'T WANT to talk about it, and that was okay with him. She didn't want pity or even affection, she just wanted to be held and to forget, and that was okay too. Whatever she wanted, whatever she needed. They lay down on the bed, and she fell asleep in his arms. To his chagrin, she had only a moment of peace before she began to scream and toss in her sleep. He got up to give her sufficient space, sat in the chair beside the bed, and welled up as he absorbed her suffering as his own.

He phoned Carmen and told him to return Clara and Dieter. He phoned the house, told Lori that her mom was safe, asleep, she'd call in the morning, and he gave her a story. He phoned his captain and weaved him the same tale. He looked back to his tortured wife, and his tears returned. He didn't know which she needed more, peace or sleep. There was no one to ask, and there never would be. Finally, with her nightmare seeming to have no end in sight, he guessed. "Honey," he softly said as he gently nudged her shoulder. "Millie, wake up. You're having a bad dream."

It took her a moment to get her bearings, after which her reaction was identical to when she first arrived at the motel. She broke into tears, leapt up from the bed, onto his lap, and into his arms. "Al, th-the things they d-did to m-m-m . . . "

"It's okay," he whispered, stroking her golden hair, but the sobs continued.

"Why c-c-can't I t-t-talk n-n-n—" She gave up trying, but the sobs continued.

"It's a reaction to the trauma, baby, that's all, it'll pass with time, I promise, don't go worrying about that too," he said soothingly, but still her sobs continued. "It's over now, baby. All over. You're safe now."

"How d-d-do you know?" she sniffled. "How do you n-n-n-know I'm s-safe?"

"Because I'll see to it," he answered with certainty. "I have to."

"What d-d-does that m-mean?"

"Let's talk about it in the morning."

"No. I want to n-n-know n-n-now. P-p-please?"

He sighed, the man of few words at a loss to explain what he knew to be true. "Sweetheart, God chose you for something special, and gave you this miraculous gift. We can't know why He did so, but there must be some holy reason."

"This doesn't feel like a g-g-gift, Al," she wept. "I don't w-want this g-g-gift."

"I know," he said, and kissed the top of her head.

A few moments passed, and she spoke again. "You n-never answered the qu-qu-qu-question. What does 'I'll see to it' m-m-ean? T-t-tell me."

"All right," he softly conceded, then reluctantly dove in. "I know people look up to me," he began with embarrassment. "They always have. I'm strong, they say, I'm brave, I'm just, I'm this, I'm that, blah blah and whatnot. And sure, yes, maybe I'm those things, but they're not qualities I ever set out to develop. I just, I don't know, have them —and for the life of me, I don't get why everyone else doesn't have them. We all had the same upbringing. It's as if God singled me out at birth to be this way, and I could never figure out why. Till now." He paused and took her hand. "Darling, God made me the way I am to serve you."

"Wh-what? Al, do you know how c-c-crazy that s-sounds?"

"I do, but that doesn't change anything. I adore you, Millie, and it's always been my greatest desire to protect you from the evils of the world, but this is something different. God gave me to you to get you ready. It's the only thing that makes sense in all this. You are my purpose. And I vow on all that is holy, and on all the love that I have for you, that I will. You will be ready."

"R-r-r-ready for wh-wh-what?"

He exhaled and smiled sadly. "For everything."

* * *

It was the middle of the night. They were both sleeping soundly when a gnawing realization stirred Millie awake. "Al! Al!" she said, nudging him. "Al, get up!"

"What is it?" he said, jumping to a sitting position. "What do you need?"

"I completely f-f-forgot to tell you. Mikey is smoking reefer!"

Al couldn't stop himself from laughing.

"You think this is f-f-funny?"

"No, of course not. Well, under the circumstance, yes, a little. Don't you?"

She briefly considered it from an objective point of view, saw the humor in it, and then got over it. "N-n-no!"

"Okay, sorry. But it's taken care of. He told me. He said he felt he owed it to you to tell me, that it would somehow get you back home. It didn't make much sense, but to be honest, we've all been a little . . . not ourselves while you were gone."

"Wh-wh-what did you d-do?"

"Threw him out off the roof."

"S-seriously."

"I grounded him for seven-and-a-half weeks. Two months for the marijuana minus four days for the confession."

"You're such a c-c-cop," she grinned. "I sh-should've called them, the k-kids."

"I took care of it. Told them you were sleeping and you'd call in the morning."

"Good." She paused. "How will I ever ex-explain th-th-this?"

"You don't. They can't know anything about it. No one can. It could put you in danger. Worse, it could put them in danger—we don't know. We don't know anything, my darling. You and I will figure this out as we go. We'll make mistakes, we shouldn't but we will, but it would be cruel of us to embroil our children in whatever madness our future holds in store. We owe them as much of a normal life as we can possibly give them, despite how abnormal our own may turn out to be."

"But I have to tell them s-s-something."

"You say it's too painful to discuss. I already gave them the particulars. A crazy man showed up at the door. Before you got a good look at him, he stuck a needle in your neck. Next thing you knew, you were trapped in a basement. Every day he brought you food, often raped you, but you only ever saw him in a mask, and he never spoke. Never said a word. One day, he stopped showing. You realized he left the door unlocked. You escaped but then found yourself on the wrong side of the tracks, completely lost. You begged someone for a dime, and then phoned me."

"What happened to t-t-teaching our children to be honest by way of ex-ex-example?"

"Well, that's out the window," he chuckled.

* * *

IT WAS COLD, it was dark, and the park was deserted. By the time Al arrived, Christoph was already seated on the pre-designated bench by the pre-designated water fountain. Both men wore heavy overcoats, hats, and gloves.

"Right on time, Alan," said the German "I assume all went satisfactorily with Mildred's return, as it did with Clara and little Dieter, thank you. Of course, my bride was a tad frightened for me to leave our home at this hour, but I assured her that all the nonsense was resolved and there was nothing further over which to worry. I assume you had a similar conversation with your lovely wife."

"You done?" Al said curtly. He had driven Millie back to Toledo the morning after the night of her return, spent three harrowing days and nights by her side, and then back to Langley on this night, so he was in no mood for Christoph's incessant jabbering. He just wanted to wrap things up and get back home before dawn.

"Down to business, I understand." Christoph removed two thick documents from the leather attache case by his side, then handed them to Al. "As requested."

"That's all?" Al asked, temper mounting. "You'd better tell me everything else was destroyed. Not a trace behind. That was our deal. And for your sake, I'd better believe you. I took your family once; I can do it again without breaking a sweat."

"I exceeded that agreement, Alan, calm yourself. As I explained at our last encounter, I couldn't simply release Mildred without cause. Too many questions would be raised, and her continued safety would be dubious at best. Instead, I altered her data. What you have in your hands is the sole file documenting the true findings as to her nature—keep it, burn it; I vanquish all possession. The other is a copy of the new, doctored file, which shows, with unequivocal certainty, that your wife's aging process and recuperative powers are no superior to anyone else.

"If you look at page four of the first document, you'll see a photograph of her abdomen one day after surgery, alongside several more photos of same taken each day going forth. By week three, all evidence of the incision is gone. But if you look at the same page on the tampered version, the official one on file with the Treasury Department of the government of the United States, her healing is gradual, like any other mortal. This is because I re-used many of the same photos—the final week-seven picture shown is really from day five. Based on this report, any trained professional would have to deduce that her tissue is forever and permanently scarred. There are many more such examples if you read on."

"This is good," said Al as he flipped through the document, understanding the pictures but not so much the math. "This is very good."

"I know."

"But what about your team? You must've had others working for you. What if they go blab that she doesn't scar or react to drugs or something?"

"As the only licensed medical doctor involved, I was the only one who examined her wounds, therefore the only one who could determine whether she scars or not." This was true. "Similarly, I was the only one with the access to witness her unresponsiveness to pharmaceuticals." This, of course, wasn't.

From the moment Al had left Christoph's home, the German contemplated phoning his superiors to find out just how much governmental oomph Al really had. But in the end, he couldn't risk it —one wrong call could tip off the wrong person, and little Dieter would be killed. The scientist would simply have to be satisfied with the knowledge that Dr. Mengele had been right all along, the unsterblich were real, and he'd just have to find another specimen with whom to prove it.

He knew that falsifying the data was a crime for which he would be imprisoned for life if caught—the Nazis would have executed him for it—but he had no choice. Most of it was easy—swapping photographs in and out, fudging a fraction of a decimal point in one direction or the other, deleting his personal notes, goals, and hopes— but then there was the morphine and young Dr. Szabo. That little hiccup required planning and finesse.

Woody came to see him that night, as instructed. The young genius entered the office to find his boss sitting at his desk, a carafe of schnapps and two glasses before him. He took his seat as he pointed to the liquor. "We celebrating?"

"Quite the opposite, I'm afraid," Christoph sadly replied as he filled their glasses. "Candidate W13-10 does not pass muster. We'll be releasing her by morning."

"Miz'iz L? No, that's impossible!"

Christoph slid the doctored file across the desk. Woody sifted through it, grimacing over each page. It had been weeks since he last looked at a compilation of the daily reports so couldn't notice that the figures had been altered, his primary responsibility having been the study of Millie's DNA and immunity systems in order to exploit her condition, Christoph the one charged with proving her good fortune to the world.

"Wait, here, look," he began his irrefutable argument. "The morphine. Look at the doses I've been giving her, yet her vitals remained completely stable. See?"

"Turn the page."

Woody did as told to find a letter of apology from their pharmaceutical supplier, forged of course. According to the letter, the most recent shipment of morphine had been mislabeled at factory, meaning that Woody had been administering placebos. The company promised to ship the correct batch expeditiously at no additional cost, offering a ten percent discount on the next order.

"This isn't possible," Woody said in dismay. "It can't be."

Christoph removed from his drawer a syringe and a small vial of sugar water labeled "morphine." He plunged the syringe into the vial, and then injected himself. He waited a moment, and then stretched out his arms to display its lack of effect.

"Does this mean that I'm unsterblich too? Or would you care to try it for yourself? Maybe you're unsterblich as well," the German chuckled lightly. "Maybe we all are."

"Okay, fine. Then why don't we just keep her till the actual morphine gets here, and then test her again? Doc, I just know in my gut she's the real McCoy."

"I'm afraid that given the results we've garnered thus far, failing to release her promptly would exceed the mandate laid out to us by the Treasury Department. Once beyond their jurisdiction, our actions could be deemed criminal."

"We're just talking a few days, a week tops. No one would know."

Christoph leaned across the desk to play his trump card, putting his hands upon the boy's like a loving father. "I know how hard this must be for you, Woodrow, given your feelings for her."

"What? No. She's a specimen, that's all."

"Really? I heard the two of you have developed quite a rather special bond, as it were, during your nightly visits."

"No! Not at all! Where'd you hear that?"

"I don't remember, maybe I'm mistaken. But if such a nasty rumor were to get out . . . a man of science doing such a thing to his subject, tsk, tsk. I may even be called upon to look into the purported felony myself. As untrue as I'm sure the allegations are, the investigation alone could be a permanent blemish on the otherwise stellar career your future holds in store. Best to accept the data which sits before our eyes and let the whole sordid matter go away, don't you think?" That ought to shut the little rapist up. "I know it's disheartening, son. How many candidates have we been through together now, how many blows? Five? Six? I've been at this game over twenty years, and it never fails to build up your hopes, and then crush your soul. But all we need is one, Dr. Szabo, and we have a new test subject expected within the week. We have our people in the field, searching everywhere every day. We'll find our unsterblich."

Woody was silent, dumbfounded, terrified. He sighed in defeat and raised his glass. "To the one."

Of course, Alan didn't need to know of such details.

"This is absolutely very good," the policeman repeated with a smile as he sifted through the top secret document in that Langley, Virginia park on that cold and dark February night.

"It is exceptionally good," the scientist boasted. "Only three people in the world know of Mildred's true nature—you, she, and I —and I assure you that I will never say anything."

Al smiled. He put his arm around Christoph's shoulders, friends once more. "No, Christoph, I don't think you will."

With that, he moved his hand up from Christoph's shoulder to his cheek, placed his other hand on his other cheek, and twisted the Nazi's head across his neck hard and fast. The sound of the crack made the birds fly out of the trees, and Christoph dropped to the ground, dead.

"I don't think you will at all," Al added as he took the dead man's wallet, watch, and wedding ring to make it look like any ordinary mugging gone awry.

CHAPTER ELEVEN

ALL THE WEEKDAY SHIFTS had been filled, and still she had to approve Katia for the eight-to-four weekend shift to keep the kids happy. Her final task was now relegated to Friday or Saturday nights only, and her window was growing smaller.

She congratulated Katia on her new employment like she had with all the others, and let Michael and Chantal walk her out. She waited for them to drive off, and then headed back to the batcave to continue her search.

She was barely going through the motions by now for it all felt a futile gesture by this point. She tried to think up a quick plan B, wondering why she and Al hadn't done so in the first place. Stupid! Got to stop making mistakes, Millie.

Something on the computer screen caught her attention, and her eyes lit up. She had to read it a second time to make sure it wasn't just wishful thinking, and then she read it a third.

"Oh my gosh!" she shrieked. "Oh my flippin' gosh!"

It wasn't a perfect match, but close enough. Eye color, good; hair color, good. She was a few years younger than Millie, but that would be indecipherable by the time it all was over; an inch too short by the records, sure, but hey, seniors shrink.

"We found her, my darling," she said to Al in the photograph. She kissed her fingers and then touched them to his lips. "We got our lady."

* * *

No one saw her slink into the loading bay from the street, for it was late and very dark. She flawlessly picked the backdoor lock and went inside. The hallway was empty, but the smell almost brought her to her knees—formaldehyde with an undertone of rotten cherries. Death. She yearned to place a surgical mask over her face, but only visitors did that. If seen, she had to look like she belonged.

She wore the proper gray Brooklyn Morgue coveralls and a blue baseball cap with her hair tucked inside and the beak tilted down to conceal much of her face. She moved with quick efficiency toward the depository where her prize awaited.

A man and woman turned the corner from the adjoining hallway, heading toward her. The woman wore the same gray coveralls as Millie—a technician or attendant like her—and the man a white lab coat—the night shift coroner.

Don't look at them but don't look away, she heard Al's voice in her head. Move fast but don't run. You're supposed to be here, and you have official stuff to do.

She could tell that the coroner was hitting on the attendant. The woman appeared uncomfortable but was subtle in her rebuking of him, presumably for fear of losing her job or missing out on a promotion or something like that.

In this day and age? Millie thought. Seriously? Doesn't he watch the news? Go online? And in a morgue of all places? How ick.

The couple brushed past her without a nod or a grunt, and Millie moved on.

She didn't realize that she'd grown accustomed to the putrid smell until she entered the room and the stench multiplied tenfold. She retained the wherewithal to close the door behind her before putting her hands to the wall to stop herself from falling, waited a few moments, then got back to work. She wheeled a gurney alongside the appropriate freezer drawer, slid out the shelf, and there she was. Jane Doe 7LR397W.

The body was wrapped in cellophane, but Millie could see the woman's face through it. Poor old lady, she thought. She knew no one would notice the corpse's absence for she had erased its entry record from the database; and she knew no one would miss the woman from the world because that same deleted record had indicated no family, no friends, no anybody. She had been found dead on Skid Row, homeless, penniless, and abandoned by all. The mere sight of her almost made Millie cry.

No, she reminded herself. This body is not the woman. The woman's true essence is somewhere else now, hopefully somewhere better. This thing before her is just the shell that once contained the lady's soul, like a cellophane bag of potato chips after the chips had been eaten. Meaningless garbage to be buried or burned.

She adjusted the height of the gurney so it was flush with the drawer. She cradled her hands under the body's shoulders to lift, but it was too heavy. She took a deep breath, summoned all her strength, and slid just a piece of shoulder onto the gurney, then spent the next five minutes shimmying the corpse bit by bit to get it in place.

Now the hard part.

She opened the door a crack to make sure the coast was clear, and then wheeled the gurney down the empty hallway. It wasn't unheard of for a body to be transferred to a funeral home in the dead of night, but it was definitely uncommon, and she'd be questioned if seen. She had her pack of lies ready, knew the names of all who worked there, but one question could lead to another and another until her story collapsed under its own detail. Best to just get the body out unnoticed.

She was about to make the final turn into the corridor that led to the loading bay when she heard footsteps. She pressed herself and the gurney against the wall, peeking out to see what's what. A tall and fat African American man was walking toward her, and he seemed angry about something. She pressed back against the wall to remain hidden. She assumed a classic karate stance, poised to attack with a savage knifehand strike. If she chopped at the man fast enough, she could render him unconscious without causing him any lasting harm.

Between violence, sex, and intelligence, Millie knew she could wriggle her way out of almost any tight spot, but came to wonder if seduction might be a more appropriate weapon in this particular situation. Even though she knew she had the skills to take out the man, if she didn't win the altercation in a snap, the fight would make noise, and the noise would bring attention.

She removed her cap to let her luscious locks fall to her shoulders, and unbuttoned the top buttons of her coveralls. The man's footsteps grew louder. She tried to stop herself from panting. She heard a phone ring.

"What the fuck is it now?" she heard the man say. The footsteps reversed themselves, getting softer instead of stronger. She heard a door open, and then close, and she hustled her way out the door.

It took her only a few minutes to get Jane Doe 7LR397W into the back of the morgue van, and then she jumped into the driver's seat. She was disappointed to find no keys in the ignition, but it only took her a few additional seconds to hot-wire the engine into a gentle start, and off she rode. No one noticed anything.

She smiled.

Guess Al was right, she thought. Garnering a dead body isn't hard at all.

CHAPTER TWELVE

"BE IT FLIGHT, FIGHT, or anything in between," Al kept reminding her, pushing her, motivating her, "the only two things you'll ever know for sure is that you'll never know what skills you'll need to survive, or when you'll need them."

Millie's training began simply enough, while at the same time, surprisingly. It was late one weekday morning. The kids were at school, and Al had phoned Morty to say he'd be coming in late. A wiry little man with big glasses and carrying a large paper bag came to the door. Al introduced him as Freddy, a "colleague," but it was obvious that he was some ex-con that Al had once helped.

They sat in the kitchen. Freddy dumped out the contents of the bag, littering the table with cheap bicycle locks. He showed her one that was split open in half so she could see its inner mechanics, latching and unlatching it with a key, and then with a hairpin. He had her try—easy as long as she could see the inside, but much harder once she graduated to the ones that hadn't been split open, where it was all about feel. At the end of the hour, Freddy said he'd be back the following week at the same time and wanted her to practice forty minutes every day, like piano lessons.

Six months later, she was ready for combination locks—not terribly difficult at first because she was allowed to use a stethoscope, but far more challenging once she could only use her natural hearing. The better she got, the more complicated the locks became. When the family moved to New York, Freddy found an associate of his to take over for him. By the time Al was the managing director at Salomon Brothers decades later, he secretly allowed her to hone her skills on the bank vault.

Very late one night, still in Toledo and a month or so after Millie's first lesson with Freddy, Al commandeered a squad car and drove her out to the desolate highway. He got out of the car, had her take the driver seat, flipped on the siren, and told her to drive two miles out as fast as she could, and then back just as fast.

Millie had always been a good, cautious driver, never climbing more than a mile or two above the speed limit. At first the high speed was scary for her, but she pushed the car to eighty nonetheless, and came to find it quite exhilarating. When she returned to Al, smiling proudly, he responded with a stoic, "Faster."

They practiced one night a week—continuing in New York even though it was trickier to get away with it once Al was no longer a cop. When she was able to drive comfortably at one-twenty, Al scattered orange cones on the road for her to avoid. Each time she plowed into one, which was most of the time at first, Al told her that she had just killed an innocent little child. This skill too she eventually mastered.

He taught her the seventeen pantomimes that give men away in a lie, and the twenty that reveal women. Only once she knew them like the back of her hand did she set out to rid herself of her own. By the time she was done, no one would ever be able to pull the wool over her eyes, and she could pull it over anyone's.

He brought her to a skuzzy yet respected tattoo artist who inked perfect replicas of nasty scars on strategic parts of her body, including the particularly ugly one on the back of her right calf. Yes, world, I scar!

It was there that Al told her of his idea to apply to college to study finance, how his GI Bill would cover much of it, and how NYU was his first choice. "Up till now, a decent job with a good house and good schools for the kids was all I ever wanted," he explained. "But you're going to need money, lots of money, and I figure the best way to make a lot of money is to learn how money itself works."

"But N-N-New York?"

"If I wanted to make cars, we'd go to Detroit. Movies? Hollywood. Money? It seems the clearest path to a fortune lies on Wall Street. What do you think?"

She saw the wisdom in it, but before she could consent, the tattoo artist butted in, "If she doesn't want it, I'll take it."

And on and on her training went. Over the years that followed, she became a master of guns, knives, swords, first aid and CPR, and explosives. The only survival skills she wasn't set out to master were the ones they didn't think of—and once they thought of it, she was set out to master that too.

Her first day at judo class was the worst for her. It began with an ill-fitting gi and a quick lesson in belt tying. The other ladies were also beginners, but bigger and less refined, and they delighted in tormenting the pretty, young flower. After twenty minutes of verbal abuse and bullying, she bowed her way off the mat, as she had been taught, went to Al on the sidelines, and told him she wanted to skip this particular skill and go home. "I-I'll never g-get this."

He smiled knowingly, kissed her forehead, spun her around, patted her on her rear, and shoved her back into the fray. "Give 'em heck, baby."

Five years later, she would receive her 1st dan black belt. Five years after that, she'd receive one in karate. Some time after that, her black sash in kung fu—all the while climbing the black belt ranks in the other styles. She would eventually meld the entirety into one cohesive kick-ass style of her own, becoming a master of mixed martial arts long before before it was even a thing.

They were in their Toledo backyard one sunny afternoon, circling each other as Millie honed her pickpocket skills, trying to remove Al's wallet without him noticing, yet trying even harder to persuade him to slow down her exhausting training schedule.

"If anything, we've got to step it up," Al answered as he noticed a tug on the back of his trousers. "Felt it."

"Darn," she replied.

"The way I figure it, we got about five years. Ten tops."

"Till wh-what?"

"Felt it."

"Darn."

"For you to learn everything you need to survive forever— forever without me."

"No, we have more th-than that. I'm not leaving you and the kids in t-ten years."

"In ten years, the kids will have left us. Felt it."

"Darn. They'll still need their mother."

"Millie, people are already talking about how young you look for your age. In ten years, it won't be explainable at all."

"I'll use m-makeup."

"Makeup is to help women look younger, not older."

"Hollywood does it all the time. I'll just study what th-they do. I mean, gosh, I'm studying everything else."

"Hmmm, that's a point. Maybe. Felt it."

"Grrrr."

"But still, it's risky."

"I'm not leaving my ch-children while they're only in their twenties."

"When then? In their thirties? Forties? Felt it. Because then there'll be grandkids you won't want to leave. Then great-grandkids. At what point will you be ready to move on?"

"When you do."

"What does that mean? Felt it."

"We'll have my next identity all set up, like you said. When you die, I'll die too and jump into it. But I'm not leaving you. That's the deal."

"Mill, you're afraid, I understand that but—"

"That is the deal. And you know what else?"

"What?"

"You didn't feel it," she said with a cheerful winning smile, tossed him his wristwatch, and walked away. Decision made, and case closed.

CHAPTER THIRTEEN

Long Island, New York
April 2017 – A Saturday Night
4 Days Since The Morgue

THE HOUSE HAD ALWAYS been a firetrap—it had been designed to be so from the outset. Chenille drapes, wool rugs, wicker furniture, hickory floors, and pine knickknacks—nothing but kindling and wood. All it took for the inferno to get started was an open kitchen window, a touch of wind, low hanging drapes, a forgotten burning stovetop, a sloppy trail of spilled gin, and an old lady who had had one too many passed out on the couch—and the fact that the nearest neighbor was an acre away didn't hurt either.

The old lady would be burned beyond recognition, of course, identifiable only by the wedding ring on her finger and the teeth in her mouth, the latter of which Millie had x-rayed and then hacked into her dentist's records in place of her own.

That had been the easy part. The arduous task had been the three nights spent ridding the batcave of all its conspicuous content, as well as two vans and a pink Corvette, and dumping them all off at random landfills around the city.

She sat in the dented Camaro on the far edge of the driveway, watching her home of thirty-five years flame into nonexistence. The trunk was filled with high-tech tech, two suitcases of clothing, and just a few personal items.

She was welling up, and it surprised her. She knew this part would be hard—it had been planned and talked about for decades—but she never expected it to be like this. She thought she had prepared herself for the soul-crushing task of leaving her children forever, her grandchildren and great-grandchildren forever, but she hadn't. It had been an intellectual preparation only.

She knew the kids would beat themselves up for not having been tougher on her regarding the caregivers, and she yearned to be there for them to tell them it was okay and that they did their best by her, but she couldn't.

At least they'll have closure this way, she reminded herself, far better than her just disappearing without a trace, her only other option. That would have been cruel. Of course, she also knew this was just more intellectualism—a rationalization in order to barrel through what was killing her.

She heard the sirens approach in the distance, and she knew it to be her cue to go. She looked to the blazing little mansion one final time as a tear rolled down her cheek.

"Good-bye, Millie," she wept softly, put the car in drive, and rode into tomorrow.

And with the death of Millie Lang, so began her epic adventure.

PART 2

STUDENTS AND SAVAGES

CHAPTER FOURTEEN

MOLLY PARKER COULD BARELY contain herself as she the strolled along the beautiful greens and browns of the UCLA campus. It was the first day of orientation, and her fifth month of her second of what would be many, many lifetimes.

She would always miss Al, of course, and perhaps the children even more, but she had done her grieving and it was time to look forward—forward without the guilt of being forever young while watching everyone she loved grow old to die.

The guilt was over, it had to be, had to be, and it was time to journey on.

It was liberating.

She was amused by all the boys and girls around her walking the campus so transfixed by their phones, for she could easily remember a time when telephones were only for rich people, when their sole use was to have a conversation, and they could never be operated more than a few feet from a wall; she could remember when her daddy had their first family telephone installed—one for the seven of them—and how excited they were to share in such technological progress; she could remember when Al brought home their first TV, and a decade later, their first color TV; she could remember when a person lost would have to ask for directions, which Al and Daddy were always too proud to do; and she could remember the time when such things as satellites and rocket ships were but silly stories in comic books and dime novels that no self-respecting person would ever read.

Look how far we've come, she marveled, and it didn't even feel from that long ago. Like yesterday. What amazing new technologies will she come to witness over the next hundred, two hundred years? It was unfathomable.

And in just a few years, she'd be an attorney. What kind? she wondered. Criminal? Civil rights? Family law? She had plenty of money stashed away so she could choose whichever branch she was most drawn to, regardless of pay, whichever she felt would most fulfill her, whichever she felt would best serve humanity.

What will I choose? she wondered.

She'd have twenty or so years of being that woman, Molly Parker, Esquire, before people would begin to notice that she didn't age, and then she'd have to move on—that was the plan she and Al had decided on from the beginning—but what will her twenty years as Molly be like? What will her new friends be like? Will she allow herself to be in a new relationship? Will she ever marry again? Have more children? What will they be like?

And what kind of life would she choose after that? And after that? And after that? What new wonders did the future hold in store for her?

She could barely contain herself.

CHAPTER FIFTEEN

THE MIGHTY BENGAL TIGER trekked along the snowy shoreline, desperately searching for the scent of caribou or elk—even a stinky fish would do at this point. The tiger heard something akin to a bear's roar, and it puzzled her because she instinctively knew that it wasn't coming from a bear. She turned to the sound—a human in dead bear fur, standing on its hind legs with its front paws outstretched like it was about to attack, its puny voice taunting her with its pretension.

The tiger hated humans. She didn't know why. They were weak, slow, and no threat to her or any of the great mammals. But how could she have known that for thousands of years they were her kind's only threat? That her ancestors had been kidnapped from a faraway land to be jailed in faux habitats for human amusement, and only regained their freedom once the human world collapsed from under their feet? And how could she have known that it was evolution itself that kept that hatred for them burning inside her? No, all she knew was that she hated them, and that this one must die.

She charged. She knew the human would run, as they all did, but she also knew she could catch it easily, unlike the swift elk or caribou who take effort. She wasn't even planning to eat the human—she just wanted it dead.

But this human didn't run. Instead, it dropped to its knees, pulled some kind of branchy-twiggy thing from its back, slid another branch in the middle of it, and then patiently did nothing at all. But as the tiger geared up for her final spring before her deadly pounce, the human did do something. The tiger couldn't figure out exactly what it was because she suddenly felt a piercing pain in her left eye. She crashed to the ground, barely able to see, but could feel her blood on her cheeks and whiskers. Then she heard some kind of "twang," followed by an immediate new piercing pain in her under-belly. One more "twang," and the tiger was no more.

The human looked at the dead animal with neither satisfaction nor remorse, removed the arrows from the Bengal's corpse, and slid them back into their quiver.

"You are not my enemy, oh great and mighty cat," began the human. "You won't even taste very good. But pickin's are slim round here, and a girl's gotta eat."

* * *

THE NIGHT AIR WAS FREEZING, but the tiger meat that sizzled over the fire on the girl's homemade rotisserie actually smelled not too bad, especially for tiger.

"Almost ready," she said to no one as she checked it. "Give it another minute."

Alone in the woods, she returned to work. She bit off the edge of the taut line hitch knot on the little tent she'd made of tiger skin, branches, and vines; used her trusted carver—a stone-sharpened flat-rock wrapped with vines around a chubby branch—to engrave an "M" into a spruce tree to signify she'd already been here in case she ever accidentally circled back; then stabbed the carver into the roasted beast to loosen it from the rotisserie.

The meat was dry and tough, but it was something.

"Maybe you won't die, girl, but you can still feel the pangs of starving to debt."

It had been a sweet day, she thought, so packed with chores that she had had no time to waste any of the sunlight in the darkness of her memories. It had taken her most of the morning to track the Bengal, just a few minutes to kill it, much of the afternoon to skin it, erect the new tent, butcher the meat into rationed portions, and then bury the extras in the snow to keep fresh. Yes, the snowy seasons puke, she thought, but it's by far the best for food preservatin.

Of course, she had the wherewithal to build her own lectric freezer for storing, as well as a nice lectric heater to keep her warmer inside the tent, but that wouldn't go over too well if a tribe found her. The gods frown on technology.

If a tribe found her, she reminded herself. *If* she could find a tribe. If.

"How long I been looking?" she asked no one, even though she knew all too well that she was in the middle of her sixteenth winter of solitude, fourteen of those having been on purpose, which had been a terrible bungle.

Got to stop making mistakes, girl.

It may not have been the biggest stupid she'd ever done, she reminded herself, but it was close. Yet after so many lifetimes bopping from one tribe to the next—twenty winters here, twenty winters there, twenty winters accepting all that ignorance and super-stition as the will of the gods—she just needed a break.

Twenty winters she'd given herself to be by herself, one measly little lifetime, and then she'd rejoin humanilly. That had been the plan.

The area that was called Baton Rouge in the old world suited her needs just fine. Never too cold in the snowy season, ample river water, and plenty of little beasts running to and fro for easy food. No tribe would ever find her there because it was a sin against the gods to enter the lands of the old world. Truth was, she knew, at one time that had been good advice—the death, decay, and disease that permeated the remaining cities that once made Merica great had become deadly to all, and practically hurl-rendering to her. But enough time had passed for the cities to heal themselves—not that it mattered a pee to the tribes because the gods had decreed it a sin to enter, period. The gods don't give reasons.

At first, her solitude was everything she had hoped. The city stood proud in its clean air, its ruins a glorious expression of what man had once been capable. Wrecks of tall buildings and small brick houses, all with heaters and colders that she could resurrect and energize in a snap; more books than one could read in a lifetime; tampons and toilets; and best of all, movies!

Oh, those glorious movies that showed that glorious world humanilly created before destroying. And all those beautiful men in those beautiful movies to ting-a-ling to. Strong, heroic men with their unique codes of honor risking their lives to save their woman and the day, so sublime to ting-a-ling to.

And all those beautiful women in those beautiful movies kicking ass and taking names in color, bamboozling their men with sexual wiles and coquettish smarts in black & white, so sublime to ting-a-ling to.

Twenty winters she gave herself. Maybe thirty. She'd see how it goes.

But after only seven of those winters, the loneliness set in. After nine, the despair. By ten, she could barely drag herself out of bed. Those once glorious movies had become an insult, a perpetual reminder of how humanilly had taken paradise and shat in it with diarrhea. By her twelfth, she could no longer tell if she was thinking or talking, and she'd spend her nights howling obscenities at the moon.

She had become, according to the spiritual principles of almost every tribe she'd latched into, possessed; and she had become, according to the science of the world in which she'd been born, crazy.

It was the falling-leaves-season of that thirteenth winter when she decided to kill herself. She wasn't sure if it would work, yet she made it her obsession still. But in the end, she couldn't go through with it—couldn't jab the carver into her temple, couldn't pull the trigger on the Glock. Was this inability to see it through part of the curse of the unsterblich, she wondered, or was she just chicken?

It was clear that the only cure for her insufferable loneliness was people. She needed people, missed people, and the paradise she thought she would find in Baton Rouge had become her prism.

And so, with hope and yearning in her heart, she left the lifeless metropolis to find a new tribe. That had been two winters ago, and she hadn't found a soul.

She finished the piece of tiger she had allotted herself, her belly satisfied but her heart barren. She tossed the bone in the fire, reached into a satchel that she had concocted from a bison gut, and took out a small photograb of her and her first man.

"What if I'm all that's left?" she asked it.

The chemicals on the picture had long since faded away, but she had kept the image alive by tracing the lines back in with charcoal or crayon or berry juice or whatever was handy at the time. She couldn't be sure if the etched image was even what he really looked like, or if his voice in her head was how he sounded, but she clung to his memory because she had to. She had had many mates over her many lifetimes, some she had loved as much as him—even though most of their faces had vaporated away with time—but she knew that if she couldn't hold onto her first, she'd be lost. She didn't know how she knew this, but she knew it all the same.

"What if it's just me, like this, alone, forever?"

"There are others," he assured her in her head as she stared at his face. "They're just hard to find, hon. Merica is a big place. You'll stumble onto someone."

"That's just talk!" she snapped at him. "It's a bad drought been going on in the sunny seasons—we see that all over the everywhere —who knows how long back it begun? Maybe everybody all starved to debt. Or maybe they migrated to new waters that had the old sick. Or maybe some lingering air-born got reactivated."

"There'd be rotting corpses and skel'tons you'd be finding all over the everywhere. You know this good as me."

She smiled. Of course she knew it. "Shut up, ya big id-it."

She cupped her hands, shoveled some snow onto the fire to

vanquish the flames, picked up the photograb, and went into the tent.

She removed her bear coat and let it fall to the ground, lying down on one half like a mattress, covering herself with the other half like a blanket—a survivor sandwich, she called it. The trickle of moonlight that seeped through the tent's flap gave her just enough illumination to gaze into the charcoal smile of her first man.

"I love you, Ool."

"I love you, too, honey."

She closed her eyes, and let sleep take her to a better place.

CHAPTER SIXTEEN

T HE HOURS MOLLY PARKER saved by no longer having to apply prosthetic makeup and hair dye every day was blessing enough; add to that the freedom gained by no longer needing to scour local databases for a ridiculously specific dead body, Molly barely knew what to do with all her spare time. If she used only half of it studying, she'd likely be putting in twice as many hours as her fellow students—and she planned to spend a whole lot more. She was out to excel.

Classes hadn't even started, but based on orientation week alone, Molly was in love with law school. She adored her shabby little single in the Weyburn dorm; couldn't get enough of the brunches, parties, and cheesy get-to-know-each-other games; and treasured meeting the other 1-Ls, her first-year peers, good smart children all.

Don't think of them as children, she reminded herself. They're not children. Stop thinking like an old lady.

It was her final challenge, she knew. The last skill she'd need for her never-ending journey. For they really were children to her—even her sixty-year-old torts professor was a year junior to her Caroline. But she knew that if she'd ever have a chance at a genuine life of happiness and meaning, she would have to embrace the essence of Molly as her true self, no matter what that essence turned out to be. She could no longer pretend the way she had pretended to be senile ole Millie or trampy vampy Mel. No, she had to actually be Molly Parker from the little town of Moses, California, a twenty-two-year-old law student with her whole life ahead of her.

She and Al never saw this challenge coming, and they should've. They had given Molly Parker an intricate, detailed backstory, complete with bank, credit card and cell phone records, an indisputable cyber presence and social media history tracing back to when Molly would have been twelve—but they had utterly missed the difficulty of removing the old lady from within the old lady.

She just wanted to fit.

Got to stop making mistakes, Molly.

She was working out at the campus gym late Wednesday afternoon. She wore the classic karate gi with a brown belt that signified a high level of skill but by no means a master, for she knew her true artistry could never be revealed, an artistry earned from more than fifty years of training while remaining her peak athletic age all the while. She had been trying to think up a spot where she could do her proper exercises in secret, but she had yet to solve that particular peccadillo. In the meantime, only basic brown-belt forms and katas, just to stay sharp.

She noticed the boy—young man—Randy—spot her from across the gym wearing a gi of his own, and a black belt. She had seen him at some of the 1-L events, although they had yet to have the opportunity to talk directly. He was a good-looking kid—young man—tall with short hair and nice shoulders. He also looked a heckuva lot like her grandson Jordan, Caroline's youngest.

Most of what she knew about Randy she had learned from the cheesy games. He was from a good San Francisco family of lawyers, had received a baseball scholarship to Stanford, nailed his LSATs, was likely the hot-to-trot alpha in his high school and college . . . and he'd been checking her out from day one.

She pretended not to notice as he approached her, and she continued to pretend when he stopped at the edge of the mat to watch her.

Oh gosh, she thought, he's going to ask me out on a date. Wait, do kids even do that anymore—I mean, do young adults even do that anymore? How can I go on a date? Even if he didn't look like my grandson, how could I date anyone? The last time I was on a date was during the Great Depression. Please go away.

She finished her kata, to which Randy politely applauded and said, "Not bad. But you seemed to have lost focus near the end. I hope that wasn't because of me."

"No, not at all."

"Yeah, it was, I think. Sorry."

"It's okay."

"Hi, I'm Randy," he said as he put out his hand. "Randy Patterson."

"I know," she said as they shook. "I'm Molly."

"I know. You're the one who did her undergrad at University of Phoenix, right? The online college?"

"So?" Molly responded defensively because she thought it was something Molly should feel defensive about.

"Oh, don't get me wrong. I think it's incredibly impressive that you made it all the way from there to here. That must be one crazy story."

"Not really. I'm just very, very smart."

"This is UCLA Law, Molly. We're all very, very smart." Molly smiled, nodded her agreement, and Randy went on. "So, listen. I don't know any other practitioners in LA yet, and I'm looking for a sparring partner. Interested?"

"Oh, gee, I don't know . . . "

"C'mon, humor me. I promise to take it easy on you."

Shoot, she thought. *He's* going to take it easy on *me*? Okay, let's get this over with, fast. "All right," she demurely consented. "As long as you promise to go easy."

They took their positions on the mat, bowed formerly, and began. As the less experienced one—ha ha—it was incumbent on her to make the first attack. She leaned sideways, unleashed a respectable sidekick toward his gut, purposely missing by a mile, and cried out in fake, unbearable pain. End of match.

"Are you all right?" he asked.

"I think I tore a darn hamstring!" she wretched, clutching the back of her thigh to continue the charade, limping and hobbling toward the nearest bench.

"Do you need some help?" he asked as he watched her suffer.

She wondered why he would even ask, and not rush in like a gentleman to prevent her from falling down—take her in his strong arms like the valiant protector he wanted to appear—but then she remembered that it was the #MeToo era where such things are considered lurid and villainous, and pausing for verbal consent to put a hand around a girl's waist, even if to help, is what good boys had been trained to do.

Poor boys.

Poor girls.

"I'm okay, thanks," she said as she convincingly hopped her way to the bench. He picked up her water bottle and brought it to her, but before she could say thank you, they heard a girl's voice bellowing toward them from behind.

"Well that was a pretty pathetic display of athleticism!"

It was another 1-L Molly had seen around, Janine something. Molly knew from the cheesy games that she'd been a high school girls bodybuilding champion, but that didn't seem all that impressive when the short-haired brunette with the pretty face was seated wearing a loose sweatshirt and jeans. Seeing her now in her taut gym clothes was a whole different kettle of fish. Almost six feet tall, with massive, defined arms and legs, her chest as much pecs as they were tits.

"I guess I should've done a little more stretching before I started."

"Yeah, guess so, princess," the bodybuilder said, then turned to Randy. "How about you and I go at it? I have no formal training, but

I can pack a pretty wallop if I do say so myself. Let me help you build up a sweat."

"Um, thanks," answered Randy, "but I think I should help Molly get home."

"No, that's okay," Molly said. "It seems to be easing up a little. I think maybe it was just a bad cramp after all."

"Well, that's a relief," Randy replied. "You know, a couple of 2-Ls were telling me about this awesome hot dog joint on Gayley Ave., on the way back to the dorm. How about grabbing something to eat and a few beers? I mean, if you want to."

Darn it, Molly thought, but Janine jumped in fast. "Great idea, Rand-o! I'm starved. Why don't you tag along, princess?"

"Um, sure," answered Molly—at least it wasn't going to be a date.

"Terrific," said Randy, meaning anything but terrific. "I'll text Josh, my new roommate, see if he wants to join us. We can make it a foursome."

"The more the merrier," added Molly, receiving a quick glance and a flash of a smile from Janine. Molly wasn't entirely sure what it meant, but her best guess was that it was the proclamation of the start of their competition for Randy.

Shoot.

* * *

JOSHUA LEONARD WONG had missed much of orientation having only arrived on campus that morning, so little was known about him. Janine put a quick fix to that, taking charge of the table and showing off her future prosecutorial skills over dogs and beer, albeit way more beer than dogs.

"Where you from?" she grilled. "What college did you go to? What was your major? What was your high school sport? What branch of law do you want to specialize in?"

Josh didn't seem to mind. In fact, he enjoyed the attention. A fifth-generation Chinese American, he was tall and obese, with straight black hair to his shoulders, a wooly black beard, an easy-going disposition, and a hearty, guttural laugh. The perfect Asian Santa Claus, Molly thought with a giggle.

"I hail from Philly, PA. Go Eagles!" he began. "My high school sport was *Dungeons & Dragons*." The gang laughed. "I did my undergrad at Penn. Double-majored in dungeons, and dragons." Laughed again. "And I aspire to be the kind of attorney that makes the most amount of money by doing the least amount of work."

He was fun, funny, and Molly didn't buy that he was nearly as lazy as he feigned, and he wanted absolutely nothing from her. She took an immediate liking to the boy—young man.

The foursome hung out till midnight, laughing, debating, pondering the meaning of life, and boasting all the great accomplishments they would one day achieve, the things Molly knew young adults had been talking about for decades but had been considered rude when she was twenty-two for real.

It was fun.

As was the next night when they banded together at Randy and Josh's bungalow-dorm with the big flat-screen TV for drinks and take-out and weed, and the night after that, and the one after that, and after that.

Janine remained abrasive to all and particularly hostile to Molly, always planting herself between Molly and Randy at every restaurant, bar, or living room, and condescendingly referring to her as "princess" in her sad attempt to show off for the boy she had no hope of winning. Molly remained romantically uninterested in Randy, who remained romantically interested in her, but she was not about to let the bodybuilder push her around.

"I bet you had a lot of older brothers growing up," Molly pointed out on one occasion, having gleaned by then that Janine absolutely detested being analyzed. "Older brothers, no sisters, single dad, no strong female influence. I'm right, aren't I?"

With the boys eagerly anticipating Janine to lash back, she surprised them by only gazing sadly down into her beer. "Yes, you are right, princess," she said softly. "My mother died when I was seven—and thank you so much for bringing that up."

A silent melancholy overtook the table.

"I'm sorry," Molly answered. "I understand. Mine died when I was four."

"Shit!" roared Janine. "My mom didn't die. I just said so to make you feel bad!"

Molly paused, and then smiled. "So did I."

The gang burst into laughter, but none hackling louder than Janine herself. "That was a good one, princess. Gotta admit, you got me. Totally got me. Nice."

Molly tipped the imaginary brim of her imaginary cap and waited for round two. Game on, sister.

Classes began on Monday with contracts. On Tuesday they had property, on Wednesday torts. That night, Randy brought a new boy into their fold, explaining that five was the optimal number for a study group, one of them to outline each of their five courses. "And this kid's smarter than the rest of us put together," he added.

Zeke Ashton was nineteen, having skipped the second and eighth grade, and completed his four-year undergrad in three. A small, fragile waif with big glasses and a speech impediment, it took all the courage he could muster to squeak out that he was an LA native and had majored in ec-ec-economics at D-D-D-Duke.

"And you want to be a l-l-l-litigator," Janine laughingly quipped.

Josh and Randy instinctively laughed along when Molly instinctively scolded them, "Come on, guys! That's not nice!" which instantly put an end to the hilarity. Apologies followed.

And thus, the quintet was forged.

* * *

IT WAS FRIDAY, the last day of their first week of school, and that meant criminal law, or "crim" as they called it. Molly met Zeke and Janine in the Weyburn lobby, and then headed to Randy and Josh's bungalow to walk to the Law Building together. There was no real reason for them to do this, but they had done so before their first class on Monday, and then Tuesday, and et cetera, so they saw no reason to stop on Friday.

They entered the lecture hall to find manila envelopes placed on the tables, arranged alphabetically according to the students' names printed on the top. It was the only one of their five courses that had assigned seating, but the bright young scholars were smart enough to figure out what was expected of them. Randy Patterson found himself seated next to Molly Parker, which pleased him a great deal.

They opened their packets to find forty-plus pages of text and photos of cases ranging from shoplifting to murder. Molly could hear Janine a few rows below moaning, "Son of a bitch is giving us a pop quiz on day one?"

Randy smiled as he shook his head. "Rookie teachers. They're the worst."

Molly could see that all the students around her had received the same material as she, but only hers had a small yellow post-it attached, which read: "Tequila Joe's Restaurant and Cantina, Encino. Tomorrow, 2:30." She assumed it nothing more than some kind of secretarial error and dug in to read the cases like everyone else.

Eleven minutes later, which wasn't nearly enough time for anyone to put a dent in the thick document, Professor Ramirez, a handsome, clean-shaven man in his late twenties donning an expensive Brooks Brothers suit and tie, entered and took his place at the podium. The students paid close attention as he spoke, but Molly couldn't make out a word. It was all Charlie Brown teacher wha-wha-whas.

The Professor glanced her way to make direct eye contact for just an instant, flashed a quick wink only for her, far too quick for anyone else to notice, then turned back to the class en masse.

An icy sweat shot up her spine, and she couldn't breathe.

It can't be, she thought. Is this a joke? That's no law professor—it's Jorgé, the Puerto Rican kid Juan added to the gardening staff after Al passed. Then it hit her that he was also a dead ringer for one of the many contractors they had hired and fired to help build the Lang mansion back in the early eighties. It hit her that he had been the bag boy at their neighborhood Whole Foods in the nineties. Like a nuclear bomb imploding within her soul, it hit her that decade after decade this man had been popping in and out of her life in different roles and seemingly trivial ways.

She had tried so hard to block out the details of those dark days as a human guinea pig that she couldn't see until that moment that all those men were one and the same—a man she had first met in a dungeon of suffering in 1965 when he sported a big burly mustache.

They found me! she screamed in her head.

CHAPTER SEVENTEEN

WHAT WAS ONCE CALLED COLORADO
5 BANANA MOONS SINCE SHE KILLED THE TIGER

THE GIRL FOLLOWED THE tracks through the brush early that morning, looking the epitome of the sinful woman. For one, she was wearing clothes, which the gods forbade on warm sunny days because it implies that people have something special to hide, when in truth they have nothing the other mammals don't have as well. It was that very vanity that collapsed the world, teach the gods. Humanilly is no better than any other creation, and in most instances, worse.

Only hunters hunting were permitted to wear clothes in pleasant weather, which for the most part meant men, and only over their loins to keep their cork and jewels from bopping round as they ran. If they had long hair, perhaps some twine to keep it tied back off their faces, that particular license varying from tribe to tribe.

Some tribes allowed women to hunt. It had once been the norm, although she hadn't come across any for a long time. She hoped the tribe she'd find would be one of those, if she could find a tribe at all.

But celestial permission aside, she too was a hunter, perhaps the greatest of ever, and so she dressed accordingly. She wore a wrap of vines over her chest to keep her udders from bouncing if she had to run, a rabbit pelt over her loins to keep out the bugs if she had to crawl, her greasy yellow locks tied in a bun, her carver nestled between hip and pelt on her left, her trusty spyglass nestled on the right, a crocodile-skin sling tucked behind her ass like a monkey tail, and a quiver of arrows and a bow slung over her shoulders.

Yet her terrible sin had nothing to do with the fact that she was hunting or clothed—evils for which she'd only receive a severe whooping. No, her unforgivable transgression was the spyglass tucked alongside her hip. Technology! A relic of the old world! A tool of the Great Seductress Satan herself! For that, both the very misogynistic tribes as well as the slightly would have her burned at the stake.

Not that it would kill her, of course. She'd been burned at the stake before, but it hurts like crazy.

She followed the tracks to the edge of the woods to a clearing of pale, dry grass amidst barren patches of earth. The herd of horses she had tracked, all small and scrawny, were grazing by the riverbank a quarter klick to the south, pecking at what little vegetation they could find. The base of the Rock'n'Rolly Mountains was to the north, with more forest straight ahead to the east. She took her bow from her shoulder, an arrow from her quiver, and took aim.

Before she had a chance to release, her target bolted. The entire herd stampeded. She crouched down to see what's the what, ready to spurt if need be, and her mouth fell open in shock.

It was people! Fuckety-fuck people causing the stampede!

She giggled in glee, then instinctively smacked her hand over her mouth to muffle the sound. She dropped to the ground and covered herself with brush, not yet ready to be seen by them, certainly not while all clothed and teched-up. She whipped out her spyglass to get a better look.

The people chased after the gaunt equines slinging stones, hurling spears, and discharging arrows from finely constructed bows. Kill after kill after kill—they were pretty good, she had to admit. Their spears and arrows were smooth and sturdy, the flint tips sharpened to perfection, their bows rugged and strong with just the right amount of bend and twang—almost as good as her own. A few of the more muscle-bound hunters were even able to thrust their spears with such force that more than half of it appeared on the other side of the dead horse's neck, an ability even she didn't possess.

Most of them were beige-skinned, as was most common in these times, but there were enough browns and pinks and ambers to insure her own pinkness not a liability. There were no women in the party, which was the absence of a good sign but not necessarily a bad one. Stay positive, girl.

After a time, one of the hunters, presumably the Shepherd, put fingers to mouth and blew an ear-ouching whistle. The others stopped cold. They had killed all they needed, and the gods would punish if they took one stitch more.

But one of the hunters didn't stop—a small one, with blotches and irritations on his face and body that the old world called acne and eczema—most likely a virgin on his first raid, overeager to achieve his manhood status.

His shot wasn't bad, she acknowledged. His spear sailed through the wind with barely a wobble, slicing clean into its target's under-belly. Status achieved, but at a perilous cost, superstitiously speaking, and he should've known better—and the men sure-as-shat should have known better than to bring him along if he didn't.

The Shepherd grabbed the virgin, shook him, scolded him, back-fisted him in the face to knock him to the ground, then dropped to his knees and begged the gods to forgive his own depravity and wickedness. The other men followed suit and echoed his pleas, although not in unison. For this was not a rehearsed group prayer, but an individill's cry for mercy, each member of the tribe being personally and collectively responsible for the actions of all others.

The girl was not surprised by it. She had seen the likes of it plenty, the differences between tribes residing primarily in its minu-tiae—names of gods, of legendary warriors, details of the same para-bles—but the upshot was that these people were mere products of their time. Backward, scared, superstitious, and stupid.

"We did it, Ool," the girl whispered joyously to nobody. "We found one."

* * *

SHE KEPT her distance as she followed the hunters while remaining inside the forest's edge just in case. Their catch hung upside down, tied by vines and bundled to spears that they balanced on their shoulders as they walked, two hunters per horse.

The men made their way toward the foothill face where two others of their tribe were posted as sentries, dressed for battle as the others but with hollowed moose antlers tied to their necks that they could blow out as a warning cry. The hunters greeted the sentries one by one with officious fist pounds, brushing past them and into a crevice in the mountain wall—not much more than a crack really, but still large enough for the tallest of them to slip through without folding in his arms or ducking.

Cave dwellers? she wondered. A prudent choice in the snowy season no doubt, but cold and damp the rest. Why would anyone want to live in a cave during the sunny season? What's wrong with these people?

She waited for the last of the hunters to disappear, and then set her sights on the sentries. She scoped out two fist-sized rocks, removed sling from ass, and prepared to launch. She knew precisely which part of the men's heads to strike in order to kill them, which would hurt and antagonize them, and which would knock them out for a spell. She aimed for the latter.

Woosh, woosh, thwack, woosh, thwack! They were down. That easy.

She cautiously approached them, checked their pulses, and calculated in her head precisely how much time she'd have before they'd come to. Ample. She made her way into the cave.

It was thin—not a cave but a passageway, she realized, brisk and wet as expected, but with sunlight shining in from an opening on the far side. She dropped to her knees and crawled on from there, making herself small as small was, as she approached and peered through to the other side.

It was beautiful!

A rolling grassy meadow, klicks wide in all directions from the center, surrounded by a crystal blue lake on one of the four sides, with plush forests along the other three that jutted up against smooth mountain walls, utterly impossible to climb to the up or down. The only way in was by boat, which the gods forbade, or through the cavey-tunnel where any invaders or predators could be picked off one by one and massacred with little effort.

Rings of wooden cabins abounded. There were two in the middle, surrounded by a circle of nine round those, a circle of more round that ring, and on and on. Smatterings of honeybees fluttered about. Apple, peach, and apricot trees bloomed; blackberry and raspberry bushes flourished; sweet baby corn stalks sprouted randomly up from the ground all over; and wild plants and herbs abundant in healing properties grew everywhere.

Some of the women had already started skinning the fresh kill their hunters had brought them, while others sat by their cabins trimming their husbands' shaggy hair and beards. Little girls sat on floating docks as they netted whiskered-fishies from the lake, and even smaller ones filled wooden buckets with the gods' waters to nourish the grass and food-bearing plants. Young mothers nursed newborns, while others bathed toddlers in the peaceful blue waters. Men and boys practiced their slinging, spearing, arrow-bowing, and hand-to-handing, while a tall, attractive-looking man offered pointers, tips, and humor to the younger ones with good-natured smiles and playful shoves to the ground, and they seemed to adore him for it; and all the little fires in front of the cabins cooked some concoction of something in little clay cauldrons that hung over fires, and it smelled scrumptious.

Fruit, corn, honey, fishies, proximity to meat, wooden cabins, impeccable security—this is what one would have to call a rich tribe, thought the girl. She had been with poor ones—always hungry and on the run from some peril or other—and in-the-middle ones too, but nothing beats rich. Some concepts never get tired.

Yes, she smiled, I could live twenty or so winters in a joint like this.

CHAPTER EIGHTEEN

I RON MANACLES HELD HER in place while a mad scientist thrust steel daggers into her flesh. Unyielding shackles kept her prisoner as a buck-toothed monster-boy straddled her thigh. Stars and stripes. LBJ. Torture. Rape. Torture. These were the images that flashed through Molly Parker's brain as the professor-slash-janitor-slash-everything prattled on in his incoherent Charlie Brown wha-wha-whas.

Randy's concerned whispers of "are you all right?" were barely wind in her ear, but she felt his shove on her arm, and then noticed the piece of paper on which he wrote, "u ok?"

Darn it, she thought. Pull it together, Molly. Keep your stuff inside. Don't let them see it. Too many hard questions to answer. Pull it together! Now!

She forced a smile and wrote back, "Bad shellfish, breakfast."

Her instinct was to run, to get the heck off that campus as fast as she could. The heck with Molly Parker—she'll start over, be someone else. Go! Run! Now!

But logic prevailed. They'd expect me to run, she realized, that's what they want me to do, likely a couple of agents waiting to abduct me right outside that door.

Come to think of it, how did they find me? The only possible way was that they were watching me when I was Millie. But then why haven't they tried to abduct me until now? And why here of all places? None of this makes sense!

Calm down, Molly. Just keep your cool and wait to see what happens next.

Run!!!

By the time class ended, her full coloring having yet to return, Randy remained worried about her, and shared his concern with the others.

"I just need to l-lie d-d-down," she assured them.

Shoot, she thought. It's back.

She grabbed Randy's arm quickly, rested her head on his shoulder, leaned her body against his as if she was about to faint, and let him support her as he and the rest of the quintet walked her home, her eyes darting in all directions on the lookout for any agents. She knew it wasn't nice to lead Randy on like that, but she had to divert attention away from her sudden stammer—and judging by the popping eyes on her new friends' faces, it seemed to do the trick. For the rest of the walk, she answered their questions only by nodding yes or shaking her head no.

"If you need anything," Randy said when they arrived at her room, "we're just a text away. All right?"

Molly pressed her hands together in front of her chest and bowed her head in gratitude, namaste style. She locked the door behind her, put her ear against it to hear her friends' footsteps fade off, and then she sat down on the floor, and cried.

* * *

As the day wore on, she struggled to come up with a solution—but how can one find a solution when one doesn't understand the problem? It made no sense that they'd been watching Millie all this time only to abduct Molly here and now. And if taking her was their intention, why'd they let her leave the Law Building at all? Why reveal themselves and then allow her to run?

Maybe it's not a "they," she considered, maybe it's only a "he." Maybe the professor-slash-et-cetera is acting independently. Clearly he's just like her; maybe he only wants to help. But then, once again, why now? He'd have had plenty of opportunities to introduce himself to her over the decades, and ole Millie sure could've used such help from time to time. No, that theory made no sense either.

Nothing did.

Yes. The prudent thing was to run. Every fiber of her being told her so.

No. If they tracked her here, they could track her anywhere. They're likely watching her at this very moment. She looked fearfully out the window. She didn't see anyone, but that didn't mean anything. No, if she ran, she'd be looking fearfully out windows for the rest of her very long life.

The only way to solve the problem was to find out what the heck was going on, which meant following the instructions on the post-it and going to meet the man . . . which could be exactly what they want her to do.

Got to stop making mistakes, Molly—yet all options felt like a mistake.

She noticed the time and texted Randy that she wouldn't be joining the gang on this particular Friday evening, claiming that she was still feeling a little woozy.

The others of the quintet convened at Randy and Josh's bungalow, as per usual. *Game of Thrones* was playing on the flatscreen but with volume muted. They'd seen the episode multiple times, and their thoughts were on Molly.

"Some of those p-pictures P-Professor Ramirez had us look at were p-pretty gruesome," offered Zeke. "They sure b-b-bothered me."

"Actually, I found them pretty cool," Josh chuckled his confession. "But yeah, that makes sense. Maybe one of the gorier images got to her."

"No, Molly's too tough for that," countered Janine. "She may seem all prim and goody-goody on the outside, but that girl's got a fire in her belly."

"Oh no," Randy gasped as the ugliest of thoughts entered his head, and then he said no more because he didn't want it to be true.

"What?" Janine demanded. "Say it."

"Maybe it's not that one of the gory cases got to her. Maybe one of them . . . like . . . *happened* to her. Maybe she was a victim of a . . . you know, a rape or something."

"Oh shit," whispered Josh.

"Yeah, oh shit," echoed Janine. "That's gotta be it. Fuck. The poor kid."

With no further evidence for the future lawyers to go on, they settled on that as the explanation—it made a lot more sense than bad shellfish for breakfast.

Janine left shortly thereafter, far earlier than usual. She headed back to the dorm and knocked on Molly's door. "Hey princess, it's me, Janine. How we doing?"

Darn it, thought Molly. What does she want? "S-s-sleeping," she lied.

"I was just about to make myself a pot of tea. Care to join me?"

"Sleeping," Molly repeated.

"No worries. If you change your mind and want to talk, you know, like, girl-to-girl, just bang on my door. Don't worry if it's too late. Anytime is good. 'K?"

"Th-th-thanks."

"You sleep well, Moll," Janine told her, and then walked away.

Well that was uncharacteristic of her, thought Molly.

CHAPTER NINETEEN

"I DUNNO, OOL," THE GIRL sighed. She shoveled a large hole in the forest as second thoughts ran rampant. The photograb stood on a rock, held in place by two small stones. "You'll get all faded away again, and I just got you looking so pretty."

"You can etch me back in when you come back," he replied as if no big deal.

"What if I do it wrong? What if I already done-done it wrong?"

"What it matters? As long as I'm with you."

"I guess," she said, paused, and asked, "What if they don't take me in?"

"They'll take you in, hon. You know the math. One man with ten women can make ten new people a winter, but one woman with ten men can still only make one—and likely at a net loss 'cause the men'll kill each other off to be the one to seed her.

"Now, if you were a man, that'd be a tale of a different color. Then they'd assume you a spy, and automatical kill you. But no tribe would ever put a potential mommy in peril by making her a spy. They all know that, and so do you."

"Yeah, great epoch to be a woman in, all right," she groaned.

"Just do what you always do. Learn as much as you can and then make them feel like you belong, like you're no different than they are. You'll be fine."

"Maybe I should go back to Baton Rouge. Yeah. Baton Rouge wasn't so bad."

"Baton Rouge was awful. You tried to kill yourself."

"But I didn't!" she barked. "I can nab and break me one of them scrawny horses. I know how to do that, you know. Ride into town like a civilized lady."

"You're just getting butterflies, baby. Happens every time you go to latch."

"Why should I fuckety-fuck have to?!" she demanded as she jabbed her shovel into the dirt to quit digging. "I was a lawyer, for fuckety-fuck sake! Twice. A lectric engineer. A baby gene designer. Chief resident of ER at Boston General."

"You think I don't know this?"

"I founded the first robot parts and service shop in all of Europe. Built it into a giant."

"Tell me when you're finished."

"I lived fifteen winters on a hydropod on Mars. Was mayor of Albany at the outbreak of the Collapse—mayor of the capital city of the richest state in the mightiest land in the history of the world."

"So why didn't you stop it?"

"No one could by then. You know that. The stopping had to have started long before. But I saved plenty-pon-plenty lives, and none of this is the point."

"Then what is the point?"

"I'm too good for these id-its! Too smart, too strong, too accomplished, too fuckety-fuck everything!"

"Baby, this could be what you've been searching for all this time. What you had before you lost it, found it from time to time then had to give it up again. Family, by blood or otherwise; a home; Toledo two-point-oh. It's what you want, what you've always wanted."

"I dunno . . . "

"You'll make good friends. You always do. Deep, loving friendships—"

"Which I won't remember."

"You'll birth and raise beautiful children who you'll love and adore—"

"And abandon."

"And who knows? Maybe you'll even get shacked to a good man."

"Ha!"

"It's happened before. You know it has. Even the worst of social structures can render quality individills."

"They beat their wives, Ool!" she blurted. "And women aren't allowed to know how to fight, so I won't be allowed to defend myself. They'll burn me if I fight back. Skilled as I am, I can't take a whole tribe with arrows at me from a distance!"

"You don't know that about this tribe. You saw nothing to tell you they beat their wives."

"It's how it was with the last three. It's the way things are now, Ool, the way they've all become."

"You told me your last tribe revered their women. Wouldn't even let them leave the safety of the homestead because motherhood is too sacred to be put at peril. Women are their most prized possession above all else, is what you said."

"'Possession' was the word you should've heard most. It's like . . . remember telebision sets? The early ones? Everybody loved, loved their telebision sets, but when it begun to act up, they'd give it a big hearty thwack on the side till it behaved. That's how it is these days. Husband gets upset, thwack-thwack-thwack on his woman."

"Then don't do anything to upset him."

The girl gasped. "Ool! That's a terrible thing to say to me!"

"Honey, look at me," he said gently. She turned to the photograb with indignant fury, and he continued. "When you watch me as I speak . . . do my lips move?"

She paused, thrown by the question, and then she laughed a little laugh. "Shut up, ya big id-it. I know you're not real, okay? I know you're just my magination. But talking to you like this helps me sort things out."

"Good. So in terms of all the very excellence advice I been giving . . . who's really been doing the giving of it?"

"Me," she begrudgingly admitted.

"Good some more. Because you're halfway to crazy, my darling, and we can't let you get all the way because there'll be no one round to bring you back home.

"Besides, maybe this tribe's different. When you described their homestead, you made it sound all serene and picture-esky. So maybe they're good folk, right?"

She sighed. Maybe, but in the end, she knew it didn't matter. She was losing her marmalades, it was a fact, and only real kinship with real people could keep her sane, get her sane, make her sane, no matter how gods-awful those people turn out to be. Ool was right on that. She couldn't take another sixteen winters alone.

She couldn't take one.

She sat beside him and forced a little smile. "So best friends and babies, huh?"

"It won't be so bad," he encouraged. "And hey, c'mon, it's only a matter of time till the good Lord reveals why He blessed you so."

This time her laugh was big and loud. "Serious?" she cackled through the woods. "You still believe that diarrhea? After all we've seen and been through?"

"I'm not talking about the backward people's superstitious hooey-ha. I'm talking about the one true God, our Lord and Savior Jesus Christ."

She shook her head in fond amusement, and tittered, "I love you, Ool."

She finished digging the hole, tossed her tools and weapons inside, and turned sadly back to the photograb. "Guess I'll see you in twenty winters or so."

"You take care of yourself now, y'hear?"

She nodded stoically, put the photograb in the satchel, the satchel in the hole, and filled it. She covered herself with dirt, then rubbed her front and back against a spruce tree to render cuts on her skin.

She picked up a sharp stone and tore it deep into her right calf along the line of her tattooed scar, then another along the tattooed scar on her left shoulder, then bashed the stone to the side of her head to draw blood. She took a deep breath and limped bravely into her next lifetime.

* * *

THE TWO HUNTERS trekked home after spending the morn observing a troop of chimpanzees. The one named Thunder was tall and handsome, with brown, falcon-like eyes, and big, clumsy muscles that lent him an air of superiority when he walked. The one named Leaf was small, with green eyes so pale they barely seemed to have any color at all. Both had seen twenty calendars, and both had many scars.

They'd discovered the troop by accident many calendars prior and had been slipping away from their dwelling to study the beasts ever since. They made no mention of them to their Sorry, their Holy One, or to any of the Community, claiming only that they were on search for new meats. One time they happened to stumble upon a herd of antelopes; another, a stray pair of baby elephants; most recently, the skinny horses, but the chimps were always their true objective.

"Did you notice how he is so helpful to his youngers?" Leaf expounded, now far from the troop's earshot so able to speak aloud. "Did you notice it?"

"You point to this every time," Thunder replied.

"And every time tis so," Leaf countered, "and every time important. Follow. We know it permitted to make homes because the birds do; we know building with wood an allowable technology because the beaver does; and by observing the way of the chimp, we'll come to know the blessed manner to usurp a Sorry."

"I know, I know. But me, I'm ready now."

"You are no more ready than our young chimp chum."

"He looks ready to me. Almost big as his Sorry, and bigger each day."

"Perhaps, but if he moves now, his Sorry's support will band together to slay him back, while his own support remains too young and small to be of consequence. But as he waits, his support grows older and stronger, while his Sorry's grows older and weaker."

"And he knows this thing how?"

"He doesn't know how we'd know. Only umanity is cursed with thought. The chimp is intuited by the gods. Usurp as he, and you too shall be in harmony-with.

"The youngers already worship you, Thunder. Keep at how you teach them, with humor and charm. And keep pecking at Clearsky. As long as you remain within the laws he can take no retribution against, and tis to our advantage when he seems weak to his support. So peck, peck, peck. But above all, stay patient. Remember, others have tried this before, and always Clearsky has prevailed."

"Are your toes getting frozen, old chum?"

"My toes are hot as yours, old chum, but you must heed my counsel of patience. Must heed the lesson of the chimps that the gods have put before your eyes. Some day one will succeed at his usurp, and then we'll know how to carry out ours. Tis a lesson the ones who opposed Clearsky before you were not given."

"No, old chum," chuckled Thunder. "What they weren't given was you."

Leaf smiled, flattered. "Twill be a glorious day for us all, my future Sorry."

"But what of the Holy One who's blessing I'll need to anoint me as the one truly chosen?" Thunder asked. "The chimps don't teach us that."

"I'm working on it."

Thunder smiled. He had no doubt his chum would deliver for he'd never met a man so clever, and that's when he noticed the critter in the distance. "What's that?"

Leaf scanned the plain. "I don't see anything."

Thunder nodded a silent command. Both men raised their spears above their heads and separated to approach the thing from opposite sides.

"Tis a man!" Leaf shouted as they drew closer.

"No, tis a woman," Thunder corrected. "And she's hurt." He

knelt beside her, and gently rolled her over. She was bruised and cut. Dried blood caked all over. She moaned. "Shhh," he whispered as he tenderly brushed her hair off her face. "Shhh."

"She's pretty," observed Leaf.

"Yes. If we get to keep her, I call dibs."

"As intended by the gods," deferred the smaller man, who immediately set upon conjuring a way to turn the discovery of the woman to politic advantage.

The men tucked their spears under their arms. Thunder grasped the girl's thighs; Leaf her shoulders. They lifted, and then carried her home as they chitted on.

Their accent was different from her last tribe, the girl observed, their grammar more stilted and officious, some of their slang foreign to her ears, but it wouldn't be too hard to put on. She'd developed quite the knack for such things over her many lifetimes—and she didn't have to be pat off the bat, just close.

She opened her eyes just a slit to study the man in front of her while still maintaining the air of debt's door. He's a looker this one all right, she noted, and very nicely hung. He was the one she saw teaching the young ones when she spied on the tribe from the cavey-tunnel the other day, the one all the children adored.

Yes, his dibs on me are most welcome.

* * *

SHE SPENT the rest of the day in the Holy One's cabin—a sparse four-bedroom in which everything was made from wood, clay, or animal. She lay on a feather-stuffed, elk-skin mattress atop a wooden gurney, and continued to feign unconsciousness so she wouldn't have to answer questions until she had a stronger sense of how to best fit in. Next to the gurney was a bench on which sat clay bowls, jars and cups, and a pile of maple leaves. On the far side of the room was a fireplace, a poofy sofa, and a small table on which lay a faded, half-completed jigsaw puzzle of a cartoon moose and squirrel, an almost-completed one of Michelangelo's Sistine Chapel with just one piece missing, and a plate of that yummy-smelling concoction.

THE GIRL WHO WOULDN'T DIE

The Holy One, whose name was Horizon, was a bony, wrinkled, old man with a beard so thin and white that he seemed almost clean-shaven. He dunked a handful of moss into a bowl of what smelled to be corn alcohol, then patted it over her open cuts. He doused the maple leaves into a bowl of honey, then pressed them against her torn skin until they stuck—the honey acting both as wound-addressing agent as well as adhesive. One after another, he pressed, until all the cuts were bandaged, except for the deep gashes on her calf and shoulder, which Horizon deemed to require stitching.

The girl was impressed that he knew about infections and disin-fectants.

Meanwhile, the Holy One's disciple prepared for the next stage. Sandy was a lanky young man of seventeen winters. He yanked out three pieces of his shoulder length hair and braided them together, yanked three more to braid those, three more to braid those, then braided the three braids into a robust thread.

Horizon took a duck fibula—a tiny bone sharp on one end with a teeny hole at the other—out of the cup of alcohol and proceeded to run the thread through it. He was about to pierce into the girl's calf when the disciple interrupted. "Shouldn't we have her drink of the hooch to help numb the pain?"

Hooch, the girl repeated in her head. She hadn't heard it called that for a very long time. Good to know. And they pronounce it 'hoo-ché.' Good to know.

"She already sleeps, young Sandy," said the master. "There lies no sense in waking her only to render her drowsy."

Lies no sense. Not 'there's no sense,' or 'makes no sense.' Lies no sense. Got it.

"Of course, master," Sandy replied. "I should've deduced that. Apology."

'Apology,' not 'I'm sorry,' but 'apology.' And they say it 'aplo-gee.' Does that mean that 'thank you' would be 'gratitude'? Or, 'grate-tee-tude'? Probably.

The stitching process hurt a little, and the old man's unsteady hands only made it worse. Didn't matter though. The deep gashes would soon vanish without a trace, but the ink of her ancient tattoos would remain, showing her to be a normal mammal that scars like everybody else.

* * *

As the post-noon wore on, or 'after-lunch' as they said it, many of their tribe came to take a gander—men considering her as wife, women assessing their potential new sister. They would enter without knock or announcement, as if free reign into the Holy One's cabin was a welcome norm. One of those who came was Thunder. He placed a clay vase of petunias on her bedside table, and then left.

The girl saw it through the slits of her eyes, and thought, aww, that's sweet.

Many of the children were mesmerized by the stranger. One of them inched cautiously toward her and ran her tiny fingers along the girl's locks to see what an outsider's hair felt like. Sandy tapped at her hand. "Cease such, she's healthing," he affectionately reprimanded. "Away, Daughter-of-Love. Away, little ones." The children scattered.

From what the girl could glean thus far, it seemed that men's names were derived from aspects of nature. There was Thunder, Horizon, and Sierra on the complimentary side; Drizzle, Pebble, and Stumpy at the other extreme; with names like Leaf and Sandy hovering in the middle. Contrarily, women's names were based on traits of personality—Playful, Love, and Share-y on the good; Dour, Brash, and Petulant on the not-so. The girl set her mind to coming up with her next new name, something that would fit their paradigm without seeming threatening to them.

Another who came to gander was the virgin-boy she'd seen at yesterday's hunt, the pimply one who killed the horse after the killing had been deemed done. The gossip she overheard informed her that he was a son of the Shepherd, which they called "the Sorry," and the tribe had granted him his manhood status at the prior night's Gathering, along with the less-than-flattering moniker 'Skinny Horse'—a perpetual reminder of the dubious manner in which his status had been achieved.

For this tribe, like so many others into which she'd latched, didn't name their young until adulthood since so few made it that far— their coming of age commencing upon first blood for a girl, and hunt or war's first kill for a boy, his first attempt permitted only after his thirteenth winter, or 'calendar' as they said it. Till then, girls went by 'Daughter-of-mother's-name,' and boys 'Son-of-father's-name.' The period between a boy's thirteenth calendar and first kill they called 'manling,' not 'virgin.' It could last a day, or calendars.

Nonetheless, Skinny Horse had come of age, was likely still single, and desirous of wife. Ugh, she thought. Even if she didn't get to be with Thunder, the notion of being shacked to this one was downright hurl-rendering. He was too young. True, in reality they were all too young, but this one was too-too young.

Like the little girl before him, Skinny Horse reached out and ran his fingers through her hair. Sandy admonishingly slapped his hand. "She's healthing! Away!"

"Slap me not like a child, Sandy," he blustered. "I am man now."

"And I am apprendix to the Holy One, Skinny Horse." The new man twinged upon hearing it. "You've had your little look-see, now away."

Skinny Horse glared at him indignantly, and then huffed off.

'Apprendix,' thought the girl. Not 'disciple,' but 'apprendix.' Got it.

She sensed the dusk approach and knew it time for her show to begin. She blinked her eyes open, and groggily asked, "Where-where am I?" She looked into Horizon's withered face. "Who are you?"

"Shhh," said Horizon. He held a cup of water to her mouth, and she drank.

"Gratitude," she said. "But how did it come to pass that I am in this place?"

"Our hunters found you dying on the plains and carried you to our dwelling."

"Are you hungry?" asked Sandy, as he picked up the clay plate. "You must be."

"Star-ved, kind sirree, gratitude."

Sandy fed her the stew, which was as delicious as it smelled—

apricot, peach, and maple syrup over a hearty base of whiskered-fishie, which they called 'pussy-fish,' exquisitely spiced with sage and thyme. "What will become of me?" she asked.

"You will take lake-wash in preparation for the night's Gathering where you will tell of how you came to be where you were found," Horizon answered dispassionately. "The Sorry will have consult with our men, and then decree you embraced into our Community, or banished, or slain."

"But stress not much," added the apprendix. "I can envision no reason why our Sorry wouldn't embrace a healthful woman of proper birthing age, for there is no doubt we can use such contribution."

"Praise the gods," said the girl.

"What is your name, woman?" asked the Holy One.

"I am called . . . Mellow."

She smiled. It felt nice to have a name again.

CHAPTER TWENTY

ENCINO, CALIFORNIA
SEPTEMBER 2017
THE DAY AFTER HER FIRST CRIM CLASS

TORTURE. RAPE. TORTURE.
   The images flashed even more vividly as Molly tapped on her phone to give the Uber driver five stars and a tip. She got out of the car with dread and forced herself into the San Fernando Valley cantina. She wore a white, cotton t-shirt, purple harem pants, and sneakers—lithe, pliant attire in case she had to fight.

But the Professor must be a friendly, her brain told her gut for the eleven-thousandth time. It's the only thing that makes sense. That has to be it, has to be.

Rape. Torture. Rape. Torture.

Professor Ramirez sat at a booth in the back wearing black jeans and a Grateful Dead t-shirt. There was a close-to-full pitcher of margaritas on the table, a half-full glass in front of him, and an empty one across. He saw Molly enter and waved his arm to get her attention. She unzipped her purse to check that her can of mace and

Saturday night special were still inside, the gun's safety off. She left the purse unzipped and went to join him.

"You w-w-wanted to s-see me, P-P-Professor?" she stammered tepidly.

"Francisco," he warmly corrected. "Please, Molly, sit." She took her seat across from him as he filled her margarita glass.

Doesn't he know I'm immune to alcohol? she wondered. Wouldn't he be too?

"Do you know who I am?" he asked.

"You're my t-t-teacher."

"Cute," he acknowledged with a smile. "Of course, yes, I am that, and in more ways than you can imagine, but you know what I meant. Who am I?"

"You t-tell me."

"Relax, Molly, I'm not here to hurt you," he assured her, putting his hand on hers as a comforting sign of friendship. She immediately jerked it back. He raised his arms in an innocent mea culpa. "I'm sorry. I shouldn't have done that. But I promise you, Molly, I am your friend. I've been so for a very long time. No one's coming after you. Everyone who was involved with Dr. Mueller's experiment is dead or too old to care. I know this because I kept tabs on them. For now, I'm just trying to determine how far back your memory of me goes so we can proceed from there."

She sighed. What's the point in playing games? "You were the j-j-janitor."

"That's right. Cheers," he said as he raised his glass. "And no, liquor doesn't affect me either, to answer your unasked question. I just like the taste. Don't you?"

"You can read minds too?"

"No, I just figured you'd be wondering because I'd be if I were in your shoes."

She said nothing in reply, only looked at him blankly, resenting the heck out of his friendly demeanor, while he continued to stare at her and smile.

"What?" she demanded uncomfortably.

132

"I just can't believe I'm actually sitting here with you, all revealed like this. I've been waiting fifty years to talk to you. Sure, that's a drop in the bucket in terms of how long I've been alive, but fifty years still passes like fifty years. You'll see. Anyway, I'm sure you have a slew of questions for me, so fire away."

"So this isn't s-some elab-b-borate plot to abduct me again?"

"No. But you knew that, or you wouldn't have come to see me. Next question."

"Promise?"

"I swear on the souls of my thousands of children, and theirs, and theirs."

With that, Molly leaned across the table and punched him in the arm.

"Ow!" he chuckled. "What was that for?"

"Why'd you have to come out to me so . . . so . . . dr-dr-dramatically?!"

"I like dramatic," he laughed on. "You and me, we've got to keep things hopping. You'll see. Besides, there was absolutely no manner in which I could've revealed myself to you that wouldn't have given you a severe jolt or two. Now, I'm sure you have other questions for me that are a little more, let's say, profound."

She paused, then softly asked, "C-c-can we die? Like, ever?"

"There you go," he smiled approvingly. "I was a warrior in most of my early lifetimes. Severely injured more often than I can count, yet here I sit. But that's not exactly scientific, is it? So I suppose the official answer has to be, I don't know."

"Why did you wait so long to r-r-reach out to me?"

"My initial plan was to wait a whole lot longer so you could experience a few more lifetimes on your own. I didn't want to make myself a crutch for you, rob you of developing the vital instincts you'll need to survive going forward."

"What changed your mind?"

"Weakness," he answered with a self-deprecating grin. "Selfishness. It's been so long since I've been able to be my real self with someone. Even when wrangling my way into the mad German's project, I never expected him to find someone like me. Best case, I figured I'd maybe learn a little more about what I am, and why. But then he found you. For the first time in forever, I didn't feel alone. And as soon as your results were conclusive, I set into motion the events that led to your release."

"P-prove it."

"Let's see. Did Al ever tell you about an anonymous correspondence with cut out letters from *Reader's Digest*, *Life* magazine, and *Playboy*?"

"Yes!" she said in complete surprise. "That was you?"

"A lot was me."

"What else?"

"A lot."

"Name two."

"The night you were stealing your Jane Doe, and that big fellow was heading toward you, but his phone conveniently rang to draw him away . . . You're welcome."

"You were the one who phoned him? How would you know to do that?"

"Because while you were hacked into everyone else's computer, I was hacked into yours. You had morgue surveillance on your system, so I had it on mine."

"That's c-creepy."

"Yeah, but in a good way."

"Okay, what's another example? You said two."

"Actually, you said two, but all right." He paused a moment, and then continued. "Molly, why did you choose to study the law of all things? Why not medicine? Why not biology or genetics to learn why you are the way you are?"

"I want to be as far from that world as p-possible, thank you very much. Medicine will be next. But we figured the world will keep ch-changing, so it'll be easiest for me to adapt if I have a solid under-standing of how s-societies function . . . and that's the law."

"I couldn't agree more. But what on earth made you think of that?"

"Oh, um, hmm, good qu-question. Oh yeah. It was this online

article Al and I stumbled upon years ago. It called the law 'the b-building blocks of civilization.'"

"Once again, you're welcome."

"No way!" she giggled. "You got that article in front of us?"

"Wrote it for you, actually."

"Wow," she sighed, finding it almost too much to absorb. "Okay, one more."

"Nuh-uh. You said two. Brand new kind of question now."

"Okay," she conceded. "You said that you waited s-so long for me . . . does that mean there aren't others like us? Just you and m-me?"

"Like the mad German said, it's not as if we advertise. So, once again, don't know."

"There's a lot you don't know."

"There is," Francisco said with a smile. "But there's also a lot that I do."

"Tell me one. Give me some tips, advice, oh ancient wise one."

"Ask me anything."

"Could you please give me some tips and advice?"

He laughed, and then so did she. "Okay, um . . . Keep up your hacking skills. It may not seem important now, but tech progresses fast. By the time you need to—"

"On it. I can tell you right now where war will soon break out, and what corporate mega-merger is being secretly negotiated. Also, my great-granddaughter is getting way too promiscuous for my taste, and it's killing me."

"You'll get used to that. I don't even check anymore once I've moved on."

"How can you not? I'm never going to not check."

"'K," he smiled knowingly.

"Don't be smug. What else you got?"

"Okay. Let's see. Keep a low profile. Be a lawyer, sure, but not the kind that can get famous. And at all costs, keep your face off the internet."

"I'm pretty careful."

"Be exceptionally careful."

"Why? You said Christoph's project is done with and no one's after me."

"What if some future scientist independently comes up with the same theory? And what if, in this hypothetical future, there's some kind of facial recognition software that can take a single photo of a person and instantly scour the entire web and all its history for a match?"

"That doesn't sound very likely."

"Neither did the internet before the internet."

"Good point. I'll be exceptionally careful. Next?"

"Next. Um, okay. Al was a good man. Don't ever forget him."

"I don't need you to tell me that."

"Yes, Molly, you do. You're going to have a great many lovers going forward, husbands, boyfriends, partners—the words for it will change as society does, as will the social constructs around it, but where there's love, there's love—and you'll love many of them as much as you loved Al. Nothing wrong with that.

"But after enough lifetimes, the past can grow hazy, memories blend together like repeating dreams. You come to regard your recollections as impossible because no one can live as long as you think you have. It must be your brain that's at fault. You'll believe yourself mad even when you're not, which is, in itself, madness. But those beautiful memories of your first love—the small moments, the smells, the touches—will reconnect you to your origins, the you who you were before you started all the pretending. And of all the narratives that will duplicate and echo through your mind, your beginning will remain the only one of its kind.

"The memory of your first love will ground you, Molly. Al will ground you, always, and without him you'll be lost."

"Gosh," she whispered. "That's good. Do you remember your first?"

"Of course."

"Tell me about her."

"No," he said, breaking eye contact for the first time, his lips curving into a bittersweet smile. "She's just for me," he said sadly, and then he said no more.

Molly let his melancholy permeate in silence. She studied him as his shoulders sagged down, as his eyes welled up. She tenderly put her hands on his and softly invited, "It's okay. If you need to talk about her, I'm the one you can talk to."

He violently yanked his hands away. "I said no!!!"

She jolted back, not realizing how enamored she had become of the man until that very moment when he frightened her.

"I'm sorry," he said quickly. "I shouldn't have reacted like that. I'm just not used to . . . I don't know . . . being myself, my full self, with someone."

"It's okay. I'm the one who should apologize," she answered. "You said no. I should've respected that."

"Don't worry about it. Hey, know what I like even more than margaritas?"

"What?"

"Ice cream."

* * *

"So how old are you?" Molly asked as they strolled down Ventura Boulevard, she slurping on her pistachio almond, he on his mint chocolate chip.

"Have you heard of the Punic Empire?"

"Um, I think so."

"Carthage?"

"'Course. That's who Rome beat to become, well, to become Rome. Right?"

"It's a tad more complicated than that—take a history class some-time—but yes. Carthage was the capital city of a great and mighty empire, where I was born to a family of little means, near the end of its glory."

"Wow, that's old all right. Wait. Then how are you Puerto Rican?"

He laughed. "Francisco Ramirez is third generation Mexican-American, and conflating the two is a microaggression I must now report to the PC Police."

"Busted," she laughed along.

"Genetically, I'm what you'd call Arab, and lived as such through most of my lifetimes in the Middle East and then Europe, but it's safer to blend in America as a Latino these days. Come to think of it, you might have a bit of a handicap there."

"What do you mean?"

"Me, I can blend into all kinds of groups given my skin tone and facial features. I've been Muslim, Jewish, Zoroastrian, Sikh, now I'm Catholic, albeit not practicing. But you're white, and white is white no matter how you slice it."

"I don't think white as an okay thing is going away any time soon."

"'K," he smiled.

"You're being smug again."

"Busted," he laughed. "Next question."

"Okay," she said, and then took a moment to phrase the one question that was the most important of all. "What's the point of it?"

"As in, what's the meaning of life? Is there a God?"

"As in, so we get to live a really long time, maybe forever. Why? So every twenty years we have to leave everyone we've come to love, anything we may have built, just to start over from scratch? For what purpose?"

"Again, don't know—but in that way we're not much different than anyone else. So, we choose our purpose. Be a lawyer, a doctor, a farmer, a homemaker, join the Peace Corps, the military, live a life of celibacy, follow up with one of debauchery. Buck the system. Be the system. I've done 'em all. In time, so will you. We choose our purpose, Molly, if only in order to have one."

"So what's your purpose this go-around?"

"Isn't it obvious by now? You."

She sighed uncomfortably, and then giggled a little giggle. "I've got to tell you, Professor, this is not at all how I expected my first week of law school to wrap up."

"I know," he giggled along as he wolfed down the last of his sugar cone and tossed his napkin into a trash bin. "What would you like to do now?"

"I don't know, maybe I should head back. Why, what'd you have in mind?"

"Well, Molly . . . if it's okay with you . . . I'd really love to kick your ass."

* * *

THEY STOOD in the backyard of his Encino Hills Spanish style two-story, circling each other on the grassy lawn next to the pool. Her hair was tied back in a ponytail, her shoes and socks off, and she was glad she had dressed for a fight. Francisco had swapped out his jeans for a pair of sweatpants, his feet and upper body bare, his exquisite musculature something Molly had to remind herself to ignore.

She thrust a swift sidekick to his chest, which he blocked with ease, returned with a double-roundhouse kick to her stomach and head, which she off-angled and parried with ease, returned with a knifehand strike to his throat, which he blocked and answered with a headbutt to her forehead, from which she dropped underneath, rolled away, and then sprang back up to her feet.

They laughed as they repositioned themselves for the next onslaught.

"You know, you're the second best at this in the world," he smiled, "and I am thoroughly enjoying the competition."

"Funny, I always thought of myself as first best," she cockily replied as she began to circle him once more. "Been at this fifty-two years, you know. Neither Bruce Lee nor Mr. Miyagi got anything on me."

"Fifty-two years, eh?" he responded, poising his body in a scorpion-like defensive stance unfamiliar to her. "What do you think happens after two-thousand-one-hundred-and-seventy-nine?"

"All right, old man. Impress me."

Without warning, he leapt and unleashed a ferocious flying butterfly kick at her face. She ducked, spun, and countered . . . and they were off to the races.

"Not bad for a youngster," he smiled mid-combat.

"This all you got?" she taunted. "No wonder the Romans kicked your behinds."

"Careful," he cautioned. "That dig's still a little close to home."

"Sorry," she replied, then charged with a barrage of wicked front kicks that he blocked handily.

"I'm starting to get the feeling you're not giving me your all," she panted.

"I just want you to feel you're doing well."

"The heck with that, fossil-boy. I want your best!"

She never saw what he did, but the next thing she knew she was lying prostate on the ground, regaining consciousness, barely able to breath.

"You all right?" asked Francisco, holding out his hand to help her up.

"So you can beat up an old lady," she wheezed. "You must be so proud." She slapped away his hand, sprang to her feet, and circled him once more.

And on the battle waged, beyond the afternoon, through the dusk, and into the pale darkness of the LA night, pausing only occasionally for him to teach her a new trick from an ancient technique devised by unheard of peoples lost to history.

By the time the light was too dim to properly see, he had her pinned down in an inescapable hold that she had never come across in all her years of study, with his index and middle fingers perched an inch from her eyes.

"Stop struggling like that," he advised as he panted from fatigue. "In a second, you'll be blind. What do you do?"

"Learn braille?" she panted back.

"Do you want me to teach you or not?"

"Okay. What do I do?"

"First, dislocate your shoulder."

"How do I do that?"

"You've never done that? We can do that. Watch." With that, he used his free arm to demonstrate the ancient art of self-dislocation. It looked inhuman.

Curiously, she followed his example. She gently rolled her shoulders like a yoga exercise, then quickly and violently jerked one shoulder forward while yanking the other back with equal force. She felt a sudden "pop" and a brief, mild pain, but her arm had an odd flexibility she never knew possible. "Holy mackerel!"

"Good. Now you can squirm that arm out of my hold—your enemy will never notice because he's focused on your eyes, won't even consider it because the human arm isn't supposed to work like that. Good. Now reach up, and grip onto my balls."

"Shouldn't you buy me dinner first?"

"You know, brat, if you snark me like this in class, I will fail you."

"Okay, okay," she replied, panting with a smile, then did as instructed.

"Lightly!" he screamed.

"Sorry."

"No, no, that was good, actually. In battle, you squeeze as hard as you can, but today is for educational purposes only. So, your enemy reacts. You keep squeezing, and now you can wriggle your healthy arm free." He took hold of her hand to move it through the drill. "Hard knifehand strike to the cave of his mouth, like this. His head snaps back. You recoil fast, separate your fingers like this, and BAM into the opposing edges of his throat, jutting through his pharynx, and he's dead." He paused. "And I'm done." Exhausted, he allowed himself to tip over to the ground, landing at a diagonal to her with the tops of their heads almost touching, forming a human "V."

There was a brief moment of silence as they both tried to catch their breath, which Molly broke by huffing, "Thank you for all this, Francisco. Really."

"No, thank you, Molly. Really," he graciously huffed back.

Another silence, which she broke again. "In that last move you showed me, what else could I do instead? I don't want to ever actually kill a person."

"If you have to kill 'em, you kill 'em."

"No, I'd prefer to find another way. I'm never going to kill someone."

"'K."

"Shut up."

* * *

Two thousand years, Molly marveled in the back seat of the Uber on her ride home. He was born before Rome was even a thing, before the printing press or indoor plumbing or anything was a thing. The notion she could be that old someday was too much to fathom, so she turned her attention toward the other amazing lessons he gave her, particularly what he said regarding Al.

It wasn't that she'd ever consciously decided to stop thinking about the only man she'd ever loved, but with the hardship of letting go of Millie, the difficulty of truly embracing Molly, and the awesome excitement of law school, she'd felt it best not to dwell on him. Francisco, bless his soul, taught her that was incorrect.

Dwell she should, so dwell she shall—it was the loveliest of training drills she ever had to endure. She didn't need to close her eyes to see Al's smiling face or hear his tender voice inside her. He was young and healthy, old and frail, everything in between, and beautiful in all versions. And she didn't need that old Polaroid to imagine his touch, but she yearned to hold him in her hands all the same.

"Get off at Sepulveda," she told the driver. "I want to make a stop."

By the time they arrived at the Van Nuys storage facility, she decided not to have the driver wait—may as well do some hacking drills as long as she's here.

She yanked up the door of her extra-large unit, then closed and locked it behind her before flipping on the lights. The teraflops and analyzers were on their tables as she had left them three days ago, the bulletin boards and maps on the walls, the books in stacks underneath, the file cabinets in the corners—the "mini-batcave" she'd been calling the place. She noticed the generator was getting low on juice, and she'd have to tend to that in the next day or so, but she was here for Al now.

She looked to the bulletin board beside the desk, but the photo wasn't on it. Odd, she thought, she could've sworn that's where she'd tacked it. Thinking back, she didn't remember actually tacking it, but she didn't remember not tacking it—one of those automatic tasks one does without thought so the memory doesn't stick, like locking a car door or turning off the coffee machine. She looked to the other bulletin boards, nothing.

She swept through the files on her desk and tables, then every file in the file cabinets, and then leafed through all the books.

Where the heck is it?

CHAPTER TWENTY-ONE

Long Island, New York
5 Months Earlier
The Morning After The Night Of The Death Of Millie Lang

WHAT HAD BEEN A CELEBRATED palace just the evening prior was by morning a dilapidated teardown. Windows were punched out by the pressure of the fire hoses, the front door kicked in by first responders, almost half the roof gone, and the air itself scented with the stench of disaster. A pair of firefighters patrolled the ruins to ensure there were no lingering embers buried beneath any of the rubble, and two uniform cops stood by the once-grand entranceway puffing on their smokes while they waited for the forensic team inside to finish up.

A shiny blue BMW cruised the majestic driveway to stop inches by the front door. The driver got out and looked around. A short, stocky, mid-fiftyish man with a comb-over that failed to hide the Florida-shaped birthmark embedded on his scalp, he wore an expensive watch, expensive shoes, and what had been an expensive suit nine years ago when he bought it that now just looked frumpy.

"Hello, boys," he told the cops. "How you screwing up my crime scene today?"

"No crime here, Pete," one answered. "Just a tragic mishap that killed a sweet old lady. You guys ain't wriggling out of a payout on this one."

"Says you," Pete answered. He took a step back to get a wide-angle view of the catastrophe, made a mental note of the tire tracks coming in and out to cross-reference against the kosher visitors, and snapped some pictures on his phone.

Peter Mailor was considered one of the best insurance investigators in all New York, his powers of observation and deduction matched only by his ineptitude at nine-ball. In fact, a big chunk of his exorbitant salary would almost always find its way into the hands of pool sharks, another into the hands of high-priced call girls.

"Boys," he nodded to the policemen, and sauntered inside.

Cops didn't like Pete. Once an up-and-coming NYPD detective, he had been a bitter, arrogant blowhard with little regard for the law he served. He'd lock people away with glee, but only to show off, to pronounce himself superior to the sleuths around him. If ever praised for a job well done, he'd downplay his accomplishment only in order to belittle the fool who complimented him in the first place.

He knew what they thought of him and he didn't care. He'd help them out of a jam from time to time, sure, but never because he was kind but rather because he enjoyed having them in his debt so he could lord it over them. He'd watch all the saps buddy-buddy each other as they relished in their bogus friendships, oblivious to the fact that they'd be abandoned as dirt the moment they were in need. It was a lesson he had learned the hard way as a little boy, and again even harder in his teens.

So when his drinking began to spiral out of control, his higher-ups saw it as the perfect excuse to oust him, even though the boozing hadn't affected his job performance a lick. No one stood up for him. Even the ones who pitied him for his sad, self-fulfilling prophecy stayed quiet. To Pete, it was just the way of the world.

Not long after, he secured an entry-level investigator position with Kingston-Benefit Insurance. Between his high intellect and low morals, he excelled. No one was better at helping the monstrous conglomerate slither its way out of making good on a claim, and so he climbed the corporate ladder fast. The brass didn't care how much he drank or how rude he was as long as he got the job done, and that suited Pete just fine.

The inside of the house was an even bigger mess than the outside. Shattered glass abounded. Costly rugs were reduced to sheets of dust atop scorched, cracked floors, and handwoven wicker chairs to grainy powders. The grand oak bookcase had vanished from the charred wall, its literary classics rendered black and illegible.

A duo of forensic specialists was packing up to go as Pete entered the home. "Gentlemen," he issued as he began to snoop around. "Care to give me a head start?"

"Hey Pete," began the older, senior specialist. "So, okay. Old lady lives alone. Kitchen window open, stove on, no one nearby. Wind blows a flame onto a roll of paper towels, flares up to the curtains, yadda yadda."

"And get this?" added the junior. "She was hammered. Slopped a trail of booze all over before she passed out on the sofa. That's what spread the spreading."

Pete crouched down low and sniffed the floor. "Gin," he said. "Nolet's. Nice."

"Body's with the coroner," continued the senior. "Kids've been notified to come in to ID, not that it'll do much good. Anyway, that's it, and we're out of here."

"Mind if I stick back and poke my nose around?"

"Couldn't stop you if I wanted to, but I'm telling you, you won't find nothing nefarious. Was just a sad accident. What good people pay their premiums for."

"I still got to cross the i's and dot the t's," Pete said with a smile. "It's why I get the big bucks . . . and you don't."

"Fuck you," replied the senior specialist, and the duo left.

Pete moved methodically through the ruins, opening doors and drawers, not sure what he was looking for but knowing that there was almost always something. He opened a cupboard to discover the liquor cabinet and stopped cold. "Well, hello."

Two bottles of Cristal, an unopen backup of Nolet's, Johnny Blue, Absolut Elyx, Don Julio Real, and lots of fancy-shmancy wines. "This investigation's going to take a long, long time," he assured himself as he poured a tall one.

He shot back a swig of the Johnny Blue and kept bottle in hand as he crossed into the kitchen. It took him only a moment to ascertain that the forensic guy's story held water, but that didn't necessarily mean that the fire was an accident. He snapped some pictures, then went back to the living room to check the upstairs.

The seat and padding of the escalator-chair had melted away, along with the previously ornate stairwell banister. He stomped his foot on the oak step to make sure it wouldn't splinter from his weight, and it seemed strong enough. Still, he stuck to the edge where the banister had once been as he climbed.

The second floor wasn't nearly as bad as the first, but still pretty singed and stinky. He made his way into the master bedroom, one of seven he had to check.

It was clean and the bed was made, consistent with the theory that the old woman passed out on the couch. He rummaged through the drawers and closet to find nothing telling, and then headed into the bathroom.

He began with the medicine cabinet in the hope that the old woman kept some fun painkillers to pilfer, and he was sadly disappointed in that regard. He swung the shower door open by rote with no real expectation of finding evidence of arson, but tiny shards of slimy stringy things on the floor caught his attention. He picked up a piece. Gooey, plasticky. Some kind of latex? Why? He took a Ziploc from his pocket and placed a few of the shards inside for the boys in the lab to figure out.

Still, he wanted to know. He took a gulp of the Johnny and held the Ziploc up to the light as he leaned against the interior shower wall, when the wall itself budged. He put the baggie back in his pocket, pressed his shoulder to the wall, and pushed. It pivoted open with relative ease, and he walked through to the other side.

He found himself in a large, barren space with red brick walls, completely untouched by the fire. There were a bunch of tables with nothing on them, a couple of chairs, some TVs bolted into the bricks, and nothing else.

What the hell?

There was a big, rectangular hole in the floor in the far corner. He crossed over to investigate and looked down. It was an elevator shaft, the elevator itself four stories below. The firefighters had long since shut off the power, so he proceeded to climb down the ladder within. As his eyes reached floor level, he happened to notice something behind one of the tables, a piece of paper of some kind pinned between a table leg and the wall. He climbed back out of the shaft to learn more.

It was an old black & white Polaroid of a man and woman in bathing suits, with a hand-written caption "Miami Beach, 1954." He fixated on the woman's face as the wheels in his head began to spin and clang, the memory files of his computer brain popping open at dizzying speeds, until he realized what he was looking at.

"Holy shit," was all he could say.

* * *

PETE COULDN'T REMEMBER the last time he thought about the file, yet still he knew exactly where it was—top left shelf of the garage below a stack of boxes of old tax returns and bank statements. He'd left his car on the street in front of his two-story Queens home where it would likely get ticketed or towed, but it allowed him to dump all the useless crap onto his empty garage floor. He had bigger fish to fry.

He found the box he wanted, worn and tattered, one corner collapsed from the weight of the junk that had been above it, "parent stuff" sloppily written on its side in red magic marker. He carried it into the house, plopped it on the kitchen table, and rummaged through its contents. A bunch of useless tchotchkes, hospital bracelets and little phonebooks, two filled-to-the-brim photo albums labeled "Clara and Christoph," and a third barely started labeled "baby." At the bottom was the manila envelope. He read the words emblazoned upon it, words he hadn't seen for a very long time, words that boasted a name he had tried so hard to forget:

For my son Dieter Mueller, to be opened on his twenty-first birthday.

Peter Mailor took a glass from the cupboard and the liberated bottle of Johnny Blue from his briefcase. He filled the glass, shot it back, sat at the table, yanked the dossier out of the envelope, and quickly flipped through its pages until he came to the first photo of Millie, sad and scared and strapped to a hospital bed in 1965. He placed the Polaroid of her and her husband from eleven years earlier beside it. He picked up his phone, scrolled to the pix of dark-haired Mel that he had taken at the pool hall only four weeks prior, and placed it between the two. He stared at all three.

There was no question they were the same woman.

He took another shot and began to read, starting with the handwritten letter that was paper clipped to the dossier's cover, welling up as he went. It wasn't the first time he read the embarrassing pages, although the first time in a long time, and the very first with its contents validated, so perhaps not so embarrassing after all.

To my beloved son, my Dieter,

If you are reading this, it means that I was not blessed with the privilege of watching you grow into the fine young man you must be by now, and that shall be the greatest regret of my abbreviated life.

I watch you play in your playpen as I write this letter. You're two-and-a-half years old, and you're happy. You're smiling as you explore the range of movement of the arms and legs of your little soldier doll, like a true scientist. So smart, so beautiful, so innocent, so white, so filled with potential. The world shall be your oyster.

I must leave for a meeting soon, one that may result in my assassination. I have explored all my options, but I find myself with none that can save me. I am boxed in. My only hope is that my suspicions are misguided and that the man I must meet lacks the intellect to see or the courage to pursue his best self-interest. I am not optimistic.

You will hear terrible things about me as you grow. I will be presented to you as a lunatic or a monster, a co-conspirator of the Holocaust. Hogwash, all. I have always been a man of science, as was my father before me, as was his before his, and as I assume you are on your way to becoming now. My life's work was dedicated to the eradication of disease and the betterment of mankind. But not everyone desires such blessings for the world, and it is for this reason that I will likely be murdered.

Enclosed is the chronicle of my crowning achievement. There is, at most, only one other like it. The copies that I have left with the Treasury Department, my current benefactor, have been doctored to invalidate my results. I did this for your protection.

I cannot envision the state of genetic science in the year 1985, at the time of your reading. I cannot predict whether my breakthroughs have been discovered and so rendered commonplace, or the knowledge I pursued never learned at all. If the latter, if my computations are too advanced, my hand-written margin notes will give you an accurate sense of the man I was, and of the benevolent goals I aspired to achieve.

I must go now. My hope is to return within the hour to destroy this letter in the embers of our fireplace. If that does not come to pass, I beg your forgiveness for my absence from your life. I pray it's been a happy one thus far, and I have no doubt that it will be a successful one going forward into your future.

With all my love and prayers for you, my little Dieter

Your father
Christoph Wilhelm Mueller

The wet that had been growing in Pete's eyes dripped down his cheeks. "It was all true, you crazy Nazi bastard!" he wept. "All this time it was true! I'm so sorry I never believed you, Christoph. Father. No one did. We . . . I didn't know! How could I have known?!"

Pete downed his glass, refilled it to empty the bottle, and read on. As Christoph had predicted, the science was incomprehensible to him, but the margin notes said it all, accentuated and confirmed by the handwritten notes of another scientist who signed his name "Woodrow G. Szabo."

His father had been a genius, Pete understood at last. A hero. A martyr.

He turned back to the page where he had left the three photos of Millie, realigned them neatly to see, once again, no difference at all. He clenched his teeth as he glared.

"Got you, you bitch."

CHAPTER TWENTY-TWO

THE DWELLING
THE NIGHT OF THE DAY SHE GOT HERSELF FOUND

THEY SAT IN A SERIES of rings around a circle of little fires that, in turn, encircled a single, jagged boulder roughly fifteen hands tall called the Condemnation Rock. The innermost of the rings was for the men; behind them sat their wives—sometimes one, sometimes more; behind the women, their children. Mellow sat in the second ring, directly across from the Sorry, with no one in front or behind her.

At a glance, she calculated about fifty adult men or less, and about a hundred adult woman or more, on the small side for a tribe but not terrible given their natural, impeccable security.

It was the fifth day of the moonth of sloth in the calendar of the god of waters, proclaimed the Holy One, who then proceeded to lead the congregants in group prayer and song. A few were somewhat familiar to Mellow—old world tunes she once knew but with melody and lyrics askew—and others of which she had never heard the like, but she did her best to learn quickly and join in as if she belonged.

With prayer and song dispensed, the Sorry took reign of the ceremony. Clearsky was a man of average height, bald on top, with more than fifty calendars behind him. His scarred, leathery skin covered a brawny muscular body, exuding the image of a man who had seen many combats and won them all.

The matters discussed ranged from the commonplace to the barbaric. There was much talk about corn and horses; new updates regarding the proper food-bearing plants by which to relieve themselves; a woman named Love had recently birthed a still and continued to suffer a sick that wouldn't health despite the Holy One's best voodoo; and some squabbling over cabins—those closest to the center marking a man's status, the two center ones belonging to Clearsky and Horizon.

A feeble old man named Gazelle confessed that he was no longer able to hunt and had therefore become a burden to the Community. In accordance with their holy laws, Gazelle anointed his eldest son, his closest male relative, to put him to rest. With cutter in hand, the son helped his father to his feet, walked him to the Condemnation Rock, and had him lean against it. Horizon rose, sprinkled drops of corn hooch upon the old man's head, and yodeled a blessing commending him for his piety and service. The son raised his cutter to the heavens, mumbled a soft prayer of his own, and then slit his father's throat. Everyone softly banged rocks against other rocks in sad applause and deference while the son carried the body away.

For Mellow, it was nothing new . . . just sad and pointless.

She could tell they were reserving her for the climax of the ceremony. She was confident it would go her way based on what she had thus far observed, but the butterflies in her tummy fluttered nonetheless. It's just positive energy, she reminded herself, harkening back to her days as a Broadway chorus girl.

Thunder would occasionally glance her way with warm, encouraging smiles, assuring her that all will be well. It helped, and her return smiles told him such.

None of that was lost on the woman seated behind him, a handsome woman of thirty-two calendars who glowered at Mellow with a painful glum. Mellow understood. She'd been a second wife before and had seen the pangs of rejection a woman endures when cast aside for what is new, but she also knew such feelings pass. She'd been a first, too.

At one point, Clearsky turned the discussion to the notion of whether their use of bows and arrows could be considered a form of technology, and the Great Drought their punishment for it. Most of the men had observed the other primates throwing stuff, but never had they seen any construct one thing to hurl another. No decision was to be made that night, said the Sorry, but they were each to consider imposing a temporary halt in the practice to see if the gods reward them with rainfall.

Mellow knew the outcome in advance for she had witnessed such stupid far too often. One generation decides to experiment with a new notion—almost always regressive—and then remains too frightened to return to the prior, better approach. The next generation follows suit because it was how their fathers did it. The next accepts it as tradition, the next as the will of the gods, and for the next any deviance is a holy sin punishable by death.

It was how the world got so fuckety-fuck.

* * *

"MY PEOPLE WERE A GODS-FEARING PEOPLE," she began. "We lived in harmony-with, and the gods shed their pity upon us for it. Our river flowed strong, our rains rained when time for rain, our produce was plentiful, and our meats grazed in abundance.

"But one night, the night of the last banana moon like the one above us now, the gods changed their minds, and shook our lands. The ground opened. Our river flooded above its banks. Boulders crashed down upon us from the mountainsides."

"Can such a thing be?" the Sorry asked the Holy One with a hint of suspicion.

"Yes, my Sorry. Tis taught of deep in our lore. One of the gods' most angry of sanctions. Mellow, what the gods punished your people with is called 'earthquake.'"

"Earth cake?" asked the former Caltech seismologist with feign confusion.

"Quake."

"Quake," she self-corrected. "Earthquake. Twas a terrible earthquake. Even our bravest warriors ran affrighted and shouting. And the next thing to which I was aware, I awoke, my head hurt, and it was lumpy." She began to sniffle. "Everyone was dead. My husband, my warrior sons, my daughters, their babies, all dead."

Yes, I'm a woman whose children make it to adulthood, was what she was really telling them. Chew on that!

"I cried from dawn to dusk and back again. I was scared, hungry. Our foods were ruined so I went on a searching. I found a little blackberry bush, scarfed it empty, but twas not enough to fill my fill. I journeyed on, found a tiny more each day, but never enough. I knew not to where I headed, only followed the path of food as I found it until my weakness grew too strong and I could follow no more, and so I laid down upon the earth to await my death, where your brave warriors found me. Praise the gods."

An unsettling silence ensued, for they all knew in their hearts that a similar fate could strike them too at any time, knew that the gods were almighty, and fickle.

"A sad tale indeed," the Sorry said, returning human voice to the Gathering. "But what has yet to be determined, Mellow—and must be determined—is why the gods turned on your people. You seem a strong woman of proper hips and hearty uterus who can certainly aid to reinforce our numbers—as a rule tis all we require—but your people did sin, must've had sin in their souls, and the Sorry of this Community cannot risk you a carrier of their infection."

"I know not how we displeased them!" she fake-sobbed. "I know not why the gods spared me and me alone, know not why they led me to you!" she wailed as she gave them the clue that they'd need to bring it all home . . . she hoped. She could provide the answer herself, but it would be much better if they got it on their own.

"Tis not a fair to ask her such a thing, my Sorry," defended Thunder. "She's but a woman. How could she know the secret transgressions of her Sorry or Holy One?"

Nope, thought Mellow, that's not it, but gratitude for the trying.

The men of the Community proceeded to fire off questions about her people's use of bows and arrows and other technologies. She replied to each with the tribally correct responses as they veered further and further away from the answer so obvious.

She shot a quick glance to Thunder, a flash of a nod with urgency in her eyes—Say it! Thunder understood the plea but remained at a loss.

During this, Sandy leaned forward and whispered something into his master's ear. The Holy One nodded consent, and the young apprendix spoke.

"The woman cannot speak of what she didn't see, no matter how many different ways we ask it," he insisted. "We can't know why the gods turned on her people. All we can know is what they put before our eyes, and here is what they put. They spared only she; they led her to us; and she's a healthful birther. It must be therefore reasoned that the gods did this for reason, and that they wish us to embrace her into our fold."

There ya go! thought Mellow.

Agreeable murmurs followed as the men discussed the apprendix's very salient point. Clearsky looked to Horizon, who nodded. He turned back to the most elderly of his wives, who nodded too. He rose and reached out to her—a sturdy, leathery woman of more than forty calendars—and helped her to her feet.

The woman held out her hands to Mellow. "Come."

Mellow rose, walked to her, and took her hands. "I am Dour," the woman sternly declared. "First wife to the Sorry, First Moma of the Community, moma to all she's, and moma twice to she's without moma. Kneel before your Sorry, my new daughter, kiss his feet, and I will prompt you of what to say." Mellow did as told, and Dour continued. "You are my Sorry, and may the gods take pity on my Sorry."

"You are my Sorry, and may the gods take pity on my Sorry," said Mellow.

"I vow to the gods to live my life by the ways of my Community, to serve the whims and desires of its men with energy and humility, only my Sorry's wishes will supersede theirs, and only my husband's his." Mellow repeated.

Clearsky smiled, took her hands, and helped her to her feet. He kissed her on both cheeks, then her lips, and passed her back to his wife.

Dour put her hands on Mellow's shoulders. "You are us now, my daughter," she said, "with all the rights and hardships of the she's of the Community."

Everyone banged rocks against other rocks in welcoming applause.

"And now you must wed," Dour went on, and turned to the men. "Who amongst you wish Mellow to live under your protection as moma to your children?"

Leaf jumped in quickly. "I believe the answer to that question requires no debate. For is it not our law that a new man be given first wife upon first opportunity? Can it be coincidence that the gods gave us Mellow but a day aft Skinny Horse came of age?"

Mellow could tell he was lying for she had never lost that particular skill, but she couldn't for the life of her figure out why. She shot a quick, exasperated glance to Thunder. What the fuckety-fuck? Thunder smiled back and nodded assuredly.

"I have pondered the same, chum Leaf," smiled Skinny Horse. "Yes, I will take Mellow to my protection, and I praise the gods for delivering me a wife so fetching."

"Not so quickly," Thunder calmly interjected. "'Tis also law that a hunter be entitled to the treasure of his catch. I found her, and so she is mine."

The Sorry's heart skipped a beat, for he instantly saw the trap that Leaf and Thunder had set for his son—a trap he knew was actually intended to diminish his own standing. He could see that the others remained unaware, so he sought to buy himself a little time till a winning strategy was revealed to him. "You already have a wife, Thunder," he said wearily, as if Thunder but a petty annoyance.

"And you have three," Thunder said pleasantly. "But yes, our laws seem at odds, as they do from time to time. So I issue challenge. Skinny Horse and I will combat, and the gods themselves will decree who shall receive fair Mellow's hand."

There was an audible gasp among the congregants, for such a combat would be ludicrously one-sided, and they wondered how on earth their Sorry would save his son from the inevitable trouncing.

"Are you so intent on antagonizing your Sorry?" Clearsky asked Thunder.

"Is my Sorry so intent on antagonizing his mightiest warrior?" parried Thunder.

"Marriage is not a thing of game!" The Holy One shouted to Thunder and Leaf both, seeing through their ploy. "Our laws are given us by the gods, whip-snaps!"

"Tis the gods' laws upon which I rest my claim," Thunder humbly replied.

"And please don't bring me into your little squabble, oh righteous one," Leaf added innocently. "I proclaimed from the start that Mellow should belong to the new man, and my position remains where it started."

Mellow could still not decipher what Thunder and Leaf were up to. She got why the Sorry was trying to stall on behalf of his son, and she assumed the Holy One was just suckling up to the boss—not the first time church and government were in cahoots. All she knew for sure was that she was in the center of a high-level rivalry, which was a perilous place to sit on her first night.

"Of course," Thunder taunted amicably, "this can all be resolved without wound or shed of blood if little Skinny Horse wishes to cower her to me."

"Enough!" Clearsky reprimanded, then calmed himself. "It's been a long Gathering. Let us put this squabble on a table until—"

"I accept the challenge!" shouted Skinny Horse.

"Quiet!" the Sorry snapped at his simpleton son.

"No, Pupa, I accept it with relish'n'mustard!" insisted Skinny Horse then turned to his darer. "Tis law for her to be mine, and the gods will see it so!"

Thunder smiled winningly. "I s'pose we'll find out."

Dour leaned forward to whisper something into her husband's ear, but he raised his hand to silence her.

"A challenge for Mellow's hand has been challenged, and the challenge accepted," the Sorry proclaimed. "The combat will be held in light of day aft the morrow's luncheon.

"The Gathering is shut."

CHAPTER TWENTY-THREE

Los Angeles, California
December 2017

Life for Molly Parker was strolling along splendidly. Her first semester of law school was winding to a close, and she was pretty confident she had kicked rear end as planned. Of course, if her grades turned out too good, she'd have to hack into the school computers so as not to bring any undue attention upon herself—straight A's across the board would be adjusted to include several A-'s with a spattering of B+'s. On the other hand, if her assessment of her smarts was wildly off and she received mainly C's, she would leave them intact and accept the sad truth about her mediocrity—but she wasn't going to cheat up.

Life needs problems, although small ones. If too catastrophic, the whole existence thing can become unbearable. But a life with no problems at all can put one in a mind-numbing rut, and existence can grow monotonous to the point of pointlessness. We all require a gentle flowing stream of small, solvable problems and petty annoyances in order to be happy, and that's exactly what Molly had.

She never found that Polaroid, and it bugged her to no end.

Randy got the message by mid-October. Their friendship flourished, which was good, and he found a girlfriend, which was good in theory but not really. Audrey was an undergrad and a stunning young lady. The daughter of a successful movie producer and his third trophy wife, she was spoiled, entitled, manipulative, and treated Randy like he owed her something. Molly couldn't stand the girl.

"Why can't he see her for what she is?" Molly asked the others of the quintet.

"Have you gotten a look at her?" Josh chuckled. "Oh man, he sees it all right."

"Oh come on," Molly answered. "Randy can attract pretty girls other than her. He's handsome, brilliant, sweet. He's like a gosh-darn Kennedy."

"He's a total nerd," Josh replied. "I'm crazy about the dude, but let's face it."

"Please. He was a star college athlete."

"Jock-nerd. It's rare, I admit, but not unique. Look at his interests. *D&D*, video games, *Game of Thrones*, comic books, more comfortable in a library than a party, and can't talk to girls worth beans."

"He has no trouble talking to me."

"Only once he stopped trying to land you. Remember how lame he was with you at first? 'If ya want, if it's okay, shucks, shucks.' And also remember, Audrey picked him up, not the other way around."

"I think ole Joshua here has a point," added Janine. "If you had given him a shot, there'd be no Audrey. It's all your fault, princess."

"Hey, don't pin this on me," Molly laughed. "I'm here for books, not boys. Made that clear from the start. Kick your behinds and go home. But really, do you guys like her?"

"No one likes her," Janine quipped. "I don't think Rand-o even likes her."

"I think, for Randy, it's the ch-challenge," Zeke offered. "The c-c-conquest."

"Trust me, dude," Josh asserted. "It's the pussy."

Molly shot him a look. "You know, you can be very vulgar sometimes."

"You love me."

"Two things can be true at once," Molly said, paused, and continued. "I think we should go talk to him, all together. I mean, really, he could do so much better."

"Stop being his mother, princess!" Janine scolded. "Maybe it works differently where you come from, but here in the civilized world, friends don't tell friends who they can date. If we do as you suggest and he stays with her, he'll resent us for not liking his girl. If he dumps her because of us, he'll blame us if he ever has second thoughts. No. He does what he does, and we do nothing except be here if and when our friend needs us."

It was an odd response coming from Janine, Molly thought, for the bodybuilder never stopped pining for the boy, continuing to nudge her way between him and Molly at every study session or opportunity. Janine had an obvious vested interest in Randy being single again, so what's up with that?

Molly's opinion of Janine had done a full one-eighty since their first encounter four months ago. The girl remained cutting and unnecessarily competitive, true, but Molly had actually come to enjoy the verbal sparring. Janine had a good heart, and she didn't even mean half the mean things she said. Yet more than that, she was part of the quintet, Molly's new family.

Later that night, the gang was streaming *Highlander* on the big-screen in the bungalow, a gory 1980s cult classic about an immortal Scottish warrior who must murder all the other immortals because only one gets to remain alive.

"This is ridiculous," Molly smiled. "Hated it the first time, hate it even more now. Why do the immortals have to kill each other? It's so stupid."

"It's the rule," Janine laughed as if it obvious. "Said so right in the opening card."

"The characters didn't see the opening card," the budding attorney laughingly countered.

"Even so," Janine counter countered. "Sean Connery tells it to him later."

"Well, who told Sean Connery? And why do they have to listen? Why don't they all just get together and agree to not to kill each other anymore?"

"Because then there'd be no movie, duh."

"Molly, if you just accept the rules, it makes total sense," added Randy.

"Shhh! Here comes the best part!" Josh shouted excitedly. "It's totally sick!"

Molly turned to Zeke. "You should cover up your eyes, honey. It is pretty sick. I'll tap your shoulder when it's safe to look again."

"Th-thanks."

"Is that it?" asked Randy. "The violence bothers you? Molly, we don't have to watch it if—"

"No, I'm fine with that," Molly interrupted. "It's just that this is not how a real immortal would ever behave."

"What?" Janine laughed. "What?" Randy, Josh, and Zeke laughed together.

"You guys know what I mean," Molly laughed along to cover her little flub. "It's illogical, that's all. But, fine, watch your silly movie. I'll shut up." The others returned to the screen; Molly sighed, moved to the kitchen area, and texted Francisco, "Ever seen *Highlander*?"

The return text came only moments later. "It's ridiculous."

"That's what I said."

"Still on for Saturday?"

"Wouldn't miss it for the world. "

Molly had been going to Francisco's Encino home almost every Saturday since their first meet. They'd spar, eat, laugh, drink without being able to get drunk, and be their true selves in ways they could never be with anyone else. He was always a perfect gentleman, and it bugged her to no end.

As midterms wrapped up, she told her friends that she'd be going up to Moses for the holidays to spend time with her sick mom —Molly Parker's only living relative—but in truth she was going to

Francisco's private island near Tahiti so he could get her started on sailing and skydiving.

As to sailing, she didn't get the joy of it a lick. Hated, hated it. Her hands burned from the ropes, and the boom kept whacking her in the back of the head.

"You're not ducking low enough," Francisco smiled patiently after one particular whack, his hand fixed firmly on the skiff's tiller.

"Last time you said it was because I wasn't crossing over fast enough."

"Both," he replied matter-of-factly. "Coming about."

She dropped the line to the deck, bent low, and crossed from port to starboard, only to be whacked again before picking up the starboard-side line. Francisco did his best to stifle his laugh.

"It's not funny!" she scolded.

"It is, actually. You're just not seeing it. Sheet it in tighter."

She tugged the line in as she tried to ignore the cuts and blood droplets forming in her hands. "Why is this fun? Why would anyone take this up for fun?"

"It's a lot of fun once you get the hang of it. For me, I had to learn it because it was my job during a couple of lifetimes."

"Like, in the navy?"

"More like the merchant marines, but less legal."

"What does that mean?"

"I was a pirate. Coming about."

Her mouth fell open in shock. She stared at him in disbelief as the jib began to flap uncontrollably in the wind.

"Coming about!" he repeated like a roar.

She dropped the line and darted back to port only to get whacked again. She pulled the sail in tight, and they were off and running once more.

"That time was because you weren't paying attention," he admonished.

"You were a pirate?" was her only response. "An actual, literal pirate? You're not speaking metaphorically, like you were a businessman who raided other companies? You're saying that you were an honest-to-goodness, for real, yo-ho-ho pirate?"

"Twice. The first time, I was about to enlist in the Armada when a buddy pointed out that while both gigs have you getting ordered to kill strangers, pirate ships offer a profit-sharing component so it pays way better."

"So you killed people for money?"

"I'd been killing people for God, King, and country for centuries. I didn't see much difference."

"For country, maybe I could appreciate, but for money? That's just cold-blooded murder. You're a good person, Francisco, at least I think you are. Didn't it tear you up inside?"

"All those who fell by my sword would've died hundreds of years ago anyway."

"That's not the point. Gee, I could never do that."

"That's because you already have money."

"I mean at all. For any reason. No way, José. I would never, ever, *ever* take another person's life."

"Wrong. Molly, when you find yourself in a situation in which you have to kill, you have to kill. I've told you this."

"And I told you, no. There's always another way. Next topic."

"Coming about."

She dropped the line, ducked as low as she could, and made her move, clearing the swinging boom with an inch to spare.

"There ya go!" Francisco said encouragingly. "See? Sailing's not so hard."

"I still hate it."

"I know."

Yet despite her disdain for sailing, her first crack at skydiving was even more tumultuous. The classwork was pleasant enough, learning to fold her parachute relatively simple, and knowing Francisco would be physically clipped to her back gave her a calming sense of security. Still, she was scared, so she stalled, and she stalled, and she stalled.

"Look, I can see why you think it's a skill I should possess," she explained one starry night as they roasted marshmallows in their little fire, "but the odds of me ever having to escape some bad guys by jumping out of a moving airplane are pretty remote, don't you think? For that matter, needing to sail away to safety one day is pretty unlikely too."

"Oh, that's not why I want you to do these things. That's your husband talking."

"What do you mean?"

"Don't get me wrong. I respected Al to no end. He did his absolute best to ready you for your great adventure, but he couldn't get it the way you and I get it."

"I don't get it." He laughed a little laugh, then so did she. "Seriously though, I don't."

"It's the experience of things that matters, Molly. Once in a while, you've just got to feel the sun on your face and the wind at your back as you glide through choppy waters; the pumping of your heart as you plummet to the ground with nothing more than blind faith that you packed your chute right. You've got to push yourself to do the things that Millie never would've, because if you remain in your comfort zone whenever survival permits, your forever is going to be very, very boring."

"I'm not bored yet, gramps."

"Suit yourself. I'll cancel the pilot."

"Thank you," she nodded, thought about it some more, then sighed reluctantly. "No, I should know how to do these things. Al would be right. I might need these skills someday. Let's do it."

"That's my girl."

It was the last day of their vacation when she found herself soaring fourteen thousand feet above the ground with Francisco clipped to her back. She had every intention of going through with it . . . until she looked down. "Are you out of your flippin' mind?!" she shouted into her mouthpiece for him to hear through his earbuds. "I'm not doing this!"

"You're ready, Molly," he said calmly into his own mic. "Trust me."

"Why should I trust you?! You were a gosh-darn pirate!" She looked down again. "No way, José! We'll get killed!"

"We don't die, remember?"

"Even better. I'll snap my neck and be stuck in a wheelchair for all eternity."

"Molly, again, if you don't want to do this, you don't have to."

"Good. I don't want to." He just looked at her. "What?!" she demanded.

"Nah, I think you want to." And with that, he leapt out of the plane, bringing her along with him.

"I hate yoooooooooooooo!!!!!!" she screamed as they plunged downward. "Pull the cord! Pull the cord! Pull the cord!"

"It's too early. You learned this."

"You're a terrible, terrible man!"

"Try to enjoy the thrill of the free-fall. Feels like we're flying, doesn't it?"

"No! It feels like we're hurtling toward a brutal disgusting death! Pull it! Pull the cord! Pull the cord!"

And on she screamed until he finally asked, "Think I should pull the cord?!"

"Yes, you idiot!"

"Or should we wait a bit longer? We can wait a bit longer."

"Pull it, for crying out loud!"

"As you wish."

The sudden intensity of the deceleration was startling to her. She'd been foretold of the sensation, but feeling it was another matter. She was aware of Francisco pointing out various things he was doing that he wanted her to observe, but her focus remained on the ground below whizzing toward them at a brisk twenty-six feet per second—the cars starting to look more like cars than ants, the trees more like trees than broccoli.

"Get ready for touchdown!" he shouted.

She bent in her knees and raised her legs as she'd been instructed, saw his toes touch the ground, and the next thing she knew she was lying in the center of a bullseye on Mother Earth's soft grass. They detached themselves from the chute and removed their helmets. Molly stood up and stared at him in disbelief.

"I'm sorry," he began with a light chuckle, "but I really thought you'd—"

"That was awesome!" she shouted as she broke into giddy laughter. "Oh my gosh, it was crazy!" She jumped up and down like a little girl. "I want to go again! When can we go again? I want to solo next time! Can I solo? That was awesome, so awesome!"

Francisco could only laugh.

* * *

IT WAS the last Sunday before the start of the new semester when it happened. The boys were off at the bungalow playing *Dungeons & Dragons* for money, which the girls had no interest in, so they hung out in Molly's dorm room, devouring veggie chips and cheap Chablis while they sat on her floor re-binging the first season of *Mad Men* on her laptop, a twenty-first century TV drama about life in the 1960s.

"What is wrong with this chick?" Molly sighed, referring to the Betty Draper homemaker character. "She has everything. Why's she always so mean and mopey?"

"Here we go," Janine chuckled. "Don't you ever watch something just to watch it?"

"I'm just saying," Molly chuckled along, enjoying in advance the verbal spar to come. "What's her problem?"

"Well, first off, her husband's cheating on her."

"Nuh-uh," retorted the future attorney. "She doesn't know that yet. All she knows at this point is that he's gorgeous, rich, and he takes great care of her."

"Exactly. Why does he have to take care of her? She's smart, capable. It must be so frustrating for her to be stuck at home with those little brats all the time."

"They're brats because of how she treats them. She's a terrible mother."

"Because she has the potential to do so much more with her life, to be so much more, but the sexist world she lives in won't allow it."

"Oh please. That is so twenty-first century people shoving their values on people they know nothing about. This chick grew up in the Depression. She and her family lived in a tent in a park through most of her teens. She went days without food at times. And when all that's finally over, her husband goes off to war, and she's got to go work in a darn weapons factory."

"Yeah, and soon as the men get home, she and all the other women get fired."

"Who gives a hoot? It's a factory! Loud and smelly and sweaty and ick. And now she gets to live in a beautiful home in the burbs with a beautiful husband and go to PTA and church meetings till the cows come home. You're saying that's not a way better life? So, to repeat, what is this chick's problem?"

"You know, you're ten years off actually. She's like thirty, and it's 1960."

Molly paused to do the math. "You're right. I am. Okay, so her formative years were spent living in a tent in a park and starving. My point still stands."

Janine laughed a little laugh, and then looked at Molly with an odd smile.

"What?" Molly asked.

And that was the moment when the bodybuilder with the short brown hair and pretty face leaned in, touched her hands to Molly's cheeks, and kissed her gently on the lips. Molly was too stunned to do anything.

"Oh," said Molly.

"Been wanting to do that for a very long time, princess," Janine said softly.

"Oh."

"Are you okay?"

"Um. I'm not sure."

"Well, did you like it?"

"I'm not sure. Um. Try one more."

Janine leaned in again, adding a little more passion to the soft kiss, as well as a few more seconds. She pulled back.

"So, you're gay then, right?" asked Molly.

"Boy, you catch on quick," Janine chuckled.

"Then why were you after Randy all this time?"

"I was never after Rand-o, stupid. I was after you. I was into you since that first day in the gym. I wanted to beat the crap out of him to show off for you."

"Oh," said Molly as she tried to process it all. "Hmm. All right, try one more."

The next kiss had even more passion, more seconds, and just a little touch of tongue. Janine pulled back.

"Then why've you been so mean to me all this time?" Molly asked.

"I didn't think I was being mean. I thought we were playing. You give as good as you get, you know. I thought you were enjoying the game too."

"Hmm. I was, actually. All right, try one more."

The next kiss had more passion still. Molly wrapped her arms around the muscle-bound girl and used her own expert tongue to do some masterful probing of its own. When Janine began to pull back, Molly held her tight and kept her close.

"You can stop stopping," she whispered . . . and so began her next adventure.

Molly's brain flooded with thoughts she'd never thought as the girls removed each other's tops, her heart and loins flooding with feelings she never felt as she explored the feminine for the first time.

Janine moved her lips down to Molly's neck, then her breasts, tummy, ultimately reaching her thighs. She pulled off Molly's jeans and panties then slid her tongue inside her princess, up and down and all around, and effortlessly knew precisely where the clit was to be found.

Molly writhed in delight, but she had been gone down on before. Yes, Janine was wonderful, wonderful, holy moly! wonderful, but if she was going to experiment, she was going to experiment! She pivoted her body along her rear end like a lazy Susan, neatly tucked her face under the bodybuilder's privates, and went to work, and to play. The college girls moaned in mutual ecstasy as their months-long competition transformed into welcome shivers between their legs, and glorious quivers throughout their beings.

Well look at me, smiled the ninety-four-year-old lady.

CHAPTER TWENTY-FOUR

RICHMOND, VIRGINIA
APRIL 2017
1 WEEK SINCE THE DEATH OF MILLIE LANG

DAMN NEW YORK NUMBER again. Everyday lately! Can't this bozo take a hint?

Woody wouldn't answer a phone if he didn't recognize the caller ID. He hadn't for years. Jinny used to give him heck about it all the time before she passed. God, he missed her.

It wasn't so much the telemarketers that the buck-toothed biologist had been trying to avoid, although that was a pleasant bonus, but rather the reporters, and then when they started to ease off, the journalists who wanted to do a more in-depth piece on the evils of Big Tobacco, and as they slipped away, the documentarians. In not too long, he reckoned he'd be dodging historians. The irony was that he never even smoked.

This house is too big for me on my lonesome, he thought. I should move.

He browsed his vinyl record collection and reached for Johnny Cash, then changed his mind in favor of Patsy Kline. Jinny's favorite.

He smiled. They fought about that too, which to listen to. He almost always won. Today, he let himself lose.

I can't sell this house, he thought. Jinny loved this house.

No sooner was *Crazy* blasting through the speakers did the blue BMW pull up and park on the curb. New York plates. The caller. Had to be. A short, stocky fellow got out and headed up the walkway.

"Goddammit," Woody muttered. "All right, boy, you want to play? Let's see if we can't have us a little fun."

He went to his den, assessed his vast collection, then chose the pump-action shotgun. He crossed to the main foyer and opened the door with the weapon pointed at the stranger before he could even knock. "What the Christ do you want?"

"Dr. Woodrow Szabo?"

"Who wants to know?"

"My name is Peter Mailor. Before I legally changed it, it was Dieter Mueller."

"Never heard of either of you." He pumped the gun and took aim. "Now, git."

"Christoph Mueller was my father."

"No kiddin'?" Woody smiled as he lowered the shotgun. "The baby."

"Yes, the baby. And I have something for you, something I believe you'll appreciate a great deal."

"Shoot, your daddy used to talk about you all the time. Come on in."

* * *

"Well kiss the virgin mother on the mouth," Woody good-naturedly whistled as he skimmed the file. They sat at the picnic table under the juniper trees in his backyard, sipping on mint juleps. "I knew it. Told him not to let her go. Begged him."

Look at the old geezer, Pete reflected. With all the money he must've made, he couldn't bother to fix those chompers? Jesus.

Be nice, Pete. You need him. "So the science is valid?" he asked respectfully.

"You're darn tootin'. Of course, this isn't the document your daddy showed me on our last night together. The one he showed me said Miz'iz L wasn't unsterblich at all."

"Miz'iz L?"

"Mildred Lang. I called her Miz'iz L. I was a kid, and got to admit, had a little bit of a crush on her. They hadn't come up with the term 'MILF' yet, but boy oh boy, was she. So, why didn't you bring this to me when you first got it?"

"You have to understand what it was like for me growing up, sir —learning my father was a madman, a Nazi, right hand to Mengele, and then my mother . . . "

"Yeah, I heard about that. What a thing, eh? I'm sorry."

"Long time ago. So, when I first read the document, I just assumed it more madness."

"Never even looked into it?"

"I did, actually," he groaned. "I'm an effing retard if you must know the truth. I recognized her photographs because I'd met her years earlier—at least I thought I did, then I thought I didn't, now it's pretty clear I did. I tracked down your Miz'iz L that first day I saw those pictures, and surveyed her for a month, but all I found was an ordinary old lady living her life. Plus, she had this big scar on the back of her leg, which the document said she couldn't have, further evidence it was all bullshit. I mean, sure, there was a similarity to the young woman I once knew, but having to choose between two different women having similar features or the crazy rantings of a Nazi lunatic, well . . . fuck me, right?"

"No, I can see how a man could arrive at such conclusion," Woody offered. "Me, I gave up on it too. Had to. One day I come to work, there're new agents all over the place. They tell me the project's done with and to go home, then I read in the paper your daddy'd been killed. I reckoned Treasury just got plum tired of footing the bill—the man had been at it twenty years. Reckoned he fought them to let him keep the program going, threatened to take his findings public if they didn't do as he willed, so to keep him quiet, they done him in. Then all his old Nazi-Mengele stuff from the war starts coming out in the papers, like they're distancing themselves from him by hiding him in plain sight, leaking to the press one juicy story after the next so no one will pursue the real one. I was scared. Went underground for three years. Might still be there now if Big Tobacco hadn't plucked me out of oblivion."

"Well, thank God they did, sir," Pete offered back. "Dr. Szabo, I came here to bring you this document, proof positive of your fine work, so you can start this project up again, and I will do everything in my power to help make it so. My only condition is that I have free reign to observe all tests and experiments that you perform on her."

"I don't know, son, those experiments can get pretty ghoulish at times."

"Counting on it," Pete replied with a subtle grin. "Do we have a deal?"

Woody paused, exhaled as he considered. "I'm retired, you know. I'm seventy-three years old, and tired. Tired and retired. On the other hand, I don't quite cotton to the notion of being remembered as the fellow who spent his life disproving the link between cancer and smoking—a lot of folks didn't like that. But history has a way of letting great accomplishments override everything else. No one thinks of Gandhi as a pervert. Being remembered as the man who ended sickness and death? Yeah, I think I'd like that. Jinny would like that. Okay, son, count me in."

"Excellent. Where do we start? I can find her for you, but I don't know anyone in government to grant us the financing."

"I only know a few, and I'm persona non grata with those I do," Woody chuckled. "But government wouldn't pick up a tab on a humanitarian cause these days anyway. Different times. But I do know some very rich, old, sick men."

"Why would they be interested in a humanitarian cause?"

"Let me explain it this way. Do you know what the HIV virus does?"

"Kills people."

"Yes and no. It invades the DNA, messes with the immunity system. People who die from the AIDS don't really die from the AIDS—they die from something they wouldn't have died from if they didn't have the AIDS. So, what if HIV has some kind of sister-virus? But instead of hindering the immunity system, she improves it? Instead of rendering it useless, she renders it invincible? If that's the that, a transfusion of Miz'iz L's blood could, theoretically, make the recipient unsterblich too. A lot of dying billionaires would pay a pretty penny for such a treasure."

"You guys were working on this in the sixties?"

"Hell, your daddy was working on it in the forties. When the AIDS epidemic broke, a whole half of our research was validated. You don't know how hard it was for me to keep my yap shut and not go bragging about it all over town."

"Then, perfect. You get us a sugar daddy, and I'll go get us our girl."

"No, son, it doesn't work that way. These men, they have their own way of doing things. They don't know you. They'll have their own people to put on it."

"I don't mean to brag, sir, but I'm one of the best investigators in the country, maybe the world. Whoever your guys hire, I'm better."

"Maybe you are, maybe you ain't, won't matter to them no how. This is how it's going to go or it won't go at all. But rest assured, son, one thing I've learned in my travels is that when big money is motivated, there ain't nothing that can't happen. So just sit tight. It ain't a matter of if, only when."

CHAPTER TWENTY-FIVE

THE HONKYTONK WAS SURPRISINGLY boisterous, thought Mellow, particularly after such a contentious Gathering. The music from the drums and whistle-bones was peppy, the singing mostly on key, the dancing fun and sloppy, and the hooch plentiful. Of course, as a husbandless woman, Mellow was to enjoy none of it.

The First Moma held a torch in one hand and Mellow's hand in her other as she led her to a cabin in the fourth ring. "I'm very disappointed in you, Mellow."

"Apology in advance, First Moma, but what did I do wrong?"

"Don't play me as dunce. You think no one saw the smiles of flirt and eyes of goo-goo you cast upon Thunder? A combat is the result of your slutty. Have your before-people never taught you of the Great Punishments?"

"Of course they did," lied Mellow. "All know of the Great Punishments." I shouldn't have smiled at him in public like that, she told herself. Stupid. "But Moma, Thunder cast eyes and smiles upon

176

me first. Is a woman not to return a warmth to a man? Apology, but I know not all your ways yet. Tis a hard."

"Hrmph," was all Dour said in return, leaving Mellow to worry whether the First Moma would wind up foe or friend, and what the upshot of either could be.

They arrived at the cabin and stepped onto the porch. Dour knocked on the door and turned to Mellow. "Sunburst has but one wife, and she has taken to a sick. You will be of his cabin to fill her duties till you're wed."

The door opened. It was the little girl who had stroked Mellow's hair. "Hi!"

"Is your pupa about?" asked Dour.

"Yes," answered the moppet who Mellow calculated at around six.

"Then go fetch him, child!" snapped Dour.

"Okie!" the girl shouted merrily and ran off.

Dour could see the fret on Mellow's face, misread it, yet it touched her still. "Stress not much, Mellow. Sunburst loves his wife, has even stopped attending Gatherings to be by her side. Tis unlikely he'll call you to his night chamber. He's a good man."

"Gratitude," Mellow replied, paused, and asked, "Is Thunder a good man?"

"No."

Before Mellow could respond, the girl returned with her pupa, a brick of a man with firm defined muscles, shaggy unkempt hair, and bags of plagued sleeplessness under his eyes. "Yes?" he asked.

"Sunburst, this is Mellow," Dour began, and proceeded to explain how it came to pass that the outsider had been embraced into the Community.

"Welcome," he said suspiciously.

"She's unwed. Clearsky deemed her to you for a brief to take to Love's tasks."

"That's what I thought," said Sunburst. "No."

"Sunburst, tis your Sorry's decree."

"And tis my cabin," he insisted. "The Sorry has no dominion

over the insides of another man's cabin. The gods will give my wife back to me, I know it, but I will not risk encouraging them the notion that I'd be content with replacement."

"Sunburst, the women of the Community have covered your wife's duties, for tis what we do. But now there's one who can give respite for half the morrow—"

"Why only half of it?"

"A challenge has been challenged, and the challenge taken. Aft the morrow's luncheon, Thunder and Skinny Horse will combat for Mellow's hand."

Sunburst roared with laughter. "Seriously?"

Mellow could see why the sad man had been given his name. Despite his obvious troubles, his laugh was joyous, infectious, and a light shone from his eyes as he chuckled. "Dour, you can't let your poor boy go through with—"

"He is a man now!" Dour said prickly. "His name is Skinny Horse, and I am well aware of the nature of the combat. Let us return to the matter of hand."

"If just for one night and half-day, tis a fine. Welcome to my cabin, Mellow."

Dour left without a word, just a huff. Sunburst led Mellow inside. Torches illuminated the two-chambered cabin. "You are my guest, Mellow, not a replacement," he admonished. "You'll fill Love's chores, and that is all that you will do for me. Get?"

"Yes, kind sirree. I get."

"Daughter-of-Love. Take Mellow to your chamber and dress her a bed. Come the morrow, you'll show her our cupboards, and she'll take charge of the break-fast."

"Yippee!" the moppet shouted, grabbed Mellow's hand, and dragged her into another room. "I'm so happy I can know you, Mellow! I didn't think I would." The space was crammed with bunk beds on which lay moose-hide mattresses, only one of them dressed. "I never met anyone from beyond the dwelling before! Nobody has!" She opened a cupboard, took out sheets and blankets, and proceeded to prepare the mattress next to her own. "Except for the men who combatted the heathen tribes those calendars ago, but they never took to talking with them. So tell me all! Tell me, tell me, tell me!"

Mellow clutched an edge of the sheet to help, answering, "The story of how I came to be amongst you is a sad. I conveyed it at the Gathering, and I wept. One weeping per night suffices, don't you think?" The little girl dolefully nodded, and Mellow went on. "But I want to know about you, Daughter-of-Love."

"Me?" the girl asked, both flattered and flabbergasted. "I'm just regular."

"Not to me," she said as she sat on her freshly made bed. "To me, nothing and no one here is regular."

The sound of quiet sobs began to emanate through the wall. Daughter-of-Love leaned toward her, and whispered, "You can't speak of that. Men don't cry."

"I know."

"Truth be, they do," said the little girl as she sat on her bed. "Proof be, he does. But they're supposed to not. And he'd be very angry at me if I spilled the beanery."

"What does he do when he's angry at you?"

"He looks at me like this." She squinted her eyes and scrunched her face. "And he says," she adopted the lowest voice she could muster, "'I'm very saddened by your conduct, Daughter-of-Love.' And it makes me sad.'"

"He doesn't hit you?"

"Pupa? Nuh-uh. I know some pupas hit, momas too, but not mine. They just speak at me like I already know properly, like I already dripped first blood."

"Does he hit your moma?"

"No, he loves her too much. Tis why he cries now. He fears she'll die."

"And you don't fear so?"

"She always healths. She had a still before me—that would've been my big brother; then me, healthy as stew; then a misk, so we don't know what it was; then this one, my little sister. Tis a sad." She reclined on her side and bent her knees to her chest like it was a slumber party. "So, you're to wed Thunder? Luckeeeee!"

"Only the gods know," Mellow replied humbly. "The combat will determine."

"Nah, Clearsky's not going to let his son get pulverized. He'll get him out of it, like always. No one likes Skinny Horse, you know, at least none of the youngers. He thinks he's big stuff just because his pupa is Sorry, and now he brings disgrace to him. Tis a bad for everyone, except you and Thunder."

"What do you think of Thunder, Daughter-of-Love?"

"He sure looks dandy, don't he? All the boys of my calendars wish to be just like him when they get their status. And he's so nice to all us youngers. In truth, me and Son-of-Stone are hopefuls but—"

"Hopefuls? Tis a what?"

"Son-of-Stone is my best chum in the world, and we hope to come of age same day so we can wed each other. A far throw, I know, but my moma and pupa were hopefuls so tis a possible. But if I bleed before he slays, a girl could do a lot worse than Thunder's third—and you and I will be sisters! That'd be a colossal yippee too, no?"

They heard the front door open, and footsteps enter the cabin. "It's Horizon and Sandy, come to check on Moma!" exclaimed Daughter-of-Love. "Let's go watch!"

Mellow let the little pixie excitedly lead her back to the entrance chamber where they sat on the sofa. The door to the other bedchamber was ajar and Mellow could see the procedure getting started. Love lay asleep on a large, double bed, her hair greasy, her body drenched in sweat. Sunburst sat on a chair beside her, clutching her hand in both of his, hiding his tears deep inside his eyes. Sandy stood on the other side, applying cold, wet maple leaves to her forehead.

The Holy One moved to the foot of the bed as he shot Mellow an irate glance to show that he too blamed her for instigating the combat to come. His displeasure expressed, he hunched over and pulled down the covers, then spread Love's thighs apart to reveal a discolored vaginal area filled with pus and foul-smelling discharge. Even from her distance, Mellow could diagnose that the woman suffered from chorioamnionitis, a vaginal infection that, if not properly treated, could absolutely lead to a stillbirth, if not the eventual demise of the moma as well.

The Holy One scooped his fingers into a clay bowl that sat on the dresser and spread a greenish-yellowish poultice over the infected area. Mellow could tell from both the color and the flowery, anti-septic odor that it was derived from yarrow—not the best plant around for the job but adequate in a pinch.

He pulled the blankets back over her, ordered Sunburst out of his way, and proceeded to pour a pungent decoction from a clay pitcher into a clay cup. Mellow inhaled the earthy, bitter aroma, and instantly knew it to be of burdock root.

No! she shouted in her head. Tis far too weak for its intended purpose, and she had spotted at least two others in the dwelling that would do a far superior job.

The Holy One nodded to Sandy who moved Love up to a sitting position.

"Wha-a-a-a . . . " the woman mumbled. "Let me sleeeeep."

"Shhh," soothed Sandy. "You'll sleep soon, Love. Shhh."

He tilted her head back and pressed his fingers to her cheeks to open her mouth. Horizon poured in the medicine, and then Sandy leaned the woman back down. The Holy One put the back of his hand to the woman's forehead, his fingers to her neck, and then his ear to her chest. He brushed his tongue up and down against the roof of his mouth, making sad clicking noises, and sighed. "We'll keep at what we do, Sunburst, but tis now in the gods' hands alone."

A miracle she survived this long if that's the treatment you've been giving her, thought Mellow. She looked to the little girl beside her to see quivering lips and ever-widening eyes, despite her prior optimism. She looked to the father, a decent man in an indecent time if all she heard was to be believed, and she had seen no reason not to. She looked to the woman, dying of a thing for so long not fatal, and from all that Mellow could tell based on husband and child, Love must be a quality person too . . . and that was the moment Mellow decided to save her life.

* * *

"I KNOW of what I do, Moma," Skinny Horse whined in the entrance chamber of the Sorry's cabin. "I could not show myself coward on but my second day as man."

"Then you shall show it on your third!" Dour forcefully replied. "For you will not go to combat against Thunder. You are too small and weak in the comparison."

"But I needn't be the victor. If I face him true, brave all the punishment I can bear and then tap out, my courage will be forever unquestioned. Perhaps I'll even—"

Clearsky burst in. "What is this chitter?!" He turned to Dour and motioned for her to kneel. "I'll scold at you shortly." He turned to his son. "You're a man now, and still you suckle upon moma's booby? She is your caretaker no longer! You are hers! Caring for our momas is what men do. Tis the gods' law. And as the parent owes the child no explainings, a man owes his moma none as well. How can you not know this?"

"Apology, Pupa. Tis a difficult habit to break."

"Perhaps. Break it still."

The new man nodded shamefully. Clearsky sighed and put his hands on his boy's arms. "You had to accept the challenge, son. I know. You couldn't let your pupa take your battle, much as I wished. Sometimes men have no choices, despite what women think. Now, you have a cabin of your own. Go to it. This is your home no longer."

"Yes, my Sorry, gratitude," and he was gone.

Clearsky turned to his wife. "And you! You know better than that."

"I do," said Dour, craving with every fiber of her being to burst into tears, yet too proud to display such weakness. "But I can't lose him, Clearsky. How many sons have I lost to war, to hunt of beast? All but one is the answer. I cannot watch another of my egg perish. I've seen forty-three calendars, and I can make child no longer."

Clearsky well knew his wife and could feel the tears she refused to shed. He hugged his arms around her head. "You won't lose him. His strategy has merit. He won't get the woman, but I wonder if she's not more trouble than she's worth."

"Yes, it seems as such," Dour agreed.

"Come. Let us go to my bed," he said as he helped her up.

"Tis not my turn."

"I make it your turn. You need me tonight, and I you." He took her hand and led her to his bedchamber where a pregnant woman of twelve calendars sat on a wooden rocking chair, sewing skinny-horse hide into snowy-season boots.

"A change to plan, dear Whisper," Clearsky said. "But I vow to make it up to you."

"As you desire, my husband, my Sorry," Whisper hoarsely replied and then left.

Clearsky took his senior wife in his arms and kissed her softly. Dour massaged the back of his neck with one hand and slid the other down to his stick and stones . . . only to find nothing of consequence.

"Clearsky?"

He took a step back. "We do not speak of this," he decreed.

"By the gods! You worry about Skinny Horse as I do!"

"No, he'll tap out and be fine. It's not that. And we do not speak of this!"

"Course not, my husband," Dour assured him. "Come." She led him to the chair and had him sit, moved behind him, and rubbed his neck and shoulders.

"I shouldn't have proclaimed him a man," Clearsky confided. "He's not ready."

"Then why did you?" she soothingly queried, if only to get him to open.

"He slayed aft the buzzer. Either twas a valid slay and he's man by the gods, or invalid and deserving of thrashing. There is no middle, and I didn't have the heart to sentence him to a thrash. I've been too soft on your final son, my Dour, I know."

"He'll be fine. A wise man once said, 'his strategy has merit.'"

Clearsky smiled, paused, and confessed, "Thunder's coming after me."

"Yes, it seems as such," sighed Dour. "But you've been come after before."

"I was younger, and stronger."

"And dumber," she smiled.

"Perhaps," he laughed. "Perhaps not. I proclaimed our son a man despite the Community's discord, allowing Thunder to wrangle the others into saddling him with that ridiculous moniker. I stepped right into his trap without even seeing it. But I couldn't make two self-serving decrees at the same Gathering. 'Skinny Horse.' Bleh."

"There are worse things than an unflattering name."

"You would know, Dour," he smiled.

"Hey!" she giggled as she playfully slapped him on the arm.

Clearsky laughed along for a moment, and then grew serious again. "I must be vigilant ever forward. Cannot drop my dukes against him by a smidge."

"A tragic that you cannot just slay him now."

"Ah, if but I could," Clearsky mused. "But a Sorry cannot slay a man only because he doesn't like him. The gods would lay curse upon me, and my support turn. No, I have to wait for Thunder to make error, and only then can I put him out of our misery."

"It will come to be. Thunder is impetuous, and not smart."

"But his friend, that Leaf, is cunning as a techno-demon of the old world."

"And so you shall slay him, too. Close your eyes to imagine it." He did. She moved her hands over his chest, stroked his nipples, and sensually whispered in his ear, "You shall slay them both, and it shall be glorious." He smiled. "Bloody and heinous and glorious." He moaned. She moved a hand to his inner thigh and gently massaged. "Brutal and ugly, and the songs of your valor will sing forever in our lore." His breathing grew heavier. She took hold of his stick, rock-like and strong now as the gods had designed it to be. "Glory to Clearsky," she said as she rubbed. "Glory to my Sorry." She moved in front of him and sat on his lap for him to enter her. "Blessings to my husband . . . my hunter . . . my killer . . . " And on she praised, writhing in pleasure along with him, yet the one thing she didn't say, the one thing she'd never utter aloud, was just how much she loved him. She'd never display such weakness.

* * *

MELLOW MADE certain that pupa and daughter were fast asleep before she got out of bed and left the cabin. Barring an owl and a few crickets not a peep was heard, as the Community seemed snugly tucked in for the night. Between the illumination of the dazzling stars and moon, her extraordinary sense of smell, and lifetimes of experience with just this sort of thing, the darkness proved little handicap for her.

Sunburst's cabin was closest to the trees by the north wall, but the plant she needed was by the eastern near the cavey-tunnel. She headed toward, into, and through the closest thicket in complete silence—another skill she had mastered long ago—taking the less direct route so as not to be seen, just in case. It didn't take a rocket scientist to deduce that women weren't supposed to know how to do what she was about to do.

As she approached the curve where north met east, she noticed Thunder shadowboxing out in the clearing by the little fires, gearing up for the morrow's combat. She squatted low to the ground to watch him.

He wasn't very good, she realized. For one, he used only his upper body, and made no attempt at all to fight with his legs. His punches and elbows had tremendous force, and he was surprisingly quick for a man of his bulk, but he left himself wide open for counterattack with every assault he made.

Still, he was a pleasure to watch—not so much for the artistry but his configuration. Oh, that lovely configuration.

Get to work, Mellow.

She made her way onward till she came to the pungent, white and yellow flowers she sought. They were beautiful, but more importantly, plentiful. Why on earth would the old man use burdock when he had bloodroot? How uneducated at his job is he?

She knelt to the ground, used her hands to gently dig around the plant, and then pulled it out en masse. She peeled away the petals and stem, leaving only the root in her hand, and contemplated if she should dig out another. She decided that hiding but one would be risk enough, and that she'd come back when she required the next. With root in hand, she began her stealthy trek back.

As she re-approached the curve near where Thunder trained, she noticed a figure sitting in the dark by a tree; then she noticed it was the apprendix; and then she noticed that he was ting-a-linging himself to her likely future husband.

So startled was she that she forgot her training, took an instinctive step backward, snapping a twig in the process. Sandy immediately turned to her.

"What are you doing here?!" he barked with a whisper as he leapt to his feet.

Got to stop making mistakes, Mellow.

"I had to make poopy," she innocently whispered back. "What are *you* doing here?" she added not-so-innocently.

"I'm not doing anything! You're far from Sunburst's cabin, woman!"

"I got lost. What are *you* doing here?"

"What's that in your hand?" he demanded, regarding the bloodroot.

She had a solid alibi prepared, but under the circumstances she felt it safe to ratchet everything up a notch to see how it played out. "With my before-people, Holy Men studied the gods and the lore, but twas the women who healed." Out in the clearing, Thunder finished his drills and returned to his cabin. "My moma was Healer of our community, and I her apprendix. I know better than Horizon of how to cure Love." She paused, and added, "So, what did you have in *your* hand?"

Sandy's eyes darted back and forth like a trapped little bird. He yearned to appear stern but couldn't shed the terror growing inside him. "A woman should not attempt such. Tis the way of the heathen who worships the demon. I must tell of this to my master."

"Then I'll have to tell of what things I saw."

"You saw nothing," he replied with trembled voice. "Nothing!"

"I saw you being in love with Thunder."

"They-they—no one would believe a woman's lie such as that."

"Not at first, but suspicion would fester. You'd be watched, and in time, you'd be found. You know it so."

He whipped his head from one side to the next as he desperately searched for a response, as if his way out lingered somewhere in the air. With his greatest fear come to fruition, he exhaled deeply, defeated, drained, and he dropped to the ground. "I'm so bad," he whimpered.

"You're not bad," Mellow smiled warmly, putting her hand on his shoulder to console him. "You're as the gods made you."

"No, I'm not," he told her. "I tried to be good. I promised I would. Promised I'd overcome my thirst for men. But I didn't! I couldn't! The Community will have me bagged and drowned in the lake for this, and I shall burn inside the Earth's core till time is a thing no more!"

"No, you won't. You know, with my before-people, twas considered a completely normal. Some men lay with men, some women with women."

"But the gods destroyed your before-people."

"Good point," she said, keeping her little laugh inside. "But that was only recent. Since the start of my before-people's lore, twas how it was, and the gods smiled on us for generations."

"Why?"

"You're the one learned in such matters. You inform me. But it seems to this brain-addled woman that one could only be as the gods wish us to. A hawk cannot be a lion, and a lion can't be a pussy-fish. The gods decide what we are, not us."

"I never thought of such in such manner," he considered. "But even so, the Community still will have me bagged and drowned for this."

"How would they know? I won't tell them."

"Why not? I'm sick. Your holy apprendix is sick. Tis your duty to say of it."

"You are not sick. There is nothing sick about you." She took his hand and helped him to his feet. "Perhaps tis the reason the gods led me here, so I could tell you so. Perhaps tis why you alone saw that I must have been brought for purpose."

He paused, considered. "But how do I know you won't ever tell? Even if by accident? I've lived in fear of being found out for so long when no one knew, and now someone knows. A woman no less. How can I know it won't slip out?"

"Trust me," she smiled. "I'm very good at keeping secrets."

CHAPTER TWENTY-SIX

Santa Monica, California
Summer of 2018

MOLLY AND JANINE MOVED in together in May, shortly after finals. It was a lovely second-story one-bedroom in Santa Monica, only a few miles from the beach, which their balcony and windows didn't face. Neither had ever lived with a lover before—unless Molly counted Millie's husband as a "lover," which she didn't—so both were nervous. To calm their anxiety, they made love before unpacking.

Molly knew the risk of taking on a roommate given her Saturdays with Francisco and her late-night hacking sessions at the storage facility, both of which she couldn't explain and neither of which she was willing to give up. She had many lifetimes ahead of her and had no desire to live them like a nun, so she decided to take the bull by the horns and nip any potential problems in the bud.

"There's something I have to tell you," she confessed as they lingered in bed. "I should've told you before but I was, I don't know, embarrassed."

"What is it?"

"Okay, so, growing up, I was alone a lot. I was an only child in a tiny town with a single mom who worked her behind off 24/7 to raise me. There weren't a lot of kids my age, and the ones that were, well, let's just say they weren't as intellectually curious as I was, so I had no friends—other than a boyfriend here and there, but those never lasted because they were pretty intellectually uncurious too. I didn't mind. It was how things were, and I came to like being alone. It was normal for me. So, then I get to law school, and there're people everywhere. And now I'm sharing my living space, my bed, with someone. Don't get me wrong, I'm super excited we're taking this step—but sometimes it'll be too much, and I'll need to wander off on my own."

"To where?"

"I don't know. Nowhere. Everywhere. Walk on the beach, museums, movies. The point is, for us to work, I need you to be cool about it."

"You mean, I can't even ask where you're going?"

"Of course you can ask. You just can't—I just don't want you to—I'm sorry, I know this is weird."

"Hey, it's okay. We all have our issues. Long as we're confessing . . . I snore."

"Holy moly, do you ever!"

Janine chuckled. "Other than that, princess, I'm perfect."

"Not even close, Bluto," Molly smiled as she snuggled in closer. "But I'm kind of smitten by you anyhoo." And they made out some more.

Of Molly's ten courses, she received a B+, an A-, and the rest A's. She got Francisco to cite her legitimate A in crim as a B so she wouldn't have to hack into the school computer. In the end, she was pleased with her results—excellent but not too excellent. Janine did a smidge better and took great joy in lording it over her.

Josh spent the summer in Philly with family and friends, and then returned to find himself a quaint studio apartment in Westwood, walking distance from the campus. Zeke spent his time off exploring Africa with his parents, and then moved back into the dorm. Molly was to spend the last week of July and first two of

August on Francisco's private island but told everyone she was going back up to Moses to be with her bedridden mom.

Janine was seated at the kitchen table scrolling Reddit on her laptop when she was told of the trip, it being Molly's turn to make the cappuccinos.

"Want me to come with you?" Janine offered "I'd love to finally meet her."

"Not yet," Molly answered, "but thank you, that's sweet."

"You know, you've met my family a bunch of times."

"Yes, and they're great, but Mama's not doing very well these days. It's just not the right time for me to come out to her."

Janine looked to the floor and mumbled, "Are you embarrassed of me?"

"Gosh no! I adore you to pieces, Bluto! You know that. I just want Mama to be a little stronger before I, you know, shock her to death. Please understand. Please?"

"Of course, no, I get it. Coming out can be hard, especially to parents. Just know, if you need me up there, for any reason at all, I'll be on the first plane out."

"I do know. Thank you."

"You're welcome. And on that note," the bodybuilder grinned as she reached into the briefcase by her foot. "I have a little something for you." She removed a small, gift-wrapped package and handed it to Molly. "Happy b-day, princess."

A smile exploded on Molly's face. She hadn't told anyone, had almost forgotten herself, but yes, it was official—she was ninety-five! Her ninety-fourth birthday had been spent all alone, en route to LA, between homes, between identities; ninety-third, watching her husband wither to bones; ninety-second, learning of his diagnosis. It was to be her first happy birthday in a very long time, and the gift almost brought her to tears.

"How'd you know?" she asked.

"Chalk it up to my exemplary investigative skills," boasted Janine. "Also, it's on your Facebook page, stupid. Cake's in the fridge. Angel food. Boring, but your fav. Now, come on, open. It's not much but, you know, girl on a budget, best I can do."

"I love it in advance," Molly beamed as she tore off the wrapping to find a framed 5 by 7 selfie of the two girls in bikinis that Janine had taken at the beach two weeks prior. A chill shot up Molly's spine. "You promised you'd delete it," she accused. "I mean, I don't want it to ever get online for Mama to see."

"I did delete it, but I printed one out for you first. Toss it, burn it, it's yours."

It was all Molly needed for her smile to return. She looked around their small space. "It should go . . . right . . . over . . . there!" She placed the frame on the little table next to the balcony door as she examined it. "Aw, I look good, don't I?"

"Yes, I do," the bodybuilder quipped back.

Molly giggled and sat on her lover's lap. "Thank you so much, Janine. I love it."

"My pleasure, Molly," she answered. "So, twenty-three, huh? Feeling old yet?"

"Not yet," she said, and they kissed.

* * *

RANDY SPENT HALF the summer back in San Francisco. In early July, he and Audrey moved into a ritzy three-bedroom on the twentieth floor of a high-rise in Brentwood. The gaudy space did not fit his personality one iota, nor could he afford his half of the rent based on the monthly allowance his parents were sending him, but Audrey said her father would cover the balance. Randy said he didn't feel right about that. Audrey wept that if he really loved her he'd do this for her, and he buckled. Everyone knew this story because Audrey would brag about it at parties.

"You really have to start standing up for yourself," Molly told him a few days after the couple's first Brentwood soiree. It was roughly eight months since he and Audrey had started dating, and Molly couldn't take it anymore. Despite the well-meaning advice of Janine, Josh, and Zeke to butt out, she felt someone had to set their friend straight. The two sat in their favorite hipster café sipping on lattes, and she tried to be as delicate as she could. "You're too good to let her treat you like that."

"What're you talking about?" he answered. "This is how we get along. It's who we are. You and Janine go at it all the time, and I don't get on your back."

"I'm not getting on your back," she apologetically replied, platonically putting her hand on his, "but I care about you, bro. I can't imagine you're happy like this. Besides, Janine and I go at each other. Your relationship is pretty one-sided."

"I'm being polite. What do you want me to do? Call her the c-word?"

"No, don't do that. But you don't have to let her walk all over you."

"She doesn't. I don't. Look, I know the two of you never hit it off—"

"This isn't about me and—"

"Shhh! I'm talking now! You two have been like oil and water from the start. But I love you both, so I want you to try to get along with her. Please. She's a good person once you get to know her."

"You love her? Really? Like love love her?"

"Yes. I mean, I don't know if I'm going to marry her or anything—"

"Thank goodness for that."

"This is what I'm talking about! Audrey is my girlfriend. I love her, and I want you to love her, too. If you can't do that for me, then keep your damn opinions to yourself because I don't want to hear them. Okay?!"

"Okay," she said humbly. "I'm sorry. This didn't go at all how I wanted it to."

"No, I'm sure it didn't."

"Hey," she tapped on his hand so he'd look her in the eye. "I really am sorry."

"It's okay," he softly accepted.

They hung out for another hour, talking, laughing, dissing Season 7 of *Game of Thrones*, dissing HBO for making them wait two whole years for Season 8, and speculating on how amazing that final season would be. By the time they left, their conflict was behind them and their friendship solid as ever.

That night, Randy told Audrey about the conversation in yet another attempt to get his two favorite gals to get along better.

"I think Molly's great," Audrey innocently claimed. "She's the one who has a problem with me, and I don't know why. I try and try, but she's got some bug up her ass about me. You think it's because she was into you before she went gay and thinks I stole you? Baby, I didn't steal you." She took his hand. "We met, and it was magic."

"Yes, it was," Randy agreed. "Is."

What a bitch that Molly, thought Audrey. Meddling in my love life? Who the f does she think she is? Oh, she'll regret this.

"But for you, baby, I'll try even harder," she said. "I promise."

CHAPTER TWENTY-SEVEN

THE WATER BOILED IN the clay pot over Sunburst's fire-pit. Mellow snapped the bloodroot in two and watched the dark-red liquid ooze into the clay bowl before her, then used the handle of a cutter to crush the body into a fine powder. Although unlikely at this hour, if anyone were to see her, she'd say that she'd grown anxious in her new surroundings and felt a cup of tea would help her sleep. She'd offer them some. Hopefully, they'd decline. If they partook, they likely wouldn't enjoy the tart, bitter taste. If they did, well, then she'd have new patients to care for.

She poured the boiling water into the bowl, mixed the decoction until the powder dissolved, and then went inside. She poured a tiny amount into a clay cup and hid the remaining decoction under one of the floor-logs.

With cup in hand, she stealthily snuck into the master bedchamber. Sunburst snored loudly, which was a good sign but by no means a guarantee he'd remain asleep. Her back-up plan, if he were to awaken, was to tell the same tale she told Sandy. Given what she'd learned of Sunburst thus far, it seemed more likely that he'd let her save his wife than out her to the others as a heathen to be bagged and drowned. Still, there was no guarantee. Still, it felt a risk worth taking.

She knelt by Love's side, slid her hand behind her neck, and raised her head.

"Whaaa . . . " moaned Love.

"Shhh," Mellow whispered as she poured down the medicine. "Shhh." She rested Love's head back to her pillow, crept out, and then into the bed to which she'd been assigned. She set her internal alarm clock for three hours hence—another skill she'd perfected over her lifetimes—and drifted off to sleep. She awoke what felt to be only seconds later, popped out of bed, gave Love a second dose, then returned to wake Daughter-of-Love to start on the break-fast.

As instructed, the little girl took Mellow to the "cupboards," which weren't really cupboards at all. Fruit was kept fresh by leaving them on trees, captured fish remained pristine by keeping them alive in netted-off areas in the lake, and the last of the skinny-horse meat held its vigor in honey-sealed elephant-belly sacks that nestled in the cold overnight waters.

The pixie babbled away as they labored, spouting every detail that popped into her head—the boys she liked, those she didn't, and her strategy of timing her first bleeding with Son-of-Stone's first slay so they'd be named at the same Gathering and wed to one another. Mellow could only smile.

Under Mellow's tutelage, they prepared a razz-berry, blackberry and pussy-fish ragout seasoned with a dash of peppermint, with a side of seared skinny-horse bacon. By the time Sunburst took his seat at the picnic table by the fire, his morn meal was ready. Sunburst looked to his daughter and tapped on the table. Daughter-of-Love left Mellow by the fire and went to sit across from her pupa.

Mellow removed the cauldron from the flames, dished the ragout onto clay plates with a wooden ladle, and removed the bacon from the searing rock with a cutter. She brought two plates to the picnic table, and poured the apple juice from a clay pitcher into Sunburst's cup, as he dug in.

"This is very tasty, Mellow," he said. "Finely done."

"Thank you, kind sirree. Now if I may have my leave, I'll eat alone indoors."

"No, tis a fine. You've done well by us, woman. You may sit at my table."

"A great privilege, but perhaps tis not best. What if the gods see us together and come to think you've taken a—what was that word you used—'replacement'?"

"Yes. Tis a point of wisdom. Have your leave then."

She bowed her head, picked up her plate, and went inside. Course, the reason she gave for eating indoors had nothing to do with anything she'd said, but with the two outside it was the perfect opportunity to tend to Love once more.

It was Love's third dose so far, and she actually opened her eyes for a few moments before drifting back to sleep.

* * *

IN PREPARATION for the morn hunt, Sunburst donned on his zebra-hide crotch-cover, tucked his sling into his left hip, cutter to his right, and his four favorite spears in hand. He returned to his bedchamber to stand by his wife's side to whine a little prayer to beg the gods to health her.

"I'm hungry," Love said groggily.

A colossal smile shined suddenly upon Sunburst's face. "You're a'what?"

"Hungry," she repeated, her eyes blinking open. "Fetch me a meal, husband?"

"Yes, you're hungry, course!" he replied gleefully. "Daughter-of-Love! Come quick! Your mother speaks of her hunger!"

"Why is my hunger of such news?" she asked weakly.

Sunburst dropped to his knees and took her hand. "You have slept for many days, Love my love. You have spoken no more than two words at once; and would eat only what the Holy One could force inside you."

"Many days?" she asked, and then looked down to her tummy as memory returned. "And the baby? What of the baby?"

Sunburst couldn't speak it aloud, only shook his head and looked to the floor.

She sniffled. "Boy or girl?"

"It matters not, my wife."

"What was it?!" she bellowed despite her fatigue.

"A girl."

She wept softly, lacking the strength to cry as hard as she felt it— and that was the moment Daughter-of-Love burst in all bubbly and giddy. "Moma! Moma!" she shouted as she hugged her and kissed her. "You're up! I knew you'd health! I told everyone!"

"Oh, sweet daughter, tis not time to rejoice. Your sister did not come to be."

"We know that, Moma. We grieved for her, and then the grieving faded way. But I never knew her. Twas you for whom we were all so affrighted."

"Daughter-of-Love," interrupted Sunburst, "go fetch the Holy One and tell him the blessed news; and tell the Sorry I won't be partaking of the morn hunt."

"Husband, no," said Love. "Tis your duty."

"You are my duty this day. I'll be security, and Clearsky will make the swap."

(Although the Community hadn't seen another tribe since the Great Drought began four calendars prior, it remained their custom that only a third of their men go off to hunt, the others remaining back in case of attack. It was largely a symbolic by this point, but it seemed to be what the gods wanted.)

Sunburst continued to his daughter. "Go."

"Better not leave me again, Moma!" she giggled as she ran off. "Yippee! Yip! Yip! Yippee!"

"I remain hungry, my husband," Love yawned.

"Course. Apology. I'm too joyed to think it properly." He turned to the door. "Mellow! Come!" Back to Love, "I prayed for you, Love my love, so hard did I pray."

"And the gods answered you, my love-in-return. Sent me an angel who poured cups of health into my mouth as I slept. An angel with flowing golden hair and warm, azure eyes."

The notion popped into Sunburst's brain like a flash. Could it be that Mellow was an angel come to save his Love as reward for his pious life? No, it couldn't. It would mean that her tale of her before-people's undoing was a fib, and angels don't fib.

Then who was she to have such powers if not an angel? A demon? As grateful as he was to have his wife back, she'd be damned to burn inside the Earth's center till time was a thing no more if saved by dark spirits. No. Better to be embraced into the gods' bosoms on this day then live forty calendars more to suffer such a fate. If a demon was amongst them, she must be destroyed.

"You beckoned for me, sirree?" Mellow asked as she entered the chamber.

"Is this your angel?" Sunburst suspiciously asked his wife.

Love's mouth fell open in shock upon seeing Mellow. Mellow looked back with desperation in her eyes, shook her head, put her finger to her lips. Shh. Please?

"I said, is this your angel, woman?" Sunburst repeated sternly.

"No," Love answered. "I said an angel. This is a woman. I said my angel's hair was golden, not yellow. And he had wings. Wings like a swan. And his image was translucent to the eyes, like a glorious shadow of brightness. Who is this person?"

Sunburst exhaled a hearty sigh of relief. Mellow was no demon, and his wife was free to live. Praise the gods. "Her name is Mellow," he told her, and then explained how she had come to be among them. "You're a boon charm to my cabin, Mellow. Gratitude. Now, go fetch my wife her break-fast."

With his focus off her face, Love looked to Mellow and winked. Mellow smiled back, then turned to Sunburst. "Right away, kind sirree," and she sprinted out.

* * *

Sᴜɴʙᴜʀsᴛ sᴛᴏᴏᴅ ɪᴍᴘᴀᴛɪᴇɴᴛʟʏ by the window as Mellow fed Love the remainder of the ragout. After only four spoonfuls, Love turned her face away. "Tis aplenty."

"Push to take a tad more," urged Mellow. "Tis beneficial for your strength."

"Stop such, Mellow," Sunburst chastised. "You're a charm, yes, but a woman, and not learned in such matters. We'll await direction from Horizon."

"Perhaps one swallow more," said Love as she shot her husband a bratty grin.

Sunburst chuckled. "Yes, my wife has returned indeed." He looked out the window then back to Love. "Our daughter is a good girl but given easily to whimsy. I'll fetch the Holy One myself." He turned to Mellow. "You stay and tend to my Love."

Mellow waited until Sunburst was gone before she put her hand to Love's forehead. "Boon. Still too warm for my liking, but not as burny as last night." She squeezed Love's wrist. "Praise. You'll remain weary for a moonth or so, and I want you to stay in bed for a half-moonth after that. Feign weakness if you must to avoid your chores. You're well on the trail to recovery, but by no means out of the forest."

"Are you an angel, Mellow?" asked Love. "Are you my angel sent to me?"

"No. I am but a woman, as you spoke it. My moma was the Healer of my before-people, and I her apprendix. But I fear the men of the Community will not take favor with a woman possessing such knowledge as I have, and will thrash me for it, or worse."

"Stress not much, Mellow," Love said as she took her physician's hand. "We she's have to stick together . . . and I'm very good at keeping secrets."

Mellow smiled.

* * *

Tʜᴇ ᴍᴏʀɴ ᴘʀᴏᴄᴇᴇᴅᴇᴅ with little event. Daughter-of-Love went off with the other little girls to net more pussy-fish from the lake, while

Mellow gathered up the break-fast dishes, bed sheets, and blankets to take to the lake for washing.

Many of the women were already by the waters when she arrived, bathing toddlers, washing one thing or another, trimming each other's head-hair. Some of the chitter dealt with the blessed news of Love's recovery, but the bulk was about the upcoming combat. Would Skinny Horse cower? Would the Sorry exceed his authority to intervene on his son's behalf? Would the new man be foolhardy enough to fight the goliath? Playful, a decidedly gregarious young woman with robust scars of whooping upon her back, took it upon herself to enact the battle, along with a spot-on impression of Skinny Horse whining for mercy, all to the laughing delight of everyone. Mellow did her best to keep her reaction in the middle, smiling just enough to not seem a twig-in-muddy-ground but not so much that anyone would think her proud for being the source of the conflict.

The show ended abruptly when Dour arrived to start on her own chores, and the women quickly returned to their tasks in silence, Playful being particularly flushed with guilty. The First Moma had seen enough of the silly girl's performance to find it offensive, knew it within her right to punish the lot of them for the insult, but girls will be girls. She decided it best to let them wonder if she'd witnessed any of it, and let their fear of her wrath be their punishment.

Not long after, Mellow sensed a shadow looming over her. She looked up to see Thunder's wife glaring down upon her with bitter eyes and no words.

"Hello," Mellow said pleasantly to break the uncomfortable. "I'm Mellow."

"I know," answered the woman. "Everyone knows. I am called Kindness."

"A delight, Kindness."

Another uncomfortable followed, and Mellow could tell the woman had something more to say—a threat, a warning, a stay-away-from-my-man, a something. She knew it pointless to respond preemptively, so she waited for what was to come while she planned possible responses in her head.

Kindness sighed, made a decision, and then huffed away saying no more.

* * *

SHE HAD one last chance to give Love her next dose before the combat was to begin. Sunburst sat on his porch whistling a merry tune as he whittled the blades of his spears to new sharpness. Mellow returned with the now clean blankets and dishes and offered to trim his head-and-face-hair, if he'd like. He said he would. She told him she'd be right back after she got the proper cutters from inside. He never noticed that it took far longer than it should've because he was in too boon a mood.

* * *

THE COMMUNITY SAT in rings that after-lunch just as they had the night before. Thunder and Skinny Horse, donning their hide crotch-covers, each stood on a single knee across from the other and held their open palms toward Clearsky.

"A challenge for Mellow's hand has been challenged," began the Sorry, "And the challenge accepted."

"Victor or loser," proclaimed the Holy One, "may the gods render pity on you both for we are all, us all, but the gods' mistake. Begin."

Gasps and murmurs abounded for most everyone had been certain that the mismatched match would never occur, but Clearsky didn't even try to save his son from the thrashing.

Thunder moved to the center of the circle, arms raised to the sky, roaring as if he'd already won. The young men and their wives, manlings, boys, and girls cheered for their hero, and he smiled graciously upon each of them. Mellow found the adoration shown him impressive, and a little sexy.

Skinny Horse seized the opportunity and charged at Thunder's back. At the last moment, Thunder moved a half step to his side and stuck out his leg for Skinny Horse to trip over. Thunder's fans laughed. Clearsky's supporters groaned.

"Trying to pull a quick one on ole Thunder, are we?" the big man pleasantly asked. "I say we keep our combat clean. What say you?" He held out his hand to help the new man up. Skinny Horse accepted the offer, whereupon Thunder yanked him, thrust out his foot, and tripped him to the ground once more. "Rule number one. Never trust an adversary." He turned to Clearsky. "Shame on you for not teaching your boy such." He turned back to Skinny Horse, and again held out his hand.

Skinny Horse slapped the hand away, slithered backward so out of Thunder's reach, and then stood. He readied his fists in fighting stance, and circled Thunder as he looked for an opening. Thunder merely rested his hands lazily on his hips while pivoting to keep the new man in front of him. "Are we going to combat, or dance?" he teased.

As far as Mellow was concerned, she could have done without the bravado—Thunder was going to win; he didn't have to humiliate the kid. Still, alphas will alph.

"Your hubris will be your undoing, Thunder," accused Skinny Horse.

"And your fear yours, Son-of-Clearsky."

"I fear not the likes of you. And my name is Skinny Horse."

"Oh, apology. I thought you'd be embarrassed by that ridiculous moniker, but if Skinny Horse you insist, Skinny Horse it shall be, Skinny Horse."

"Shut up."

"Have you grown rattled, Skinny Horse? Rule number two is—"

"Shut up!"

"Tell you a'what. I want you to do well. So to help you regain your composure, I shall grant you free punch." He clasped his hands behind his back.

"Is this another of your trick?"

"No, but even if so, with my hands behind me, you should be quick enough to pop me well before I can respond. But trick tis not. I vow this by the gods."

With fists raised, Skinny Horse cautiously moved toward him. Thunder made a quick little gyration of his shoulder, and Skinny Horse flinched back.

"Just funny-ing, son," chortled Thunder. "Now proceed. Show us the skills inherited from the cum of a Sorry."

The new man moved in fast, jabbed to the mouth, and backed off just as quickly. Thunder spit out a touch of blood, then turned to Clearsky. "Not terrible. He cracked no tooth, which one should on free punch, but still." Back to the new man. "Well done. I see your confidence grow, little one. Come, I'll give you another free."

"By the gods?" asked Skinny Horse.

"By the gods," nodded Thunder, his hands returning to behind his back.

Skinny Horse moved in as before, waving his right fist poised to deliver another blow to the mouth—and no one saw him drop his left hand to his side, wind up, and deliver a powerful upper cut to Thunder's stones. The big man's eyes sprang wide in bewilderment, and he dropped to his knees, gasping.

The new man dashed behind the brute, wrapped his arms around his neck, and squeezed. Thunder dropped face first to the ground, as Skinny Horse choked on.

Clearsky, Horizon, and all the seasoned hunters smiled approvingly.

Then Thunder tilted left and then rolled right so he was on top. He jerked his head up and then smashed it back down into Skinny Horse's face, shattering the nose. He planted his knees upon the new man's forearms, and punched. Hard with the right, vicious with the left, vicious with the right, hard with the left.

The boy tried to tap out but his arms were pinned. His face grew mangled beyond recognition as consciousness left him, but still Thunder pounded on.

"Enough!" shouted Clearsky.

"The boy has yet to tap out," Thunder said matter-of-factly as he punched away.

"He's mind-numbed!"

"He has yet to claim me victor, and so I am within my rights.

Unless the Sorry wishes to exceed the authority bestowed upon him by the gods for his own self-serving purpose. Do you? Do you wish to put yourself above the gods, Clearsky?"

"You are a demon!" shouted Horizon. "A manipulator of the gods' ways!"

Thunder merely smiled at that. He stood, lifted Skinny Horse above his head, and carried him toward the Condemnation Rock. He paused for dramatic effect, perching to crash the new man's spine into the boulder's sharpest edge.

"One," said Thunder as he smiled to his Sorry, daring him to intervene. Men hissed and booed. Women cried. Some turned away. "Two," Thunder counted on.

"Don't!" shouted Leaf. Thunder looked to his best chum, the wisest man he'd ever known. "Don't do it," Leaf pleaded softly, gravely. "We don't need it. Don't."

Thunder smiled at his accomplice, then turned back to the rock. "Three!" He threw the boy down strong. Sounds of cracking vertebras echoed through the valley.

The sobs reached a fevered pitch. The seasoned hunters shouted curses. Thunder's fans didn't know what to think. Only Clearsky and Dour remained stony, refusing to give the brute the reward of their tears; and Mellow could only wonder about the sadistic animal she was soon to wed, and how she had misjudged him so.

Skinny Horse's body slid to the ground with a thud, wedges of bone jutting out his back. Thunder put his hand to the new man's neck. "Still alive, but he'll never walk nor hunt again. A burden to the Community indeed." He turned to Clearsky. "Now, who might be his closest male relative to perform our holy rite?"

The Holy One moved to the young man, examined his back and legs. He turned to Clearsky and nodded woefully. Thunder's words had truth.

"You'll pay for this, Thunder," Clearsky seethed as he picked up his cutter. He moved to the unconscious boy, lifted his son to a sitting position, and slit his throat.

Thunder raised his arms and roared to his fans in victory. They tepidly banged their rocks, still uncertain how to feel. Leaf, as appalled as any, knew something had to be done to save Thunder from his impetuous gaffe so he took his rocks and banged with fervor. "Triumph to Thunder! Yip! Yip!" he cheered, nodding license to the youngers, making it okie for them to celebrate their champion once more. "Hail his might and virtue! Yippee! Yip, yip, yippee!"

One by one, then two by two, and then five by five, the youngers joined in, relieved for the permission and clarity. "Triumph to Thunder! Yippee! Yip! Yip! Gods praise Thunder! Yippee!"

Mellow could not have been more repulsed.

The seasoned hunters looked to their Sorry in dismay. How could he have been so impotent in saving his son from such a pointless end? Could this be the same man who'd led them to so many victories in battle? Had he lost his vigor to age? Had the gods' favor on him been altered? Is he the cause of us being plagued with drought? Their reactions were not lost on Clearsky.

Thunder breezed his way toward Mellow and reached out his palm. "I ask not for your kneeling on this day as is our custom, my enchanting bride," he smiled. "I beg only for your hand."

"Wait!" trumpeted the Sorry. "I issue challenge for her!"

The gasps of shock amongst the congregants were audible—but at least Clearsky was going to do something, even if too little too late.

"You wish to combat me, my Sorry?" Thunder grinned.

"Playful! Fetch me my cover!"

Thunder beamed as he looked upon the Community, soon to be his Community. His eyes fell upon Leaf, who shook his head in desperate plea. We're not ready. Don't do it. You'll ruin all for which we've toiled these many calendars. Look around. Don't do it!

Thunder's first instinct was that Leaf was being overly cautious, as was his usual, but then he scoped the seasoned warriors who'd come at attack upon his win, and those who'd rush to his defense. Leaf held truth again. Few of his team were ready.

"My dear, Clearsky," he said good-naturedly. "I'd no more combat my beloved Sorry than the gods themselves. I cower to you. Mellow is yours."

Mellow sighed in relief. Neither Dour nor Clearsky were fan, that was a certain, but still better than marriage to this horror show.

"Go kneel before your husband-to-be," the First Moma instructed her. "For we do things proper in our cabin," she added for Thunder's benefit.

Mellow did as told, kneeling before the man for the second time in two days.

Clearsky sighed in regret. It was the combat he wanted, not the woman; wanted to legally slay his nemesis before all and be rid of him once and for boon. Thunder's cowering was something, truth, but a symbolic at best. He looked down to Mellow—she was the reason his son had to die by his hands. She's trouble, this one. He could feel it. He never should've let her in. He turned to Thunder. "I don't want her. She's yours." He kicked dirt into Mellow's face and proclaimed, "The Gathering is shut."

* * *

MELLOW AND THUNDER'S wedding followed immediately after Skinny Horse's funeral. Few over twenty calendars attended. Even the Holy One opted out, commissioning his apprendix to perform the ceremony.

Conversely, every young man and his wife, every manling, boy, and girl old enough to walk showed up. They whooped and hollered as the ritual proceeded, banging stones and cheering, often drowning out Sandy's words entirely, and going downright ape-poopy when the couple cemented their vows with a kiss.

The honkytonk that followed was celebratory and joyous. While the young men hovered round the groom, the women and girls were all over his bride, finding her an intriguing mystery they yearned to treasure. Daughter-of-Love felt a special pride for having already forged a friendship with their glamorous new princess.

Mellow was polite and cordial as she answered their questions, all the while studying Thunder across the way as he bantered with his fans, chuckled with his disciples, topped off their cups of hooch, and flattered that they too could've defeated Skinny Horse without troubles. He was so good with them, so affable and charming, not at all the fiend she had witnessed only hours earlier. It occurred to her that he'd always been warm and sweet to her as well, and it bothered her. It had been a long time since she couldn't make sense of a man.

* * *

HE HELD her hand in his as he led her to his cabin in the first ring. "I have much joy regarding this day, fair Mellow," her new husband said softly in his deep, alluring voice. He lifted her into his powerful arms and carried her over the threshold. "Much joy indeed." He gazed into her eyes and kissed her. A gentle, loving kiss.

For the most part, his cabin was similar to the others she'd seen, wood, clay, and animal, but with unusual sparkling stones decoratively placed on windowsills and cabinets. Could it be that her despicable beast had the quiet soul of an artist?

He opened the bedchamber door and carried her in. It was larger than the ones in Sunburst's home, with still more rare gems scattered about, and an oversized bed with an exquisite stone headboard glistening turquoise and green.

He put her to her feet, touched his hands to her face, and smiled. "My wife, so beautiful you are. I have been truly blessed."

She had to admit, he had a killer smile. "You're too generous in your words, my Thunder," she feigned her admiration. "For I am the one who's been blessed."

He put his hand to his chest, then whipped it out to smash his knuckles across her face! She spun as blood spewed from her nose. "I got the better of this bargain, not you! Me!" he shouted. He grabbed her shoulders and pinned her against the wall, groping at her bosoms, mauling at her genitalia.

"You don't have to be this way, my husband," she groaned. "I give myself freely to your pleasure."

"This is how I take my pleasure, woman!" he responded with a new darkness in his eyes. "At least how I do today." He clutched her wrists in his powerful hand, and back fisted her again with the other.

"Now speak no more!" He threw her onto the bed, yanked her legs apart like a dead chicken, and shoved himself inside her. She grunted from the pain, and he slapped her. "Not a sound!"

She could take him easily, she saw. So many openings he left her, so many opportunities, but that would only reveal that she knew things a woman shouldn't know, which would lead to the men of the Community overwhelming her en masse, which would lead to her being bagged and drowned. No. She simply had to endure the torment of his clumsy blows and the sloppy gyrations of his oversized stick.

And then she remembered the trick. She had used it before in situations like this, albeit not for many decades. She learned it in the old world—even in the old world it had been considered ancient.

Go away, Mellow, she told herself, go away. Shh, shh, relax. Go away. Relax and go away. Shh, shh, shh. Go away, away, way, way, way, way . . .

Everything was white. She stood on an ocean of cloud. Thunder's grunts and thrusts were outside her like a numbness, heard but not heard, felt but not felt.

"Over here!" she heard a man shout from afar. It was Ool! He was dressed like a man of the old world, all dapper and snazzy in his white tuxedo jacket and bowtie. His slacks were black, and his black footwear shiny.

He held out his hand to beckon her toward him. She moved slowly, unable to run to him, much as she wanted to. The cloud beneath her feet gave way like sponge, making titty-bitty squeaks with each step. She took his hands. He smiled and kissed her forehead. He raised her arm and twirled her round like the dance people danced when they knew how to dance. He put his arm behind her back and dipped her down to the cloudy floor, softer than soft could be.

He brushed her hair from her eyes, and she put her hands to his face. She could feel his skin, actually feel it, the smoothness and the tiny imperfections, too.

"I love you, Millie," he said.

Yes! she remembered. That was my name, my first name, from

my first lifetime, the one with him, the name I've been copying all this time. That's who I am. I'm Millie!

He leaned in to kiss her as she opened her mouth in anticipation, happy tears dripping down her cheeks. "I love you so much, my darling," she wept.

"I said shut up!" shouted Thunder, plunging her back to reality. He grabbed her ears, rammed her head hard against the stone headboard, and all went black.

It would be three days before she'd regain consciousness, during which time Love would die due to inadequate medical care.

CHAPTER TWENTY-EIGHT

Santa Monica, California
More Summer Of 2018

MOLLY DIDN'T WANT JANINE to drive her to the airport, but other than a few "that's not necessarys" and "you don't have to bothers" there really wasn't much she could say to dissuade the kind gesture. So they hopped into Janine's beat-up green Camry, kissed a fond farewell by the LAX curbside, and Molly went inside.

She got in line for airport security where she stood for fifteen minutes to make sure Janine was long gone, and then went back to the curb where Francisco awaited in his shiny red Lamborghini. He drove them to the Van Nuys airport where they boarded his private jet, and personally flew them to his private island. Along the way, but only when the weather was clear, he let her pilot. It was thrilling.

It was on that same trip that she made her first solo jump, which she'd been looking forward to since Christmas. She loved it even more than expected, staying in free fall a little longer than Francisco had instructed just to mess with him, or to show off. With fear gone, it really did feel like she was flying.

"Now!" Francisco shouted into his mouthpiece, free-falling in front of her with his hands on her shoulders. "I said now!" he repeated with growing intensity. "Pull the cord now!"

She stuck out her tongue at him and smiled boldly. It felt nice to be on the brave side of the dispute for once.

"Stop kidding around, you brat! Pull it or I'll pull it for you!"

Well, we can't have that, she thought.

Woosh! The sudden deceleration from the opening parachute was no longer a startling sensation but more like a welcome visit from an old friend. As she floated gently to the ground, she reflected back to the terror she felt before her first tandem jump, and then started to giggle when its ridiculous similarity to her wedding night ridiculously popped into her head.

She and Al had made out more than a few times by then, had even engaged in some heavy petting on occasion, but the actual deed remained a complete mystery to her. An exciting yet terrifying mystery, and far more terrifying than exciting. She even wanted to back out at first, but she knew she couldn't. Like it or not, it was her duty now. So she lay back and let Al do all the heavy lifting, remaining utterly conscious, nay suspicious, of every move he made, every squeak of the bed springs, every chirp of a bird on the other side of the window, unable to enjoy any of it . . . until it was over and she realized just how marvelous it had been.

"Oh my gosh, oh my gosh! Al! Let's do that again!" she shouted, having yet to learn that men need time to reboot. "I'll be better at it this time! I promise!"

Molly landed her first solo jump less than four feet from the target's bullseye in a perfect drop'n'roll. Her paratrooper-husband would've been proud.

As to sailing, she was slowly but surely getting the hang of it, but still hated it.

The skiff cruised lazily along the shimmering waters as the ocean winds cooled down the heat of the golden sun in the blue-blue sky above. "Coming about," Francisco announced.

Molly crossed to starboard, clearing under the boom with ease while still resenting the sting in her palms as she yanked in the line, and wondered if this was a good time to ask her burning question.

"Something on your mind?" queried Francisco—of course he'd read the curiosity on her face.

"It's okay," she answered with a decided change of heart.

"Ask."

She wanted to ask, wanted to know, but she didn't want to embarrass the man, so she asked something else entirely.

"How can you be so sure there aren't others like us?"

"I'm not sure. I never said I was."

"But don't you wonder? I mean, maybe you already met one, but how would you know? You couldn't. Or would you? It's crazy-making, isn't it?"

"I had a friend in Baghdad once, my best friend in that lifetime actually. I was a physician, he a teacher of philosophy—of Viking descent, I think. Little details tend not to stick. You'll see. It was the time of Al-Zahrawi, the father of modern surgery—"

"It had a father?" she interjected with a giggle. "Funny, I never thought of surgery as something that would need a parent."

"Everything has a parent in one way or another. Anyway, this Nordic fellow and I were very close. Our wives were dear friends, our children played together. But as usual, eventually, I had to move on. Coming about.

"Flash forward a few centuries. It's the heyday of the Renaissance. I'm a painter living in Venice and—"

"You were a painter during the Renaissance? Who? Were you famous?"

"I painted houses, Molly, get over yourself. I owned a small company with six workers under me. We were hired by a travelling dignitary to touch up his newly purchased villa, but he seemed so reminiscent of my old friend, same face, same voice, I was almost certain it was him. Or was it simply my faulty memory engaging in wishful thinking?

"We hit it off immediately, he and I—another sign he was who I suspected. We'd spend hours talking into the night, night after night, drinking his wine, staring off to the sea, uncommon as it was for nobility to fraternize with the merchant class.

"On one of those nights, the topic of immortality arose, but we spoke around it only in hypothetical circles. We agreed it would be a curse not a blessing, agreed the bearer of such a curse would live in constant fear of being discovered, and that he would need to acquire a great many survival skills over his many lifetimes.

"But neither of us copped to it. I had already spent one lifetime locked away as some kind of demonic vampire, so no, my nobleman had to admit it first, and he didn't. Perhaps he had the same fears as I, or maybe he was just a normal with a keen imagination. No way to know. I left Italy the next morning frightened that I had divulged too much, and I never saw him again."

"That's so sad."

"Only a little, and only if I let it be. You'll see. Coming about."

One afternoon, they sparred in the waist-deep waters of the warm Pacific. It was grueling and exhausting, far more difficult than fighting through air. After five punishing hours, they lay panting on the sandy beach when Molly finally mustered the nerve to blurt the question she'd been too bashful to ask.

"So after how long does an unsterblich's sex drive go away?"

Francisco laughed. "Excuse me?"

"I know you like me, and you've never . . . you know . . . tried anything."

"You're with someone."

"I know, but before that. I gave you tons of signals, and nothing. I mean, I'm not wanting you to do anything now—I'm staying faithful to Janine, absolutely—but I've been wondering about it. Worried, to be honest. When does it go away? More specifically, how much time do I have till I lose mine?"

"It doesn't go away," he assured her. "My sex drive is live and kickin' as ever."

"Oh. Are you gay?"

"Nope. Tried it a couple of times, didn't care for it."

"Oh. So, it's me. You're just not into me. I read it wrong. How awkward for me."

"Not at all. Molly, I've been in love with you for more than fifty years. You're beautiful, smart, funny, kind, sexy as all get out. But I gave myself a purpose these past few lifetimes, I told you that. You are my purpose, so to cite a modern version of an ancient adage, you don't shit where you eat."

"You probably should've stopped after 'sexy as all get out.'"

Francisco laughed, then so did she.

One morning after breakfast, they spent their time at the island's shooting range. It was her favorite of all the activities they did together for it was the only one in which she was just as good as he was—there's no such thing as better than perfect. Also, he had such cool weapons.

That evening after dinner, they spent their time honing their hacking skills. Molly had never co-hacked before because Al never thought it a skill that he himself would ever need. It was a blast! Together, they learned more about the inner workings of the Trump administration than anyone outside of government had a right to know, and more than most inside knew. It was on that same night that Molly had her mother, Greta Sharon Parker, who never existed, pronounced dead of pancreatic cancer by a Dr. Robert J. Mulroon, who didn't exist, at the Plumas County Hospital, which did. The moment she hit "enter," officially rendering Molly Parker an orphan without a single living relative in the world, Francisco passed her a box of tissues and asked if she was all right. Molly could only laugh, then so did he.

* * *

MOLLY RETURNED HOME and wept as she told Janine the sad news about her mom. Janine's response was impeccable, and she kept her petty bruised feelings—which she knew were petty—to herself. She hugged her partner, consoled her, let her cry on her shoulder, and she remained impeccable for a whole six hours.

"Can I ask you a question, princess?" Janine tentatively asked later that night. They were lying in bed, Molly re-reading her favorite Jeff Abugov sci-fi novel, Janine unable to focus on her J. Kenner romance book.

"Of course you may, Bluto."

"Why didn't you tell me about your mom?"

"It was the first thing I told you when I got home."

"I mean, while you were there. Why couldn't you pick up your phone and clue me in? Even a text. I would've been on the first plane out for you."

"I know, and that's precisely why I didn't."

"Baby, we've got to be there for each other. How do you think it makes me feel being shut out like that? If we can't rely on each other, what good are we?"

"You think this is about your feelings?"

"I'm just trying to talk. Why do you have to shut me out of everything?"

"I don't shut you out of everything, I shut you out of this!" Molly snapped at her, and then made herself well up as she went on. "Mama was so proud of me. This is a woman with no education, abandoned by her husband, her parents, raised a child all on her own, worked a double shift as a waitress in a seedy bar-and-grill, and still somehow managed to get her baby into UCLA Law. Now you want me to tell this feeble, churchgoing lady, on her deathbed, that her pride and joy is nothing but a big fat lesbo? And don't tell me she wouldn't know. She'd know. She'd see how we look at each other, and she'd know. She wasn't educated, but she was smart!"

"There's nothing wrong with what we are, princess. It's 2018, for chrissake."

"I know there's not. And in time, she would've come to know it too. But she didn't have time! Okay?! Any other questions to make this all about you?!"

"No," fumed Janine.

"Then good night." Molly rolled over and turned off her light.

"Fine." Janine rolled over and did the same.

Molly felt awful. Playful banter aside, it was their first real argument, and she faked it. She'd never faked an orgasm with Janine, only a fight. Weird. She wondered how she would feel if the shoe were on the other foot, if Janine shut her out, and she knew she wouldn't like it one bit. She had overplayed her hand. She'd been mean.

"I really do appreciate you wanting to be there for me," she said softly by way of apology. "Just knowing so made it feel like you actually were there."

"Good," Janine grunted.

Another pause, and Molly added, "You know, we've never had make-up sex."

"Maybe another time. I'm too mad at you right now."

"Well, if you were happy with me, it wouldn't be make-up sex."

Janine stifled her laugh. "Good-night, Molly."

"So, turns out Mama left me a pretty fat insurance policy. Covers the rest of my tuition, living, and some extra on top. Want to help me buy a car tomorrow?"

"What is wrong with you?" asked Janine, rolling back to face her. "How can you think about a car right now? Your mother just died."

"She sorta made me promise. She always dreamed of owning a black Hummer, but that's not me. So, what's between a black Hummer and a pink 'vette?"

Janine laughed despite herself. "You crack me up, princess," she said as she moved on top of Molly, no longer able to stay angry.

Molly smiled, rolled them over so that she was on top. "I sure do, Bluto."

It was Molly's first experience with make-up sex, and it more than lived up to its reputation.

* * *

IT WAS the final Thursday night before the first week of classes. Janine was reclining on the sofa with a glass of white wine, scanning Netflix for something good to wa when the buzzer rang. She opened the door to find Randy, Josh, and Audrey.

"We were just chowing down at the Promenade," Josh began. "In the neighborhood, so we figured we'd drop by. How's my favorite couple?"

"We're not disturbing you, are we?" asked Randy.

"Not at all. Come on in."

They entered as Josh shoved a six-pack of Dos Equis into her arms. "My mamacita always told me never to show up at someone's door empty-handed."

"I already started on some Chardonnay but knock yourselves out."

"More for us, excellenté," said the Asian Santa.

"Where's Moll?" asked Randy.

"Who knows?" Janine sighed. "Out."

"Oh no," said Josh. "Trouble in porn-paradise?"

"No, it's just something she does. You wouldn't know it from hanging with her, but that girl needs more private time than anyone I've ever known."

"She just goes out and you don't ask where?" Audrey asked in feign bewilderment, the moment she'd been waiting for suddenly presented.

"I did at first, but it was always something stupid or boring, so I stopped."

"Wow, you are so much stronger than me, Janine. If my Randy took off for no good reason, I'd so assume the worst, so confront him about it." She turned to Randy and added, "So you'd better watch yourself, mister." She quickly turned back to Janine, as if to correct a terrible faux pas. "Oh, I'm sorry. I didn't mean to imply that Molly's cheating on you. I'm sure she's not. I'm only saying that if Randy ever acted how she's acting, I'd think he was."

"Dude, let it go," Josh sighed with an ironic chuckle.

"What, we're just talking. I'm confessing my insecurities. I'm not saying Molly's cheating on her. I'm saying the opposite."

"Audrey, maybe that's enough," said Randy.

"Molly is not cheating on me!" Janine attested firmly, annoyed by the annoying girl, as usual. "She was very upfront about all of this from the get-go."

"Exactly," Audrey innocently agreed. "So, let's assume the best. Molly's story is totally true and she's totally not cheating on you. I'm just trying to say how amazingly cool you are to take it all on dumb faith like that because I couldn't, nor could any girl I've ever known. You're a very strong woman, Janine. A toast to you, my sister."

"Uh-huh," said Janine. She saw through Audrey; they all did. The manipulative pampered rich bimbo was just trying to cause suspicion and stir up trouble. The bitch of it was, as far as Janine was concerned, it was working.

* * *

FOR THE FIRST several weeks of their cohabitation, Molly had been very careful to make sure she wasn't being followed during her secret excursions—a skill Al had taught her well—even instructing her Uber and Lyft drivers to make quick detours from time to time after spotting a green Camry through the sideview mirror. She knew the story she'd given Janine was flimsy at best, and she wouldn't have blamed her an iota if she'd chosen to verify it for herself. The fact that Janine trusted her so completely only made Molly cherish her all the more. But as time went on, her countersurveillance grew lax. Had she applied only a fraction of her skill while she drove to Francisco's Encino Hills home that particular Saturday in her brand new, six-year-old Mustang convertible, she would have spotted the Camry in a second. But she didn't. Instead, she focused on the spidery LA freeway roads as she sang along to the Bruno Mars vocals that blasted from her new old speakers.

Across the 10 and up the 405 the two cars rode, and Janine felt terrible. A relationship must be built on trust—she believed that to her core—yet she was the one violating that trust. But the further they drove, the more her suspicions grew.

She wouldn't, thought the bodybuilder, not Molly. Not squeaky-clean Molly. No way. Not her.

Off the 405, merge onto the 101, exit Balboa Blvd.

Encino? What the hell's in Encino?

She followed the Mustang into the hills, and watched it pull onto a circular driveway close to the mountain peak. She pulled over a half block back and turned off the engine. She watched as Molly got out of her car with her gym bag; watched her saunter up the steps to ring the doorbell; watched, a moment later, their 1-L crim professor open the door to greet her, hug her, and lead her inside.

"Oh, fuck you, girlfriend."

CHAPTER TWENTY-NINE

THE DWELLING
3 DAYS SINCE HER WEDDING NIGHT, THEN 3 MOONTHS MORE, THEN 3 CALENDARS AFTER THAT

MELLOW BLINKED OPEN HER eyes only to endure a pounding in her head and a ringing in her ears. She lay on a bed in a wooden cabin, at least she thought so—everything was blurry, fuzzy as a peach skin, walls and floors wobbling and spinning as if gravity itself was on vacation. She reached behind her head to feel a big maple leaf covering a bulge the size of her fist. Just the touch of her finger to it hurt.

"Welcome back," said a woman seated on a stool next to her.

Who was she? Mellow asked herself as she willed the woman into focus. She looks familiar. Kitten? Captain? Kindness! Yes, her name is Kindness. She's my husband's wife. His name is . . . is . . . Thunder. Who am I this time? Mellow. You're Mellow.

"You slept long and too long more," said Kindness. "We were fearful for you."

"What—what happened?" Mellow asked weakly.

Kindness dipped a handful of moss into a clay bowl of warm water, and then dabbed it to Mellow's forehead as she gently spoke. "Never confess your affection to our husband unless he proclaims it first . . . specially not during relations."

Yes, no, it hadn't been Thunder to whom she had expressed her love, but Ool—though Kindness didn't need to know that. "He's a monster, isn't he?"

"Not always. Often during relations—his moma was a bad woman—and he grows savage when he feels unrespected, but sometimes he can be sweet. So loving and sweet. And when he takes you to his bed that way, wooo-hoosh—he'll be all you dream a man of his girth to be. Strong and powerful, yet with a touch soft as mink. He'll say he loves you, and mean it, and that's when you must say it back . . . but this advice you won't need because the words will flow from your lips without the trying.

"One just can't predict from moment to next which he'll be," Kindness continued, "and the sweet shows its face far less than the cruel." Not only did Mellow know the type, she knew the proper psychological term for it. "I wanted to warn you that day at the shoreline, hoped you'd see it in my eyes, but I couldn't say the words for fear it would put my children with him in danger. We are not permitted to gossip of the goings-on of our cabin to those outside it. So strong apology I give to you."

"Stress not much, Kindness. Tis not as if I had choice who I wed."

"A truth," Kindness agreed, and then smiled to alter the tone. "But now you're my sister, my dear little sister with the funny talking voice from far away, and I'll protect you as my own. Tis my duty, and I won't disappoint."

"And tis mine to remember that you are our husband's first, and tis you who sets the rules of the cabin. I too will not disappoint."

"I know you won't."

"Oh!" Mellow exclaimed as she remembered. "How fares Love?" Kindness' smile vanished. She broke eye contact, looked down sadly, and shook her head. "Aw, fuckety-fuck," Mellow muttered.

"You say a'what?" asked Kindness.

"Nothing. Just remark my before-people used upon hearing a bad."

"Yes, but what was it? Speak it again."

"Fuckety-fuck."

"Fuckety-fuck," Kindness repeated curiously. "And tis to express sorrow?"

"Sorrow, anger, self-stupid, stubbed toe in the dark, all the bad feelings."

"Fuckety-fuck. Hmm. Tis new to us. Say something to make me feel bad."

"Umm . . . our husband is cruel, and there's nothing we can do about it."

"Fuckety-fuck!" Kindness shouted angrily, paused, and then giggled. "Yes. It works. Fuckety-fuck."

Despite her continued dizziness and pounding head, Mellow couldn't help but giggle along. It hurt, but so what? "Fuckety-fuck," she laughingly agreed.

"Fuckety-fuck," Kindness repeated as she took Mellow's hand for them to titter as one, and thus their sisterhood was forged.

* * *

EVERY SIXTH NIGHT, on the nights when Thunder lay with Kindness and the sky was at its darkest, Mellow would sneak out of the cabin and stealth into the woods to meet with Sandy the apprendix. It was his idea, but she didn't mind. Despite her initial need for blackmail, she had grown quite fond of the boy.

For his part, he adored her. She was the only person with whom he could be his true self, and they could talk about anything. Almost always he'd try to impress her with his knowledge of the lore and legends that his master had taught him. Sometimes she'd instruct him on the medicinal properties of various plants of which Horizon remained unaware, and he'd take credit for his "discoveries" as he boasted them to his Holy One. And sometimes they'd chit about nothing at all.

"I never cared for the strawberry," he pontificated one night as they sat in the dark by their favorite tree, mindlessly plucking the fruits off a vine and popping them into their mouths like popcorn of old. "Don't like how the seeds get stuck in the teeth."

"I like its sweetness," she replied.

"I as well, but not worth the bargain."

Sometimes their mundane chits would tangent to the politic.

"My master would disapprove of me spending time with a woman," he confessed one night. "He'd think it too much a temptation for me. Ha ha."

"Ha ha," Mellow repeated with a smile.

"Specially with you. He still blames you for the death of Skinny Horse."

"Twas not my bad," she said sadly. "You know that."

"You're a woman. To the Holy One, all bad begins and ends with woman."

"And to you?"

"He's my master. I learn what he teaches."

"One day you shall be Holy One. Should you not learn to learn for yourself?"

"Tis in the lore given us by the gods, Mellow."

"Is it? Or is it how Horizon decodes the lore given by the gods? He would also decode the lore to say that your urges are of sin and sick. Me, I say not. All the Holy Ones of my before-people said not." Sandy paused and furrowed his eyebrows, and Mellow could almost hear his brain clanking. "Consider," she smiled winningly.

And sometimes the apprendix just needed to yak.

"My moma died in my fifth calendar, birthing what would've been my little brother. Pupa thought it below a man to tend to children, and there were no unwed women for him to wed. I tried to learn from the older boys, but they would only tease me . . . until your husband came along. He reached out his hand and began to teach me what a man must know, what my own pupa wouldn't, and the others fell in his line. Tis when I discovered I like boys. Maybe tis why I became the way I am."

"Tis not. Tis only because the gods decreed to make you so. I've told you this."

"You have, but tis a hard to accept."

"Easier, I'd think, than tis something unholy about you."

Sandy considered for a moment, but it remained too difficult still. He shook it off and returned to his story. "Thunder and Playful were hopefuls in those days. The three of us and Leaf would skip stones in the lake and tell funnies in the night. When Thunder and Playful would start to smooch, Leaf and I knew it our cue to go, but I'd sneaky back and watch from behind a bush and yearn that twas my lips pressed to his.

"Not long after my ninth calendar, Playful had first bleeding. Clearsky took her as his new second, his previous second having recently perished in a birthing. Thunder was mortified, but he could do nothing to it for he had only twelve calendars and had yet to go to battle—we were in war then. He had no status, no name of his own.

"One night, Dour found Thunder and Playful smooching in the woods. At the next Gathering, before all, she reprimanded Playful with harsh whip, shrieking that a wife of the Sorry must forego childish chums. In tears, Playful vowed to the gods to adhere. She never spoke to me, Leaf, or Thunder again.

"Thunder flew into a rage of insolence and brooding that frightened all. Even the Sorry didn't wish to contend. Only his moma's husband would scold and thrash, but soon his fists grew too bloody from the punching, and he too let young Son-of-Heat be.

"With my one best chum absent from me in his despair, and my other having vowed to never speak with me again, I had no one once more."

"What of Leaf?"

"Leaf was never my chum. He had always competed me, for he alone wanted to be Thunder's preferred. With Thunder gone from us, Leaf and I had no bond.

"I was lonesome. I sought counsel from Horizon and Rainfall, the apprendix before me. Their insights warmed me. I was fascinated to learn the things of Heaven and ground, and my passion delighted them. When I learned that men of spirit were not permitted to lie with woman, I knew I found my calling. Not permitted? Ha ha, it would be my fuckety-fuck alibi! I trailed Rainfall every day, as if I was the apprendix's apprendix, and Horizon said he would consider making it official.

"Twas round that time that Thunder passed his thirteenth calendar. The men brought him to battle, and he achieved status that very day. Twas unheard of! And not in the manner of Skinny Horse did he achieve it, nuh-uh, but with courage and valor did he save many of our warrior's lives; and took more than many from our enemy.

"He was named Thunder that night without hesitation or debate —some say because of the thunderous manner in which he combats, others for the threatening storm that looms above him always. But there was no question he was of thunder.

"Kindness' husband had perished in that same battle, and she was given to him that night. She was twelve calendars his senior, and beautiful without wrinkle or scar. Even though Playful had been his hopeful, most thought Kindness a higher status pairing—and Thunder loovvves status. His rage was vanished the morn next, and his smiles continued well beyond. He didn't even show upset after the mysterious deaths of his new children that he inherited from Kindness' before-husband."

I'll bet, thought Mellow, but knew better than to express her cynicism aloud. "So you got your chum back," she said instead. "All is good once more then, yes?"

"No," Sandy answered sadly. "When he learned of my association with the Holy Ones, he called it a betrayal, and flew into new berserk. 'How much time have I wasted on you?!' he screamed as he punched me and shoved me to the ground. I didn't get, I still don't. He began to tease me to the other boys—the ones from whom he once protected me—and praised them, praised them, when they hurt me.

"I hated him. I hate him still . . . and yet I crave him . . . to the god of love do I crave him . . . which makes me hate him all the more."

The apprendix paused, and then gazed into her eyes as his own grew cold. "I'd slay him if I could, Mellow," he vowed. "If the gods permitted, I'd slay him as he sleeps, and I pray each day for their permission." He lay his head upon her shoulder. "I love him, Mellow. I hate him. He's so pretty. I want him dead."

Mellow put her arms around the boy, stroked his hair, and sighed, "I get."

* * *

THE WOMEN WADED knee-deep in the crystal blue lake as they performed their daily chores. Mellow took care of the household washing while Kindness taught Daughter-of-Kindness how to bathe little Son-of-Thunder-2, Son-of-Thunder-1 having by then seen enough calendars to join the older boys in the hunt-and-combat games.

Among the others alongside them were Shy, a demure teen who said little and focused mainly on the suckle-feeding of her twin babies; Candid, a pleasant woman whose frankness Mellow always appreciated; and Brash, a tall, cocksure one who's only captivating trait was that she didn't care what anyone thought of her.

Brash's first three husbands had died in combat and so was considered a bad charm. She was given to Leaf on his seventeenth calendar, the night of his first slay. She was nineteen calendars his senior. She loved to boast how she reigned supreme in her cabin, and delighted in Mellow as a new audience for her overtold tales. " . . . and with one little frying pan struck to his mushy little head, he never took superior to me again," she laughingly concluded. "Always best to get saddled to the weak ones."

"Don't listen to her, Mellow," chuckled Kindness. "Brash likes to talk hard, but you've seen her at the honkytonks. She's just as submitty as us all."

"That's because Dour would have me thrashed to new scars if she knew the truth of it," Brash countered and turned to Mellow. "Fear your husband, yes, for he is strong and large, but tis the moma-of-all-she's who should truly terrify. They say that when she was Clearsky's third, it was she who slayed wives one and two in their sleep so she could ascend to First Moma, and twas not the gods at all."

"Who says that?" whipped Kindness. "Only you say that, Brash."

"Many say it for tis a truth," Brash insisted. "Tis the only possible if you ponder it, for wives one and two were good and kind. Why would the gods take them so young? And on the same very night?"

"No one knows whether tis a truth or not," offered Candid. "Tis a rumor of gossip only, and you know it to be so, Brash. But either way, Mellow, you do need to take heed. Dour can be harsh, no query on that, and she still blames you for the demise of her last and final son. Tis in her eyes always."

A sudden wave of nausea struck Mellow with a jolt. Her stomach churned, her body lurched, and her break-fast flew out her mouth in a vomitous stinky red. Kindness and Candid took quick hold of her arms and helped her to shore, Mellow sicking all the while. Kindness knelt beside her to hold her upright and patted her on the back.

"Stress not much, Mellow," she soothed. "The First Moma would call for no thrashing without cause, and that business with Skinny Horse is moonths behind."

"No, tis not it," Mellow panted. She had seen far too much sad and bad for the likes of Dour to bring her to sick; nor was her nausea due to anything she ate for she had never once suffered a food poisoning, even in eras when most food was poisonous. She never even had a flu. But she knew from so many lifetimes the precise cause of her ferocious puke. It happened every time, and only at such times.

"I'm with child," she told them.

* * *

SON-OF-THUNDER-3 WAS AN EXTRAORDINARY LITTLE BOY. After only four moonths he was crawling; by six, walking and making simple words like "moma" and "pupa"; uttering full sentences not long after that. At little more than two calendars he held the maturity of one with four, banged drums and whistled whistle-bones skillfully as any, could count to ten, and had a delicious sense of humor to boot. "When is a door not a door?" he asked one day when the crowd was large enough to warrant a big funny.

"I don't know, Son-of-Thunder-3," Mellow smilingly indulged. "When is a door not a door?"

"When tis ajar!" the toddler shouted with a cackle so contagious that everyone in earshot couldn't help but laugh along. Only when the laughter subsided did he turn to Mellow and ask, "Moma, how can a door be a jar?"—which only made everyone laugh all the more, which only made him cackle even louder.

A brilliant, good-natured klutz, he'd live in his head and wobble into trees and trip over rocks, popping himself right back up with a giggle, "Did it on purpose!"

"You're such a goofball," Mellow would playfully tease.

"Yes, I'm a goofy ball," he'd good-naturedly laugh along.

Mellow knew that in a different era Son-of-Thunder-3 would've grown up to be a world class scientist or cellist or billionaire entrepreneur, a success at anything he wanted, but he was beginning to ask questions, his congenial manner starting to give him away, and she worried how much longer she could keep his secret a secret.

Late one morn, Daughter-of-Kindness and Sons-of-Thunder-1-and-2 were off performing their children's chores. Son-of-Thunder-3 played near the firepit while Mellow and Kindness diced the pussy-fish and produce for the daily luncheon.

"Certain you wish to task so?" Mellow asked her. "I'll take gladness in tasking for us both. Don't push, my sister."

Kindness was in her fifth moonth with child, and all were worried for her. Even though she'd birthed seven healthy children (four of whom Thunder had slain,) she'd seen thirty-five calendars, an age where the gods don't help so much.

"Gratitude, Mellow, but my mind would go to mushy if I did nothing at all," she said when she noticed Son-of-Thunder-3 lying on the grass staring wide-eyed into the sun. It was an odd sight, and Mellow saw her sister's curiosity.

"Stop that, 3," Mellow scolded. "You'll hurt your eyes."

"My eyes aren't hurted, Moma," he said innocently. "I like the warm on them."

"Up! Now!" she insisted, then quickly turned back to Kindness to steer the conversation away from the boy. "So, how went exam with the Holy One?"

"He spoke that all fares well, which relieves; and First Moma tied acorn to thread and spun it over my belly to determine it male. Thunder will be beyond himself—four boys to one girl! For Dour is correct on such at least half the time."

"Yes, she's a very wise woman," Mellow quipped.

"Shhh," Kindness conspiratorially smiled back.

In lieu of staring at the sun, 3 threw a stone into the air and held out his hands to catch upon its descent. The stone fell to the ground with the boy snapping his palms closed only after hearing the thud of its landing. Again, Kindness found something odd about it, and again, Mellow saw so.

"Come, 3!" she clamored. "'Tis time for your bath."

"You already bath'd'd me on this day, Moma," he said as he fumbled in the dirt in search of the stone that lay but a fingerbreadth before him.

"I said now!" Mellow commanded.

But it was too late. Kindness had seen the likes of the sight a hundred times or more, but it's true meaning only hit her then, and it hit her hard. Her mouth dropped open in shock and dread, and she turned to Mellow hurt and bewildered.

"Just one more try," beseeched the boy as his hand stumbled upon the stone, and as Mellow looked to her sister in pleading desperation. "I can do it, Moma, I can!" the toddler insisted as Kindness noticed Thunder approaching.

"Listen to your moma, boy!" she yelled. "Or get the back of both our hands!"

"Yes, Auntie," 3 grumbled, and then shuffled despondently toward his moma.

Kindness turned to Mellow and whispered only, "We'll chit," for Thunder was too near for anything more to be safely spoken.

"The hunt was slight," the great hunter grunted as he dropped three teeny squirrels onto Kindness' lap. "The Great Drought is strong for Clearsky has lost the gods' favor. One rodent to be cooked and added for the Holy One and apprendix, two in our supper. And

I want a foot rub." He turned to Mellow. "You." He started into the cabin, pausing only to smile and tussle his son's hair. "You're a tough little one, ain't ya, l'il goofball?" he said fondly, and went inside.

Except Son-of-Thunder-3 wasn't really a goofball at all. He was just an exceptional little boy who happened to have been born blind —Mellow had spotted it in his first days of his life—blind in a world where a man's only value lay in his ability to hunt and fight, any male lacking in such to be slain as a burden to his people.

CHAPTER THIRTY

SANTA MONICA, CALIFORNIA
SEPTEMBER 2018
THE NIGHT OF THE DAY JANINE FOUND OUT

"Fuck you, girlfriend," said Janine.

Molly had barely walked in, barely flipped on the lights when she heard the cuss and saw Janine on the sofa in her pink flannel jammies, a near-empty bottle of Smirnoff balanced between her thighs.

"You were sitting in the dark?" Molly asked.

"I don't know what pisses me off more," Janine continued with a slur. "That you're a lying cheat, or that the sick bastard only gave you a B."

What did Janine see? Molly wondered, and when? And how? It didn't matter though. Whatever she saw, there was only one conclusion she could have drawn.

"What're you talking about?" she asked innocently, trying to buy time to come up with a believable story, even while knowing there was none to be had.

"I saw it, okay? I followed you to Encino and saw you hug the prick and go inside."

"Oh that. All right, I know what it must look like—"

"Yeah, it looks like you're fucking our crim teacher."

"I'm not. I went to see him back in January to try to get him to change my B. He wouldn't, but we started talking, and we kind of hit it off anyway. I didn't tell you because I was afraid you'd think what you're thinking now. But we're just friends."

"Right, because Miss Prissy-l'il-white-farm-girl must have so much in common with Mr. Urban-Mexican-prosecutor-man. What riveting conver-fuckin-sations you must have."

"Look, you're drunk—"

"Not drunk enough."

"Why don't we get you to bed and talk about it in the morning?"

"You think I'll be less pissed at you when I'm sober?"

"Maybe not, but you'll be more lucid."

"Fuck you, I'm going to bed." She stood up and staggered toward the bedroom. About to topple over, Molly caught her, and helped her the rest of the way.

"It's all right. I got you."

"No, you don't 'got me.' You had me, and you lost me. Bitch."

"Shhh," Molly soothed as she eased her love into their bedroom, into their bed, and then lied down next to her.

"Oh no, no," said Janine. "I am not sharing my bed with you. No, no, no."

"It's my bed too, honey."

"Fine. Then I'll go sleep on the couch." She got up, staggered some more, and grabbed onto the dresser to keep herself from falling.

"All right," Molly said. "I'll take the couch." She helped Janine back to bed, pulled the blankets over her, and left.

* * *

MOLLY AWOKE EARLY the next morning, made herself up pretty as a picture, took a quick run to Trader Joe's, and returned to prepare a hearty breakfast of avocado, gruyere and salsa omelets, blueberry-chocolate pancakes, real Vermont maple syrup, turkey sausage, honeydew, bold coffee, and tomato juice with celery stick, with two Tylenols and a glass of water at Janine's spot.

When Janine walked in, she saw the spread and groaned. "You've got to be kidding me. You think a fancy meal is going to make up for what you did?" She remained standing as she picked up the Tylenol and water. "You know, I have a good mind to report that son of a bitch. End his career and ruin him."

"Please don't. It'll reflect badly on me too."

"Maybe it should," she grunted as she downed the pills.

Molly moved to her, took her hands in her own. "I am so sorry, Janine, but what you saw was not what it looked like. I promise."

Janine yanked her hands away, seemingly ready to fly into another cussing fit. Instead, she took a deep breath, a few steps back, and spoke softly. "I knew you were straight when we hooked up, okay? Maybe it's tough giving up boys, I wouldn't know. Maybe if you had come talk to me about it, we could've figured something out. Maybe I would've given you some kind of hall pass or some-thing. I don't know what I would've done. But to screw around behind my back all these months, lie to me all these months, lie to me even now after you've been caught red-handed—"

"Janine, I never slept with him."

"Don't insult me! Don't insult my intelligence. At least give me that."

"Look at me. I swear by the grace of God that I never had sex with him, never even kissed him. Look into my eyes. Do I look like I'm lying?"

Janine took a moment to study Molly's face. "No, you don't. Which only tells me what a talented liar you must be. What else have you been lying to me about?"

"What can I do to prove it to you?"

"You mean, what do I need from you? Okay, here's what I need. First, I need you to admit the truth. I don't know if I'll forgive you after that, don't know if I can, don't know if I want to . . . but I know for sure that I won't if you keep lying to me."

"Janine—"

"Shut up. After that, if I choose to forgive you—if—I'll need you to pick. Him or me—you don't get both. If it's me, you never see him again. Ever. You don't talk to him, you don't text him, if you get him for crim next semester you transfer out. And I'll be watching.

"If you choose him, well . . . " She paused, considered whether she really wanted to say what she wanted to say, and then said it. "I love you, Molly. There's something about you, some crazy mysterious thing inside you that I don't understand, but you're not like anyone I've ever known. I feel special just being in your presence. So if you choose him, if it turns out I'm nothing more than some kind of lesbo experiment for you, so be it. Maybe we can stay friends. Maybe. After the hurt goes away, maybe.

"But I'm not going to beg, I won't be lied to, and I will absolutely not let you keep playing me for a fool."

Molly looked to the floor, unable to think of a single word to say that could make things better.

"You got twenty-four hours to make a decision," continued the bodybuilder. "Till then, stay the fuck out of my face." And she walked out.

Molly threw the elaborate breakfast in the trash then cleaned the kitchen.

* * *

FRANCISCO WAS surprised when his doorbell rang early that Sunday afternoon, and even more so to find Molly standing there with sad eyes and too much makeup for daytime. "What's the matter?" he asked. "What happened?"

"Janine dumped me."

"Come in."

He led her inside, sat her on the sofa, put up a pot of tea, sat down beside her, and had her tell him everything.

"Well, she didn't exactly dump you then," he observed after the tale had been told. "Sounds like she doesn't know what she wants to do."

"Did you miss the part where she said I can never see you again? Oh, maybe she'll change her mind when I explain how I desperately need you in my life because you're the only other unsterblich in the history of the world. Think she'll believe me then?"

"Do you love her?"

"What's that got to do with anything?"

"Just answer. Do you love her?"

"I don't know. Maybe. She's not Al."

"No one's ever going to be Al. We covered this."

"What I mean is, with Al, like, everything was easy. We each had our own departments of the stuff we were in charge of, and we always trusted each other to take care of it right. With Janine, we share everything, and everything's like a contest. Don't get me wrong, it's challenging, exciting. Boy-oh-boy, you have to be on your toes with that one. She's so smart, and witty, and tough, and beautiful, and she's got such a beautiful heart too. I just treasure being with her."

"Sounds to me like you love her."

Molly paused, reflected. "Maybe I do. Yeah, I think I do. No, I do. I do."

"Then it's settled," he said. "You and I have to call it quits for a while."

"Wait, what? No! That's not what I meant."

"Molly, your relationship with Janine is an experience you want, so one you have to have. If I wasn't in the picture, you'd choose her in a heartbeat."

"I wouldn't have to choose at all if you weren't in the picture."

"Exactly, and I shouldn't be. Listen, this thing we're saddled with is hard. New adventures are the only thing that makes it palatable. Staying with me, choosing me every time a new lover gets jealous, your eternity will get very stale very quickly."

"You've told me that, and I don't care."

"But I do. I've become the crutch for you I was always afraid I'd become, and in more ways than you can even see. I made a mistake, Molly. I was weak, and I was selfish. I'm so sorry for that. Now, go to Janine and tell her that you love her, and that you and I are over."

Molly let the words sink in, stood, put her hands on her hips, and said, "No."

"Trust me. This is for your own good."

"No! I'm ninety-five years old, Francisco, and I'm scared. I was scared while I pretended to be old and watched my husband die, and I'm scared now as I stand here pretending to be young. I never show it, don't even face it because that makes it even scarier. I just dig in and do what I have to do and pretend I'm not scared—and that's my biggest pretend of all my pretendings every moment of every day.

"So, no, Francisco, you don't get to send me away." Despite her best efforts, she began to well up. "You're the only person like me in the world, so, no, you don't get to send me away. Maybe showing up to me as you did was a mistake, but you did it and you don't get to undo it. It'd be like . . . like . . . putting a sandwich in front of a starving kid then yanking it away and saying, 'it's for your own good.' It's mean!

"I can't do this by myself, Francisco. I can't lose you. I won't!"

He put his arms around her. "Shh, shh, no, shh, you won't lose me, Molly, not ever. I'll just go back to keeping tabs on you like I've done since 1965, guiding and helping you from afar. When this thing with Janine runs its course, whether it's a college fling or a death-do-us-part or an anything-in-between, I'll return to you.

"You and Janine—you and anyone for that matter—will only ever have as long as you have. You and me, we have forever."

She didn't know what more to say for she'd said everything she had. "But, but . . . how am I going to practice my martial arts?" was the best she could come up with.

"You'll figure it out."

"How am I going to—"

"You'll figure it out." He stroked her hair. "You're stronger than you know."

"I'm not. I just pretend I am."

"Shh," he said as he gazed into her eyes, and she into his, and neither were aware of their faces growing closer ever closer until their lips touched, until their mouths opened. Their arms squeezed tight around each other as their year-long suppressed desires could be contained no longer—and it wasn't just the way that his tongue massaged the inside of her mouth that drove her wild, but that it was in a way she'd never felt a tongue move before. She didn't even know it could.

Can someone climax just from kissing? she wondered.

* * *

SHE'D HAD many sexual partners in her life—one man she loved, and one woman too—but never had she experienced anything like him. Holy smokes! He knew things, did things she never could have imagined, carnal techniques and artistry lost to history, his loving prowess possessing the same magical wonderment as his fighting skills.

She lay naked beside him in his bed, panting harder than she had after any of their most rigorous of sparring sessions. She felt drained and empty, yet full and complete. She noticed that he was also panting hard, and it pleased her. Seventy-seven years of intimacy may not be two thousand, but she had learned a few tricks along the way too. Their eyes caught, and the smiles they smiled were bittersweet.

"Are you still going to send me away?" she asked, longing to hear the answer she knew she wouldn't hear.

"I'm sorry," he whispered sadly. "I shouldn't have let this happen. I'm sorry for that too."

"Then this is really good-bye?"

"How about . . . 'see ya later'?"

"I like that better," she purred as she nestled her head upon his chest. "You know what, Professor?"

"What?"

"You sure have a messed-up way of ending a relationship."

He laughed a small laugh, a sad, gallows laugh, and then so did she.

CHAPTER THIRTY-ONE

The Dwelling
The Morn Kindness Figured It Out

H E WASN'T THE FIRST broken that Mellow had brought into the new world. She once had a son born with half an arm, but he grew to be master of sling and spear with the other. She once had a daughter who was unable to walk, but her uterus was strong so she held value. One son had been born deaf, but twas the early days of the new world, not long after the Collapse, before umanity went all fuckety-fuck.

She had loved all three—loved all her children, in fact, even the ones who came to be not so deserving of it—but her heart went out to Son-of-Thunder-3 most. Perhaps because he was so remarkable in so many ways, or perhaps because he'd grow up to be so helpless in the only way that mattered anymore. Perhaps both.

So she kept his condition secret, buying time to come up with an idea that would spare him from his Community's laws—at least a better idea than the terrible one she had from the start. When he began to walk, she taught him to count steps so he could move from one spot to the next by memory. When he began to talk, she placed

various objects in his hand and told him its name, its color, its properties. "Tis a needle of pine and tis green, smell it." "Tis a razz-berry
and tis red, taste it."

"What does green mean, Moma? What's red?"

"I'll explain that when you're older," was always her answer, for
she couldn't let him know that his world of darkness made him
different from the others. He was too young to grasp the concept of
"secret," and too chitty to keep one if he did.

But her time was running out, or had already run out, she
couldn't be sure.

The luncheon that day was among the most intense she could
remember for she simply couldn't deduce in which direction her
sister's heart would land. A wonderful woman Kindness was, true to
her name, a loving mother and auntie; twas hard to imagine she'd
support the slaying of an innocent child. On the other arm, Kindness
was a devout woman and committed to the ways of her Community.

Mellow tried to read her face, but the answer wasn't on it.

The only saving grace was that Thunder was oblivious to the
tension, which was unusual for he was among the most perceptive of
people she had ever met.

Something was up with him, the sisters knew. For more than a
moonth he'd seemed distracted—no, anxious, as if awaiting something he wanted but didn't know if he'd get; or get but didn't want.
In bed, he'd been neither the cruel Thunder nor the sweet,
performing his husbandly duties responsibly, mechanically, as if
endeavoring to plant another seed in her soil while his thoughts
wandered to the elsewhere. Kindness being already with child, he
had no relations with her at all.

Aft the luncheon, Thunder left with Leaf on another of their
meat-recon campaigns. Son-of-Thunder-1 walked his little brother to
his first hunt-and-combat game. Kindness instructed Daughter-of-
Kindness to gather the fish and produce for the evening supper,
reminding her to gather two-fold for it was their cabin's day to make
meal for the Holy One and apprendix. Kindness started on the skinning of the hares while Mellow went inside to put Son-of-Thunder-3
into his crib for nap.

"Why is Auntie Kindness cross with you on this day, Moma?"

How could he have possibly picked up on that? she marveled. Wow.

"Tis of an adult nature," she answered. "I'll explain when you're older."

The boy giggled. "Tis what you always say about everything."

"For tis always true," she giggled along, tickling and kissing him. "Nighty-nite."

But her good cheer shifted back to fear and dread as she returned to the fire-pit area. Kindness was by then gutting that first hare, so Mellow sat beside her and began to skin the next in silence, deferentially waiting for the senior sister to speak first.

"Your son is blind, Mellow," she said at last. "You know it, you've known it all along, and you kept it from me. What have I ever done to earn such distrust?"

"Apology," Mellow said shamefully. "But I feared to tell anyone."

"Since when am I anyone?"

"You're not." She dropped to her knees and wrapped her arms around her sister's legs. "Please, Kindness. Speak of it not. I beg you!"

"Shhh," Kindness empathized as she lifted Mellow back up to her seat. "I get your love for the boy, I do, but the efforts you seek will only delay what's inevitable."

"Not undoubtedly. For two calendars and more I've searched a method to save him, and I'm not ready to retire the trying."

"But there is no method. Thunder would never approve it. He cares far too much for his status to relinquish his duties on behalf of a weak."

"I know."

"Your only other option is the Sorry, but you'd have to ask the First Moma to do your asking, and Dour still blames you for Skinny Horse. Even if she took your cause, she'd never convince Clearsky who slayed his own son for the same law."

"I know, I know. I gave up on those as solutions long ago."

"What others can there be?"

240

"I don't know! But I feel in my heart that the gods will reveal one to me. I just need more time. Please, don't speak of this."

"Course not, my sister. Tis not my tragic to speak. I thought you knew that."

"Gratitude, Kindness, so gratitude."

"But my advice to you is to tell our husband still. When you joined us, Mellow, you vowed to accept our ways. This is our way. 3's blind cannot be hidden forever, and he'll be slain to the god of the broken soon or late. Yet if you opt to put the Community above your wants before his plight revealed, your own status may rise. Telling of the boy now can be a good for you."

"Will consider, dear Kindness. But still, you'll chit not of it?"

"My lips are stitched together," Kindness promised, and Mellow could tell that she was saying a truth. She wanted to kiss the woman, but she knew better.

* * *

MELLOW COULDN'T RECALL EVER SEEING Thunder so perpetually smiley. He was pleasant and loving through the supper, complimented both his wives, laughed and cajoled with the children, and even helped clear the picnic table afterwards. Whatever he'd been waiting for, he clearly got it.

Aft the supper, he proclaimed that it had been too long since he'd pleasured Kindness. He affectionately told her go to his bed to wait for him, then took Mellow by the hand and walked her to her chamber. He looked warmly into her eyes and said, "I'm glad we're wed, Mellow. You've been good wife to me."

"And you the best husband for whom a woman can dream," she lied.

He kissed her softly on the lips, and then returned to Kindness.

Mellow went inside where 3 lay in his crib, mumbling incoherent goobly-ga's as he slept. It brought a smile to her face, and then a frown. What do I do?

Kindness' moans began to emanate through the walls, growing louder as her ecstasy mounted. Yes, twas the sweet Thunder this night, thought Mellow. She sat on her bed, briefly happy for her sister till her own dilemma bashed back into her brain.

She'd spent more than two calendars searching for a better idea than the one she had from the start, and she had failed to find it. It was now but a matter of time till the others would discover her son's broken, just as Kindness had; a matter of time till Kindness' belly swelled to the brim and Thunder would lie with Mellow only. If she and the boy were ever to flee, it had to be this night.

It would be a diarrhea life for Son-of-Thunder-3, she recognized. He would never have a friend, never lay with a woman. He'd know only his mother and the dead concrete city he could never see. She'd introduce him to beautiful music, course, teach him braille so he could read those glorious old-world tales—or would it be cruel to expose him to the concept of others when he'd never meet another soul, to beautiful lands he could never fathom, to adventures he could never take?

Was Kindness right? Should she simply accept the ways of her adopted Community? Should she spare her baby from his inevitable loneliness and drudgery?

She didn't realize that she'd been softly weeping when she heard the thud of the boy plopping onto the floor aft climbing over his crib's rail. "I told you not to do that," she scolded. "You'll hurt yourself."

He hopped up on the bed beside her. "Don't cry, Moma," he said as he wrapped his teeny arms around her. "It'll be all right. It'll allll-llll be all right."

She smiled. In that moment, she knew what she had to do, what she'd always had to do, what she should have done calendars before. She picked him up, put him back in his crib, kissed his little forehead, and got back into bed. She set her internal alarm clock for two hours hence so that Thunder and Kindness would be fast asleep when she'd begin their getaway.

It will be a diarrhea life for him, but it will be a life. Little Ool will have a life.

* * *

SHE AWOKE with a buzz of adrenaline. She went to the kitchen, poured a titty-bit of hooch into a cup, and returned. She nudged the boy awake and told him to drink.

He took one sip and gagged. "It's dia-ra-ra!"

"It's medicine."

"I don't have a sick."

"And we want to keep it that way. Drink." He wrinkled his nose and scowled at her but did as he was told. She swaddled him in his blanket, and then used twine and slings to prepare the papoose.

"Are we going somewhere, Moma?" he slurred sleepily.

"Shhhh. Shhhh."

By the time he was secured to her back, the little chitterbox was out cold.

She crept out her chamber as it occurred to her that despite her overall contempt for the Community, she'd actually miss it. She'd miss Sandy to pieces, course; miss her dear friends Candid, Shy, and even Brash; miss Daughter-of-Love, the adorable little pixie who had come to lean on Mellow as her de facto moma; and she'd miss Kindness most of all. She yearned to say a real good-bye to her but what would she say? She kissed her index and middle fingers, pressed them to Thunder's bedchamber door where her sister slept this night, and left.

Through the rings of cabins and into the woods she stealthed till she came to the tunnel opening and went inside. It had been three calendars since she'd felt its cold dampness, since she'd been outside the dwelling at all, but as she neared the opening on the far side, she noticed flickerings of orange. A campfire?

The sentries! She'd completely forgotten about the sentries!

"Who's that?!" she heard Thunder shout.

She hit the ground fast and lay still as still could be.

Got to stop making mistakes, Mellow!

"Tis nothing," she heard Leaf say. "You're being paranoidal."

A frighteningly long pause followed as Thunder waited to hear a single sound more. "Perhaps," he finally conceded.

Abort! Mellow screamed in her head. Mission abort! Get back to the cabin! There's no telling what Thunder'll do to me if he finds me trying to desert, but little Ool's condition will be found for certain, and for certain he'll be slain.

But Thunder will hear me if I move but a fingerbreadth—he's impeccable in that skill. I just have to lay quiet and wait them out.

But we're on his path home! He'll find us upon his return. Or the replacement sentries will find us when they come to relieve.

She was stuck, trapped, and all she could do was listen, watch, and hope against impossible hope for a miracle.

"I was with good cheer all day," she could hear Thunder gripe to his chum. "From the moment we saw the blessed event I was with good cheer, and now you seek to ruin it? Why not simply ruin it when the boon news first arrived and spare me the false happy?"

"It remains boon news," insisted Leaf. "Jubilant news. And I seek to ruin nothing. I do but what I always do, which is to plan."

"Or is it to stall?"

"No, tis to plan," Leaf replied, insulted. "Thunder, please. Seek reason. We must-must-must solve the Horizon issue in advance if we wish our final success."

The small fire rendered just enough illumination for Mellow to see the two men sitting on large rocks, and their words made it clear that they were plotting some kind of plot—she just couldn't make sense of what it was. Maybe she could leverage it against them somehow. Blackmail? Trickery? Something? Anything? One way or another, she had to reckon herself a way out of this death-trap.

"To fuckety-fuck with the Horizon issue!" Thunder bellowed. "For so many calendars you've tried to solve that puzzle, but perhaps tis a jigsaw with no final piece. For so many calendars you've said that when a chimp-cub grows to defeat his Sorry, it will be the gods showing us the proper manner in which to usurp, their decree that tis my time at last. Patience, you counselled always, patience, patience, yackety-yak. And lo'n'behold, on this day of glorious days, our little chum is victorious. Tis my time, Leaf, by the gods decree, according to the words of you!"

She was reminded of the day they found her. This chit seemed similar to that one, although she couldn't be sure for their accent and slangs were still foreign to her ears back then. How long have they been at this? And what exactly are they at?

"Even in victory, Thunder," Leaf countered, "without anointment of the gods, without Horizon's proper blessing, you will never be considered the one true Sorry."

"If the gods favor me to win, that in itself is their anointment."

"Perhaps, but without proper blessing, half your support will not accept it."

"Then I will slay them."

"Oh, will you? You'll first slay half the men of the Community who support Clearsky, and then slay half of the half that remains? Who'll be left for you to Sorry?"

Titty-bit by titty-bit the info compiled in Mellow's head to lead her to a story, to see their plot, and then her own plan began to take form. The more she imagined upon it, the stronger it became, till it was perfect. Lemons-to-lemonade, absolutely perfect!

If she could pull it off.

Thunder sighed, and then forced himself to a hard decision. "Leaf, my chum. You are the cleverest man I've ever known. But you're a slight man, no fault of yours, and so not proficient in the ways of combat. Your frozen toes are rational."

"I do not have frozen toes! I speak truth, Thunder! You must heed me!"

She used the loud of Leaf's protests to drown out the removing of her papoose, gently laid her baby on the ground, and kissed his rosy cheek.

"Stress not much, Leaf," Thunder went on with sympathy. "You'll always be my most trusted advisor, but to the advice you give now, no. When the combat begins, find a lonely spot in the woods to hide. When it ends, return to your rightful place by my side. Done, and decided."

"Thunder, I implore. We cannot win this without Horizon on our team."

"He is wrong, my husband," Mellow pronounced as she emerged from the tunnel. "You don't need Horizon."

"What're you doing out here?!" Thunder blared as he leapt up from his rock and raised his arm to strike. "Are you dropping eaves on me?!"

She squinted her eyes in anticipation of the blow to come but stood her ground nonetheless. "You need only the Holy One."

THWACK! was the sound of the knuckle-side of his hand whipping across her face to send her reeling to the ground. "You fool! Horizon is the Holy One!"

Mellow spit out some blood, and then responded. "He is today."

"You babble, woman," he shouted as he grabbed her hair, yanked her to her feet, and wound up to strike again. "This will teach you to drop eaves on me!"

"Wait," Leaf interjected calmly, curiously. "Woman, explain yourself."

"Don't embolden her, my chum," cautioned Thunder.

"No, she may be onto a thing," he replied, then turned to Mellow. "Proceed."

"If the Holy One is slain during the combat, Sandy ascends to the position."

"What it matters, dunce wife? Sandy is no more ally than Horizon!"

"Wait," Leaf repeated, considered, then looked to Mellow. "Sit," he told her, then turned to Thunder, "You, too." Mellow did as instructed. Thunder glared at his diminutive co-conspirator who simply nodded back matter-of-factly. Thunder grunted then did as advised, and Leaf turned back to Mellow. "Why do you presume that Sandy would bless Thunder after we've slain his beloved master?"

"Because he's my chum."

"Is he now?" Thunder growled suspiciously. "Since when is this?"

"Since my first days amongst you. We kept it secret from all so Horizon could not object. But stress not much, husband. We had no relations. I vow it to the gods."

"And I should simply take a lying woman's—"

"Thunder, later to that, please," Leaf urged, then back to Mellow.

"So perhaps he's your chum, but he's none to Thunder. Why would he do Thunder's bidding?"

"He wouldn't. But he'll do mine if I ask nicely."

Thunder and Leaf looked at each other, simultaneously shrugged and turned back to her. "Ask."

"But I want something in return."

"You'll have the back of my fist again if you don't go do what you offered."

"Upon his ascent to Holy One," Mellow went on as if oblivious to the threat, "Sandy will nominate our son as his apprendix. You, Thunder, the newly anointed Sorry, will confirm him to the position, and then you will gift me to Sandy to rear the boy, for such duties are beneath a man."

"Interesting," he said. "No. Now go do what you offered."

"I shall not."

"Then I shall thrash you."

"You thrash me anyway."

"Then I shall slay you."

"Then I shall be freed from your thrashings." She watched as Thunder fumed, and she let the moment sit—she was actually enjoying herself. "Tis a good bargain for you, Thunder; and you, wise Leaf, know it to be so."

"I see no reason to give up a wife," insisted Thunder.

"After your victory, you'll have half the women of the Community to choose from, including Playful, your once hopeful. What need you of me?"

"Then I see no reason to give up a son. 3 is a strong little boy, and smart too, may earn himself to be my heir. And I like him. He makes me chortle. No. But I'll tell you a what. In exchange for this service, since you want away from me so badly, I'll gift you to another—any man of your choosing, if he'll take you. But my son will remain in my cabin and reared by Kindness. I will not give up a potential heir."

Mellow sighed before telling him what she so didn't want to tell him, but she knew it a necessary risk. "3 will never be your heir, Thunder. Our son is blind."

An ominous silence bombarded. Thunder reflected to all his

many joyful moments with the boy and came to see that his wife's words indeed held truth. Old curiosities suddenly made a new sense, and it trampled on his heart. "How—how long have you known of this?"

"What it matters? Tis so."

"He'll never hunt nor combat," said the pupa with a sad crackle in his voice. "A burden he'll surely be. I must slay him. By the gods, I must."

"Or . . . you can simply grant him to the Holy One in exchange for his blessing upon your victory. Thunder, the news of our son's broken is known only to us three, and I'll see to it that it won't be shared to any till he's firm in his new standing. No one will ever know that you spared a weak."

"How can one be apprendix without sight?" asked Leaf.

"That would be for the Holy One to determine, wouldn't it?"

"Yes, it would," Leaf acknowledged pensively, then turned to Thunder. "Tis a good bargain. With the boy sightless, you give up nothing . . . except a wife you're willing to gift off anyway."

"Tis the principle. I will not be bullied by a woman."

Leaf leaned in, slapped his hand on Thunder's knee. "We're ready, my future Sorry. We weren't a moment ago but we are now. Tis the final piece of the jigsaw. Perhaps tis why the gods put Mellow on our path those calendars past. They are telling us tis time. Your time. Make the bargain."

Thunder took a moment to consider, then sighed with a shrug. "Fine. Done, and decided."

Now the hard part, thought Mellow.

* * *

MELLOW WASN'T AT ALL surprised by Sandy's initial reaction the following night when she told him of her scheme. "No!" the apprendix shout-whispered as they sat in the dark by their favorite tree. "I can't even fathom you to ask me such."

"I ask you only to save my son," she pleaded. "Tis the only way there is."

"Apologies re your boy, Mellow, but his condition is the gods' doing, and the slaying of him their law."

"Nuh-uh. Their law is to slay those who burden the Community. Men of the gods are not required to hunt or combat. He'll be no more burden than you or Horizon."

"No! Still, no, no, no. I will not be accomplice to usurp, specially one that puts Thunder at helm. You know my thoughts on him. No. I must warn of this to my master."

More than not wanting to have told Thunder about 3's sightlessness, this was a card she particularly didn't want to play. She knew it a diarrhea thing to do, but her baby's life depended on it. "Then I must warn him of your sickness."

Sandy's mouth dropped open in shock. "It would be my death sentence," he gasped. "And you've always proclaimed it not a sickness."

"Tis not, but only you and I know so."

He looked at her with devastating hurt, her betrayal tearing at his insides. "I thought you were my chum."

"And I thought you mine. Save my baby, Sandy my chum. Save your own life."

"My life is only in risk because you place it there."

"Be as it may, vow you'll say nothing of this to your master, vow to anoint my husband upon his victory, and vow to make 3 your apprendix. Or, have your secret out by dawn."

"What if Thunder is defeated?"

"Vow it to the gods, Sandy. I need you to vow it now, right now."

"But, but . . . how could a blind even be an apprendix?"

"We'll reckon on that when the time comes. Now, please, do as I beg you."

"I don't know enough to be Holy One! My learning time was too short. No!"

"You are already expert at legend and lore, and I can mentor you re healings. I know far more than Horizon. You know I do."

"And I'm to parade myself as apprendix to a woman? Chit of humiliation."

"No one will know it. It will seem natural for me to be by your side because natural for your apprendix to be by your side, and I by his as his nurturer."

"No, no, no! I cannot sit quiet to watch my master slain."

"Your master is boon as slain already," she said sadly, "and there's nothing you can do to save him. But you can save my baby, and you can go into the lore as the wisest Holy One of ever. Or you can be disgraced and bagged and drowned.

"Save my baby, Sandy. Please. Save yourself. I beseech you, dearest chum."

The apprendix could barely speak. His lips began to quiver, and his fury turned to tears. "I can't!" he wailed. "Horizon has been so good to me! I love my master! I despise Thunder! I can't! Can't! Won't, won't, won't . . . "

"Shhhh," Mellow soothed as she took him in her arms to offer comfort, for it was his tears, not his words, that told her exactly what she was so desperate to hear.

He would do as she bid, and her baby would get to live a proper, respectable life.

War was imminent.

CHAPTER THIRTY-TWO

THE LAST THING JANINE wanted was to go to some rich kid's party.

It had been a rough month for the girls. After leaving Francisco's place, Molly returned home to confess her love, admit her sin, and beg her partner's forgiveness. It turned out more heartfelt than she expected, for although making love to Francisco had felt so right in the moment, in retrospect it felt so wrong. Her shame was genuine.

Still, it was difficult for Janine to accept. She sought to rationalize the affair as some kind of bi thing that she couldn't understand, but it wasn't enough.

"I want to forgive you, Molly. I do."

"Then do."

"What if we say . . . for now . . . that I'll try?"

"I'll take it."

And so the quasi-forgiveness was granted. Janine remained cold to Molly for the rest of that day and beyond, and Molly remained relegated to the couch.

The next day was Monday, the official start of second year, civil procedure class. Given the ongoing lack of conversation, Molly said she'd understand if Janine preferred to drive to campus in separate cars. Janine was adamant that they drive together, and then didn't say a word the entire ride.

After class, upon returning home, Janine took her textbooks to the kitchen table to begin the required reading. Molly joined her, at which point Janine went to the bedroom to complete her reading alone. Molly knew better than to follow.

And on it went, day after day, week after week, Janine keeping an eagle eye on Molly's whereabouts while barely uttering a sound. To her credit, she never stopped struggling to find her way back to trusting the girl she so loved, the girl who had so thoughtlessly crushed her. To Molly's credit, she hung in and dealt.

It wasn't exactly an "intervention" when the boys of the quintet showed up to insist that Molly and Janine join them at the ritzy bash a family friend of Audrey's was throwing that weekend, but it sure felt like one. By this point, they all knew what Molly had done (although not with whom), but none could stand seeing their dear friends so perpetually miserable together.

"You can't stay home every night and not talk to each other," urged Randy. "You have to change this pattern, or you may as well just spare yourselves the agony and end it right now. Is that what you want to do?"

"No," Molly answered quicky.

"No," Janine mumbled softly.

"Then get off your collective ass and say you'll join us," asserted Josh. "Look, you'll go, you'll get hammered, maybe start talking about what you need to talk about. Maybe even start laughing again. So, what say you, and it better be yes?"

"I'll go if she goes," Molly volunteered.

"Why wouldn't you?" grumbled Janine. "Maybe you'll meet a nice fella."

"J-Janine," Zeke interjected. "That's not h-h-helping."

"Come to think of it," Janine went on, "aren't you better off going without me? Your chances of scoring dude or chick grow exponentially if out as a single."

Molly responded sadly. "I'll do whatever you want me to do."

Janine sighed. The last thing she wanted was to go to some rich kid's party.

"Fine," she conceded. "I'll go."

After the boys left, Molly began to make up the sofa bed. Janine started toward their bedroom, but then stopped in the doorway and turned to her. "Hey, listen. I don't mean to be a bitch, okay? I know I'm being one, and I just can't seem to stop myself."

"It's all right."

"Anyway, I'm sorry for it. I should be better than this. I know I should."

"No worries."

"Thanks." She went into the room and closed the door behind her.

Molly nestled under her covers and smiled. Progress?

* * *

THE PARTY WAS in full bloom by the time the girls arrived. Molly wore a blue buttoned-down silk blouse with a black pencil slim skirt, ankle strap heels, light makeup, hair down and straight, which she knew was one of Janine's favorite looks for her. Janine wore a black tank top and sweats, which she knew wasn't Molly's.

The swanky Mount Olympus home boasted marble floors, pitched ceilings, glass walls, panoramic views, and original Italian art. The crowd was young and rich, the music upbeat and loud, and the air thick with marijuana smoke. From the other side of the vast space, the girls could see Randy and Audrey chatting in a small group. Audrey noticed them, waved, and headed toward them. On her way, she latched onto the arm of a tall, good-looking, twenty-five-year-old in a black Armani jacket and tacky Bermuda shorts and dragged him along. Randy followed.

"Hi! So glad you decided to show!" announced Audrey, giving

each girl an air-kiss to the cheek. "Guys, this is one of my oldest, dearest friends, Billy, our host. Billy, these are two of my best buddies in the whole wide world, Janine and Molly."

"Welcome to my humble abode," Billy said pleasantly, then turned to Audrey with an impish grin and mouthed, "Wow."

"Relax, playa," Audrey giggled. "They're gay. Well, she is. She's bi, but trying real hard to be lesbian only because she—"

"Jesus Christ, Audrey," moaned Randy. "Enough."

"What?" Audrey asked innocently. "We're all friends here."

"You have a beautiful home, Billy," Molly said to change the subject.

"Yeah," he chuckled. "Having an asshole absentee daddy with major guilt issues sure pays off in the end."

"Oh stop," Audrey said as she playfully slapped him. "Your father's a doll."

Before Billy could say otherwise, two young women bearing significant face metal and cleavage, one with purple hair, the other green, approached them. "Billy! Are we playing or what?"

"In a sec," he told them, then turned back to Molly and Janine. "Strip nine-ball in the billiards room—a host's duties are never done. So, beer in the kegs; spirits at the bar; munchies, weed, and coke, well, pretty much everywhere. If you smoke cigarettes, keep that outside on the deck, would you? Enjoy."

And that's the kind of party it was.

MOLLY AND JANINE had been at the gala little less than an hour, drinking in silence at one of the little ice cream tables, a silence which Janine eventually broke only to point out that it was Molly's turn to go get the next round. It would be Janine's fourth.

Janine's excessive consumption over the past month concerned Molly, but she knew better than to mention it. Instead, she decided to match her this night so it would be her fourth too. Maybe the booze combined with the festive atmosphere would loosen Janine up enough to truly talk things out, or laugh with her, like Josh had said.

"Two vodka-and-crans, please," she told the bartender as she filled two small hors d'oeuvre plates with smoked shrimp blinis, seared duck crostini, and a generous helping of lobster jalapeño poutine. The drinks were poured in due time, and Molly returned to the table to find an attractive red-haired girl in her seat, rolling a joint. Janine and the girl were smiling and laughing, and Molly was glad to see Janine happy again, for a minute.

"What's going on?" Molly asked good-naturedly as she put down the plates and glasses.

"Oh, is this your seat?" the redhead asked politely as she began to rise.

"No, it's okay," Janine told the girl. "She doesn't own it." The redhead sat back down, and Janine turned to Molly. "Excuse us. We're talking."

It took Molly a moment to fully grasp what Janine was actually telling her, and then said only, "Seriously?"

Janine replied with an icy glare. Molly raised her open palms to her shoulders in surrender, spun on her heels, and walked off. She found an open stool by the bar, far enough to seem like she wasn't watching them, but close enough to watch them.

She kept her hurt inside as it was obvious what Janine was doing, obvious what the cold stare meant—"If you can, I can"—which was ridiculous! She had always taught her four children, and her eight grandchildren too, that two wrongs don't make a right. If Janine took this young woman to bed out of spite or revenge, there would be no coming back from it, no matter how drunk she was. Two wrongs don't make a right!

"Are you okay?" she heard a male voice ask.

She turned to see Billy and a tall, buff young man. "Of course," she answered.

"I disagree," Billy warmly replied. "More than anyone I've ever seen, you look like someone in desperate need of company," he added as he sat on the stool to her right.

Molly was about to politely decline his offer when she noticed Janine putting the lit joint into her mouth, flame-part first, and sensuously blow the smoke into the redhead's mouth, their lips barely a millimeter from touching.

Molly turned to Billy. "Busted. Yes, I'd love some company right about now."

"Cool," Billy answered. "This is my friend Bruce. Bruce, Molly."

"Hello, Bruce."

"Nice to meet you, Molly," Bruce said as he took the stool to her left.

Molly could peripherally see Janine glaring at her and replied with the same icy look she'd received only minutes earlier—I can play this game too, Bluto! She turned back to Billy with a smile. "So, what gave me away, honey?"

Janine flipped her the finger, took the redhead by the hand and led her out to the deck.

Molly had no intention of taking up with either young man and made that very clear to them from the outset, yet still, she had to admit she was enjoying the attention. The boys of the quintet were her bros, God bless 'em, to Francisco she'd always been like a project, and it had been a long time since she'd allowed a man to fawn over her. It was fun; harmless, innocent fun. So she let them ply her with drink and weed as they laughed their way through silly, flirty games of twenty questions and never-have-I-ever.

But her assessment of the situation could not have been more wrong, for what she didn't know was that Billy had slipped a roofie into her drink when he first sat down. What Billy and Bruce didn't know was that it wouldn't affect her one iota.

And the fun rolled on.

"Never have I ever . . . " Billy mulled with a naughty grin, little more than an hour after their games began, " . . . been with two guys at once."

Molly chuckled at the outrageous boldness, and then decided to do the kid one better. "You mean only two at once, or does more than two count?"

Billy practically did a spit take. "For real?"

She looked back at him with a coquettish "you'll never know" smile when a sudden wave of nausea struck her with a jolt. Her stomach churned and her body lurched forward. She instantly knew the cause for she had experienced such a thing only four other times in her life, a lifetime ago.

She slammed her hand to her mouth to keep the throw-up down but knew it only a temporary measure. She bolted up from her seat and scoured the space for a bathroom. She spotted one, but the line was five deep.

"Come," said Billy as he rushed her to a small bedroom and the bathroom within, knowing her ailment to be a common reaction to a roofie-booze-and-weed mix. She barely made it to the toilet when chunks of the fancy food flew from her mouth, its force so explosive that dollops of puke and toilet water splashed back at her.

Billy knelt beside her and held her hair behind her. "Shh, you'll be okay. You just overdid it a little." When the hurling finally subsided, Bruce handed her a wet washcloth to cleanse her face.

Her breathing was heavy. The room was out of focus and dark, despite the bright phosphorescent lights. There was a bad taste in her mouth, and she smacked her lips. Bruce held out a Dixie cup of water and Listerine. "Here, swish this around."

Her hand quivered as she reached for the cup. She swished as instructed, and then spit. "Thank you," she said weakly. "I think it's passed. I'm okay." She started to get up but was still a bit shaky. Billy grabbed onto her arm to help. "Thanks again," she said. "I think I just need to lie down for a minute."

"That's probably a good idea," Billy agreed as he led her out of the bathroom and helped her onto the bed. Bruce closed the bedroom door. Billy removed her heels. It felt nice.

Still a little dizzy, she looked around to find something on which to focus to help regain her steadiness. It was a small room, she observed—a bed, dresser, closet with sliding mirrored door—a maid's room, a servant's room. Billy sat down beside her and began to unbutton her blouse.

"What are you doing?" she asked.

"Nothing," he said as he began to fondle her breasts over her bra. "You're hallucinating. You drank and smoked too much. I'm not even here."

I'm not even here. The words had a familiar ring to it, an eerily terrifying familiar ring. "Stop that," she said as she swatted his hand away like an annoying fly.

"Shhh," he soothingly replied as he pinned down her arms, as Bruce reached up her skirt and proceeded to pull down her panties. "You beautiful little slut," Billy smiled as if a compliment and began to kiss her tits.

You've got to be kidding me, she thought; and then she snapped.

She dug her skull deep into the pillow and then thrust it forward hard and fast to bash her forehead into Billy's nose. The boy screamed and spurted blood as he flew back. She kicked up her knees and drove them into Bruce's jaw. He tipped to the side and down to the floor howling. She sprung off the bed and landed with her knees crashing into his chest. And then she punched, and punched, and punched.

"Nazi!" she screamed. "Kidnapper! Torturer! Villain!"

She could sense Billy sneak up on her from behind, and she let him. The instant she felt his hand on her shoulder, she grabbed it, pivoted, and flipped him over her back, sending him soaring through the air and into the mirrored closet door. He hit the floor hard as shattered glass rained down upon him.

Despite the closed bedroom door and the blaring music, those closest to the room heard the crash and raced inside, Josh among them. By this point, Molly was standing with her foot pressed into Bruce's throat, blood spewing from his mouth as he gagged to death; one hand squeezing Billy's neck as she held him pinned to the wall, elbowing him in the head with her free arm, one swing after another.

"Fiend! Torturer! Nazi!"

Josh, like everyone else, had a pretty good guess as to what must've provoked the event. With his kickass friend seeming anything but at risk, and possessing no fighting skills of his own with which to lend a hand, he opted to do the next best thing. He pulled out his phone and began to record.

Janine was still out on the deck when the crowd by the doorway caught her eye. She moved into the house to satisfy her curiosity, and then realized that the screams she heard were Molly's. She shoved her way into the bedroom and was horrified at what she saw. Molly was about to kill these boys!

"Nazi! Torturer! Villain! Kidnapper! Nazi!"

"Molly! Stop!" Janine shouted, but Molly was too far gone to hear it. The bodybuilder barreled through the crowd to peel her away from the boys, yet the moment Molly felt another hand upon her, she clasped onto it and pivoted again, ready to maim yet another tormentor. "Moll! It's me, Janine! Princess, it's me!"

The fact that it was a woman's and not a man's voice gave Molly just enough pause to turn to look at Janine, and the distress in her lover's eyes was enough to whisk her mind back to the present. She let go of Billy who dropped to the ground sobbing, took her foot off Bruce's throat, and let her own body go limp.

"I'm sorry!" she trembled as she buried her head on Janine's shoulder, as the reality of what she did sunk in. "I don't know what happened to me!"

"Shh, shh, it's okay," hushed Janine.

"No, it's not!" Molly sobbed on her shoulder. "I don't know what happened!"

In the ten months they'd been together, Janine had never seen Molly so scared, so vulnerable, so lost; had never until that moment felt that Molly actually needed her—and it was in that moment that all was forgiven, truly and forever. "It's all right, princess," she said as she held her lover tight. "Your Bluto is here, and she ain't going nowhere ever again. Your Janine is here."

THE PARTY THINNED out shortly thereafter as only those involved awaited police and ambulance. Randy, Josh, Zeke, and Audrey offered to stay with Molly, but she said that as long as Janine was by her side, she'd be okay. They said they'd check in on her the next day.

Molly couldn't tell which frightened her more—her total belief that she was in 1965 and that Billy and Bruce were her ancient tormentors, or that she absolutely would've ended their lives had

Janine not stepped in; that she could be capable of such a thing. She wasn't. She couldn't be, couldn't be.

Pull it together, Molly, she told herself. No time for tears. Cry later. What now?

"Listen," Janine softly began as they sat on the designer couch in the now deserted living room, "it was self-defense, no question, but you crossed a line, princess, a big line, and you could face charges too. They could call it attempted murder. Assault for sure. You'll get off in the end, I think, but you need a lawyer. A good one. I know you don't have the scratch for it, so if Ramirez—sleazeball that he is —will take you on pro bono, I'll be okay with it. I'll make myself okay with it. All right?"

Molly let the suggested scenario play out in her mind and knew she couldn't let it come to that. "I'll be back." She got up and headed to the maid's room.

"No! Princess, you can't talk to them. As your acting attorney, sort of, no!"

"I took the same crim class you did, Bluto."

"I got an A, you got a B."

"I'll just be a sec," Molly smiled and went into the room. Janine followed.

The boys were lying on the bed, bleeding, swollen, bones cracked and fractured. The purple and green haired young ladies from before fawned over Billy, two other freaks over Bruce.

"So, here's the thing," Molly began. "You fellas can press charges against l'il ole me for almost beating you to death—how embarrassing for a dude—and I'll charge you with rape. Your daddies are rich and famous so this'll be big, our faces plastered all over the place. I don't want that—I'm shy—and I know you don't want it because it'll destroy your lives forever. So, how's this instead? Leave me out of it. Tell the cops you did this to each other—figure out why amongst yourselves—but if I don't press charges, and you don't press charges, there are no charges. Whaddya say?"

With their lips too swollen, their teeth too shattered, and their vocal cords too ruptured to speak, they nodded their consent.

"Lovely!" smiled Molly. "A pleasure doing business with you

creeps. I wish you a slow and painful recovery." She turned to Janine and said, "Let's go."

Josh, back home in his Westwood studio apartment, didn't know any of this, of course. All he knew was that some rich fucks tried to violate one of his favorite people in the world, and they got pummeled for the effort. He was so proud of her. She was a goddamn hero! A cautionary tale to assholes everywhere, and it was a tale that had to be told. With the best of intentions in his heart, he posted his recording to his Twitter feed so the world would know how amazingly awesome his sister was. The accompanying text read simply: "They tried to rape her. Watch out, dicks! You could be next."

The clip went viral in a flash, seen by thousands before the sun even rose and by millions more before it set again, including a frustrated mid-level sleuth at an elite private detective agency hired a year before by a consortium of tobacco barons to locate a certain unsterblich girl.

CHAPTER THIRTY-THREE

The Dwelling
Six Days Since Her Midnight Chit With Sandy

The first rays of sunlight had just begun to poke above the horizon as Leaf marched onto the clearing, spear in one hand, wooden shield in the other, sling and cutter nestled between crotch-cover and hips, with streaks of war-mud drawn on his face. He came to a stop, officiously pounded the blunt of his spear to the ground, looked up to the pale moon, and screeched like a monkey.

One by one, Thunder's supporters left their homes—all dressed for combat as Leaf was. The oldest of them had seen twenty-five calendars, the youngest barely eight, for Thunder had promised the children early manhood status if they could slay on his behalf. One by one, they arrived at their pre-designated spots round pre-designated cabins, pounded down their spears, and waited in disciplined stillness.

The wives of the Community began to flow from out their cabins to start on the break-fast, paused at the ominous sight, and then worriedly raced back inside.

With all the men, manlings, and boys in place, Leaf screeched again. Thunder emerged from his cabin, dressed for combat as well. He made his way to the clearing in front of Leaf and pounded down his spear. His soldiers grunted and pointed the tips of their shields toward him in solidarity, then back to the front door of their assigned foe.

The warriors who supported Clearsky, having been awoken and informed of the recent development by their wives, stepped out their cabins, also combat ready. Each found himself facing two young men or manlings, backed up by two or more youngers who kept their distance with rocks poised to sling. Despite the dismal odds, the seasoned warriors remained steadfast with shields up and weapons pointed. They showed no fear for they felt none, while many of Thunder's had to gulp down their jitters.

A handful of men came out their cabins baring neither cutter nor sling and placed their spears on the ground to signify neutrality. They had no love for Thunder, yet had, over the calendars, come to perceive Clearsky as weak and unwise. They'd combat for neither and leave the outcome to the gods. The young soldiers assigned to their cabins turned and sped off to their next pre-assigned position.

Horizon stepped onto his porch holding a megaphone of clay. He knew exactly what to do for he had seen many such attempts in his long reign—some successful, some not. One thing he knew for certain was that whether Thunder won or lost, he will never be anointed as Sorry. The Holy One wouldn't allow for it.

"Women!" he announced. "Fetch your youngers and fetch your-selves to my cabin! My purity will stand as shield against ancillary harm, and the gods will protect all those within my walls. Come! Now!"

The women grabbed their children by the hand, picked up their babies, and scurried toward the old man's house, the older children scurrying behind them.

"Moma, what's happening?" 3 asked as Mellow ran with him in her arms.

"A usurp is to begin," she answered. "Your pupa attempts to be the Sorry."

"Yippee! I hope he gets it."

"Shhh," she cautioned. "We'll be awaiting among some who hope otherwise so we mustn't speak our hearts aloud."

"Then my lips are stitched together, Moma."

Sunburst stood resolute by his cabin, shield up and spear pointed, surrounded by youngers he once considered good. Among them was Son-of-Stone, his daughter's hopeful, but he'd be giving the boy no special privilege for it.

"Awaken, Daughter-of-Love!" he shouted, keeping his eyes fixed on his adversaries "Get you to the Holy One's cabin! Up! Up! Now!"

A few moments later, the nine-calendar-old girl stepped sleepily onto the porch. "Pupa? What goes on?"

"Get you to the Holy One's cabin!" he shouted. "Go now! Run!"

Her eyes fell upon her hopeful, and she was mortified. "Son-of-Stone? You take arms against my pupa? How could you?!"

"Go!" hopeful and pupa shouted in unison. "Now! Run!"

The little girl's eyes welled up, but she did as she was told.

With the women and noncombatant children secured inside, Horizon and Sandy positioned dutifully on the porch, all was still for longer than anyone's comfort. The silence deafened. Even the birds and crickets seemed reverent of the moment.

At last, with great pomp and purposeful dramatic effect, the Sorry stomped out. He sized up the situation peripherally only, as if this feeble attempt at usurp a petty annoyance at most. Yet he could see the numbers and he knew that twas bad.

He had felt this day coming, had been preparing for it for calendars. He had done all he could to keep his supporters behind him, had even attempted to secure additional alliances among the newer, younger men. He had no idea how ghastly he had failed; no idea that Thunder would stoop to enlisting children. Smart. Vile yet smart, albeit unlikely the gods would reward such sin. Then again, one never knows.

"So you find the courage to face your ending, young Thunder," he demeaned as he majestically made his way to the clearing. "You were a self-indulgent brat as a child, and now a sinful usurper who brings children into the mix." He stopped three paces before him and stomped down his spear. "So, how wish you to proceed? How wish you to die this fine morn?"

"I take no qualms with the olden who call you chum, old man," Thunder replied, "as long as they accept my position once you live no longer. Contrarily, if the gods should happen to smile upon your wrinkled buttocks, my supporters will turn back to you once more. I propose clean combat, you and I alone, no weapons nor props, to the death and square and fair, and to the victor goes the Sorry's cabin."

"Uggggh!!!" Thunder's supporters boisterously grunted their agreement.

"Accepted," Clearsky declared, showing no sign that it was actually his preference. "You and I alone, to the death and square and fair. And my support, as well, will be yours should you find victory . . . which you won't."

"Uggggh!!!" Clearsky's supporters grunted their agreement.

Leaf bowed his head in deference and backed away. Thunder and Clearsky dropped their shields and spears to the ground. They removed their cutters and slings from their hips and dropped those as well.

"A challenge for the Sorry's cabin has been challenged!" the Sorry proclaimed, "And the challenge accepted with relish'n'mustard!"

"Victor or loser," the Holy One megaphoned from his porch, "may the gods render pity upon you both for we are all, us all, the gods' mistake! Begin!"

The upstart and the champion circled each other with hatred dripping from their eyes and bloodlust sweating out their pores. Thunder leaned forward as he moved, his arms dangling in front of him like a bear. Despite the fact that he was younger, taller, and of greater reach, gone was the cockiness he had displayed against Skinny Horse those calendars ago for he knew the pupa to be a foe of worth.

Inside the Holy One's cabin, some women prayed while others wept, yet none spoke their desires with words. Dour offered comfort to those whose husbands stood by Clearsky, while Kindness did the same for those whose kin fought for Thunder. Few had the stomach to stand by the window to watch. Mellow was among those who did, her baby in her arms, Daughter-of-Love by her side.

Mellow's emotions clashed and tore at her insides. She loathed Thunder with all the loathing she could muster, and she had no strong feelings for Clearsky one way or the other. The fact that he didn't like her didn't make her not like him—course, it didn't endear him to her either. Yet she desperately needed Thunder to be victor, for if Clearsky should win, her baby would be slain by simple virtue of being his father's son, his lack of sight not even an issue.

So she watched and silently rooted for the man she despised when something caught her eye, and she felt a sudden, awful pang in her gut. While Thunder stalked as a bear, Clearsky positioned himself as a tiger, then as a snake, then a crane—he was practiced in martial arts! How could that be? she asked herself. Why wouldn't he have shared his skills with the others? For moments just such as these, she answered herself.

Thunder saw an opening and charged, but Mellow could see it was a ploy, a trap! Clearsky hopped a mere step to his side and thrust a ferocious sidekick to Thunder's midriff, the speed of the charge making the kick twice as powerful as it would have been on its own. Thunder bent forward clutching his belly but remained standing. Clearsky took the opportunity to thrust a straight kick to his head.

Wrong move, Mellow mused. His face is down, you dunce. Don't make your kick from the only place he can see it. You had him and you messed it. Praise the gods.

As predicted, Thunder caught hold of the leg and pushed Clearsky back hard. The Sorry hit the ground, sprung right back up, and the circling began once more.

A blue belt at best, she deduced, and clearly self-taught. She could take Clearsky with ease, she knew. The question was, could Thunder?

This time it was Clearsky who charged—a jumping swivel kick to Thunder's face, and it landed hard! Thunder went down but managed to grab hold of Clearsky's ankle as he fell, taking the Sorry down with him. Despite the blood gushing from his mouth and a few loose teeth, he bit madly into Clearsky's calf. Clearsky screamed and tried to yank it away only to have Thunder spin them over so he was on top. He pressed his knees into his Sorry's shoulders to keep him put. Clearsky struggled to free himself but Thunder's mass was too great. The upstart delivered a powerful fist to the nose, another to the jaw. Clearsky lurched up his legs, wrapped them around Thunder's neck, and leveraged them both to their sides, keeping Thunder trapped in his scissors, squeezing and choking. Thunder thrashed and writhed but couldn't escape the hold. His breath was running out, his consciousness waning.

The Sorry lifted his legs up to raise Thunder's head, then bashed it down to the dirt. And again, and again. Blood trickled from Thunder's temple. "You fool!" panted Clearsky. "Did you really think the gods would choose you over me?!"

And with all seeming lost, Clearsky suddenly jerked upright, the point of a spear jutting through his shoulder!

"Now!" shouted Leaf, the thrower of said spear.

All at once, boys hidden behind bushes slung rocks at Clearsky's head and torso. All at once, Thunder's soldiers by the cabins stabbed at their unwitting opponents. All at once, teen-men and manlings converged upon Clearsky, slashing their cutters into his flesh. The Sorry flailed to fight them off, even landed a few good punches, until Leaf snuck up behind him, slit his throat, and the Sorry was no more.

And all at once, Mellow breathed a sigh of relief. Course Thunder would insist on winning by a cheat. She kissed 3's forehead and held him tight.

For his part, Sunburst had responded quickly and valiantly to the deceit. His shield went up the moment he saw Leaf's spear enter Clearsky's shoulder, fending off rock and spear alike. Liar! Trickster! were his thoughts as he used spear as sword to jab death into two of his assailants, only to have four more emerge. He didn't know for whom he fought, only that a chiseler such as Thunder should never lead. A rock flew into his jaw and drew blood as he slayed the third manling. A spear stabbed into his side as he slayed the fourth and fifth. Only Son-of-Stone remained fighting before him, while the little ones continued to sling rocks from a distance.

"I don't know what to want!" Daughter-of-Love wept to Mellow, turning back to the combat, then away again. "My pupa and hopeful combat to the death! I love them both! I love them both hard! What should I want? I don't know what to want!"

"Shhh," was the best Mellow could think to say to comfort the girl. "Shhh."

"What if they both slay each other? I'll have no one! No one!"

"You'll have me," Mellow said as she put an arm around the girl. "Always."

In one fluid motion, Sunburst let go his shield, tossed his spear to his left hand, dropped to his knees, seized his sling, grabbed a handful of rocks and slung them at the boys in the distance, fending off Son-of-Stone with spear-in-bad-hand all the while. One by one, the sniper-children went down, Son-of-Thunder-2 included. Sunburst had no idea if they'd been slain or harmed, and had no time to wonder, for as he dispensed with the last of them, his eyes averted for but a moment, he felt the blistering heat of Son-of-Stone's spear searing in and out of his thigh. Without pause, he thrust his elbow up to the younger's jaw, sending him crashing to the ground.

Wounded and exhausted, Sunburst hobbled toward him. Son-of-Stone lay on his back as he pointed up his spear, but even injured, Sunburst was too skilled for the boy. With little difficulty, the greater warrior used his spear to knock the weapon from out his enemy's hands, and then moved its tip upon his chest.

Son-of-Stone exhaled in defeat and laid his open palms by his ears to accept his fate with grace. "You combat like a god, pupa-of-my-hopeful. If slain I must be, honor to be slain by the likes of you. Tell Daughter-of-Love I died well."

"Pupa! No!" Daughter-of-Love screamed. "Please, Pupa! Don't! Don't!"

No one ever knew if Sunburst heard his daughter's pleas over the chaos of battle, or if he felt her heart in his own, or whether he simply couldn't bring himself to slay a defenseless child for the sole crime of being seduced by a wicked charismatic. He flipped his spear backward and smashed the blunt at the boy's head, rendering him unconscious; then he dropped to the ground, placed spear at feet in surrender, and allowed himself to suffer the anguish of his many wounds.

And the combat raged on.

Not all of Clearsky's supporters had been as fortunate as Sunburst. Many perished the moment Leaf shouted "Now!"—never aware they'd been bushwhacked. Others battled without conviction as the one for whom they fought had already been slain, and so they perished as result; some dropped their spears in surrender for that very reason; and no one but Mellow saw that it was Thunder himself, revived and back on his feet, who threw the spear that ripped through the Holy One's chest, the slay that compelled Sandy to his knees, weeping in shame.

When the last of Clearsky's support at last capitulated, and the only sounds left to hear were the yelps and sobs of the agony of the wounded, a ferocious shriek rose above it all. "No!!!!!"

Dour stood on the Holy One's porch holding Kindness in front of her with a cutter pressed to her throat. "You will not be the Sorry, Thunder! Another man, yes, for Clearsky is no more, but not you! The men of the Community will choose in accordance with the gods. Drop your spear to submit, or watch your wife die!"

"Dour, no!" wept a terrified Kindness. "Please, First Moma, don't! Moma, please!"

Oh fuckety-fuck! thought Mellow. Do something! Save her! Think!

"Please, Moma, don't! Please!"

"Dour, my chum," Thunder said calmly, smiling his most amiable smile while simultaneously raising his spear to throw at her. "You're upset. I get. This day of days must be a sad for you. Tis for many. But Kindness is First Moma now. You more than any know the punishment for bringing damage to a First Moma."

It occurred to Mellow that although she could never display her fighting prowess against a man, defeating a woman would bring no suspicion as long as she dumbed down her skills. If Thunder could hold Dour's attention just a little longer, she could stealth behind the widow and take her out before Kindness came to harm.

"Hold him," she told Daughter-of-Love as she put 3 in her arms.

"To where you go?" asked the little girl.

"Shh. You'll see. Stay here."

Outside, the conversation continued. "Kindness will not be First Moma, Thunder," Dour went on. "For you will never be the Sorry!"

"Look around, ole chum," Thunder charmed as Kindness wept and howled. "I already am. The gods have willed it."

"The gods have willed you nothing for you won on a hoodwink." Blood began to trickle from Kindness' neck and her sobs grew ever louder. "Now submit and drop your spear, or your wife will perish this very moment, along with your unborn son."

Mellow was close enough to make her move when she saw Thunder sigh and lower his weapon. He was going to acquiesce!

"You have me at disadvantage, ole chum," he said softly, then leaned low to his side and whipped his spear in a submarine release with perfect upward trajectory that sliced through Kindness' belly and into Dour's heart, slaying all three.

Mellow's mouth fell open in shock, and she dropped to the floor.

"Tis done," said Thunder. "Tis won."

"Uggggh!!!" his warriors shouted victoriously as they stomped the blunt of their spears to the ground. "Gods pity the Sorry! Hail to our Thunder! Yip, yip, yippee! Hail Thunder!!!"

CHAPTER THIRTY-FOUR

Santa Monica, California
October 2018
The Morning After The Party

It felt nice waking up next to Janine again. Even though the girls had shared their bed, they hadn't actually "slept together" because the prior evening had taken too much out of them. Still, it felt nice waking up next to her.

Janine blinked open her eyes to see Molly's smiling face. "Hey."

"Hey back," said Molly. "How ya feeling?"

"Little hungover. Not too bad."

"I'll get you some aspirin."

"No, I'll get it. You stay in bed. I want to make us a special brunch today."

"Let's make it together."

"Remember that morning after I found out about you and Ramirez, and you whipped up that lavish breakfast because you stupidly thought it would make up for your unforgiveable behavior?"

"Yes."

"My turn." She kissed Molly's forehead and started out.

Molly sighed contentedly when the nausea blasted inside her once more. The pregnancy! With everything else that had happened, she almost forgot. The moment Janine was gone, she raced to the john and let 'er rip! It was as bad as ever.

Only once it eased up did she realize that she had to let go of all that came before and focus only on what's next. She had to tell Francisco, of course. He was the father. He had a right to know. She had to tell Janine; her partner had a right to know too. Would she stick around to help raise the child alongside her, or will she hate it as a constant reminder of the infidelity? Will Francisco want to be involved?

Do I even want to have a baby right now?

The question shocked her the moment she thought it. In four other pregnancies, the notion of getting an a-word would never have even occurred to her.

But that was Millie, she reminded herself. She was Molly now, a different woman in a different world. There was no logical reason for her to abandon the career she sought in order to raise another child. Perhaps she'd want to someday, but twenty-three was too young, and ninety-five too old. Yet despite her decades-long contempt for the God she loathed, the word "sin" kept rattling in her brain.

And then she was struck with a new terrible thought. What if the baby was like her? Jeez Louise, what if it was unsterblich too?! None of her children to date had been so cursed, but their father was a normal. Do two immortal parents beget another? If so, would an a-word even take?

She decided not to say anything to anyone until she decided what she'd do.

She splashed some water on her face, brushed her teeth, threw on her robe, and headed into the kitchen. Janine was at the table, hovering over her laptop.

"Holy crap, Moll," she chuckled, "you've got to take a look at this."

Molly turned to the screen to see herself beating the life out of Billy and Bruce with skills that would put Jet Li to shame. The clicks and shares were off the charts, and positive comments abounded. "Go Molly!" "UCLA rules!" "Molly Parker is my hero!"

"Oh, for goodness sake," she moaned.

"You're famous, princess," Janine gushed.

Molly sat down, closed her eyes, and dolefully shook her head. "I don't want to be famous," she sighed. "I never wanted to be famous. Gosh darn it."

* * *

EVEN AFTER DR. MUELLER'S project shut down, Francisco Ramirez, Esq., then Julio Garcia, janitor, remained worried for Millie. He knew that only a handful of people were aware of the experiments—a couple of congressmen and their aids, a few bureaucrats, the nurses, orderlies, and federal agents. He felt it safe to assume the political folk would stay silent about their part in the morally reprehensible program, the agents and orderlies were oblivious to the science they served, and the nurses had nothing to gain by going after Millie. The only wildcard was young Dr. Szabo, so Julio felt it prudent to keep a watchful eye on the lad.

At first, it was a simple matter of old school espionage, posing as Woody's friendly neighborhood mailman, his cleaning lady's boyfriend, his shoeshine boy, even once reprising his role as a janitor at the Academy of Tobacco Studies. With the advent of the internet, it all became easier, albeit way less fun. The last time he checked in on the bilogogist was shortly after Al died. Even before beginning the task, he expected it to be little more than a symbolic, anal precaution. He was right.

When he saw Josh's video clip on his Facebook feed that Sunday morning, his first impulse was to wonder how Molly could have been so reckless to allow this to happen. Hadn't he taught her anything? His second impulse was to check in on Szabo. He didn't expect to find anything, considering it yet another symbolic, anal precaution, but better safe than sorry. He booted up his teraflop, saw that his last check-in ended on December 2, 2016, so he dug in and started on the 3rd.

It was boring and tedious for Szabo reveled in a life of predictable monotony. It wasn't until Francisco's second day of searching that he spotted something unusual. April 2017, the day after the death of Millie Lang, a series of phone calls from a New York number, multiple times a day that continued for more than a week, all unanswered. He tracked the number to an insurance investigator named Peter Mailor who worked for the same company that covered the Lang estate, and who just happened to have been the investigator assigned to the fire. Mailor's credit card statements showed that he booked a round-trip flight from La Guardia to Richmond, Virginia, where Szabo lived, and the unanswered calls ended abruptly.

Francisco phoned in sick to work and slept very little for the next three days.

Shortly after Mailor's return to New York, Szabo made a series of calls to retired chairmen-founders of the major tobacco conglomerates, all old, dying men. His credit card statements showed that he took numerous trips to Winston-Salem throughout that summer. By early autumn, phone conversations between Szabo and the tobacco barons abounded, as well as conversations between Szabo and Mailor. In October, Szabo founded a nonprofit which he dubbed "Project Heracles," receiving multi-million-dollar donations from each of the barons to erect a state-of-the-art biotech laboratory just outside of Richmond. Separately, the barons contracted a clandestine private detective agency comprised mainly of ex-CIA and mercenaries. As the year went on, the frequency of the calls slowed, but the donations continued, construction of the lab continued, and the monthly payments to the detective agency continued.

That was until four days ago, the day Josh's video posted, when there was a sudden flurry of calls amongst the parties. The agency's travel log showed a plane chartered from Richmond to LA, due to arrive any minute now. The manifest showed two names Francisco didn't recognize, with a return flight booked for later that night, the third name added to the manifest being that of Molly Parker.

Francisco knew it had always been Mueller's and Szabo's hypothesis that a transfusion of unsterblich blood could render the recipient with the same magical properties, which would explain how Szabo was able to convince the dying billionaires to get behind him; and it wasn't much of a leap to assume that the insurance investigator found something incriminating about Molly in the ashes of Millie's home and then brought it to Szabo who decided to resurrect the project. But how would Mailor have comprehended the importance of whatever it was he found? How could he have known about Szabo's connection to it? Question, question, question.

The answers didn't matter though. The bad guys were coming for her, there was no doubt about that. Molly was in danger, and it was his job to protect her.

* * *

IT NEVER OCCURRED to Molly that anyone would be coming after her for any unsterblich reason. She and Al had let go of that particular fret years ago, and Francisco had confirmed that all who'd been involved in Christoph's project were by now dead or too old to care —but that wasn't why she stopped going to her classes.

She was embarrassed. She sat alone in bed and watched the video clip over and over as she chastised herself for her complete loss of control. She read the comments and tweets and posts and reposts touting her as a hero, a champion of women everywhere, the new symbol of the movement, and that just made it worse. She read the backlash too, the negative, misogynistic ones that dubbed her an ugly, man-hating dyke who should hook up with a real man to get the beatings she deserved, but those didn't help either.

Got to stop making mistakes, Molly.

She knew that if she couldn't tolerate the praise the World Wide Web was showering upon her, the inevitable face-to-face accolades she'd receive on campus would be too much to bear. Best to wait a week or two and let the craziness die out, for the next big thing to consume the cyberworld's imagination. In the meantime, Janine will keep her up to speed as to what she'd miss at school.

Janine. Boy-oh-boy, had she been impressive! For one, the 2-L's handling of the media was like that of a seasoned pro. She told the cackling throngs that swarmed the front of their apartment building that Molly was resting, which was true, and promised that she'd grant interviews by the end of the week, which wasn't. She told them that all inquiries must be directed to her only, and that anyone who disobeyed her rules would get nothing. The busybodies promptly dispersed.

She was even able to convince Molly to forgive Josh, at whom Molly was furious. The bodybuilder's contention was that Josh meant well, that most people would be happy for such acclaim, and if the clip prevented only one asshole from being an asshole, saved only one girl, that in itself would make it all worth it.

It was a solid argument, Molly had to admit. My lady's going to be a heck of a lawyer someday.

Her phone rang. Francisco again. Fifth time in the past half hour. She declined it, as she had the others. She opened her voicemail and deleted his message without listening to it, erased his new text without reading it. She knew what he had to say, and she didn't need to hear it—she could berate herself just fine on her own, thank you very much; and she certainly didn't need to explain to Janine, who'd been sneaking peaks at her call list, why she spoke to him after promising she wouldn't.

What am I going to do about the baby?

She turned her attention back to her laptop to make herself more miserable when the doorbell rang.

She got up from the bed and went to look through the peephole —two middle-aged men in brown suits, one tall and buff, the other taller and buffer. "All press requests are supposed to go through my spokesperson," she told them through the door. "She made it very clear that anyone who bothers—"

"We're not the press, Miss Parker," said the buffer one, and they held up badges. "Detectives Rogers and Martinson, LAPD. We'd like to speak with you."

"I already told the police that I won't be pressing charges."

"Yes, but we're investigating a related— May we come in?"

Something didn't feel right, but she couldn't put her finger on it. On the other hand, the last thing she needed on top of everything else was trouble with the police. "Sure," she said, and opened the door.

The men entered. "The boys who assaulted you are facing charges in another matter, Miss Parker," said Detective Martinson. "We were hoping you'd be willing to testify on the woman's behalf."

"Or at least answer questions to assist us with background," added Rogers.

They're lying about something. "Um . . . can I see your badges again?"

The men removed their badges and showed them to her. Molly studied them carefully, only to realize that she had no idea what an LAPD badge was supposed to look like. Even a bad fake could dupe her. "Um, okay. What are your questions?"

"We were hoping you'd come down to the station with us."

"Um . . . no. Let's do it here. Can I offer you fellas some coffee?"

"It would be much better if we did this down at the station."

"Yeah, but, um, I don't want to."

"Trust me, Molly, it'll be best this way. Come on, let's go."

"Am I under arrest for something? If so, show me the warrant."

"Molly, you're making this much more difficult than it needs to be," said Martinson as he amicably put his hand on her shoulder. She swept it off with a rudimentary circular block.

These aren't cops, she realized. "I changed my mind. I'm not talking to you." But if not cops, who are they? You know exactly who they are, Molly, don't be dense. "Please leave my home," she told them.

"Molly, you're going to come with us," said Rogers. "One way or the other."

"Gentlemen, gentlemen, please," said Francisco as he breezed cheerfully into the unit. "Is there a problem?"

"Who are you?" asked Martinson.

"I'm Miss Parker's attorney," he smiled as he gave them each his card. "Professor Francisco Ramirez, Esquire, at your service. And you are?"

"Detectives Rogers and Martinson, LAPD."

"Charmed, I'm sure." He turned to Molly. "Are you okay?"

"What are you doing here?"

"I thought you might need some help."

"I got it covered."

"Guess I wasted a trip then. Detectives, may I see some badges?"

Martinson looked to Rogers. Rogers considered something for a moment, then replied to his partner with a subtle nod. Martinson nodded back, then turned to Francisco. "Of course, Mr. Ramirez," he said as he reached into his jacket.

"*Professor* Ramirez," Francisco corrected.

"Professor Ramirez. But honestly, Professor, we only want to ask her a few questions regarding another case."

"Fair enough. Direct the questions to me, and I'll decide which—"

Even with his attention squared on Martinson, had Francisco gotten more than five hours sleep in the past three days he would have noticed Rogers removing his Beretta from its holster; but he hadn't so he didn't. BANG! The unsterblich collapsed to the floor with a thud, blood and brain bits pouring from his open skull.

Molly was too shocked to scream.

Rogers turned his pistol toward Molly's chest. "No more games." He turned to Martinson. "Cuff her."

Pull yourself together, Molly! Pull it together! Now! Now!!!!!

"I know why you're taking me," she seethed as Martinson made his way behind her. "But do you? Your boss is going to be pretty darn miffed if you kill me."

"Yeah, they mentioned something about that," the buff-but-less-buff-one replied as he re-aimed his gun at her thigh, as the other punched her hard in the eye just because he could.

"Gee, you boys think of everything," she said.

She put up no resistance as Martinson yanked her left arm behind her and clanked the metal bracelet over her wrist, whereupon she shot her right elbow straight up to his jaw, grabbed hold of his head with both hands, dropped to her knees, and flipped him over in front of her. Rogers reacted only a split second too late, firing his pistol and nailing his partner in the belly. Martinson screamed as the blood gushed from his stomach. Molly popped back to her feet, leapt over the howling Martinson and delivered a dastardly roundhouse kick to Rogers's wrist, knocking the gun out of his hand with the CRACK of a bone—moved in, two open hand chops to the sides of his head, and the man was down, and out cold.

BANG! A bullet ripped into her shoulder, and she too was down.

She could see Martinson lying on the floor, whimpering in a pool of red, his smoking pistol pointed at her in his shaking hand. She rolled over fast, grabbed Rogers' gun, and pointed it back at Martinson as she lay on her back. She waited and watched for all of a few seconds as the hemorrhaging man's strength waned, and his arm dropped to the ground. She crawled toward him, easily removed the pistol from his hand and said, "What I'm about to do won't kill you, but what your partner did to you might—that's on you boys, not on me. Got it? On you, not me. I'm only hurting you." Then she bashed the barrel of the gun to his head to knock him out.

She tucked both guns into the back of her jeans and crawled frantically to her unconscious mentor. "Francisco, Francisco," she said as she tapped his face. "Wake up. Wake up, Francisco. Talk to me." She checked his pulse, and there was nothing. "Wait, no. You're not dead. You can't be. We don't die. You and me, we don't die." She put her ear to his chest, no beat. Her cheek to his mouth, no breath. "Stop it! You can't be dead! I need you!" she shouted. "I can't do this by myself! I told you that!" She shook him, as if trying to wake him from a drunken sleep. "You're the father of our baby, Francisco! I'm going to have it! I'm going to have your baby! I want to raise it with you! You're not dead, Francisco, you can't be! Unsterblichs don't die! Stop it!" She kissed him, kissed him hard, as if a kiss could bring him home, as if fairy tales were true. She put her ear to his chest again, nothing. "You promised we were forever! 'Be with Janine this lifetime,' you said, 'but you and me are forever!' That's what you said! You said forever! WAKE UP!!!"

She heard sirens approaching in the distance. Someone must've heard the gunshots and called the police. Of course they did! She had to go, and fast. This would be impossible to explain if the cops were legit, and it was a toss-up whether they were or not. Treasury was in on it the first time.

279

She took Francisco's hand in hers. Kissed it. "Thank you so much, my darling."

She crawled back to Rogers, scoured through his pockets to find the handcuff key, and removed the bracelet from her wrist. She got up and wrapped a dish towel around her shoulder—she'd remove the bullet later but for now she couldn't afford to leave a trail of blood.

She grabbed her purse and moved to the balcony to make her escape when her eye caught the framed 5 by 7 of her and Janine on the little table, her birthday present, two hot chicks in bikinis in love. Her first impulse was to take it so she couldn't be identified, but then remembered that her image was plastered all over the internet anyway. She put two fingers to her lips and touched them to her lover's face.

She looked at her own image in the picture and sighed. "Goodbye, Molly Parker. I liked being you." She paused. "God damn it."

She moved onto the balcony, leapt over the rail down to the grassy lawn two stories below to land in a perfect drop'n'roll, and ran angrily into her next lifetime.

CHAPTER THIRTY-FIVE

MUCH OF THE AFTERNOON had been consumed with the burning of the fallen and many of their sons—the little brothers of those who combatted for Thunder being spared of their pupas' sins. The stench of the corpses still lingered in the air.

"Oh, great gods," hailed the new Holy One in the center of the Gathering, the new Sorry kneeling before him, "here is Thunder, whom you have chosen for us to follow!" It was the sixteenth day of the moonth of gluttony in the calendar of the god of air.

Mellow sat awkwardly in Dour's old spot, 3 on her lap, Daughter-of-Kindness behind her. The men remained dressed for combat and would remain so for three days hence, as was their way. Nine of Thunder's best soldiers stood in strategic locations round the circles in case of retribution. That too was their way, although no one expected such. For even to Thunder's most ardent detractors, it no longer mattered that they didn't like him. The gods had made their choice, affirmed by the Holy One's blessing. Twas clearly the gods' plan all along—and any man who'd sacrifice his wife and unborn son in service to the holy plan must surely be a man of great piety. Even Sunburst was reconsidering his prior assessment of his new Sorry's character.

"Grant him the wisdom to sorry us wisely!" Sandy continued. "Grant him pity when he fails, for he is but man, vile and worthless, the gods' mistake as we are all. Ugggh!"

"Uggggh!" repeated the throng.

"Rise, my Sorry," Sandy continued. "Rise to take your place in our lore."

Thunder did as told. Sandy kissed him on the cheek, then the forehead, then the other cheek, a perfect triangle. "May your reign be long and peaceful."

"Much gratitude, my Holy One."

Sandy backed away to sit at the Holy One's spot. Thunder, who according to custom was supposed to return to his spot as well, didn't. Instead, he remained standing in the center of the circle, one by one making eye contact with all, establishing a style of leadership different from his predecessor right from the start.

"Twas a day of great courage and even greater misfortune," he began. "I myself lost a wife, two sons, and a child unborn. I feel you grieve with me, my chums, and I pray you feel my grieving with you back. But this day was destined to be, as the gods had foretold it to Horizon so many calendars ago, as Horizon had foretold it to me when I was but a boy.

"Clearsky had grown weak and unwise. We all saw it. Even those who loved him saw it. His time had ended, by the gods' will. And in accordance with their will, we must set aside any animosity that may still linger within our hearts, and come together once more as a Community united, strong, and rich.

"Many of our youngers have become men on this day of days, so the morrow's Gathering will have many namings, and many betrothals. The morrow aft the morrow will bring us many weddings. Yet before we can relish'n'mustard in the joy to come, there remains a matter that must be attended.

"The slayer of Horizon must pay for his crime! Holy Ones are of the gods, beyond and above any threat of spear or stone! Beyond politic! Stand to make yourself known, criminal!"

Everyone looked around, but no one said a word.

Smart, thought Mellow. Must've been Leaf's idea.

"Sinner!" Thunder went on. "Coward! Stand now to be bagged and drowned!" Nothing. "Then may your afterlife be one of pain and suffering."

He paused for dramatic effect to signify a complete change of tone and topic. "Son-of-Thunder-3," he said warmly, "come now to your pupa."

Mellow kept her smile inside. Her plan had played out to almost perfection, the death of her beloved sister an unexpected tragic of unnecessary cruelty, but she had learned long ago that one must endure the bad with the boon. Her baby had been saved.

She helped the toddler off her lap and pointed him in Thunder's direction. "Just walk straight," she whispered in his ear.

"Come, my son," aided Thunder. "Come to your pupa. Just follow my voice. I'm right here."

Wait, thought Mellow. Why's he saying it like that?

"Here I am, Pupa," 3 said upon arrival.

"Boon. Now kneel to your knees before me."

"Much gratitude, my Sorry," Sandy began as he stood to begin the next sacred ritual. "For the gods indeed have instructed me to nominate—"

"Hold on," Thunder interrupted, and then turned to the Community at large. "It has come to my attention that my cherished son, my beloved son, my only living son, lives without sight.

"But," began Sandy. "Wait, what?"

No! Mellow shouted in her head. Impossible! He wouldn't!

"The child will never hunt," Thunder continued with a sadness, "never combat, and shall live as a burden to us all. With such a heartbreak in my chest, I, his pupa, am obliged still to obey the laws given us. For even a Sorry cannot put himself above the gods' laws." He moved behind the boy and removed his cutter from his hip.

"No!" Mellow screamed as she sprang from her spot and charged.

But before even two strides were taken, she fell to the ground with a blistering pain in her thigh from the spear that had been hurled into it. She looked up to see three young men surrounding her, each with weapon pointed at her and ready to throw, each steps beyond her reach.

"Harm her no further," Thunder gently commanded. "She is First Moma now. May her insolence this night be forgiven as the melancholy of a grieving parent." He put his cutter to the boy's neck, and said, "Die well, my son." Then he slit his throat.

He turned to Mellow with a barely detectable smile that only she could see. "Don't you ever dare to bully me again," it said.

She glowered back with an expression that he couldn't understand because he had never before seen it on a woman's face.

"You will die tonight, in your sleep, by my hands," it said.

THE HONKYTONK WAS SURPRISINGLY peppy given all the funerals that day. Thunder was at his charming best, lavishing gratitude upon those who supported him, flattery on those who opposed, accepting the compliments he received with just the right amount of feign modesty. Mellow could tell he'd be the sweet Thunder in bed tonight, if things got that far, which they wouldn't.

"Gratitude for being dutiful tonight, Mellow," he said as he took her in his arms for the ceremonial slow dance of Sorry and First Moma. "I know you have anger at me, but I had to do what I did. You can see that now, can't you?"

"Tis a hard, my husband, I admit, yet I'll effort. I'm proud to be First Moma of my Community, and I want to be a good one for my Sorry."

"You will be," he smiled. "I know it, my beauty."

"You flatter me, Thunder, but tonight you seem to flatter all."

"Much politicking required after a successful usurp. To truth, I should probably return to it."

"Course. Let me take your cup to fill."

"Gratitude, but perhaps I should slow it. I need to keep my wits with me."

"Oh no. You seem not hoochy at all, and you deserve to be joyous on this night of nights. Have one more, if only to let your humble wife render you with glad."

"Tis a fine," he smiled at her. "One more, but none after." He kissed her gently, she took his cup, and off she went.

His decision to taper off was a set back, Mellow thought as she limped to their cabin, but nothing that a blast of crushed valerian root couldn't take care of. She ground the proper dosage into his cup of hooch, decided it best not to take chances, and then doubled it. In not too long, Thunder was slurring his speech. Shortly after, his balance grew shoddy. Mellow assumed the protective First Moma role as she had seen Dour so often do, announced that their Sorry had honkytonked enough for one evening, and ordered two warriors to help get him to their cabin and into his bed. They did as she commanded. She watched them return to the celebration through her window then grabbed a cutter from the kitchen drawer and went to their bedchamber to slay the son of a bitch.

She clutched the cutter in both hands as she raised it high to the sky to plunge down hard into his heart when a voice popped into her head.

"Don't do it!" shouted the voice. It was Ool.

What's he doing here?

"Give me one fuckety-fuck reason why not?!" she yelled back in her head.

"Because dying in his sleep is too good for him."

"What does that even mean? No. I must slay him now. He slayed 3, he slayed Kindness. He does not deserve to live. No! No one will discover my deed till the morrow, and by then I'll be long gone from this dreadful place."

"And to go where? Another community? They'll be just as bad, you know that. To be on your own again? Alone for all eternity? Mad and suicidal forever?"

"Stop it! I have to do this! He has to pay!"

"Think! Honey, think. Today was the best day of his life. He won his war. Was blessed as the Sorry. Adored by friend and foe alike. For him to die now, his final thoughts and feelings will be those of joy and bliss." Her hands began to tremble. "No, he must agonize physically, torture emotionally. And when, and only when, the unenduring pain of it all brings his eyes to public weeping, then he must die."

"I like that," she admitted. "How?"

"We don't know yet, but tis our purpose now. Yes, we will be their First Moma, play the dutiful wife and take our husband's thrashings, all the while seeking to fulfill this lifetime's mission." He paused to let it sink in, then, "Put the cutter down, baby."

She nodded, placed her weapon on the bedside table, dropped to her knees, put her face right up to Thunder's, and whispered aloud. "I will see you disgraced before your Community, husband, peeled of all dignity, watch you cry like a little baby girl, and then laugh and laugh as you die so very slowly by my hands. And this I promise on the souls of my hundreds of children, and theirs, and theirs, and on and on."

Only three times in her many, many lifetimes had she made a vow on the souls of her progeny, and she'd kept every single one.

PART 3

FUGITIVE AND
FIRST MOMA

CHAPTER THIRTY-SIX

Santa Monica, California
October 2018
Moments After Jumping Off The Balcony

I T WAS TOO RISKY to try to get the Mustang from the underground garage so she sprinted ten blocks away from her building with no particular destination in mind, then slowed to a less conspicuous brisk walk as she hatched her next move.

No one seemed to be chasing her at the moment. Most likely the bad guys' higher-ups had yet to learn what went down, but they will soon. On the assumption they'd try to track her via her bank and credit card transactions—it's what she would do if she were them—she tapped her phone for an Uber to take her to LAX. During the ride, she scanned her mobile for flights. There was a multiple leg headed to Hamilton, Ontario with a change of planes in Chicago scheduled to start boarding in forty-five minutes. Perfect.

She charged the purchase to her MasterCard and downloaded her boarding pass as the car pulled up to the United curbside. She tapped the driver five stars and a healthy tip then darted in. She hid her Saturday night special in the ladies' restroom, tossed Rogers' and

Martinson's pistols in a trash bin, crossed through security, withdrew five hundred bucks from the ATM, converted an additional thousand to Canadian dollars via her credit card, then returned to the ladies' room for her gun. She cracked apart her cell phone, threw the pieces into four separate bins, then exited back to the curb where she hailed a taxi to take her to her storage facility in Van Nuys. She paid the cabbie in cash.

She didn't know precisely who was after her but she hoped they were smart. Much easier to trick smart people. Dumb people can get lucky.

She pulled down the storage unit door, looked around and sighed—all that lovely tech she'd have to leave behind for she had to travel fast and light. How long had it taken her and Al to put the system together? It was her last tactile memento of him, the only thing she still possessed that he had actually ever touched, and it was hard for her to let go.

Get over it, girl! Move!

She pulled off her top, dragged an oversized first aid kit out from under one of the tables, grabbed a thick piece of rope from within and placed it between her teeth. She used a scalpel to slice into her shoulder to expand the area the bullet had entered, and then used her fingers to worm around inside the wound as she searched blindly for the slug, biting hard on the rope all the while, her eyes filling with tears from the pain. At last, she stumbled upon the bullet, yanked it out, then dropped to the floor, panting to catch her breath.

Rest, she told herself. Just for a moment.

No, she told herself. No time. They might know about this place.

She put the rope back in her mouth and bit hard once more, stitched closed the opening in her arm with surgical thread, then taped a large swath of gauze over it, grimacing and panting all the while.

Rest, she told herself. Just for a moment.

No, she told herself. Stop asking.

She stood, got a pair of scissors and the proper L'Oréal products out of a file cabinet drawer, and watched herself in the mirror on the wall as she sheared away Molly's luscious, golden locks to above her ears, then dyed it a naturalistic red, taking proper note of the time.

She applied green and yellow concealer over the black eye Detective Martinson had bestowed upon her, piled a healthy dose of foundation over that, then checked her work. She could still see a remnant of the shiner but only because she was looking for it. No one would notice at a quick glance.

She used a brown eye pencil to dot freckles onto her face and arms, green lipstick on her lips.

She opened another drawer to retrieve her new outfit; kicked off her sneakers and pulled off her jeans. She put on a pair of leopard skin pants, a tight pink t-shirt so sheer you could almost see through to the nipples, a Mickey Mouse wristwatch, humungous, orange-tinted sunglasses, and scuffed old Hush Puppies on her feet—an ensemble Molly Parker wouldn't be caught dead in.

She grabbed hold of a large, stained backpack and looked inside to make sure the fifty thousand dollars in cash was still buried under the bundle of clothes at the top, and that the tacky leopard skin purse (to match her pants) still contained the proper IDs. She sighed again. She and Al had spent years mapping out every single detail of Molly Parker's life—this new chick had a driver's license, birth certificate, social security card, a fabricated Montana address, and a never used Visa. That's it. Five things. No school records, no employment records, no bank account or email address or relatives or anything. She barely existed. Then again, Molly never really expected to need her.

Poor excuse, girl. You should've worked harder, better, smarter. Next time.

She took her gun, can of mace, and the recent five-hundred-dollar withdrawal out of Molly's purse and packed them into the leopard skin, the one-thousand Canadian into the bottom of the backpack, then unplugged her electric drill from its charger and proceeded to annihilate her hard drives.

"It's okay, Al," she said sadly as she put a hand to her heart, "you're still in here."

She checked the time. Thirty-two minutes since the dye. Forty would've been better but good enough. She grabbed a jug of Evian, held her head over a bucket to wash away the excess chemicals, then strapped on the backpack, slung her new purse over her shoulder, locked up her unit for the very last time, and tossed the bucket into a nearby dumpster.

It took her less than fifteen minutes to walk to the Sherman Oaks Galleria and into its underground parking lot, less than five to find a vehicle whose owner had left his parking stub in the cupholder, less than one to unlock the door with a hairpin, and even less than that to hot-wire the blue Corolla's engine to a gentle purr and drive off.

By the time she hit the freeway it was almost four and the rush hour traffic was making her crazy. She had wanted to be out of LA long before, but she took solace in the fact that if she can't move forward neither can any of her pursuers. Besides, with any luck, they were all busy waiting for her flight to land in O'Hare right about now. Despite her fears, the image of it made her chuckle.

By the time she hit Palm Desert, the sun had already set. She pulled off the freeway and drove aimlessly through the town until she found a Best Buy. She went inside, grabbed a local newspaper, and picked out last year's model cell phone, registering it to new-girl's name and address, requesting a 406 Montana area code. She did her best to conceal her jitters while she waited to see if the system would accept her never-used credit card. It didn't.

"Oh, that's strange," she said. "It went through just fine earlier today."

"Yeah, the system's been a little wonky lately," said the clerk. "Let me try again."

"Oh, that's all right, I'll just give you another card," she told him as she peered into the leopard-skin. "Oh drats, it's in my other purse. I'll come back."

"Oh, there it goes," smiled the clerk. "Went through. You're all set."

Good, she thought. Now the girl has a phone number. That's six things.

She headed back into her car, opened the paper to the classified section, then hunted for secondhand motorhomes for sale. The

THE GIRL WHO WOULDN'T DIE

Corolla would likely have been reported stolen by now so time to get rid of it, and she knew better than to check into a hotel anytime soon.

She found an ad for a 1999 Georgie Boy Landau priced at just under thirty thousand dollars. She had no idea what a Georgie Boy Landau was, but she liked the lack of flashiness that comes with a nineteen-year-old vehicle, and the price seemed comparable to the other ads. She phoned the owner to see if he was home, and he was. She asked if she could come see it now, and he said she could.

She drove just a little way until she found a sleepy, little side street with no parking restriction signs. She pulled over, got a screwdriver out of her purse, removed the license plates from the Corolla's front and rear and shoved them into her backpack to be disposed of at some future location far away. She strapped the backpack to her back, purse over her shoulder, walked the couple of blocks back to the main drag, then hailed a taxi to take her across town for the RV.

Edna Eldar was a sweet old lady, short and frail and on a walker. She answered the door with a warm smile, invited the girl in and offered her a glass of iced tea, apologizing for the wait to come because her husband was "stuck on the crapper." But it wasn't the wait nor the old lady's course language that concerned our hero, but that the local news was playing on the TV in the living room and the story it reported was all about her!

She pretended not to hear it as it heralded " . . . law student who captured the cyber world's imagination Sunday for standing her ground against an alleged sexual assault is now the primary suspect in the murder of her professor." She pretended not to care as it described how Francisco's body had been found bleeding from the head on her living room floor and rushed to Cedar Sinai Hospital in Beverly Hills where he was pronounced dead on arrival. She pretended not to notice as the screen popped up a snapshot of her frenzied, viscous face—a frame lifted from Josh's viral video; and she pretended to ignore the overdub that described Molly Parker as "armed and dangerous," warning that anyone who sees her should contact the authorities and not try to apprehend her themselves.

There was no mention of Rogers or Martinson, she noted. These bad guys are good.

Joe Eldar came into the room and greeted her warmly as his wife returned from the kitchen with the iced tea and cookies. Neither showed any sign of recognizing her—either they hadn't been paying attention to the newscast or her hurried disguise was working. Or they were terrific actors who would call the police the moment she was gone. Hard to tell.

Joe led her outside and showed off the camper with the kind of sad pride a father might display while sending his daughter off to college. He, a former grocery store manager, and his wife, a construction company bookkeeper, had retired in the early 2000s, cashed out their 401Ks, and bought the motorhome almost new. They spent the next sixteen years roaming the country like the hippie teenagers they had always wished to be, then settled in Palm Desert a few months ago after Edna's health began to wane. The camper was their baby, he boasted, always maintained and properly serviced, always kept clean, and its registration renewed on time only two weeks prior. The girl took it for a short test drive and that was all she needed.

"I promise to take good care of 'er, sir," she assured the man.

The paperwork was signed, the cash exchanged for keys and pink, and the couple wished her well. She jumped into the driver's seat with a cautiously optimistic sigh of relief, waved good-bye, and drove off once more.

SHE NOTICED the tank was less than a quarter full as she approached the highway on-ramp. She pulled into the nearby service station to fill up, as well as to amass sacks of junk food and groceries. No one seemed to recognize her, although a couple of teenage boys seemed rather fixated on her chest.

On she drove as she scarfed down a greasy hot dog and Cheetos that she washed down with an orange soda. Amidst all the adrenaline of the day, she hadn't realized how hungry she'd been. She hadn't eaten since breakfast, and very little at that because she'd been so consumed with how her fellow students would respond to Josh's video.

This morning. The good ole days.

* * *

IT WAS past midnight by the time she rolled into Arizona. She pulled onto the shoulder and got out, poured some of her Aquafina into the sand, then smeared the mud onto her California license plates, not so much for it to appear that she was trying to conceal something but just enough to conceal it. She considered staying parked there for the night to get some sleep, but Arizona is only one state over. By now her little Chicago trick would have played itself out, and they could probably guess she'd drive to Arizona.

Arizona is so obvious, she groaned as she got back into the RV and drove on. What am I even doing here? Stupid, stupid.

* * *

THE SUN WAS STARTING to rise as she cruised through New Mexico. She pulled over, went into her bathroom, and threw up.

The nausea hadn't lasted this many days during the other pregnancies, she recalled, or is that just faulty memory? Hard to tell. She hadn't given birth for over sixty years.

She got back into the driver's seat and again considered staying parked on the shoulder to get some sleep, but decided that if they could guess Arizona, New Mexico was obviously next.

Why are you driving in a straight line? Idiot!

One more state, and then I'll rest. Veer north.

* * *

SHE BREEZED through northern Texas without even realizing it, simply struggling to stay awake. She didn't know where she was nor where she was going other than "far away," turning willy-nilly from one stretch of highway to the next. By the time she crossed into Oklahoma it was night again. Her eyes were heavy, so heavy and drooping, the outside dark, so dark and quiet, and she had no idea that her new motorhome was drifting idly off road. Only the bumpy gravel of the shoulder under her tires snapped her back to consciousness whereupon she slammed on the brakes inches before crashing into a tree.

This is crazy, she told herself. You can't risk an accident. Can't wind up in a hospital.

She turned her head back to look into her camper's cabin to see her cozy new bed beckoning to her, so soft, so warm, so inviting, and then she noticed a pair of headlights approaching from the distance. She slumped low in her seat, grabbed her pistol from her purse, and cradled it under her thigh. The vehicle whizzed past without incident.

You can't stop, she told herself. It's not safe.

You can't keep driving, she told herself. It's too dangerous.

Just rest your eyes for a couple of minutes. That's all you need. You're an unsterblich for goodness sake, a minute or two should be all you need. Yes, just for a minute or so.

The next thing she knew there was a tapping on her window. She awoke quickly to find a deputy sheriff on the other side of the glass thumping his flashlight. Through her rearview mirror, she saw the flashing lights of his squad car. She looked to the clock. It was almost two in the morning. She'd been asleep for five hours!

Got to stop making mistakes, Myla.

CHAPTER THIRTY-SEVEN

The Dwelling
3 Calendars Into Thunder's Reign

"At the start of it, the gods conjured up everything," Sandy the Holy One began. It was the first day of the moonth of pride in the calendar of the god of stars, and time for the telling of the first of the Great Punishments. Of all the Gatherings through the four seasons, this night was considered one of the two most sacred.

"The light of the day and the blackness of night did they conjure," he continued on that warm vernal eve, his sixteen-calendar-old apprendix Raven seated at his back and hanging on his every word. "The lands and the waters and the mountains and the strands; the birds and the fishes and the mammals, the reptiles and amphibians and invertebrates, all of them, and they placed them in a garden of paradise and color, and it was perfect."

It was the sixth time Mellow was hearing the hallowed story—yet another spin on a tale so old she could barely remember in which lifetime she'd heard it first, nor the particulars of how it had then been told. She looked round the fires to see the women of her Community so enraptured by the fable they'd been preached since cradlehood and she wondered if they were faking their awe as she was.

She sat behind Thunder in the traditional First Moma spot. Her eye was swollen and blue, her body bruised from her last thrashing, the Community's disdain for clothes and makeup forcing her to display her humiliation plain for all to see. No one ever talked about it, course, for it was a sin to gossip of that which transpires within another man's cabin.

Beside her sat her sister-wife Playful. Playful's daughter from Clearsky sat behind them along with Daughter-of-Kindness—Playful's many sons from Clearsky having been slain the after-lunch of the Holy Usurp along with the other traitors. Her toddling girl and baby daughter, both from Thunder, slept soundly on her lap. Mellow herself was in her second moonth with-child, her previous attempt having been beaten to misk because Thunder wanted the first son of his reign to be of Playful, his true love. Aft his new bride gave him girl then girl, he decided to let the First Moma take another stamp at birthing him a boy and let her belly be.

"And so impressed with themselves were the gods," Sandy went on, "that they decided to conjure one more conjurement, one that would be even more perfect than perfect, one to reflect their own transplendent nature back to them. But what they didn't realize was that in their vanity they had forgone the purity of their essence, and it was that vain nature they now strove to replicate. And so they conjured man, and they named him Odd'm because he had one stick; and from his foreskin they conjured woman, and they named her Even because she had two boobies."

"And so birthed from the vanity of the gods, Odd'm and Even put themselves above all the other critters as if they too were gods. Some critters they enslaved to do their toils, some they honored to attain their worship, and some they slayed just for kicks.

"And the gods saw their mistake, and they were saddened, and they sought remedy.

"And the god of waters offered to erase umanity from existence by flood, and the god of air said it would erase them by tornado, and the god of fire by fire, each god to the task in its own way. But the god of pity said, 'Tis not fitting for us to punish Odd'm and Even for they are only as we conjured them to be. Tis our mistake not theirs.'

"And the god of scorn said, 'Umanity is vain and believes itself to be great as we, and no good can come of that. Let us amend our only error and be done.' But the god of pity wouldn't hear of it, and a bargain was reached.

"Unto Odd'm and Even went the gods of pity and scorn to expound upon them the sinfulness of umanity's ways; and Odd'm and Even were affrighted by the god of scorn, and ashame-ed before the god of pity.

"And Odd'm and Even pleaded for their existence, and cried, 'We do not believe ourselves to be as gods! Nor do we wish to be for tis too difficult and no good can come of it! Give us but one chance more to prove our humility, oh great and graceful gods!'

"And the god of pity took pity upon them, and the god of scorn felt none, and told Odd'm and Even of the holy test. And it said unto them, 'We will let you prove that you wish not to be as us, that you wish to live in harmony-with like the other perfect critters we have conjured. In the garden we have forged two magnificent trees of which you may not eat, for to eat of the fruit of the first you will come to possess thought; and to eat of the fruit of the second you will gain wisdom everlasting to wield said thought till time is a thing no more; and to eat of both you will come to be as us, and that we will not abide. But if you truly wish to live as our other perfect critters, no temptation for you shall there be.'

"And Even asked, 'What is 'thought,' oh lords?'

"And the god of pity answered, 'Tis a wondrous blessing with which one can conjure grand things of astonishment and miracle.'

"And the god of scorn answered, 'Tis a terrible curse with which one can destroy all one seeks to destroy, and much that they don't.'

"And Odd'm and Even promised they would never eat of the fruit of the magnificent trees for they wished never to possess the power of the gods.

"And all was good, until it wasn't."

Mellow never imagined it would be as difficult to disgrace someone to death as it turned out to be. She'd made several efforts

299

over the three calendars, but Leaf was always by Thunder's side to talk the humiliation away before she could get any traction. She had considered poisoning Thunder's supper but there was no shame in a man dying from rotted nourishment, and worse, Thunder would never know it was she who'd been behind it, which was the whole point. She'd considered publicly chastising him at one of the Gatherings, revealing his most intimate secrets that only a wife could know, fabricating others such as he often failed to stiffie when stiffing was required or that he wept out for his Moma in his sleep. She'd leave him no choice but to give her public thrashing, only this time she'd combat back so all would see the great warrior pulverized and slain by a girl. How embarrassing for him! But with further reflection she realized that upon seeing her combatting skills the Community would simply deem her a demon so there'd be no real shame on Thunder, and she'd only be bagged and drowned in the lake for her troubles.

Should've slayed him in his sleep when you had the chance, Mellow. You got greedy.

Even slaying him in his sleep was no longer an option for Playful slept always at nights by his side. Her sister-wife would awaken with screamings from the blood and carnage to muck-up her getaway, which would also lead to her being bagged and drowned.

Just keep thinking, Mellow, she told herself. You'll come up with something.

"And it came to pass," the Holy One continued, "that the curiosity Even possessed from the start grew more than she could bear. What could it be this thing called 'thought'? she wondered while she sat under the shade of the branches of the magnificent tree. How could it be so glorious as the god of pity described yet so dastardly as proclaimed by the god of scorn, and both at the same time?

"What must it be like to be as the gods? she wondered. Clearly it would be too great a burden to feel all their might, but just a taste of such insight would surely satisfy the craving, just a teensy nibble of the fruit. Who would know?

"And Even looked about the garden to make certain not another critter was in sight, and she scampered up the trunk of the tree of thought until she came to the lowest hanging fruit. And she pulled herself up and sat upon its branch and picked the fruit off the branch and bit into it, and she smiled. For she knew thought, and she thought it was good.

"She took another bite of the fruit and she closed her eyes and she saw how to bury seeds in the earth to cause her favorite foods to sprout up from the ground like magic. She took another bite and saw a world brimming with her children, so many of them and all grown-up, and she knew how to build for them glorious homes of brick and steel and glass. Another bite and she knew how to craft exalted machines that rolled on grounds and floated on waters and flied in airs; another and she knew how to forge mighty projectiles to rain fire and gas and death upon any who sought to harm her precious children. All sorts of technology did she come to see, and she smiled for she thought that thought was good.

"And she knew that she must share her new gift, for thought was too delicious a magic to keep to oneself and it would be too lonesome to possess such a gift alone.

"And Even brought unto Odd'm the remaining portion of the fruit of the tree of thought, and Odd'm said they must not eat of it for they had made promise to the gods; and Even said the gods would never grow aware, and that thought was good, and he'd know this if he'd ever had one; but Odd'm wouldn't sway.

"And Even sat down beside him and pushed tears from out her eyes and said that Odd'm would join her on this adventure if he truly loved her, and Odd'm's heart grew soft.

"And she made her voice tender and said words of warmth and kindness, and she rubbed his neck and his chest and his stick, and his stick grew hard.

"And she pursed her lips and she eased them toward his and she told him that she loved him; and he pursed his lips and he eased them toward hers and he told her that he loved her too; and she turned her head away so that all he could kiss was her cheek.

"And she said unto him, 'Prove your love for me, Odd'm. Eat of the fruit of the tree of thought and I will prove my love back to you tenfold with methods you can yet imagine.'

"And Odd'm yearned for her love, and so he ate of the fruit, and he came to know thought, and he closed his eyes and he smiled for he saw all the visions Even had envisioned, and he thought that thought was good. And abundant with thought and lust did Odd'm and Even express their love for one another with methods that could never produce offspring.

And the gods were saddened, and they argued of what to do, and a bargain was reached.

And Odd'm and Even cummed each thrice before the blue sky darkened to black and the birds sang no more, and the gods of scorn and pity appeared before them.

"And the god of scorn shouted, 'You pathetic critters!'

"And the god of pity wept, 'You poor, pathetic critters. But umanity will not be erased on this day, I have seen to it, for you are our mistake not your own.'

"And the god of scorn shouted, 'But no longer shall you live in our perfect garden of paradise and color, for you, our mistake, will never be perfect like our other perfect critters who flourish in harmony-with.' And it turned to Even and said unto her, 'For your wickedness and deceit, the ecstasy of birthing which was given you at conjurement will henceforth instead be one of pain and anguish, yet you will hunger to feel its torment nonetheless; and for every moonth that you carry no child you will bleed from the cunt as a reminder of this day, and you will feel cramps of the belly and kookies of the brain.'

"And it turned to Odd'm and shouted, 'And you who knew right from wrong yet did wrong still, the weakness for coupling you have shown on this day will remain a weakness for you always as a reminder of your failing; and the wiles of Even and her daughters will hold dominion over you and your sons from this day forth; and never again will man cum more than once per conference, and then require time itself to regain his capacity.'

"And Even said, 'That's not as bad as what you gave me.'

"And Odd'm cried out, 'Punish her not, oh lords our gods, for I love Even with all my heart and loins, and even moreso since you gave her dominion over me. Punish me with the pain of birthing instead for I should have been stronger in my resolve to protect her from her curiosities. Tis my fault. I alone am your mistake.'

"And the god of pity was touched, and the god of scorn felt none for it saw only more weakness in Odd'm, and it said unto him, 'The gods cannot undo what we have done, but if you wish to take punishment for Even's wickedness, so be it. Henceforth, the burden of man and woman shall rest upon man alone. Tis now for man alone to risk demise against the great beasts for tis he alone who must bring the meats to his family; tis for man alone to risk demise in wars against his brothers for he alone must bring safety and status to his cabin; and tis for man alone to insure that umanity lives not as gods but as the other perfect critters we have conjured; and for every sin cast by woman, be it of ignorance or willful deviltry, the gods will lay their wrath on man, for tis upon man to teach woman well.'

"And the god of pity said unto the god of scorn, 'Tis not a fair bargain to give woman dominion over man and then make him responsible for her ways. Tis a task un-possible.'

"And the god of scorn saw that the god of pity held truth, and it said, 'We will give man greater size of body and greater vigor of strength and speed to subdue woman's power over him.' And it said unto Odd'm, 'Use your advantage wisely, first man, for woman will bring you to your end if you don't. Teach such to your sons, and theirs's to theirs's so that they can teach it theirs's to theirs's.

"Now gather your things, you both, and depart my perfect garden.'

"And the gods of scorn and pity did vanish, leaving only the silent blackened sky behind, and Odd'm was taller than before in height and muscle. And Even said unto Odd'm that she knew of hidden corners in the garden where they could live without the gods seeing, and Odd'm silenced her with his words for he was affrighted by the power she had been given over him and affrighted of the burden the gods had lain upon him to heed. And Even spoke again and Odd'm punched his knuckles to her nose and she bled from the face and she fell to the ground and she wept; and she came to see the wisdom of the gods' lesson and the role as lesser they decreed her to take for her wickedness; and she crawled to her husband and she kissed at his feet; and the blackness of the sky gave way to blueness and sun, and the birds sang their songs once more.

"And all was good, until it wasn't," closed the Holy One. "And so ends the telling of the first of the two Great Punishments."

Keep thinking, Mellow, she told herself. Just keep thinking.

"The Gathering is shut," said the Sorry.

CHAPTER THIRTY-EIGHT

---

3 Miles Outside Dukane, Oklahoma, Population 7200
October 2018
After The Deputy Tapped His Flashlight

MYLA TOOK A MOMENT to size up the lawman before lowering her window, which she knew she had to do. Tearing off would only bring suspicion where there might otherwise be none.

He was a paunchy fellow, mid-thirties maybe, average height, Dallas mustache, overly bushy eyebrows but otherwise ordinary-looking face. She knew it wouldn't be much of an ordeal to take him out quickly and quietly if it came to that, but the handgun by his side was strapped snugly in its holster so she was pretty sure he wasn't expecting trouble. She had no intention of giving him any.

"Hi," she greeted pleasantly.

"Are you all right?" he asked with a light, slow drawl she recognized as not Texan.

I thought I was in Texas. Where am I?

"Yes, I'm fine, thank you. What seems to be the problem, Deputy . . . " she paused to read the nametag on his shirt, "Deputy Wimpton."

"You don't look fine by the looks of it. Your nose's right up close to that tree and your ass's sticking way out onto the road. Oh, and it's 'Vinton' not 'Wimpton.' Typo on the tag. County won't spring to fix me a new one. It's all right."

"Yes, Deputy Vinton, of course. And you're correct, Deputy Vinton, I almost had an incident. I was so sleepy, but I jammed on the breaks just in the nick. I thought it best to get some rest before moving on, but I'll be on my way now, thanks."

"Oh no you won't," said the deputy, causing a momentary twinge in her gut, "not if you're all sleepy like that. There's a trailer park up ahead a mile or so off road. Easy to miss. I can lead you there, help you get checked in. Wait." His face went stern. "Have you been drinking?"

"Absolutely not, Deputy Vinton. I promise."

"Good. So you just follow me to the park. If you happen to lose me, hang a louie on the dirt road by the *Star Is Born* billboard."

"Got it."

"To be honest, it ain't always a *Star Is Born* billboard. Not too long ago it was a *Ant-Man and the Wasp* billboard. Who knows what it'll be next? Couple of years ago it was a Reese's Country Cookie billboard, not even a movie. Nothing lasts. It's all right."

"Got it. Lead the way."

"Want me to blast the siren and flash the spinny lights for you? It's pretty cool."

"No, that's not necessary, thank you."

"Your loss. It's all right. Follow me."

He turned to head back to his vehicle, and Myla smiled. The poor guy couldn't be more harmless—and getting off the highway wasn't such a bad idea.

She snuck her gun out from under her thigh and back into her purse, got out her phone to check where she was, and was somewhat thrown to learn that she was in Oklahoma.

How the heck did I wind up in Oklahoma?

No, this is good, she told herself. Oklahoma. So random. So not a place Millie or Molly would ever think to hide so there's no reason for anyone else to think of it either. Just lay low for a little while, a spell, till you get the lay of the land and figure out what to do next.

Oklahoma. No, this is good.

* * *

NAOMI HADN'T INTENDED on working a double shift that night, but business was too booming to pass up on all that cash. Even for a Friday it had been a particularly rich night, and that was saying something. Their Bucksies had just won the first game of the season for the first time after so many years of sucking and everyone wanted to celebrate—particularly the men who got to live vicariously through the high school studs they never were or would never be again. That's where she came in, and she was exhausted as a result.

The buxom platinum blonde lumbered into the park's main office, pulled a clean envelope from the stack, wrote her name on the front, deposited three months' rent inside—last, this, and next—licked it closed and placed it in the "in" slot of the letter tray holder. Best to get rid of all that cash on something useful before blowing it on something stupid.

The old man was asleep at his desk, which was not unusual. A close to empty bottle of Maker's Mark stood proudly on his workspace, the empty glass resting lazily on his pot belly above the whiskey stain on his undersized t-shirt, with Fox News playing at full volume on the TV on the bureau yet not phasing him an iota.

She considered waking him to get him into his proper bed in the back room. She'd done so on many an occasion, just to be nice, but all she ever got in return was an earful of bellyaching from the old codger. Why bother? Let him wrench his back. What do I care?

"Chester," she whispered against her better judgement as she gently nudged him. "Chester, wake up. Time to get into your bed."

"What the hell you doing, woman?!" he shouted. "Can't you see when a man's trying to get some shut eye? What the shit is wrong with you? Who is that anyway?"

She lifted his wired spectacles off his chest and placed them over

307

his eyes. "You got to get to bed, old man. This ain't no good for your back."

"Oh, hey Naomi," he said warmly now that he could see her, and then downshifted back into codger-gear. "What the hell you doing here at this hour?"

"Come on, you, let's go," she said, then helped him up from his seat and led him toward the back room. "Time for beddy-bye."

"Why can't you just mind your own beeswax for once in a goddamn while?"

"I know, I know."

The little bell above the screen door ting-a-ling'd and Deputy Dim entered with this redheaded, freckled girl in a trampy outfit—not like Dim to be out with a girl like that, or any girl for that matter—but it wasn't the girl's trampiness that caught Naomi's eye.

"Hey Chester," the deputy said pleasantly. "Got someone here for you to check in. Hey, Naomi."

"Hey back, Dim."

"Way past check-in time," said Chester. "Read the sign. 'No check-in after ten,' and I got to go get me some shut-eye. Don't I, Naomi? Don't I got to get me some shut-eye?"

"Cut her some slack, Chester, would you?" protested the deputy.

"Rules are rules, boy, and I can't go breaking them for every strange stranger who comes crawling down the pike. What would the owner say? It's my rectum on the line here, not yours."

"I can't let her back on the road. She's like an accident in waiting."

"Put her up in your place if it's so important to you."

"She shouldn't be driving at all is the point, and I can't let her RV be sticking out onto the road. Help me out a little here, Chester."

"Would if I could but I can't so I won't."

But Naomi was barely paying attention to their conversation for her focus had been drawn to the freckled girl upon arrival, specifically her makeup. Aptly done for the most part but way too thick over one eye, and with subtle traces of purple and black under all the excessive foundation; and then there was that big bandage peeking out from under her sleeve.

Wonder how many other bandages she got under those clothes that I don't see, she mulled, and how many bruises she didn't bother to bandage up at all.

Been there, done that, she sighed. Been there, done that, and way too many dones.

Fuckin' men. Fuckin' bastards.

Poor kid.

* * *

MYLA HAD NEVER GOTTEN around to figuring out who exactly Myla was, what kind of personality she should exhibit or what kind of person she aspired to be—at least Molly had had a fully fleshed out backstory before she jumped into her. Best to play her shy for now, she decided as the deputy led her into the trailer park's office, you can always bring her out of her shell later if that turns out the best way to go.

"Hey Chester," the deputy said pleasantly.

The place was a dump, she noted, small and cramped with cracks in the paneled walls, the surfaces cluttered with papers and knick-knacks, and reeking of whiskey.

"Got someone here for you to check in. Hey, Naomi."

"Hey back, Dim."

"Way past check-in time," began the chubby old man who stood with his arm around a thirtyish-year-old platinum-haired woman by an opening that led to a bedroom.

What's up with that? Myla wondered when the TV on the bureau grabbed her attention. It was her again, same crazed picture as before, right there on Fox News for all to see, the words "breaking news" embedded at the bottom of the screen even though it was clearly a rerun from earlier that day.

I went national? she moaned in her head. National? Seriously? Doggone it.

The broadcast turned to a series of shots chronicling the crema- tion of Professor Francisco Ramirez, Molly Parker's newest victim, and then it got juicy.

In the two days since she hit the road, the tale had blossomed into a titillating media wet dream. "Internet Rape Girl," as she'd been nicknamed, had been involved in a sordid lesbian love affair with a fellow student yet cheated on her with a male professor to improve her failing grades. The lover found out about the affair and demanded that Molly end it. The teacher's response to the breakup was to stalk his sweetheart, confront her, and then attack her in a blind jealous rage. Internet Rape Girl responded to the assault as she had to all her previous assaults, with deranged violence and mayhem, ultimately shooting the teacher in the head to murder him in cold blood.

The perky anchorwoman went on to say that Parker had last been seen in the Chicago area (Myla smiled a little at that) and anyone who spotted her should contact the authorities. Pundits then came on screen to debate whether Molly was a victim-hero-role-model or a demented sociopath and threat to society.

"Help me out a little here, Chester," protested the deputy.

She noticed that the woman, the one named Naomi, was checking her out. Had she caught Molly's image on the news and recognized who she was, or was it a gay thing? Hard to tell.

"Would if I could but I can't so I won't," said the old man.

"You're just being ornery, you senile coot," Naomi blurted suddenly as she proceeded to nudge the old man to his desk. "Now you get your decrepit, rumpled butt back in your seat and check my cousin into this dump, or I'll give you reason you wish you had."

"She's your cousin?"

"Second cousin. Been waiting round for her all day." She turned to Myla. "What the fuck, girl? I was worried sick. You couldn't call? Pick up a phone?"

Myla couldn't read what the woman was up to or why, but as long as she didn't recognize her from the news, all was good.

"I'm sorry, Naomi," she said. "I took a couple of wrong turns, and then I couldn't get a signal on my cell, and by then I was so tuckered out I just had to pull over to rest a spell."

"That's where I found her," boasted the deputy. "She coulda been hurt if not for me."

"Well thank you, Dim, I truly do appreciate it," said Naomi as she moved to Myla and warmly took her hands. "At least you're safe. So how ya been, cuz? How're your parents?"

"Good, good, everyone's good. Ma and Pa send their love."

"Sweet ole things. I should call them."

"They'd like that."

"Okay, okay, let's get this over with," Chester interrupted as he reached out his hand. "Credit card, proof of ID, let's go, let's go." Myla gave the man her plastics.

"Well as long as everything's taken care of," the lawman officiously announced, "Time for me to bid skedaddle."

"Thank you so much for your assistance, Deputy Vinton," Myla told him.

"Dim," corrected Naomi. "We all just call him Dim."

"Yeah, I picked up on that," Myla said quizzically, "but, 'Dim'? Really?"

"It's short for Demetrius," Dim explained. "Folks been calling me Dim since long as I can remember. It's all right."

"Then thank you for everything, Demetrius," Myla reiterated.

Dim's mouth gaped open and he looked down to his shoes, smiled a little smile and blushed a little blush, then looked back to Myla with an authoritative, "Ma'am," and left.

A bit weird, thought Myla, which Naomi read on her face.

"It's just how he is," she offered on Dim's behalf, "but he's a sweetie."

"He's a moron," Chester chimed, then turned to Myla. "All right, Myla Callahan, sign here, here, initial here."

Myla did as told, Chester assigned her a spot, Naomi volunteered to show her where it was, and the two ladies headed out to Myla's camper in the parking lot.

"61, right down that a'way," Naomi instructed. "You'll pass the big oak and it's the first empty after that. Can't miss it. We good?"

"Yes, very, thank you," Myla answered. "And thank you even more for standing up for me in there. It was very kind."

"What else was I going to do? Couldn't let ole Chester keep one of our own sleeping out on the highway."

Wait, thought Myla. One of our own? What does that mean? Did I read this wrong? "Um . . . you do know, I mean, I'm not really your cousin, right? Like, if you're actually expecting some long lost—"

Naomi chuckled. "Yes, I know you're not my cousin."

"Then, why? What's 'one of our own'?"

"Your right eye. Your left arm. I know what you're running from, Myla. Ran from it myself far too often and stayed in it even more often than that. If women like us ain't going to lend a hand to women like us, who the hell will?"

Oh my gosh, thought Myla. She thinks I've been abused, that I'm a battered woman on the run. Oh my gosh—she's been a battered woman. Oh, the poor woman.

"You want to come in for a drink or something?"

Naomi laughed again. "You got anything to offer me in there? I'm guessing not."

"Um, well, no, not really. You know, like, 7-11 stuff."

"Tell you what. I'll be grilling me up some breakfast come a.m. Just as easy to grill for two as it is for one. I'm five spots down that a'way. Say, eleven o'clock?"

"Thank you. That's very sweet . . . cuz."

Naomi smiled, clicked her tongue to the roof of her mouth as she winked a friendly wink, and then headed off.

Myla watched her go and smiled as well.

Oklahoma. No, this is good.

CHAPTER THIRTY-NINE

The Dwelling
The Morn Aft The Telling Of The
First Great Punishment

T HE SKY WAS GRAY and threatened rain, but aft so many calendars of drought the gloom above did little to perturb the women by the lake from fulfilling their chores. They had seen such teases far too often to let it instill enthusiasms anymore, and so they toiled. That said, it was anything but a joyless morn.

"And Even wondered, 'What must it be like to be as gods?'" Playful preachified in a perfectly exaggerated impression of their young spiritual leader as the women cackled guiltily. "Just a taste to satisfy the craving, ooh, the craaaving," she moaned in mock desire. "'Just a nibble, nibble, oooh,'" she gasped as she rubbed her vagina and a breast in parodied orgasm. "Ooh, just a nibble for the craving."

The women were beside themselves—they always were when Playful dove full tilt performance mode. Even Mellow couldn't help be amused by her sister-wife's little burlesque, despite the fact that the lampoon was a mock on her dear chum Sandy, and despite the fact that Mellow never cared much for Playful in the first place.

Notwithstanding her sister-wife's artistry for funny-ing, Mellow found her a cold woman, self-centered and phony, offering little affection to anyone except Thunder who she showered with adoration, which Mellow could tell was also an act. Thunder, course, had no idea of the charade for everyone showered him with adoration these days. He loved Playful more than she'd ever seen him love anyone, except himself, and he never laid a hand on her—which only made the thrashings he laid upon her all the more severe. Playful never lifted a finger to get him to thwart the practice, and Mellow never asked her to.

She was a cold woman, self-centered and phony.

But she was funny.

"'Punish her not for I love Even with all my heart and loins,'" Playful whined her whiny rendition of Sandy's Odd'm. "'Punish meeeee with the pain of birthing,'" she continued as she lied down on her back and spread her legs in pretend labor, lavishing the original man with flurries of womanly characteristics. "Oh! Oh! Oh! It hurts! It hu-u-u-urts!"

It occurred to Mellow that some of the effeminate traits Playful was garnering upon Odd'm were really just Sandy's natural mode of talk, which had always been a tad effeminate. Not that anyone would ever suspect the Holy One of having the predilections he had, but she saw no reason to make risk on behalf of a mere funny.

"That's quite enough, Playful," she told her sister-wife.

"The baby's coming out my stick, oh lords! It hurts, it hurts! Ooh, my aching wee-wee!"

"I said ENOUGH!!!"

The First Moma's exclamation crushed the women's laughter to silence and brought the performance to rapid conclusion. "Oh, come now, Mellow," Playful said as herself. "Be not such a twig-in-muddy-ground."

"You besmirch our Holy One, Playful," Mellow reprimanded. "And you deride our holiest of tales. So when your First Moma says enough, it means enough!"

"Yes, First Moma," Playful humbled as she looked to her feet, then looked back up with a titty-bitty grin and said in a perfectly exaggerated Thunder, "The Gathering is shut."

The women roared. Mellow just rolled her eyes—at least Sandy was no longer the object of the derision, and Playful's Thunder was by far the most entertaining of her voices.

"But perchance not shut just yet," pondered Playful-as-Thunder as she clowned the crowd as far as she could take them. "Should I shut it, Leaf? What say you, Leaf? I feel the need for combat. Yes, I must slay something. Who asked you, Leaf? I'll do as I please. Done, and decided. So, who shall I slay? Hmm. Perchance you, little one," she said as she pointed a crooked finger to Daughter-of-Love. "Wish you to be slain on this fine sunny morn?"

"Oh no, don't slay me, my Sorry," the twelve-calendar-old girl laughed along. "Slay Mellow. Slay the First Moma!"

The women howled, and Daughter-of-Love beamed for being part of the show, then quickly turned to Mellow with a repentant smile and mouthed, "Just funny-ing."

Mellow smiled back fondly and mouthed, "I know."

"What say you, my wife?" Playful-as-Thunder prompted to Mellow when—

CRACK! The gray sky lit up with bolts of electrical-city!

BOOM! The gods roared their boredom with the drought from within the clouds, and the rains rained down like dogs and cats.

The women smiled joyously. They reached out their arms and arched back their backs to feel the frigid embrace of the gods' pee upon their tits.

"Praise the gods!" shouted Mellow, for Sandy had long-since conveyed to her that as First Moma it would be her duty to cheer it first. "Such gratitudes for your rains!"

"Praise the gods!" repeated the women out of unison. "Blessed be the gods' pity!"

"Hail to Thunder!" shouted Mellow. "Hail to our Sorry for prevailing upon the gods to end the horrible drought we deserved! Hallowed be his glorious name! Hail Thunder!"

The women followed suit then turned hurriedly back to their chores; for although the return of rainfall was the truest of blessings, its droplets were arctic and like needles on their skin, and they wanted to get indoors fast.

* * *

"WHO OF OUR MEN, Leaf, holds the mightiest skill at the crafting of song?" asked Thunder. "For a day such as this must commemorate me into our lore."

The stony firepits of the Sorry's cabin burned strong as the gods bombed their watery pellets upon the wood-and-baked-mud rooftop above. The Sorry and his Two lounged in the large anteroom on poofy sofas hand-crafted by Thunder's predecessor as they sipped on warmed-up hooch with crushed razz-berries laden within. (Prior administrations typically chose the Holy One as the Two, another practice Thunder opted to adjust.)

"Take heed, Thunder," Leaf replied. "The return of rainfall may not in actual be the blessing we all think it to be."

"Leaf, my most faithful of chums," the Sorry sighed with a smirking shake of the head, "why must you always excrete your excretions upon my parade?"

Leaf smiled unfazed. "That's why I get to eat the big bucks."

Thunder chuckled at that, then held out his cup and shouted toward the kitchen, "More hooch!"

Mellow, Playful, and Whisper—formerly Clearsky's youngest wife who Leaf took as his own the night aft the Holy Usurp, the night aft his wife Brash died mysteriously in her sleep—were busily preparing the luncheon when they heard the command. Whisper put down her corncob and cutter, wrapped a swath of squirrel hide round her hands and reached for the black, clay jug that simmered over the oven in the firepit. Even though she and Leaf were guests to the meal, twas her turn to serve.

"Should the men be hooching as this while daytime lies upon us?" asked the eighteen-calendar-old girl in her characteristically hoarse voice.

"Women don't ask questions as these, young lady," Mellow

corrected pleasantly. "But their hooching is of no consequence for they willn't hunt in such rains as these."

"Let them hooch it up to the high heavens, I say," quipped Playful, "so they could be rendered with a sleep to spare us our womanly duties."

Mellow held her smile inside.

"Nooo," Whisper replied with an embarrassed grin, "I love my Leaf. He's my joy. I don't wish him rendered to sleep when time for relations come." She took the jug and left.

"My former sister-wife loves her Leaf because Clearsky treated her with such a terrible that Leaf thrives in the comparison," Playful offered once the girl had gone.

"And to you?" Mellow asked conversationally. "Clearsky treated you well?"

"He treated me a fine, mostly, but I had to caution always that twas never too a fine or Dour would thrash me to no skin. It was a tender balance I had to wield, and Clearsky turned a sightless eye to all of it, lifting not a finger to protect even though he could."

"Yes," Mellow countered pointedly. "Some do that."

Playful returned to her task without comment, and the women toiled on in silence.

Thunder's arm remained outstretched as Whisper entered the anteroom and began to pour. "To the brim or to the when, my Sorry?" she asked.

"To the when," he answered then, a moment later, added, "When."

She stopped pouring and moved toward Leaf. "Your cup, my husband."

"Tis a fine, wife. My cup remains full to the half."

"But my husband is the great and honored Two. His cup must be full to the full always." She took his cup from his hand and filled it.

"Gratitude, Whisper."

"Tis a privilege to me, Leaf. Is there anything more the men desire of me?"

"No, that'll be all, sweets," Leaf answered gallantly. "Gratitude."

She leaned over, kissed him full and hard on the mouth, turned away with a giggle and headed back to the kitchen.

Leaf noticed Thunder watching him with an amusement. "What?" he asked.

"'Tis just a nice to see you happy with a woman is all, ole chum."

"She's a good," agreed Leaf. "A blessing to me my Whisper is."

"Any woman would seem blessing after your last wife," Thunder replied good-naturedly. "You should have let me slay Brash for you calendars before I did."

"I still feel a sad about such decision."

"P'shaw. Brash would never have let you and Whisper enjoy one another as you do."

"A truth," Leaf responded in doleful concession.

"So relish'n'mustard in your blessing while you have it. For me, it's 'yap, yap, yap' from my women all the time, or a deadful silence arctic as snow. Mellow and Kindness were as loving sisters, mealtimes a bliss. Mellow and Playful are as Sorrys of rival clans."

"Perchance tis time for you to take a third."

"To the gods, no," Thunder chuckled. "Last thing necessary is yet more yap, yap, yaps of shrill. My cabin is quite full with the two I've got, gratitude much."

"But you're so rarely sated. I know at times you prefer your relations with brutal, yet you've whined to me on so many a hoochy night that you receive such pleasures no longer."

"Playful is my angel," Thunder insisted. "My hopeful since before I could stiffie, before I even knew what a stiffie was. Twas but her smiles in my brain that kept me going all those calendars. No. She can be touched only softly, and thrust into only with care."

"And to Mellow?"

"Mellow," he sighed. "A fine First Moma, a truth, one all our men respect and all our women adhere, even though she's never raised a hand to a one of them. She makes me look good."

"She does."

"And when I feel amorous, she is fine to the very. No man could ask for better. But when I feel animal, she disappoints. She shows me no pain, no fear, no anything. She claims the gods take her into their embrace without her asking, but for me tis like I'm thrashing upon a corpse. Does it satisfy? Course, but akin to cumming in one's fist and not a woman's cunt. Pleasant, but lacking. You wouldn't get for you have no such predilections as I."

"What I get is that my best chum is less than happy, my Sorry rarely sated, and tis my duty to serve them both. So last on the topic I will add, and only for the politic of it . . . your predecessor had three wives. Why should Thunder the Great have but two?" He paused to let the point sink in, saw that it did indeed, and continued. "Now, to business."

"Yes, to business. You were about to excrete upon my parade."

"I was about to excrete no such excretions, but yes, to the rains. They'll bring nourishment to the fruits and veggies beyond our dwelling for them to grow with bounty and color."

"Course. Tis the good of it."

"And the abundance of produce will bring new meats to graze, meats that will grow large and strong and juicy, not like the skinnies with which we've had to compromise."

"Tis a good upon a good, and we shall all grow happy and fat."

"And the abundance of meats will bring men to hunt them— heathen others who will see our perfect dwelling and strive to take it from us. The rainfalls will bring war."

"You don't know this."

"Tis an inevitable."

Thunder took a moment to process the information. "Then praise," he smiled. "So be it. My reign has been too uninteresting as it stands. The first song to honor me after three calendars is one of precipitation? No Sorry will live long in the lore for that."

"You wish for war?"

"I wish for victory," he said. "I wish for glory. And both I shall have if the gods but give me a war from which to get them. So, back to the start, who best to write my song?"

Before Leaf could answer there was a pounding at the door. He rose and went to open it to find Daughter-of-Love dripping wet in her elephant-hide poncho and hat.

"I must see Mellow," she said with haste, then remembered to whom she was speaking and rephrased. "May I have audience with the First Moma please?"

"Course," shrugged Leaf. "Mellow!" he shouted toward the kitchen as he returned to his poofy sofa. "A ragamuffin for First Moma at the door!"

"Where are your manners, Leaf?" asked Thunder. "She's just a titty-bitty thing." He turned to Daughter-of-Love who remained dripping and shivering on the porch. "Come inside, little wet one. Apology for the crude-ity of my colleague. Enter and grow dry."

"Gratitude, my Sorry," she said as she stepped in. "Ahhhh, so warm," she sighed quietly as she removed her soaking hat. "So waaaaaarm."

Mellow entered hurriedly from the kitchen. "Dearest chum, what is it?" she asked with concern. "What brings you out to me in these rains?"

With a quick glance at Thunder, the girl touched her hand to Mellow's shoulder and turned them to face outside for she didn't want her Sorry to hear her. "My moma died when I had only six calendars and she never got to showing me," the scant thing blurted in hushed panic. "And Pupa's next wife didn't make it past the first summertide so she had no opportunity. And you and the others who filled the gaps did it for me but never—"

"Shh, child, shh," soothed Mellow. "Calm it, breath. You make no sense to me, Daughter-of-Love. Now take your breath and tell me what needs telling."

The younger shot another glance to Thunder then pulled Mellow down to her level and whispered in her ear with red-faced embarrassment. "I don't know how to use the indoor ovens! No one ever taught! I efforted and efforted to reckon it on my own, but the whole cabin went smoky."

Mellow's heart skipped a beat for sadness. How could I have neglected to show her such an obvious? she asked herself, then shamefully answered her own question: because it was always more expedient to simply do it for her. A terrible on you, First Moma.

"You have to open the flue first," she sighed more to herself than to her chum.

"I don't know what that means!" the girl helplessly responded.

"I know you don't. So much apology for not thinking to show you what you must know, Daughter-of-Love. The fault is mine."

"Come teach me now, Mellow? Please? Pupa will have such disappointment in me if his luncheon not prepared in proper time. He'll think me dunce-y for not knowing. Please?"

"No one will ever think you dunce-y, Daughter-of-Love, but course I'll come."

"I love you, Mellow!" yelped Daughter-of-Love as she wrapped her little arms round Mellow's waist. "You saved my life!"

"No, only your day," Mellow said warmly as she concealed her shivers from the arctic wet of the girl's poncho that pressed against her naked skin. "Wait but here while I go garner on some clothing for the wet," she added then headed to her bedchamber.

You let her down, Mellow. Of all the people to let down . . . shame on you!

The girl had had it hard, Mellow knew. Even in this hard, hard world she'd had it harder than many. Three times her moma efforted to give her sibling then perished on the last. Her pupa wouldn't re-wed for five calendars more and then his new wife, Candid, a fine woman and doting step-moma, died with-child six moonths later from complications due to preeclampsia. Mellow could've saved easily both baby and moma with a simple series of blood transfusions, an IV for fluid replacement, practices so commonplace once upon a time, but such luxuries had long been retired from the world. With the passing of Candid, all of Mellow's original girl-chums were gone, except Daughter-of-Love.

It was a tragic for everyone, and the moppet was once again left to learn the ways of a woman without a moma to teach her, once again left to perform the household chores of a wife for her pupa while still only a child herself. Mellow did as much as she could to fill the gaps for the girl, all the women did, but all had demanding husbands or needy children of their own to tend. The fact that Daughter-of-Love was able to keep hold of that bubbly, whimsical nature through it all was something Mellow never got but always admired.

Daughter-of-Love waited quietly by the doorway, secretly ogling upon her Sorry whenever he wasn't looking her way. When he happened to turn toward her, she looked away quickly as if she hadn't been watching him at all. When she sensed he faced her no longer, she set her eyes upon him once more, whereupon he'd turn back to her and she'd turn away again, and on and on until Thunder couldn't help but smile in amusement.

"There's no need for you to be fearful of your Sorry, little wet one."

"I'm not fearful of you, my Sorry," she insisted. "Forthright-and-genuine, I'm not. I'm just . . . just . . . awestruck."

"Tis a gratitude," he said graciously, "but only the gods are to be awed."

"But I saw you combat against Skinny Horse that day, and you were mighty and grand and filled me with awe. Bam! Pow!" the twelve-calendar-old shadow-boxed. "Bash! Pook! Pow! I rooted and cheered for you all the while, brief as that combat was. Crash! Biff! Boff!"

"Yes, twas a good one," Thunder grinned, tickled by the girl. "But what of my combat with Clearsky? Twas indeed a good one too, no? Who did you root for then?"

"Oh. I, um, I—"

Thunder bellowed in laughter. "You rooted for Clearsky's team? Say it ain't so, little wet one!"

"But I didn't root against you," she defended. "Twas a hard for me. My hopeful combatted for you but my pupa for Clearsky, and they warred to the death one against the other. I was so affrighted. I didn't know how to root. But in the end my pupa didn't take my hopeful's life because he loves me, and it all worked out for every-one. Well, not everyone, obvious. Not Clearsky or his team. But me, my pupa, and my hopeful . . . and you, obvious."

"You're a whimsical little puff, aren't you?"

"I dunno," she blushed and looked to the floor.

"You're of Sunburst's cabin, yes?"

"Yes. Sunburst is my pupa."

"He's a good man your pupa. He rose arms against my team, a

322

truth, but it showed loyalty to his mentor. A good man strong and true he is, one of my best. Tell him I said so."

"I will, my Sorry."

"Thunder."

She beamed. "Thunder. I will, Thunder. Absolute for certain, Thunder."

Mellow returned wearing her skinny-horse hide coat, pants, and bonnet. "Husband, I must take my remove to tend my First Moma-ly duties."

"'Tis a fine, Mellow, but make haste. I don't wish the luncheon delayed."

"I get," she answered, "but at worst, Playful and Whisper are upon it. You needn't wait for me." She picked up two ovrellas by the side of the door, handed one to Daughter-of-Love and said, "Let's go."

Daughter-of-Love followed Mellow for but a step, then abruptly stopped in the doorway and turned back to Thunder with a big smile and zealous wave. "Biiiiiiiiiiiiiiiiiiiiiiii, Thunder!"

Thunder smiled back, raised his hand and twiddled his fingers in a chummy too-da-loo. "Biiiii."

Mellow took the pixie by the hand and led her out into the wet.

"She's cute," mused Thunder.

CHAPTER FORTY

MYLA AWOKE AT TEN by the alarm. It took her a moment to get her bearings, then the nausea returned. It's been a whole week of this, she groused, this is definitely different.

Is this what happens when carrying an unsterblich baby?

She looked in the mirror to see her freckles smudged and runny. She sighed, turned on the shower, and let the horrible events of the days past rain over her with the water. She mourned Francisco's death; grieved for never being able to see Janine again, or Randy or Josh or Zeke; lamented the end of her legal career before it even started; and she fumed for having to give up Molly after little more than a year.

She got out, unplugged her phone, flipped to the selfie she'd taken the night before, then proceeded to replicate the dots on her face. She'd have to do this every morning for as long as she remained Myla, whoever that young woman is, she still had no idea.

She applied the concealer over her eye, foundation over that, threw on a pair of jean shorts, a Motley Crew t-shirt, and her orange-tinted glasses.

Just be yourself, she told herself.

Which self? The old lady self or the college girl self?

Just go. Wing it. And smile.

The grill was already heating up by the time she arrived at Naomi's patio, plates of raw breakfast foods set on the table, Naomi knee-deep in prep. A tiny, battery-operated TV was turned to FOX with the sound muted while *Moonlight Serenade* played on a boombox beside it, fading out to mix flawlessly into *Boogie Woogie Bugle Boy*. Myla brightened.

"Morning, cuz," greeted Naomi. "Right on time."

"You're into 1940s music?"

"My grub, my tunes. If you don't like 'em, you're free to eat elsewhere."

"No, I adore this stuff! I just didn't know anyone else listened to it anymore."

"Then you might have some trouble fitting in around here," Naomi chuckled. "These parts, it's country only for the good ole boys and gals, and metal for the meth-heads."

"What about a good ole boy meth-head?"

Naomi chuckled some more. "Good point. I'll look into it."

"So, what can I do to help?"

"Being spared potato-peeling duty is always appreciated."

"I'm on it."

"Coffee's on in the camper, sugar beside it, creamer in the fridge."

"Be right back," said Myla, then headed into the RV humming along to the box. It was a nice camper, nicer than hers, with framed photos of an eleven-or-twelve-year-old boy scattered about, presumably Naomi's son although there was no evidence of a child living there.

She poured the coffee as her humming turned to words, letting herself lose herself in herself for just an inkling. She added the half-and-half as her crooning grew ever louder, then headed back out belting away. Naomi smiled at the enthusiasm.

"Songs of my youth," she nostalgically confessed, then stopped cold. Careful, girl, no mistakes. "I was raised by my grandparents. It was their music, so it became mine."

"For real? Me too."

"Wow, small world," Myla said as she started on her potato assignment.

"Well, we're cousins, same grandparents," quipped Naomi. Myla smiled, and Naomi went on. "So, favorite artist of the era?"

"Um, female, them," she said, pointing to the box, "the Andrews Sisters. Male, Bing."

"Correct. And between the two?"

"Can't do it. Won't."

"Good answer. Most beautiful actress of the era."

"Rita Hayworth, duh."

"The correct answer is Lana Turner, but the judges will allow it. Best actress."

This is fun. I'm liking her. "Bette Davis."

"Correct again. You're on fire. Movie."

"*Casablanca.*"

Naomi made the ugly beeper sound. "Ehhhhh! The correct answer is *It's a Wonderful Life.*"

Myla giggled, then broke character from the game show game to show off a little for her newfound friend. "Fun fact. Did you know that *Wonderful Life* totally bombed when it first came out in theaters? It did so stinky that the studio didn't even bother to renew the copyright; then all the TV stations started putting it on their airwaves for free at Christmastime, and that's how it came to be everyone's favorite holiday movie."

"Yeah? No, I didn't know that. But dang, now you put me in the mood to watch it again. Care to join me later this aft, after you get your camper hooked up?"

"Yes, I'd like that very much."

"Cool. I'll crack open a bottle of wine. It'll be girl's night out in daytime, and Christmas in October."

"Raincheck on the wine," she began, knowing the alcohol would have no effect on her but completely in the dark as to what it might do to the baby. "I'm pregnant."

THE GIRL WHO WOULDN'T DIE

"Oh," said Naomi, then paused to alter the tone of the conversation. "Does he know? The dad, I mean."

"No," Myla answered sadly, truthfully, "and he never will."

"Well . . . I guess if you're looking to disappear, this is as good a place as any. So, how do you like your eggs?"

"However you do. I'm easy."

"Apparently so."

"Ha ha, very funny."

On the boombox, *Bugle Boy* faded out to mix flawlessly into *Swinging on a Star*. Naomi began to sing along, Myla mirthfully joined in, then both were drowned out by a roaring, off-key baritone. They turned to see Deputy Dim approaching with a grin.

"Hellowwww, women."

"Hey Dim," greeted Naomi.

"Thought I'd drop by to see how our lady in distress is faring."

"I'm doing just fine, thank you, Demetrius."

He bit on his lip to conceal his blush and smile.

"Why don't you pull up a bench and stay for breakfast, Dim?"

"Had it hours ago. I'll call this lunch. It's all right."

"Oh! Oh!" Naomi exclaimed suddenly. "Myla, turn up the TV! Pause the music!"

Myla obliged on both counts and was distressed to find that the segment which so captivated her new friend was, once again, the ongoing saga of the notorious Molly Parker. "You like this trash?" she asked with convincing attitude and venom.

"Best trash on TV," Naomi giggled. "Now, hush."

The three watched as the nation's favorite new soap opera raged on. First, live interviews with a trio of hipsters who had spotted Molly Parker in a Chicago coffee house that very morning, describing the unsettling effects that her ghastly scowls had on them. Next, a brief clip of Janine begging Molly to turn herself in. "There are people who love you, Molly. We'll help you through this. Staying out there will only make things worse for you. Please, I'm here for you, baby. Your Janine is here for you." (Keeping the cavalcade of feelings off her face was Myla's best acting job to date.) Following Janine was a far lengthier interview with a young man claiming to be a Moses, California native and Molly Parker's high school boyfriend, currently an unemployed magician living in Las Vegas. As he conveyed the trials and tribulations of his young romance with the unhinged beauty, the broadcast cut to the ever-repeated footage of Josh's video, rendering the boy's bloodcurdling words to voice over.

Naomi turned to Myla with a smile. "You know, you kind of look a little like her."

Shoot! Shut this down fast. "Oh please," Myla moaned with deep offense.

"I mean, other than the hair and stuff, you do a little."

"You take that back, Naomi. Right now!"

"What, despite what she did, she's a pretty girl."

"She's disgusting!" Myla began, unable to think of anything better, neither woman noticing Dim growing uneasy by the new insight, looking back and forth between Myla and the TV in deep, studious thought. "Even if what she did was in self-defense like some say," Myla continued, "which I highly doubt, she's a . . . a . . . she's a lesbian!!!"

"Whoa," Naomi uttered. "I never would have guessed that'd be a thing for you."

"Well, it is. Girls are supposed to be with boys and boys are supposed to be with girls. That's how God made it, and that's how it's supposed to be."

"Nope, she doesn't look like her at all," Dim finally concluded. "Molly Parker has a bigger nose, and her eyes are darker and squintier. You should apologize to her."

"Thank you, Demetrius!"

"Okay, okay," surrendered Naomi. "It was just an observation. Didn't mean nothing by it, geez, I'm sorry."

"You know what?" sighed Myla. "I'm sorry too. I shouldn't have expressed my religious beliefs so aggressively. That was rude. My relationship with Jesus is my own."

"No harm done," Naomi said, then made a fist and held it out. "Still on for *Wonderful Life*?"

Myla smiled, phew, and completed the fist bump. "Wouldn't miss it for the world, cuz."

* * *

AFTER THE MOVIE, Naomi got out her Scrabble board and the three went at it. Naomi was best by far, Myla a distant second, Dim bringing up the rear. Near the end, no letters left in the silver bag, the words "craze," "quid," and "itch" clustered around an open double word score square, Dim laid down his last tile, a measly "d," to create "crazed" and "quidditch" for a cool eighty-six points; and by garnering the values the girls got stuck with, he eked out a narrow victory. Naomi laughed, and Myla clapped.

Dim went on to win the next two games on similar flukes, at which point Naomi had had enough and suggested they play Risk because she felt like "taking over the world," but then noticed the clock. "Hey Dim, shouldn't you be getting on to the hotel right about now?"

"Oh, dang, you're right. Lost all track of time. Thanks, Naomi."

"Hotel?" asked Myla.

"Dim's father owns the town hotel," Naomi explained. "Only one in Dukane."

"My great-great-grandpa built it with his own two hands, but my Daddy's getting up in years and not doing too well so me and Charlene, that's my kid sister, me and Charlene help out when we can.

"You know, Myla, I can swing by in the morning and pick you up for church if you want. You'll never find a good place to park your camper close by. I mean, judging how you were talking before, I assume you're a good churchgoing lady. Me, I go every Sunday too."

"Oh, well, gee, Demetrius, that's really sweet but I don't want to put you out." She glanced over to Naomi in the hope her new friend would help her find a better excuse.

"Don't look at me, I ain't taking you. I don't do church."

"It's no bother, Myla. Service starts at nine, so I'll meet you by your camper at eight-thirty."

"Great," she smiled. "Thank you. I love church."

* * *

"WHO IS IT?" she responded to the tapping on her door the next morning, knowing full well who it was.

"It's Dim. We'd better get a move on or we'll be late."

"Be right out."

Church, she grumbled. It was a smart play under the circumstances, but . . . ugh.

She checked herself in the mirror, all made-up with freckles and foundation and concealer for her shiner, in her wispy little white dress, the closest thing to church clothes that she had stuffed into her escape pack, the closest thing she had to nice.

I got to get more clothes, she told herself. And groceries. And an obstetrician.

While he waited, Dim, wearing a slightly snug, seven-year-old suit and tie, drifted to the back of the RV and caught wind of the license plate. Filthy, not unusual. He scraped off a small chunk of the hardened muck to spot the California tags.

It was exactly what he didn't want to see—but heck, it could mean anything. Molly Parker's in Chicago, everyone knows that. It's on the news. It don't mean nothing, not a thing. He heard the camper door swing open, pressed the mud back into place and returned to the front. "Hey, Myla."

"Howdy, Demetrius. Well, don't you look nice."

"Heck, it's just my church uniform. Oh. I mean, you look nice too."

"Thank you, that's very sweet."

They walked up the little dirt road making idle chitchat until they reached the parking lot where Dim gallantly opened the passenger door of his squad car for her.

"They let you drive this while off duty?" the ex-cop's widow asked curiously.

"We're pretty lax about that kind of stuff round here." She got in, he closed the door for her, crossed over to the driver's side and got in too. "Want me to blast the siren and flash the spinny lights for you this time? Honest Injun, it's real cool."

"Still not necessary, Demetrius, but thank you."

"Your loss. It's all right."

* * *

THE SERVICE WAS MORE political than she remembered from her churchgoing days before severing her relationship with the Lord back in the 1960s, and the rah-rah America combined with the rah-rah Jesus allowed her to tune out and focus on what truly mattered.

So much to do, she told herself. Make a list. What with this cuckoo Molly Parker media frenzy, we could be stuck here in Dukane for months to come, not weeks, maybe years. This town could end up my baby's home.

She looked up to the church ceiling. God, she proclaimed from within her heart, don't let my baby be like me. Don't let it be unsterblich. Please let it be a normal. I know we haven't spoken for a long time, and that was on me, but spare this innocent of Your curse and I'll forgive You for Lori. Please? Amen.

After the service, the congregants milled about on the front lawn. Dim introduced her around, referring to her always as Naomi's little cousin, which she considered a stroke of good fortune.

She found her fellow churchgoers to be a pleasant, decent people, friendly and welcoming. Much of their conversations centered around Friday's football game, some on an upcoming rodeo, and only a few on the tantalizing tale of the California killer. Myla remained quiet during all but the latter, then spouted her high-handed Christian virtues to castigate the depraved murderess, even bringing the pastor's wife into the conversation at one point to back her up.

Everyone believed her, and everybody liked her.

* * *

ONCE THE NURSE checked her vitals and extracted urine sample and blood test to confirm the pregnancy, Myla's new obstetrician entered the examining room and greeted her warmly. Dr. Ruddick was a pleasant-looking millennial, which meant that the woman who'd be delivering her baby was younger than most of her grandchildren.

When is this going to stop being weird?

JEFF ABUGOV

A local Dukane girl, the good doctor received her medical degree from Oklahoma State University in Tulsa (information Myla had gleaned from the frames on the wall) where she met her husband, a Tulsa native, who she brought home with her to take over as the town pediatrician (which she learned from the woman herself). "So as soon as you're done with me, you'll be off to see him," sported the doc. "Talk about your family physicians, huh?"

Myla was at first reluctant to tell her new caregiver about the extreme nausea because of her suspicion that it was the effect of an unsterblich baby and would give herself away, but ultimately came to her senses—no sane person could reach such a conclusion. Besides, what if it was something else, some other condition the baby had? So she told what needed to be told, spewing all her fears, concerns, and complaints that she'd been stuffing inside, the alleged twenty-two-year-old stopping just shy of blurting out "because it wasn't like this the last four times!"

"Let's see if we can't get to the bottom of it," the physician said good-naturedly as she pressed around Myla's abdomen for any abnormalities, probed inside to assure that the cervix was indeed closed, then called in a twenty-something technician to ready her for an ultrasound.

Myla lied quietly on the table while they prepped as the reality of her next few years hit her with a jolt. How am I going to raise a little one by myself?! Amidst all the running and hiding and planning and lying, I hadn't even considered that! Yes, I raised four once upon a time, but I had a husband who took care of all the finances, the house, me. I had a mother and mother-in-law who were there whenever I needed them. By the time Caroline was born, I had Lori, Robby, and Mikey to pitch in. Now I have no one, no one at all, and half my attention will always be spent looking over my shoulder ready to run, and only half on the child, at most. How can I do this?! Despite everything I've learned, all the skills I've acquired, one little baby may just be too much for me.

"That explains why the nausea's been so severe," smiled the doctor. "You're having twins."

CHAPTER FORTY-ONE

Pete got little work done that day, just as he hadn't for the past several. He sat on his fancy chair behind his fancy desk in his fancy office watching the ongoing coverage of the hunt for Molly Parker—but the real reason he was pulling out what little was left of his hair was that Dr. Szabo had stopped taking his calls.

He tried again, answering machine again, no point leaving a message again. He buzzed his secretary and told her to book him the next flight to Richmond.

He arrived at the old geezer's majestic home late that afternoon. The drapes were drawn, and the blinds pulled down. He rang the bell, no answer, even though he could hear movement inside. He rang once more. Nothing. He held his finger to the button to maintain a single nonstop obnoxious chime until the door finally opened.

"Can't you take a hint?!" barked Woody.

"Never been one of my virtues."

"Get in," said the biologist as he grabbed Pete by the collar and yanked him inside. "This is the last time we see each other, last time we speak. Ever! Get it?"

"What happened?"

"It's over is what happened. This thing's become too hot. Giant clusterfuck is what it's become, and no one wants to be implicated. Our benefactors are out."

"Let me talk to them."

Woody laughed. "They barely want to talk to me anymore, let alone you. You know, when I first brought this to them, even after telling them I couldn't guarantee success in time to keep them alive, they still wanted in. Know why? Legacy. Same as me. They wanted to go down as the men who financed the man who ended sickness. Now they're accomplice to murder—a murder with a motive that'd sound downright bonkers if ever explained out loud. Some legacy, eh?"

"Can you at least tell me what happened? After that video posted, you guys had her."

"The blockheads hired a bunch of blockheads is what happened. I need a drink. We'll call it our farewell toast." He poured two schnapps as he recounted the story as told to him—Francisco's murder and the subsequent framing of Molly for it, how they tracked her to LAX, to Chicago, had four of their men waiting for her at her gate in O'Hare and two more seated on her plane to Hamilton, and how she still managed to elude them. "Then the nitwits go leak the story to some local TV station, figuring someone might spot her and phone it in; then the cable channels and big papers get wind, and they just run the poo out of it till now it's the highest-rated reality show they've ever shown. No, this thing is too hot. Everyone was fired days ago. It's over."

"Why?" asked Pete.

"Haven't you been listening? Our funding's gone."

"You know, a little while back you showed me your lab, all completed and ready to go."

"So?"

"So, who owns it?"

"The Foundation."

"And who controls the Foundation?"

Woody paused, beginning to see where Pete was going. "I do."

"What's left to pay? Staff, security. I got money. I'll cover it. How much could it be?"

"Millions—there's more to this than you think. Single digit millions, but millions."

"Oh. I don't have that kind of money."

"I do," the scientist mumbled softly, pensively.

"Then we're back in business, Doc, and your lifelong dream can at last come true."

"Except for one tiny detail. WE DON'T HAVE THE GIRL!"

"I'll find her. I told you to let me do it in the first place. Didn't I tell you that?"

"You couldn't have done any worse, that's the truth. But no, it's too dangerous."

"If you're worried about being implicated, don't be. Until I have her, until I get her into your lab, there'll be absolutely no contact between us. If I fail, you'll never hear from me again. If I get into legal trouble, your name will never come up. Why would it? All I need is your assurance that when I bring her to you, and I will, that you'll work your magic and take your proper place in history. Promise me that, and I'll track her down for you on my own dime."

"Why's this so important to you, son? None of it will bring your daddy back, and I'm the one who's going to get the glory. Why does it matter so much to you?"

Pete took a moment to consider, then smiled. "Everybody needs a hobby."

* * *

HE WAS in LA four days later, extensive preliminary research taking up the bulk of the in-between time. His first stop was the Santa Monica apartment. Molly's friends had all spoken to the press by then, giving their takes on the story, but Pete wondered if they knew anything of her whereabouts, maybe even without knowing they knew it. A longshot, but as good a place to start as any. He rang the buzzer. A moment later, Janine opened the door wearing a black tank top and boxing shorts, tall and sweaty and utterly ripped from being mid-workout.

Look at the size of this one, he noted. Wonder what it'd be like fucking a broad like that.

Get to work. "Hi!" he began all friendly-like. "I'm—"

"No," she answered after a mere glance at the frumpy man in the frumpy suit then proceeded to close the door, but Pete had his foot wedged in the jam.

"I just want to ask you a few—"

"Listen, pal, I only spoke to the cops because I had to. I spoke to that first reporter because I wanted to get a message out to Molly; then I spoke to the second one to clear up what the first lied about; then the third to clear up the second, which made it worse still. You guys don't give a damn about the truth, you just want to sell commercials."

"I'm not with the press, ma'am." He showed her his card. "Pete Mailor. Kingston-Benefit Insurance."

"Uh-huh," she said suspiciously, wondering where he was going with this.

"As you may know, Molly's dear mother passed away not too long ago, but she had taken out quite an impressive life insurance policy years prior. I'm merely trying to locate Molly to endow her the inheritance that is rightfully hers, guilty or innocent of the crime regardless."

"She got the money in the summer, douchebag. You guys are such assholes." She stomped her heel into his toes, he recoiled his foot, then she slammed the door in his face.

He limped back to his rented Subaru and came up with a new cover to give the other ones—the pretty boy, the Chinaman, and the geek—but it didn't matter. Janine phoned to warn them so none would talk to him.

Now what?

He left the stutterer's dorm room unsatisfied and walked to the UCLA campus as he pondered why Molly would have made up an insurance settlement, but his answer came easily. She wanted to buy things—a car, nice apartment, pretty clothes, duh. He already assumed she'd socked away a hunk of the fortune her bond-trading hubby had left her, but her only way to explain any influx of cash, given her cow town backstory, was to croak Mama. Smart.

But why a cow town at all? the question continued to gnaw at him. Moses, California, two hundred miles outside Fresno, population diddly. True, with a community that small, the chances of accidentally running into a legitimate resident would be minimal, but there'd be no good way to talk herself out of the lie if she did.

Did she know someone from there? Some kind of ally who helped her disappear? Seemed unlikely, but nothing this woman had done so far had been random. There had to be a reason. If there was someone up there helping her, could there be someone else who doesn't like her, who'd want to see her caught? Perhaps a trip to Moses was in order.

He arrived at the college where he stopped one entitled piece of shit after another to learn what he could. Those who knew Molly well wouldn't give him the time of day, but all others had plethora of opinions on the matter. Her snooty teachers fell into one of the same two categories.

Moses, here I come. Another longshot, yep, but not like you got anything better, kiddo.

He took the first flight to Fresno then checked into a nearby airport hotel. He went for a walk, dropped six hundred dollars at a local pool hall, then returned to his room where he searched out a nice online escort service and ordered himself a young, pretty blonde girl to get him through the night. He awoke early the next morning, rented a Chevy Impala and bought a California roadmap because he didn't trust GPS.

It was a long and boring drive, only flat lands of fields and farms and cows and horses. The instructions the GPS lady babbled through the speakers coincided with his paper map so he was quite surprised when she suddenly announced, "you have arrived at your destination." There was nothing for miles, not even a ramshackle shithouse.

He rechecked the map, which confirmed the GPS. He got out of the car, confused, and looked around the vast, empty field. He took out his phone, which also confirmed that he was smack dab in the middle of downtown Moses. A moment passed as he tried to make sense of it, then another, and then it hit him. He laughed aloud at the brilliance of it. No wonder she didn't have to worry about running into anyone from here.

Clever lady.

Now what?

CHAPTER FORTY-TWO

The Dwelling
6 Moonths Since "She's Cute"

As Leaf predicted, the return of the rains brought nourishment to the planted foods beyond the dwelling for them to sprout large with abundance. As he predicted, new meats came to feed on them and grew hefty and delicious. So far, he was two-out-three correct.

Mellow, now eight moonths with-child, had overheard titty-bits of Thunder's chits with his Two and knew he considered taking new wife. Her feelings on the topic were to both extremes and therefore cancelled each other out. On the one hand, it would be nice to have a sister she could actually talk to; on the other, she would never wish Thunder's perverted cruelty on her worst adversary. Either way, she had no voice in it and so chose to give it little energy or concern. Course, that was before she learned the victim's name.

"I contemplate the bringing of new wife to our cabin," the Sorry informed his spouses one humid eve aft the outdoor supper aft the children gone off to play. "I broach it to you both to absorb your opinions. Leaf suggests a new sister may help bridge the qualms between you two."

"A delightful consideration!" Playful exclaimed. "But I have no qualms with Mellow. She but has qualms with me."

"I have qualms with you, sister, a truth," Mellow said matter-of-factly, "yet you have qualms with me as well. No need to lie."

"I only have qualms with you because you have qualms with me."

"So you do have qualms with me. See? You lie."

"Do not dare to call me liar!"

"I called you no name, just pointed out your acts. You lie. If that makes you a liar—"

"Take that back!"

"Enough!" shouted Thunder. "This is to what I refer!"

"She tricks me into saying things I don't mean," Playful whined. "You should discipline the First Moma for it."

"He disciplines me all the time," Mellow responded. "Doesn't seem to do much good though, does it, Thunder? Maybe you should discipline her once in a while."

"Thunder! Make her stop!"

"Enough! One more utterance, and I'll discipline you both!"

"I'm in if she's in."

"Stop it, Mellow. I mean it."

"My lips are stitched."

"Good," he said. "Keep them that way. So, to marriage. I've come to find young Daughter-of-Love quite the little cutie."

"What?!" The word shot out like a bullet from the recesses of Mellow's soul.

"I think tis a marvelled idea!" exclaimed Playful.

"The girl has twelve calendars behind her," Thunder went on, "and closer still to thirteen. She's sure to come of age any time soon."

"Husband, no," pled Mellow. "Take a wife, yes, but not her. Please. Anyone but her."

"I thought you'd thrill to have Daughter-of-Love as your sister. You show quite the affection for her always, as if she was of your own womb."

"I like her, too," said Playful. "A delightful addition to our cabin."

"Shut up!" Mellow snapped, then turned back to her husband. "Tis because I have affection for the girl that I beg you, Thunder." She took hold his hands and dropped to her knees. "Please! Daughter-of-Love is so slight and small but only one of your blows could take her life away. Two for almost certain. Please, Thunder. Spare her."

"You think I have so little control of my might," began Thunder, growing peeved by the resistance, "that I could slay a soul by error?"

"No," Mellow said quickly. "No, no, no. Thunder the Great is controlled and mighty in all the regards. But please. Your First Moma begs her Sorry. Spare the girl."

"And who would you advise I take in her stead?"

"Anyone else," she said, careful to avoid naming names. "Any woman you desire."

"Daughter-of-Love is who he desires," said Playful, "and I think tis a marveled idea."

"You said you liked her!" Mellow barked, then calmed herself. "I know you like her, Playful, so aid me. I've never beseeched you a thing before, but I beseech you now."

"Our duty is to our husband, First Moma, and I think his choice a marveled choice. Had his choice been another, I would have spoken her the marveled choice."

Mellow could only shake her head in nauseous futility then turned back to Thunder. "What can I say to sway you, my husband? Anything, I'll do anything. I know you take frustration that I don't show my anguish during relations. What if I do? What if henceforth I remain in the moment and feel all my pain before your eyes? Will you spare the girl then?"

"You're able to manage this 'going-away' thing of yours?" he asked suspiciously.

She took a deep breath. "Yes," she confessed.

"You told me you couldn't. Said the gods took you unto them without your asking."

"I know."

"Well, well, well, who's the liar now? So, tonight you shall come to my bedchamber and show me at last what I wish to be shown."

"And you'll spare the girl? Only if you spare the girl."

Thunder thrust his powerful hand round Mellow's throat and squeezed hard. "First, I don't care for the word 'spare.' I'll be making the girl wife to the Sorry. I honor her, not condemn her. Second, do you remember the last time you tried to bully me into a bargain?"

"Yes," she choked out.

"And who won, and who lost?"

"You won," she coughed. "I lost."

"A lesson you seem to need taught again. So, tis settled. I will take Daughter-of-Love as my wife aft her first drop of womanhood spills."

Fuckety-fuck, Mellow, you made it worse! she screamed inside. Dunce, dunce!

"I will stake my claim at the next Gathering," decreed the Sorry. "Done, and decided."

Two days, Mellow told herself. You got two days to fix this.

* * *

THAT NIGHT, Mellow stayed present throughout her thrashing, hoping upon hope that it would please her husband enough to change his mind. Her booming wails and yelps were not pretend for the onslaught was as severe as any she could remember, despite Thunder's zealous restraint from causing any harm to her swollen belly. Aft it was over, she lay quietly next to him on his bed, his fingers lovingly stroking her hair, her head gently nestled upon his massive chest as if she didn't despise him more than anyone in the world.

"That was nice, Mellow," he panted softly. "You see? All I ask of you is to show me your honest sentiments as you feel them."

"I get that now, my husband. And this is how I shall be for you henceforth."

"Appreciate."

"So, not to bargain or bully but only to request . . . will you re-consider re Daughter-of-Love? For me? Please?"

"No," he said as he tenderly kissed the top of her head. "You need this lesson to learn, my beautiful wife, and so I must teach it. Besides, I like Daughter-of-Love. She tickles me. Twill be a joy for us all to have my little wet one sharing our cabin."

Two days, Mellow. You got two days.

* * *

"TIS AN INTERESTING QUANDARY," Sandy said later that night as he sat with Mellow in the darkness under their favorite tree. "An interesting quandary indeed."

"What can I do about it?"

"There's nothing you can do about it. Only a man can solve this picadillo."

"How so?"

"Simple, but peril-ridden. When Thunder stakes his claim, all another man has to do is issue challenge to it. But who would be foolhardy enough to challenge Thunder?"

"Son-of-Stone is the girl's hopeful."

"He is but manling, and from what I hear, not soon to make first slay. And he would for certain never challenge Thunder. Although . . . ." his voice trailed off and he smiled.

"What?"

"Oh, tis such an odds-against, not worth the mention."

"Tell me."

"If Son-of-Stone can achieve first slay to come of age before the Gathering and claims the girl first, tis an unlikely that Thunder would issue challenge to *him*. It'd look bad for a Sorry his size to challenge one small as Son-of-Stone, specially to separate hopefuls, specially more since Son-of-Stone combatted on his behalf in the Holy Usurp. No, I don't think Thunder would issue it. He's matured wise in his politic and knows well the importance of imagery." The Holy One paused, closed his eyes, and laughed. "A pity the manling remains so far from manhood. Would be nice to see Thunder not get his way for once."

"But even if status achieved, how could Son-of-Stone claim her first? The Sorry always speaks aft the Holy One."

"Only because the Holy One so invites."

"You mean you could invite anyone to speak next?"

"Don't know," Sandy smiled. "Who would say that I can't?"

"You devil! I love you!" Mellow shouted and playfully slapped his arm.

"But tis all moot. The manling is yet a man, and not a likely to be one for some time."

"Oh Sandy, I knew you'd find me the answer!" she cheered and kissed his cheek.

"Wait. What are you going to do?"

"Nothing a Holy One wants to know about."

* * *

SUNBURST'S CABIN was by now in the first ring for his status had risen large over the calendars. He never politic'd for it, but Thunder and Leaf couldn't help noting the pious man's skills as hunter and warrior. Even though he had combatted for the other team in the Holy Usurp, they knew it judicious to cement him as ally in these new and glorious times.

Mellow knocked on his door the following after-lunch and could hear the childlike giggles of Daughter-of-Love and Son-of-Stone emanating through the walls.

Children, she sighed. They're supposed to be but children at this age.

Daughter-of-Love opened the door with big smile while Son-of-Stone remained on the sofa in the anteroom fixated on an unfinished jigsaw of a dog peeing on a fire hydrant. "Mellow, hi!" the girl shouted as she wrapped her arms around the First Moma's waist. "Tis been long too long!" Only when Daughter-of-Love pulled back from the hug did she notice the fresh cuts and bruises on Mellow's face and body. "Aww, you fell down again?"

"Yes, I must learn to be more careful. So, how fares my little chum?"

"Shh!" the girl hushed with an impish grin, took Mellow by the hand, and dragged her toward the side of the porch so out of the manling's earshot. "Guess what?"

"What."

"Thunder, your husband Thunder, he likes me. As in, *likes* me, I think."

"I thought you had your goo-goo eyes cast upon Son-of-Stone."

"Course I do. I love him! He's my hopeful and will always be, right up until my hope is rendered unallowed by the gods. But he's been manling two moonths now and they say he shows no sign of making slay any day soon, and I'm twelve, soon to be woman. If I can't be with my hopeful, what girl wouldn't pray to be wife to the Sorry? Any Sorry, but specially Thunder who's so mighty and dandy looking. And you and I will be sisters!"

"Keep optimism, Daughter-of-Love. Your pupa and moma were hopefuls, and the gods timed them to wed. Tis a possible till tis not."

"Remember the day we met, and I told you how I'd coordinate my first bleeding with Son-of-Stone's first slay?" She tittered and shook her head. "Fuckety-fuck, I was so young."

"You were," Mellow smiled. "But tis still too early to give up your hope on your hopeful so I want these prayers re Thunder to come to end. Wish you to not even think on it."

"Completed!" Son-of-Stone yelled from the sofa.

"What?!" Daughter-of-Love protested then headed back inside to find the jigsaw perfect and intact. "Son-of-Stone! You said we'd do it together!"

"We did do it together," answered the manling. "Then we got stuck for you wouldn't cease jabbering; then you left and I could concentrate and I saw it so I did it."

"That's not fair," she giggled and playfully slapped him on the arm.

"Tis so fair," he giggled along.

"Tis not."

"Tell you a what," he said as he slid his fingers under the puzzle and threw it into the air for the pieces to unravel. "We start over, and this time I won't complete without you.".

"Aww, that's so sweetish," she smiled. "You tore up your dachshund dog just for me." She turned to Mellow in the doorway, boasting, "He adores dachshund dogs so. Has three and two half jigsaws of them."

"Oh, hello!" said the manling, noticing Mellow for the first time. He rose and snapped to attention. "I didn't see you there, First Moma."

"Tis a fine, Son-of-Stone, at ease," she said as she entered the space. He relaxed and sat back down. "So, you like dachshund dogs, do you?" she asked conversationally.

"Only because they're tenacious and sturdy and tough despite their lowness to the ground, just like me; and underestimated though they may be, they come to surprise all with their extraordinary prowess each and every time, just like I will."

"I have no doubt about, Son-of-Stone," she smiled, then turned to Daughter-of-Love. "I'm here for your pupa, dear chum."

"He's in the back performing the wood chop."

"Gratitude." She crossed to the back door and stepped out to find the man axing at a tree log as foretold. "Hello, Sunburst."

"Mellow," he replied a tad suspiciously. "What brings you to my cabin?"

"May I have some words?"

He sighed. Here it comes again. "The First Moma may have as many words as she wishes, but twill do no good. I know why you're here, and my brain won't budge."

"Why is it that you s'pose I'm here?"

"You're here to urge me to take new wife, as Dour did so often, as so many of the women so often do—in frankness, I expected you to effort it long before now—but I'll tell you the what that I tell them. No. Four times my seed was planted inside my Love, two almost ended her and the fourth one did. Only but once did I plant inside my Candid, and that was enough to take her life away as well. The gods' message is clear—"

"Sunburst—"

346

"Let me finish. The gods message is clear. For reasons I cannot fathom, they've made my seed too potent for a woman's womb. So, no, I will never lie with another."

"Tis not why I'm—"

"And I knew such when I wed Candid," he guiltily confessed to further his point. "Tis why I waited so long to take new wife at all. I knew I shouldn't have, but I was lonesome and succumbed to her charms, yet it was she who paid the price. I will not make that selfish again. If tis too much burden on the women of the Community to tend to me aft my daughter leaves for husband, so be it, I'll learn the ways of your chores and tend for myself. Doesn't look too hard. But no, I will not lie with another."

"Have you completed?"

"Yes. Make your debates, they will do no good."

"I'm not here to urge you to take wife, Sunburst. That is a choice for you alone, and your First Moma will defend it to the hilty."

"Oh. Um, oh. Um, gratitude. Then what brings you?"

"Four times just now you spoke of Love efforting to make child, yet you mentioned the outcome of only three."

"I love Daughter-of-Love more than anything. So?"

"Thunder intends to take her as third wife. He will stake his claim at the morrow night's Gathering." The pupa exhaled deeply, showing remorse but not surprise. "You knew?" Mellow asked.

"Suspected," he answered. "Feared. He's been speaking to her more than typical for one of his ranking, presenting her with gifts of pretty stones and flowers."

"So you get why I'm against—"

"Yes, yes, course." He closed his eyes for a moment, imagined his daughter at the hands of their brutish leader, then opened them. He yearned to offer Mellow condolence for what Thunder did on her, but what a man does within his cabin is his own affair, not to be judged or gossiped or spoken of by any other, by the will of the gods, so he said nothing.

"We have to prevent his marriage to your daughter," she told him.

"There is no means to prevent it."

"If Son-of-Stone achieves manhood on the morrow's hunt, he can stake his claim for the girl first. Thunder will not issue challenge."

"I like Son-of-Stone. He's a good boy, and an honorable manling. A fine husband to my daughter he'd be. But tis an unlikely to the very that he'll make first slay anytime soon."

"Which is why you must make it for him."

"You say a what?"

"On the morrow's hunt, lead the manling away from the other men so they can't see. If he fails to make slay on his own, you take the animal's life and proclaim credit to him."

"Tis not how we do things, Mellow. You're a good woman, a fine First Moma, but sometimes the immigrant in you shines. No, tis a break of our laws."

"Who will know?"

"I will know, you will know, the gods will know . . . and I will know."

"Tis the only way to save Daughter-of-Love. Would you rather dismiss her to a life of Thunder's thrashings?"

"Course not, and you should not speak of such aloud. But the gods have already punished me once with seed too strong for woman because of a sin I don't even know I did. What will they do if I commit one with deliberation?"

"I s'pose we'll find out."

"Do you not fear the gods, Mellow?"

"I love the gods, Sunburst, and they love me, and they love you. Save your daughter."

"I can't," he woefully sighed. "Wish to the heavens that I could but I can't. I won't."

"I think you will, kind siree," she said. "I think you will."

* * *

THE PLAINS beyond the dwelling were plush and vibrant, the grass beneath the hunters' feet soft and green. Although rookie manlings like Son-of-Stone had never seen it otherwise, the more seasoned hunters had grown so accustomed to the barren ugliness that even after all these moonths they couldn't cease their awe-ing at the gods' beautiful.

All but Sunburst, that is, who barely bothered to notice.

What business of this is hers anyway? he muttered in his head as he marched alongside the other men. Why must Mellow put this dilemma in my brain? There is no right answer, only two wrong ones. To ignore as she bids, I condemn my daughter to a life of victimhood and violence; to act, I betray my Community and my gods. If this be a test, who is she to test me? Only the gods can lay such test, yet this woman lays test on me still.

"Thunder!" he called forward. "I discern motion in the thicket. Consent to break off?"

"Go," granted the Sorry.

"Manling!" he barked at Son-of-Stone. "Follow behind my footsteps!"

"Yes, siree," said the manling.

Aid me, oh gods, the hunter prayed in quiet as he led the younger into the forest. Steer this manling true to make his spears fly straight and strong. Grant him his manhood this day and relieve me of this unpassable test. Your humbled mistake lacks the wisdom to know what you wish of me. Oh gods, I beseech you! Take this test away from me!

Man and manling trekked through the woods in silence for some time, and Son-of-Stone was at a loss for there was nothing of conse-quence in sight. What had his senior detected? He could hear his brethren's hollers out on the plains as they began to chase upon their prey, and still he and Sunburst walked on in search of . . . what?

At last, the hunter came to an abrupt halt. He pointed off to the distance where a grizzly stood on its hinds by a cherry tree haplessly efforting to capture its fruit, then he turned to the manling and whis-pered, "You."

Son-of-Stone nodded with a gulp, dropped three of his spears to the ground, and raised the fourth above his head in throwing posture. "No, no, no," Sunburst hushed softly, then maneuvered the younger's arm into a more proper form. "The deeper the backhand the more power the throw. Now, find your target on its chest. Should be no larger than a strawberry seed. Lock on it, for your spear will soar to where your eyes are fastened. And don't forget your follow-through. Keep throwing even after the weapon has left your hand. Twill assure greater power and accuracy. Got?" The manling nodded. "Throw."

Son-of-Stone mustered all he had to muster and released his spear with such a strength that his perfect follow-through sent him reeling off his feet. The javelin soared through the air with barely a wobble and struck hard into the bear's . . . arm. The great mammal howled its fury, turned to its assailants, and charged on all fours!

"Up!" shouted Sunburst. "Up and aim and throw! Now!"

Son-of-Stone leapt to his feet with spear in hand and fired. Missed. Reached for the next and fired again. Missed. Reached for his fourth and final as he noticed Sunburst standing motionless, spear in hand but by his side. Why wasn't he throwing too?

"Don't look at me!" shouted the hunter. "Throw! Aim and throw!"

The manling tried to slow his breath but the bear was so close. He threw! Missed.

With the grizzly no more than steps away, Sunburst hurled his weapon with a tremendous brawn to nail the beast between its eyes. It collapsed to the ground, dead.

Man and manling took a moment to quell their pounding hearts before moving to the corpse. Sunburst squinted hard in thought, bit down on his lip, gazed upon the critter, then took a deep, culpable breath and said, "Tis still alive. Slash your cutter across its throat."

"It seems dead to me."

"Obey your olders, boy!"

"Yes, siree," said the manling, then did as commanded.

"Well done," softly spoke the hunter. "Your first slay. A bear. Well done."

"But twas your slay, not mine," Son-of-Stone responded with a confusion. "My weapon cross its neck a symbolic at most."

"Just accept this blessing without so many words! You've made your first slay and so have come of age. Praise the gods."

"Is this a test? If test it be, I shan't accept credit where none is earned for it would be a terrible sin against the gods, but if something else, I'll follow as you advise." The hunter winced but said nothing, so the manling went on. "A pious man as you would never lead a younger to sin for that is an even graver sin, I know such, so tell me what to do and I'll do it, my siree." Still, the hunter said nothing. "Sunburst?"

"I can't," the pupa whispered with a crackle in his voice.

"I don't get."

"Yes, manling, twas a test. You passed. Well done."

The manling beamed.

And far off on the other side of the broken concrete road, a teen-age boy and his teen-age sister trotted lazily on their horses when they heard the distant shouts of the Community's hunters and came to a stop. They wore tattered cloths of twilled cotton over their thighs and woven cotton atop their torsos—what the old world would've called jean shorts and a t-shirt—muddy baseball caps on their heads and sunglasses on their faces. The girl pulled the binoculars strapped to her neck up to her eyes to check out the hullabaloo, the boy his plastic canteen up to his mouth to drink. The girl smiled, passed her binoculars to the boy, he his canteen to her. She drank, and he looked, and he smiled too.

The boss-man will like this, they both knew. They won't be relegated as mere meat-scouts for much longer. They turned and galloped away.

CHAPTER FORTY-THREE

DUKANE, OKLAHOMA
NOVEMBER/DECEMBER 2018
THE WEEKS FOLLOWING THE OBSTETRICIAN

THE FACT THAT TWINS might explain the nausea didn't rule out the possibility that one or both were unsterblich. She'd simply have to wait until they were old enough to grow old to see if they grew old. Either way, for their own safety, she'd have to move on in twenty years or so to watch them from afar like Francisco had done with her. She knew that leaving them behind at any age would kill her, but no point in living tomorrow's pain today. For now, she needed more than just herself to raise them, and they deserved more than just each other once she was gone.

In the weeks since Myla's arrival, Naomi had gone above and beyond to help her acclimate to her new home. She showed her around town, turned her on to the best places to frequent and the worst places to avoid, and even took the time to drive her to an auto dealership in Lawton one county over where Myla purchased a used Dodge pickup—a second vehicle being necessary for trailer park living, a Dodge pickup because that's what Naomi had. She took her to the UPS Store to set up her mailing address; helped her buy a new laptop as Myla played down her abilities in case word of Molly Parker's tech prowess came out, which she knew was far more likely than not; and she told Myla of the various job opportunities in town, of which there weren't many. Myla was well aware she'd have to get a job at some point to explain how she supported herself, but there was too much to accomplish first. Still, Naomi did everything she could to help "battered cuz" get settled in, even offering to counsel Myla on her presumed domestic afflictions, although putting on no pressure.

Auntie material? Myla wondered. Yes, I think so.

Myla had every intention of creating a new batcave, but Naomi was too on top of her whereabouts so for the time being she had to make do with an ordinary person's computer. It took her weeks to fabricate Paxson High School in the already fabricated town of Bartleby, Montana, and even longer to flesh out Myla herself. Like Molly, Myla would be a small-town girl of little means. Unlike Molly, she'd have no aspirations of anything grander, as evidenced by her being single and pregnant at twenty-two. She inputted a C+ average on her made-up transcripts and five years of work experience at the local Dairy Queen, planting the bogus local store onto the official corporate roster. Hacking Bartleby into the satellite systems above, hence maps and GPS, would have to wait for the better machines.

She got out her cell phone, then faked a deep, raspy voice as she recorded the DQ store manager's outgoing message. She unpowered the device, hid it in a drawer, then drove into town to buy a new phone with the local Dukane area code to use as her day-to-day. She was at last ready to seek gainful employment, and any crap thing would do.

"Is there anything available where you work?" she asked her benefactor one early Tuesday evening while getting shellacked by her at Scrabble.

Naomi chuckled. "What is it you think I do?"

"I don't know. You work nights, often late. Cocktail waitress? Bartender?"

"I'm a stripper."

"No way!" Myla giggled.

"Seedy little joint on the far side of town. Is what it is but the money's okay."

"I want to see it! Take me?"

"Trust me, Myla, you don't want to do what I do."

"I didn't say I did, but I want to see one."

"You've never been to a titty bar?"

"Never."

"Hellowww, women," said Dim as he sauntered up to the picnic table in full uniform. "Just in the neighborhood. Some teenagers were smashing beer bottles out on the highway again. Got away before I could catch them. It's all right. So, what're we talking about?"

"Myla wants to come work with me at the club."

"I didn't say that. I just want to see it."

"You know, Myla, if you're ready to start work, I have two possibles that might interest you. Better than doing what she does. Oh. No offense, Naomi."

"None taken."

"So, Agatha, one of our clerks in Sheriff Billy's office, put in to retire and is going to need to be replaced. It's Sheriff Billy's decision in the end, but I could set you an interview. Or—and it don't pay as good—the hotel can always use an extra housekeeper."

Myla considered for only a moment. The chances of someone searching for Molly accidentally stumbling into this tiny hamlet for a night was highly improbable, but not out of the realm of possibility. So, no, the only thing dumber than working in a hotel would be to go work in a sheriff's office.

"Thank you, Demetrius. Can I let you know?"

"Sure. I'll take you out to see the places tomorrow so you can make a educated decision." Before Myla could object, a woman's voice sounded a dispatch from the walkie-talkie strapped to his belt. He pressed the button and spoke. "Three-niner-two, I'm on it." He turned back to Myla. "I got to take this. I'll meet you at the hotel in the morning at ten."

"But—"

"Gotta go, duty calls." He leaned over the game board, placed Myla's "s" tile on a double word score square to create "questions" and "zest" for sixty-two points, smiled, and left.

Naomi laughed, then turned to Myla. "Just be careful with him, okay?"

"What do you mean?"

"What do you mean what do I mean? You must know he's sweet on you."

"Nooo, he's not swee . . . oh my gosh, you're right, he is."

"Of course I'm right, and I'm assuming the sentiment ain't mutual. So just don't go doing anything that can lead him on. It's easy for him to jump to conclusions."

"I won't. You really care about him, don't you?"

"When I was a kid, they had to amputate my dog's leg. He learned to walk on three just fine, and he was cute and cuddly as ever, but everyone laughed at him when they saw him go. He didn't know they were laughing at him, he thought they were just being friendly. Dim doesn't know people laugh at him either, and it breaks my heart."

Definitely auntie material.

* * *

THE NIGHTCLUB WAS DARKER than she expected, but what genuinely astonished her was that it was the girls who seemed to be in control, not the men—it was the girls who exploited the fellas into showering them with dollar bills while on stage or to dazedly hand over their hard-earned twenties for one lap dance after another. If any guy dared try to alter the dynamic, dared to merely touch an unwanted hand to any unwanted part of her, one of the many André-the-Giant-sized bouncers would show up to terrify them back into submission. The men could touch only if the girls permitted, and then only for extra. It was fascinating.

She tried to imagine herself up on that stage, smiled guiltily, then imagined it some more. What must it be like to feel that kind of control? Despite her prowess at fighting, at tech, even at seduction, she always felt at the mercy of her surroundings, of someone finding her out. Always had to be so careful, always had to lie. There was an honesty to what these girls did, a perverse honesty, true, but that just somehow made doing it all the more tantalizing.

"It's not what you think," cautioned Naomi as she saw the allure on her friend's face.

"I know."

The odds of anyone looking for me showing up in this town is so remote to begin with, showing up in this one particular establishment is astronomical.

"Let's go," said Naomi.

"One sec," answered Myla, shifting her gaze from the stage to the lap dancers and back again. If Francisco knew I was considering this . . . actually, he'd encourage me to do it for the experience. Al would have a heart attack.

"Look, if you really want to work here," Naomi sighed in concession, "I can take you to the manager. He'll likely hire you on sight. Hey, you can dye your hair blonde and say you're Molly Parker. You'll make a fortune."

"That's not funny!"

"I thought it was pretty good," she chuckled. "So, what're you thinking? Yes or no?"

Holy moly, I can do this, Myla marveled inside. I can be a stripper. Me. At least till I start showing. There's no one to stop me, no one for whom I'd be embarrassed, no reason not to. I can do this.

"So?"

She smiled guiltily, then giggled, then answered as if it was obvious. "Nooo, I can't."

* * *

THE OLD VINTON HOTEL (IRONICALLY, its name at inception) was located next to the Chevron station by the highway at the town's edge, across the street from the Foodmart and the UPS Store. Myla leaned by her pickup in its little parking lot as she waited for Dim, her excuse to sidestep her first opportunity well in hand but so far nothing to talk her way out of the second.

She looked down the street, not to learn it anymore but this time to feel it, and it felt charming. Rib joints and bars, a pharmacy with an actual soda fountain, a little movie theater, farm supply shops, a toy store, clothing outlets, even a gallery displaying the works of Native American artists. Other than the Dunkin' Donuts, Burger King, Home Depot, and Sears, all were privately owned businesses, like an America of her youth.

Dim pulled up in his squad car, parked beside her, and got out. "Hey, Myla."

"Howdy, Demetrius. Shall we?"

He led her into the rustic, picturesque lodging. Dim's sister Charlene was manning the desk—she looked just like him except for the mustache. Introductions and pleasantries were exchanged, then he took her up to the second-floor bedrooms, all quaint and lovely. He demonstrated the proper way to make a bed and clean a sink, showing off in his way, then to the first-floor rooms, which were no different. He led her through the side door to a garden that boasted beautiful local plants and flowers, a few small tables, and stacked bales of hay on which hung a circular target with bows and arrows by its side.

"An archery range?" she smiled. "I didn't expect that."

"A little something extra for our guests. They never use it. It's all right. Watch this." He put a quiver to his back, picked up a bow, then shot three arrows in rapid succession, the first striking the center of the bull's eye, the other two brushing up alongside it.

"Wow, impressive. How'd you get so good?"

"I didn't have a lot of friends growing up. It's all right. Want to try?"

"Yes!" She took the bow from his hand and got into position.

"Hold the bow so the arrow's right by your mouth. Grip here, tight but not too tightly. Pull back as far as you can without it making you shake, aim, and when you're ready, let 'er rip."

She did as told. The arrow wobbled through the air, missed the bullseye, missed the target, and missed the bale of hay. "Dang, I stink," she laughed.

"It's your first time," he said encouragingly as he gave her another arrow. "Try again." Her next two shots were equally bad, but she wasn't ready to give up. "You know," Dim went on, "when you work here, you can come down and practice on your breaks any time you want."

"Yeah, about that," she gently began, "Demetrius, I just don't think all that bending and lifting would be good for me in my condition. I'm sorry."

"Oh. Um. It's all right. But you can still come and practice. It's my hotel, I get to make the rules. I can even give you teaching lessons if you want."

"Yes," she said quickly. "Absolutely yes. I'd like that very much."

"Good. You know, a lot of people don't think it to look at me, but I got skills."

He does, actually. Yes, he does. Definitely uncle material.

"Never doubted it for a moment."

He blushed, then replied, "C'mon, we got to get you over to Sheriff Billy. He's expecting you."

"He's what? Demetrius, I never said I wanted the job!"

"Why wouldn't you?" he asked as he led her back to the lot. "It's seven miles straight down Main, you can't miss it. Just follow me."

"But I—"

"Don't worry, Myla. You'll do great." He got into the squad car and drove off.

Why is this guy doing this to me?! she hollered in her head as she got into her car and followed behind. Stop meaning well, Demetrius! I just spent a month hiding from the authorities, and now I'm supposed to walk right into the belly of the beast? This is nuts!

But he's right, why wouldn't Myla want this job? She would. So, if there's no good reason for me to not want them, I just have to make them not want me. Shouldn't be too hard for a young, unwed pregnant girl with limited work experience and a C+ average.

She arrived at the building's parking lot, pulled up beside him, got out, and was all too aware of the chronic pounding in her chest as she let him lead her inside.

Calm down, girl. Breathe. No one will think you're her. They haven't yet. Molly Parker is in Chicago. It's on the news. Breathe. And smile.

The space itself wasn't terribly different from Al's old Toledo precinct back in the day, other than being one-millionth the size. Agatha, a petite senior with gray hair and blue streaks sat at the clerk's spot on the other side of the counter while Sheriff Billy, a forty-something man, tall with significant belly, hovered over her discussing a document. Myla had met both at church.

"Hey y'all," Dim began. "You remember my friend Myla. She's here for the Agatha job."

"Give her an application, would ya?" the sheriff matter-of-factly urged the clerk then turned to Dim. "You, come with me." Turned to Myla. "Be with you in a moment, darlin'."

The men went into the sheriff's office and closed the door. Billy crossed to the closed venetian blinds and made a little slit to look out. "How do you know this chick again?"

"She's my friend Naomi's cousin. She showed up in the summer for a visit but liked it here so much she decided to stay. I think she'll be terrific for us."

"Yeah, maybe, but you do know, Dim, even if I give her the job, grateful to you though she may be, she'll still never let you inside her pretty pink panties."

"Aw, Sheriff Billy, don't talk about her that way. She's my friend."

Billy grinned—always fun to grab a chuckle at the muttonhead's expense. "Well, it sure would be nice having a little eye candy around here for a change."

"Sheriff Billy, please."

Out in the bullpen, Agatha held a clipboard and pen over the counter and handed them to Myla. "You can sit right over there, dear." Myla sat where instructed and began the task at hand. "You know, I wasn't much older than you when I started here back in seventy-six," the clerk went on. "I'll never forget the date because it was the year of the bicentennial and this little town had quite the blowout."

"Must've been something."

"I've seen five different sheriffs in my tenure. Some good, some not so much. This one, he has his good days and his bad."

"Don't we all."

"But don't let him fret you none, dear. His bark is worse than his bite."

"I don't mean to be rude, ma'am, but I think I'm supposed to complete this."

"Of course. You do what you have to do, dear." Myla returned to her task, and Agatha continued. "It ain't too difficult a job. You got to know your computers, your PowerPoint, your Excel, your whatnot. A lot of answering phones and drafting reports—sheriffs are supposed to write them themselves but this one just gives you his notes, all squiggles and chicken scratch, for you to make sense of." The phone rang. Agatha clicked the proper extension and answered, "9-1-1." She waited briefly, told the caller she'd send someone right over, wheeled her chair to the radio, sent out a dispatch, waited for a deputy to respond, then turned back to Myla. "See, nothing to it."

"Yes, I do see that," Myla smiled as a new appreciation for the post began to take form. "So, you guys are on top of everything that goes on in this town, huh?"

"Every damn thing. Place'd go to hell in a handbasket if not for us clerks."

"Even if, say, hypothetically, the police in Lawton or Oklahoma City, or the FBI or something like that, had to show up here on some unrelated case, you guys would know about it before anyone?"

"Sheriff Billy may know it a smidge before us, but we'd be the ones putting it on his schedule, so yeah, first or second."

Change of plans, Myla. We want this job!

Her interview went off without a hitch, her limited knowledge of the field based on one year of law school being a tremendous asset, although she told her future employer it was due to watching too much TV as a kid. She said everything right and Sheriff Billy seemed genuinely taken with her. The next morning, he called her Montana area code phone to check her out and, surprise, surprise, the Dairy Queen manager loved her. Myla was hardworking, she gravelly told him, kind, utterly reliable and good with people, send her my love. He called her local phone moments later to offer her the position. She accepted on the spot.

Thank you, Demetrius!

CHAPTER FORTY-FOUR

THE OWNER-OPERATOR OF the storage facility from whom Molly had rented her unit listened to morning AM radio while he went through his monthly account receivables. Only two payments were delinquent. The first was over ninety days past due so he jotted himself a reminder to get the crew in to lug the unit's contents to the auction house, ka-ching. The other was only a month late for the first time in over a year. He grabbed a Xerox of the pre-written warning letter from its pile and rolled it into his typewriter carriage to copy in the tenant's address when the name blasted him in the face.

Molly Parker. That was the name of that law student who killed her boyfriend.

The owner had no reason to recall a tenant's name sixteen months after a rental agreement is signed—by month two they're only a number—but could this be the same Molly Parker?

He grabbed his bolt cutters, headed to her unit, and cracked the padlock in two. Inside were a bunch of fancy-schmancy computers with holes drilled into them—why would someone do that?—file cabinets, books, papers. He picked up one of the documents to find an outline for an essay on property law, and another completed one on civil rights with Molly's name typed on top.

Same one all right. What'd be the odds it wasn't? This was big. Sure, the machines with the holes probably didn't work, but so what? They belonged to a famous killer. How much did O.J.'s leather gloves go for? Wait, did they auction O.J.'s gloves? Well, if they didn't, they should've. Would've been a gold mine. This is a gold mine. My gold mine.

His first call was to the police because he didn't want any trouble. He was put through to the lead detective on the case and explained what he'd found. The detective said that he and his partner would be right over, then advised him not to speak of it to anyone until their investigation was complete. The owner-operator agreed.

His next call was to KTLA, the local CW affiliate. Their team arrived twenty minutes before the cops, the camera crews from MSNBC, CNN and FOX an hour after them . . . and that's how Pete found out about it.

The excited son-of-a-Nazi caught the next available flight out of LaGuardia, landed in LA the following morning, then taxied straight to the storage place. There was a line a block long because the owner-operator had opened the unit to public viewing, charging five bucks a head for a three-minute look-see. He had announced it on cable news.

After an hour, it was Pete's turn. The technology was impressive but nothing the high-priced investigator hadn't seen before, and the holes drilled into the hard drives not much surprise at all—of course she'd do that. The papers and books only told him that she was a law student, which he already knew. The only thing at all telling was the handwriting on her outline, which he recognized as hers, which, he supposed, was something.

"Is this everything she left behind?" he asked. "Did the cops take anything?"

"Nah, they just looked around and said there wasn't anything of use to them. I think they're embarrassed by the whole thing."

"But they're letting you show her stuff like this?"

"It's my unit, no crime was committed in it, and no incriminating evidence found. As long as I wait the required ninety days before I auction off her stuff, I haven't done anything wrong. I mean, she could sue me, but I don't think she's gonna."

"No," Pete chuckled. "I don't think she will either. Thanks for your time."

What a shit job this loser's got, thought Pete, then headed back to the main road to look around. Nothing telling.

C'mon, Pete, think it through, there's always something. What do you know for sure so far? She's in Santa Monica, Ubers to LAX, buys a ticket for the next flight, yet somehow manages to get back here to destroy her hard drives. Means, either she got to Chicago and flew back, which would be stupid, and she ain't stupid, or she gets someone to do it for her. No. She wouldn't risk anyone getting a look at whatever she had on those machines. So . . . so . . . so . . . she never got on that fucking plane!

He laughed. She wasn't even on it! Clever, clever lady.

Okay, now what? She does her airport shit then taxies here, pays cash, then does her computer shit. Now what? Now she's got to hightail it out of Dodge for real. How?

She Ubers to the bus station. Nope, she can't use her phone, she's supposed to be on an airplane. She probably doesn't even have it anymore. Probably killed it.

She hails a cab. He looked around. Nope, this is LA, no cabs to be hailed. She calls for one. Nope, she has no phone. Uses a pay phone. He looked around. No pay phone in sight.

She could've walked in search of one. No, she wouldn't risk being on the street that long, she could be seen. And then what, stand around and wait till the cab arrives? Nope, no cab.

She buys a car. Or steals one. Buying is complicated and takes time, and she doesn't know how much time she's got, doesn't know if her little airport trick worked, doesn't know if they're coming for her, and she's scared. Let's say she stole one, see where it goes.

Hang on. She doesn't want to be driving a stolen car. She could get pulled over just for that. Unless it's only short term, just to get her to a bus or train station where she plans to dump it. Her options are limited so, no, not the dumbest plan in the world. Keep going.

So, she dumps the car. After a couple of days, weeks, someone gets creeped out by the abandoned vehicle in front of their house, business, what have you, and calls it in. So, find out where she dumped the car, and you'll know where she went. Which means what? Which means shit for now, but not like you got anything better. Let's see where this takes us.

He got a room at a cheap motel three blocks away, booted up his tablet, poured himself a scotch, and went to work. He found the right online police blotter on his third try—gotta love the Freedom of Information Act—narrowed the scope of his search to the day the professor was killed and a five-mile radius from the storage facility. Twenty-one vehicles were reported stolen in that narrow window, four of which were retrieved.

The first on the list was found in Santa Monica. Nope. She'd know better than to return to the scene of the crime. Next.

The second was retrieved in Tarzana. He didn't know where that was. He spread out his California road map to find it seven miles west from where the car was stolen. Unlikely she'd steal a car only to dump it walking distance from her starting point. Maybe. Let's put a pin in that one.

The third was a classic T-Bird convertible stolen off Ventura Boulevard and retrieved a block away an hour later. Couple of kids on a joy ride. Nope.

Last on the list was a Corolla that had been found all the way in Palm Desert. He looked back to his road map. The 101 Freeway was only blocks from where the vehicle was taken, connect to the 10-West and straight on till morning, Palm Desert. There's my girl!

Unless it's not. Keep going.

So, she's in Palm Desert. Does she have a friend there? Is that why she picked it? No, she would've called them to come get her so she could get rid of the hot car soon as possible. A gas station along the way would've had a pay phone. So, unlikely she knew anyone. Let's assume for now she didn't.

So, she's in Palm Desert, no car, no friends. Does she hop on a bus? Maybe, but if she was willing to travel by bus, she could've done it from LA and dump the stolen car before the theft was even reported. A bus is too enclosed for her anyway, no way to run if anyone recognized her. No, no bus.

She steals another one.

No, she just dumped a hot car, she doesn't want another one. She buys one legally. With cash. Yeah, that's what I would do.

So, she goes to a dealership—nope, again, too slow, too public. She goes online to find cars for sale directly by the owner. No, she left her computers behind. Maybe she kept one with her. Maybe she bought one along the way. Doesn't matter. Someone tech savvy as her wouldn't dare risk leaving a digital footprint. No, my tech-savvy lady is going analog all the way. She gets hold of a local paper and that's how she finds her new car.

Palm Desert, here I come.

He phoned the Alamo across the street to book a Honda Civic for the following morning, went off to shoot some pool, lost a grand, then returned to his room to scope out an online escort service and ordered himself a young, pretty blonde to get him through the night.

* * *

HE WOKE UP EARLY, grabbed a quick shower, walked to pick up his car, then grabbed a McDonald's breakfast that he ate while he drove. He arrived in Palm Desert in good time, headed straight to the public library, then straight to the section where they kept stacks of old newspapers. He plucked out the one from the day Francisco was murdered, jumped to "used cars for sale by owner," and that's when he noticed the RV section.

Yes, of course she'd get one of those. She can't check in anywhere.

He found seventeen RVs for sale that day. Knowing such ads are paid by the week, he cross-referenced his findings with those listed the following Monday. Of the seventeen, six weren't re-listed. He tore out the page, headed back to his car and got on the phone.

One by one, he called the sellers, introducing himself as Special Agent Mailor of the FBI, which instantly put them on edge, which was the point, then assured them that they were in no trouble as long as they cooperated. The first said he sold his camper to a lovely African American couple. Click. The second to a tall white man. Click. The third knew that a real FBI agent would show up in person to identify himself with a badge. Click, come back later if need be. Fourth, no answer. Fifth, to an attractive young lady in her twenties.

Bingo! . . . he hoped, then told the seller that he'd like to swing by for a more in-depth chat. Joe gave the address, adding, "But don't tell the wife I called her attractive."

By the time Pete arrived, Edna had already put a pot of coffee and sponge cake on the table. He showed his badge—which was as real-looking as any fake could be—sat where they showed him to sit, took a double helping of cake, which he found to be dry and disgusting, then complimented the old bag on its savory flavor. He pulled his tablet from his briefcase and brought up a picture of Molly.

"Is this the woman who purchased your camper?"

"No," Joe shrugged. "Wait a minute. That's that girl who killed her law teacher."

"Oh my God, no, we wouldn't have sold it to her," assured Edna. "We would've called the police immediately."

"Are you sure it's not her? Look closer."

"Well . . . similar maybe, but no, the girl we sold it to had red hair."

Pete brought up photoshop and gave Molly red hair. "Like this?"

"Shorter," Joe said nervously.

"And lighter," added Edna. "More orangey, but still red."

"This?"

Joe and Edna looked to each other, turning ashen as the possibility began to dawn.

"Ours had freckles."

Bit by bit, the Eldars watched in horror as Pete magically transformed the lovely young buyer of their precious camper into the notorious Internet Rape Girl.

"Yes, I think that's her," Joe said softly.

"But we didn't know," added Edna. "How could we have known?"

"This is bad," Pete whistled gloomily. "Aiding and abetting a known fugitive. That's what you did. And at your age. You should be ashamed of yourselves. Yes, this is bad for you folks. Real bad."

"But how could we have known?" Edna repeated with tears. "The news said she was in Chicago."

"It wasn't even on the news yet," pled Joe.

"That's right, it wasn't," added Edna. "Or was it? I don't remember."

"So what you're trying to tell me is that you're too dumb to know any better?" chastised Pete. "Yeah, I can see that. Tell you what. You're probably good people, so I'll cut you a break. Help me out here all you can, and no one has to know we spoke. But don't go double-crossing me. If I don't say we spoke, you can't say we spoke. To anyone."

By the time he left, Pete had a copy of the registration, of the pink, plate numbers, VIN, pictures of the vehicle, a photoshop of Molly's new look, and her new name, Myla Callahan. It was unfortunate that the vehicle had been re-registered only weeks prior to the sale, but still, all in, a good day.

He drove back to LA to return the rental, phoning one of his ex-NYPD colleagues along the way, one of the many who owed him a substantial unpaid debt. "The registration may not be renewed for another year," he explained, "but if it's tomorrow, I want to know yesterday. If sold, I want to know. Abandoned, want to know. Any shred of anything on it, you get it to me ASAP."

"And then we're even?"

"And then we're even."

"Done."

"I'll email you the RV stats when I get back to the hotel." Click, and he smiled.

The moment she registers that vehicle, I got her. If she sells it, I'll find her. Abandons it, I'll track her. No matter what she does from here on out, that bitch is mine.

He arrived in LA early that evening, poured himself a scotch, emailed his colleague, booked his flight home for the following morning, then went online and ordered himself a young, pretty redhead to get him through the night.

CHAPTER FORTY-FIVE

The Dwelling
Not Long After The "Test"

MELLOW WAITED FOR HER husband by the tunnel opening with flowers in hand, presumably to commend him on a prosperous day at the hunt, which he would interpret as more of her pleading on behalf of Daughter-of-Love, but really to find out what happened re Sunburst and Son-of-Stone. The outcome of their conversation had consumed her all morn, for despite her parting words to the hunter, she knew it could go either way. He was a good man who'd do anything to save his daughter; he was a good man who'd do anything to stay true to his gods. The suspense was slaying her.

The men at last began to trickle in, laughing and cajoling as they transported rotund dead mammals hanging from bound-together-spears that rested on their shoulders, or plump furry rodents they held by the ears in their hands. Near the middle of the queue entered Son-of-Stone. He beamed with a pride as he carried the front end of a spear-bundle from which hung a grizzly. Good sign to the very! Carrying the other end was Sunburst, his face blank and cold.

She caught his attention and he woefully rocked his head. Her mouth gaped open in a sadness. How could you?! screamed her eyes. He looked to the ground for he couldn't face her. End of conversation.

She spent the rest of the day racking her mind as to what man of the Community she could sway to claim Daughter-of-Love in the stead of her husband. Although she could think of many who would thrill to have the bubbly little waif as wife, she couldn't think a soul who'd dare to challenge Thunder. Sandy was right about that.

But what made matters even worse was that this was the day, of all days, that Daughter-of-Love bled herself into womanhood. She would be betrothed in the eve, wed by the morrow, her fate sealed forever, and Mellow was all out of ideas.

* * *

IT WAS the twenty-third day of the moonth of thought in the calendar of the god of stars, and all but the Sorry, his Two, and the Holy One were seated round the fires as they waited for the night's Gathering to begin. With great pomp and theater, the three leaders arrived to take their spots. Sandy glanced to Mellow with a look that asked if there was anything he should know about, i.e., did she work some nefarious magic re Son-of-Stone? She shook her head with a sadness. He looked back at her with a knowing shrug—things are what they are—then he turned to the throngs to start the service.

For the most part, it proceeded in the same dullish manner as most—updates on where to relieve bladders, squabbling over cabins, Sandy's re-telling of how their ancestors discovered their perfect Dwelling under the Sorryship of a mighty warrior named George Washington—yet underlying it all was the anticipation re Daughter-of-Love. What will she be named? To whom shall she be wed? The most exciting stuff was always saved for last.

The only variant of the service was that a young man named Forest and his best chum Son-of-Cat had completed the song that praised Thunder for ending the drought. With Son-of-Cat on whistle-bone, another chum named Son-of-Stumpy on drums, and Forest on

371

lead vocals, they hymned out the ditty to the enjoyment of all. Twas a fun little tune, fast-paced and audacious, the lyrics to the verses a tad complex but the chorus simple and easy to grasp so that all who heard it could hymn along.

> *The greatness of Thunder*
> *This hymn is about*
> *Glory to Thunder*
> *For he ended our drought*
> *Na na na ding dang dong.*

And repeat. It was so catchy even Thunder himself joined in. When it ended, all laughed and banged rocks against other rocks in approval until the quiet returned.

Next and with big smile, the Sorry trumpeted the glorious news that the gods had blessed them with a new woman, a new moma-to-be. Most were already aware for word of such things spreads fast in a Community of these numbers, but the Sorry's declaration made it official. With that, Thunder opened the flooring to suggestion, and the naming process began.

Many great nouns and adjectives were bandied about but not a one felt just right. One young hunter who knew the girl well suggested "Precocious," and even though everyone agreed it fit her personality to a tee, they also agreed the sound failed to roll off the tongue with comfort. Her own pupa suggested "Bubbly," which everyone agreed suited even better than "Precocious," rolled off the tongue just fine; but "Bubbly" was a derivative of "bubbles" which was a thing found in nature and therefore too masculine for a woman. And on it went until the First Moma—the only woman allowed to speak freely at a Gathering—softly uttered "Whimsy." All suggestions ceased, and all beamed their approval.

The final decision rested with the Sorry alone, course, but it was custom to attempt unanimity. It was almost always found—only when the process took too long and everyone grew bored did the Sorry pull his ranking. "We seem to have found consensus,"

Thunder boasted. "Is there a soul amongst us who objects to our new woman being henceforth labelled Whimsy?" No one said a word, but their grins said it all. "And you, Daughter-of-Love, do you find peace and contentment with this new moniker?"

"I love it like a madness!" she blurted, and everyone laughed, for what a Whimsy thing to say.

"Then henceforth you shall be known to us all as Whimsy. Done, and decided." He turned to the First Moma and nodded.

Mellow rose, held out her open palms, and said, "Come." Whimsy stood, crossed to her and took her hands. "I am Mellow. First wife to the Sorry, First Moma of the Community, moma to all she's, and moma twice to she's without moma. Kneel before your Sorry, young Whimsy, kiss his feet, and I will prompt you of what to say." Whimsy did as told and Mellow continued. "You are my Sorry, and may the gods take pity on my Sorry."

"You are my Sorry, and may the gods take pity on my Sorry."

"I vow to the gods to live my life by the ways of my Community, to serve the whims and desires of its men with energy and humility, only my Sorry's wishes will supersede theirs, and only my husband's his." Whimsy repeated.

Thunder smiled, took her hands, and helped her to her feet. He kissed her on both cheeks, then her lips, passed her back to Mellow, and sat.

Mellow put her hands on the new woman's shoulders. "You are woman now, my daughter," she said, "with all the rights and hardships of the she's of our Community."

Everyone cheered and banged rocks against other rocks in applause.

"And now you must—" Mellow paused because it was too painful to say. "Now you must—" She cleared her throat as if twas the reason for her hesitation, took a deep breath and forced herself to fulfill the First Moma's duty. "And now you must wed. Who amongst you wish Whimsy to live under your protection, as moma to your children?"

"That would be me!" Thunder bellowed merrily. "I have developed quite the affection for my little wet one these past moonths; and I have always respected her pupa, a mighty warrior and hunter exemplary. T'would be privilege for me to join us together in family."

"Yippee!" shouted Whimsy.

A tortuous fire burned within Sunburst's soul as he cursed himself for his failing to protect, but was then struck with a bolt of inspiration. Divine inspiration, it had to be! Yes, he had passed the gods' test after all, and they weren't going to punish him for it.

"The claim has been made," began the Holy One, "and the claim is—"

"I issue challenge!" asserted Sunburst. "I wish to keep Whimsy as my own."

There was an audible gasp among the throngs. Mellow did her best to conceal the ear-to-ear grin she felt inside her as she looked to Sunburst approvingly, screaming "Yippee! Yippee!" in her head. Sunburst nodded back briefly then turned away—he wasn't doing this for her.

"Sunburst, this is folly," said the Sorry. "She's your daughter."

"And I wish her to be my wife as well."

"But pupa, I wish to be—"

"Hush, daughter! Be you adult or child, tis not a female's place to speak here!"

Leaf turned to the Holy One. "Can he do this?"

"Whether he can or he can't," chimed Sunburst, "he is."

"Yes, tis been done before," said Sandy, "Tis chronicled deep in our lore. But take heed, Sunburst, much more than half such unions produce child with broken."

"Twill be no issue for there will be no children. Whimsy will live in my cabin to tend me as she has done, and that will be all that my new wife will do for me."

Whimsy leaned forward and whispered beggingly in his ear. "But pupa, please! I want to be moma someday."

"Shhh, child," he whispered back with a gentle, "when Son-of-Stone gains status, I will gift you to him as reward." Then he shouted, "Now sit, woman! Speak only when spoken at!"

"Sunburst, dear chum," Thunder began, "I don't wish to combat against you."

"Boon. I wish it neither. Withdraw your claim."

"You wish me to cower to you?"

"I would never use such a word at you, Thunder. I prefer 'withdraw.'"

"'Tis but 'cower' with a politic spin. I will do not one nor the other."

"Then combat we must."

Leaf piped in. "Sunburst, is slaying the Sorry your way to attain the esteemed position? Because there are better, other—"

"I have no desire of the Sorry's cabin, my Two, and no desire to slay him, but if slay him I must and fall he does, I will put the position open for a combat in which I won't participate."

"Don't do this, Sunburst," Thunder cautioned. "I implore you, don't."

"You don't."

"Then so be it," sighed the Sorry. "A challenge for fair Whimsy's hand has been challenged, and the challenge accepted. The combat will be held in light of day aft the morrow's luncheon.

"The Gathering is shut."

* * *

IT WAS PERFECT, thought Mellow as she made her way through the woods in the dead of night. Lemons-to-lemonade perfect!

She couldn't foresee who would be victorious between Thunder and Sunburst, no one could, for although Thunder was musclebound and ferocious, Sunburst was muscle-defined and intense. Thunder may have the edge on brute strength, but Sunburst had it for quickness. Thunder didn't relish'n'mustard to combat Sunburst and would be fighting only for his ego, which albeit was huge, but Sunburst would be fighting for the safeguard of his daughter, which was huger. No, twas an absolute odds-even guess who would victor, unless one of them had a little extra help, and Mellow had no reservations about pitching in.

She arrived at the patch of jimsonweed that she'd spotted so many calendars ago, sat down on the soil, and began to dig. She giggled over the psychedelic nightmare her husband would undergo after she spiked his morrow's luncheon, the delusions, the psychosis, the paranoia. Sunburst would appear to him as a demon with horns or tail, or a fiery pillar of flame, or, or, or—she couldn't know the exact hallucinations beloved hubby would envision, only that they'll be terrifying to him; that they'll make him drop to his knees and weep for mercy like a little baby girl; and men and women all will see their brave Sorry nothing but a pitiable coward. After that, he could be Sorry no longer. It was perfect.

A truth, Sunburst was too good a man to take the life of one as feeble as Thunder would appear, but twas better that way. She wanted the honor of slaying the beast herself.

She'd wait but a week so he could endure the full humiliation of having his position taken from him, and only aft he'd been properly disgraced and shamed into the lore would she add a far heftier portion of the weed to his break-fast. By the time Daughter-of-Playful-1 was by the lake bathing Daughter-of-Playful-2, he'd be retching up all that was within his belly, and then blood when there was no food left to retch. Blood will spew from out his mouth, from his nose, his ears, his ass.

"Playful, fetch the Holy One! Leave the baby in the pen! Go!" she'd shout at her sister, the final witness, so she could be alone with him by his bedside to boast that twas she who had bested him, she who had brought forth his torture and embarrassments. She'd make sure he knew his life was at its end and that it was she who had slayed him, then she'd laugh and laugh at the agony on his face while he took his last breath.

Her purpose for this lifetime will be complete, young Whimsy saved, Kindness and 3 avenged. It was perfect. Lemons-to-lemonade perfect!

* * *

THUNDER STAYED home from the hunt that morn, as did Sunburst, for both men had deemed it prudent to prepare body and brain for the combat to come. Mellow had already crushed the jimsonweed seeds into a fine powder the night before and kept it hidden in a little clay cup in the hollow of a log by the outdoor firepit. Fortuitously, it was her turn to take the cooking lead on this day, Playful being charged with the after-clean.

She prepared the grizzly and pussy-fish stew that she over-seasoned with pepper and oregano to overwhelm the bitter taste of the drug, dished four hefty portions into four bowls, a smaller one for Daughter-of-Playful-2—Daughter-of-Playful-3 being still at suckling age—and then doused the largest helping with the perfectly correct dosage of the powder—she wanted to muddle Thunder not slay him—well, not slay him just yet. The eight-moonth-with-child woman placed the bowls at their proper spots at the picnic table, took a moment to arch and rub her sore lower back, then hollered, "Tis ready! The luncheon is served!"

One by one, the family came to the table, took their seats and proceeded to dig in . . . all but Thunder who merely swished his spoon round and round in the bowl, brought a spoonful to his lips, then returned it to the bowl to swish it round some more.

"Is my luncheon not to your liking, husband?" Mellow asked.

"No, tis not that," he responded as he swished on, his mind elsewhere. "I'm certain tis a fine. It's just . . . something about my brain isn't proper for a before-combat. My heart and belly not brimming with hatred and contempt."

"You're just hungry," she said maternally. "Eat."

"He's a grown man, Mellow," said Playful. "If he says he's not hungry, he's not."

"He didn't say he wasn't hungry. He said his brain wasn't proper for a before-combat." She turned to Thunder. "You were like this the morn of the Holy Usurp, too, but Kindness urged you to eat and so you ate and found your contempt."

"I don't recall that."

"I recall it well. I was so fearful for you, my love, but then you did as Kindness bid and you became again the angry, mighty warrior we all love and fear. Twas when I knew that glorious victory was ours."

(Daughter-of-Playful-1, who was also daughter of Clearsky, cringed a little by the comment, conjured many a cutting rebuke in her brain, but kept her imaginings inside for twas not a child's place to speak at the meal table unless first spoken at.)

"Thunder, my joy-of-joy, if you feel no hunger don't eat," insisted Playful. "Perhaps tis the gods telling you something. Don't listen to *her* just because of some mis-memory she has."

"No, no, perhaps she's right," he sighed as he filled his spoon and brought it to his lips once more, then paused again. "You know what it is?" he asked rhetorically. "I respect Sunburst. Never before have I face-to-faced with one I respect. I loathed Clearsky when I combatted him, loathed Clearsky when I destroyed his son." (Daughter-of-Playful-1 cringed yet again, and yet again kept her sarcasms inside.) "I loathed every single one of those heathen others I slayed in war as a young man or manling. Each and every one." He opened his mouth to swallow, then stopped afresh. "You mustn't speak of what I say next for I have yet to broach it to Leaf, but I've been considering to make Sunburst my Two in matters military. Leaf will remain Two in governance and politic, but still he'll be crest-fallen to learn of this, crestfallen even more to learn that I broached the topic to my wives and daughters before him."

"Eat, my Thunder, you'll feel better."

"Yes, eat," he conceded, looked at the stew on the spoon but an inch from his mouth, and again returned it to bowl. "No. I must fill the brain with fury so that the body will follow." He stood. "I must find the things to despise in this new enemy." He headed into the cabin.

Mellow grabbed his bowl and raced after him. "Thunder! Just a swallow or two! Tis good for your—"

"Will you leave him be!" admonished Playful who jumped in to block the with-child woman. "He has important combat on the approach. He knows what's best for himself."

"Move!" insisted Mellow as she shoved Playful away with her free arm.

"No!" countered Playful in resistance, causing the bowl to drop from Mellow's hands to the stone flooring to crack apart. "Tis now a point of moot," Playful added matter-of-factly, then turned and headed indoor. "Husband! Don't leave without me granting you kiss for good fortune!"

"Me too!" Mellow shouted quickly. With no better idea—and making certain 1 and 2 held no eyes upon her—she retrieved the cup of the remaining powder, splashed in a touch of water and poured it into her mouth without swallowing. She raced into the cabin where Thunder and Playful kissed, peeled her sister away with force, wrapped her arms around her husband and smooched him passionately, tonguing the liquid from her mouth into his.

Thunder shoved his palms into her shoulders with such a strength that it sent her reeling to the ground, then spit out the poison. "There's an astringent sickness to your saliva today, Mellow," he told her. "You should have the Holy One give you something for it. Bleh."

He left. Playful glanced a winning glance, then returned to the backyard to lead her daughters in the after-clean. Mellow slumped her head in defeat. Sunburst was on his own.

* * *

"A CHALLENGE for fair Whimsy's hand has been challenged," said the Sorry as he knelt on one knee under the gray and gloomy after-luncheon sky, his open palm outstretched to his adversary who knelt on knee too with open palm shown back, "and the challenge accepted."

"Victor or loser," proclaimed the young Holy One, "may the gods render pity on you both for we are all, us all, but the gods' mistake. Begin."

The fighters rose. True to form, Thunder hunched forward while he circled round his enemy to render himself a low center of gravity, his arms dangling in front of him like a bear. Conversely, Sunburst stood upright like a man, leaning in but only a tad, bopping and weaving on quick feet, his right arm forward with a slight bend at the elbow, his left bent in to guard the torso. The men, women, manlings, and children watched on with excited anticipation as the men passed colorful stones, jigsaws, and other precious doodads in wager. Mellow watched on with no emotion visible to anyone while dying inside.

For no apparent reason, Thunder briefly took his eyes off his opponent to gravely look toward the tunnel opening in the distance. Sunburst glanced quickly behind him to see the what of it, and then Thunder charged!

But Sunburst had assumed it trick in advance and played into it with purpose. He bopped out of the charge's way then delivered a powerful blow to his rival's lower back kidney. Thunder jolted up with a roar, then turned round to deliver a mighty left hook. Sunburst ducked, popped up with a quick right jab to Thunder's nose, followed with a mighty left hook, then backed off before the Sorry's next swing could even reach him.

"You think the gods are going to help you, Sunburst?" Thunder demanded. "Think they'd ever put you above me?" Sunburst said nothing as he continued his bop and weave. "They put no one above me! Clearsky learned that the hard way!" Sunburst moved in like a blink. Jab to the eye, punch to the gut. Thunder swung, but Sunburst dodged, uppercut to the chin, and backed away. The Sorry glowered as he spit blood, the pain clearly smarting, the losing smarting even more. "Think you'll gain victory with these love taps?" Still, Sunburst said nothing. "Answer me!" Sunburst didn't even smile.

Bolts of lightning suddenly flashed. Booming thunders suddenly roared. The rains poured down like dogs and cats, but no one was about to go anywhere.

Thunder charged again, this time with a terrifying war-scream. Sunburst made a quick step back, thrust his hands upon Thunder's shoulders behind the neck, then used the force of his enemy's own motion to fell him to the ground face first into a newly formed puddle of mud. He patiently watched as Thunder slowly began to rise then offered a kick to his anointed leader's head to send him face down into the muck once more.

"Withdraw your claim, Thunder," Sunburst panted as he bounced, "and we'll call it a draw."

"Never," grunted the Sorry as he pulled himself to his feet, Sunburst allowing it for he was too smart to deliver a kick he knew his adversary now expected.

Thunder moved toward him slowly, menacingly, sloppily, and swung. Sunburst parried with easy pivot and returned another jab to the face, hook to the left, cross to the gut, hook from the right. Thunder stepped back with each hit, too punch-drunk to anymore thrust a swing, his eyes so covered with rain and sludge that he could barely see. Jab, hook, jab.

"Withdraw your claim, Thunder," Sunburst repeated, "and we'll call it a draw." Now it was Thunder who didn't speak. Jab, hook, strike, jab. "Withdraw your claim, Thunder, and we'll call it a draw." Hook, cross, jab, jab. "No? Nothing, my Sorry? Then tis time for me to end this!"

With the Sorry's arms drooping wearily by his side, Sunburst wound up for the final crushing blow but momentarily lost his footing in the mud. Thunder intuitively felt the pause and leapt, wrapping his arms round his enemy's ribcage mid-air as the two crashed to the ground with a splash. A single belt to Sunburst's jaw gave the Sorry just enough moment to plant knees upon shoulders, pinning the hunter helpless. Sunburst writhed and flailed to free himself, but his opponent's mass was too great.

"Withdraw your challenge, Sunburst, and we'll call it your defeat."

Sunburst raised his legs to wrap around Thunder's neck, but the Sorry had seen that trick before. He caught hold of each ankle with his hands and then bit hard into the calves, one aft the other. Sunburst screamed, and his legs fell back to the soppy ground.

"Tap out, Sunburst."

"I will never consent you my daughter's hand," he panted. "I won't!"

Thunder smeared a handful of mud onto Sunburst's face, and then deep into his mouth. "You need not give it for I've already taken it. Now, tap out." He wrapped his hands around the hunter's neck and pressed his thumbs into his throat. "I have no desire to slay the pupa of my bride on the aft of my wedding to her, kind sirree. Tap out!"

"Fuckety-fuck to you," he gurgled.

"I don't wish to slay you, Sunburst, please don't make me do so," the Sorry said even as he choked on him harder. "I sought to honor you. Tap out, you dunce!"

"Withdraw your claim or slay me."

"Then so be it."

"Noooo!" screamed Whimsy who shoved her way through the crowd and dropped to her knees by her pupa's side. "Don't be slain, pupa! Don't die! Just consent as he says!"

"Listen to your daughter, Sunburst. Listen to my lovely wife-to-be. Tap out."

Sunburst could feel little Whimsy's hand in his, and he turned to her with mud and tears. "You don't know what awaits you, my Daughter-of-Love."

"Even so, whatever bad may await me, twill only be worse if my pupa doesn't live on."

"Give us your blessing, my pupa-to-be. You will be honored for it. I vow it so. Tap out!"

"I know you think you're doing this for my boon, Pupa, but what boon can come of it if I have you no longer? Please! Don't leave me! DON'T LEAVE ME!!!!!"

Sunburst sighed, slowly raised his arm. "I want none of your honors, Thunder. Not a one." Then he patted his adversary's back three times to officially accept the marriage.

"Praise," panted Thunder. He rose and looked out upon his people. "Tis done. She's mine."

Mellow closed her eyes tight, keeping in all her sad. Can't this man ever lose?

* * *

SHE HAD SPENT SO many lifetimes concealing truths, but the feigning of good cheer at Whimsy and Thunder's wedding was amongst the most difficult. She stayed at the honkytonk that followed only as long as was considered minimum-proper for a First Moma, kissed bride and groom to commend them on their good fortune, excused herself to her bedchamber on the auspices of a tired due to with-child, then kicked herself mercilessly for being too dunce-ish to conjure a way to save the girl. She racked her mind over and over as to what she could've done that she didn't do or what she did do that she shouldn't have, as if the finding of it would make any difference. She paused to realize that if she came up with the perfect plan now that it was too late, she'd only loathe herself all the more, and then she proceeded on with the trying anyway.

She heard them enter the front door. She could tell that Thunder was carrying his new bride into the cabin as he had done with her six calendars prior, could hear his sweet words to her as they moved into his bedchamber, could hear Whimsy drunkenly swooning from said words, and then it began.

Bam! Bash! Pow! Whimsy's screamings of confusion bled through the walls, then her beggings for mercy, then her weepings from torment, and all Mellow could do was bite down on her pillow and try not to visualize. On and on it went until Whimsy's hollers ceased to sudden silence, and that was the scariest sound of all.

"Please, gods," Mellow prayed with all her heart to the deities she knew to not exist as Thunder's grunts and groans haunted her ears. "Let her live, oh gods. Let my little chum come out of this whole. I beg you each alone and all together both! Please! Let her come out whole!"

At last, Thunder let out his orgasmic roar and then there was a stillness, utter and complete, then footsteps, then a pounding upon her door. She opened it to find him holding little Whimsy in his arms, bloody, puffy, limp and unconscious. "Follow me to her bedchamber so you can tend to her," he commanded. He moved off, and she followed. "Playful!" he shouted. "Go fetch the Holy One! My little wet one has slipped on a soap and fallen!"

The next day at the morn hunt, to the surprise of most, Son-of-Stone came of age when he slung his stone strong and true into the chest of a flying eagle to make his first slay without fluke or fortuity.

The new man was named Dachshund Dog at that night's Gathering in line with his passion for the critter as well as the similarity of characteristic that he had with it.

He was but two days too late to save his true love from her wretched destiny, but it may as well have been calendars. Sometimes the gods can be pricks.

CHAPTER FORTY-SIX

As the months rolled on, Myla grew ever more comfortable in Myla's skin. She liked her, that is to say, on a moment-to-moment basis—at times it was a tad difficult contending with the woman's never-ending hypocrisy. A devout Christian lady, young, pregnant, and unmarried; an outspoken homophobe whose last committed relationship was with a girl; a proud staffer of the justice system wanted for murder.

That aside, she liked her, liked the town, liked her friends, liked her doctor. Given everything, things could have turned out a lot worse.

Her archery skills were slowly improving too. She rarely missed the bales of hay anymore and often hit the target itself, albeit at the outer rims. Demetrius was a fine teacher.

But the best part of all was that the search for Molly Parker had died down to a virtual nothing. With everything going on in the world, news outlets simply had no room for a young, lesbian murderess whose story had run out of steam. True, there was no telling what was going on with those she really had to worry about, but if they hadn't figured out where she was by now, it was unlikely they ever would. The more time that passed, the safer she knew herself to be.

Sheriff Billy was in another one of his moods that morning as rumors of his marital problems continued to circulate. The electricity in the office had been on the fritz for a few days, blinking in and out, intermittently shutting down the lights and phone system, often crashing their computers. The sheriff and deputies (sans Dim) took turns trying to repair it on their own, competing as to which of the macho men was the macho-est, until Sheriff Billy chose to take his lack of expertise out on her.

"When's that dang electrician supposed to get here anyway?"

"He's not. You said you were going to fix it yourself."

"Just phone him already! Jesus Christ!"

"Yes sir, boss, right away."

"And what's this crap supposed to mean?" he scolded as he looked over his clipboard. "'Chest tag correction'? What the heck is that?"

"Oh, that, no biggie. Deputy Vinton's name tag had a little typo so I went ahead and got it straightened out."

"That's not your call, stupid. Anything regarding budget is my call, not yours."

"Sorry, boss." She didn't let him see her smiling inside. "Won't happen again. Promise."

"Just get the dang electrician in here. And have those goddamn babies already. Jesus Christ, your jumpin' hormones are driving me batty!" He went into his office and slammed the door.

Without knowing the electrician's actual name, she flipped through Agatha's old rolodex and found it under "e" for "electrician." She'd been getting the hang of the place.

She was at her seat by the front counter, visible to the other side from the chest up only, when he walked in shortly after lunch. He was the first man she'd seen since her arrival who wasn't overweight because of bad eating or skinny as a toothpick due to drug addiction. He had broad shoulders, a square jaw, a sunny smile, and a pleasant, easygoing way about him. "You must be new-Agatha," was how he greeted her. "Jack Quinn, electrician at large."

"Nice to meet you, Jack Quinn. I'm Myla."

"'Myla.' Rolls off the tongue way nicer than 'new-Agatha.' I'll go with that. So, Myla, sounds like your wires got a little corroded. Where do you want me to start?"

She laughed a little laugh. "How would I know?"

"Right, right, I'm the expert, I keep forgetting that. So, I'm guessing . . . the wires?"

"Sounds like a plan."

"Let's find out if it's a good one," he said as he sauntered over to the breaker box. "You know, I get paid extra if I don't burn the place down."

"Better than the other way around, I suppose."

His turn to laugh a little laugh. He opened the box, examined in silence for a few moments, then closed it. "I have to check outside. Will you still be here when I get back?"

"I don't know. Depends when you get back."

"Then I'm not leaving."

"That's one way to not burn the place down."

He looked at her and smiled, charmed. She smiled back, touché.

And so it went for the next three days, Jack moving from one area of the building to the next, trucking away for parts and then returning, he and Myla both reveling in their lighthearted repartee whenever proximity allowed, and Myla couldn't get enough of it.

"So, Dim tells me he was the one who got you this job," he said out of nowhere late one afternoon, the faulty wiring mended, packing up to go. "Are you guys a thing?"

"No, Demetrius is a dear friend. Been a great help to me since I got here, but a friend."

"Good. I've known the guy since grade school and love him like a brother. He had it hard growing up—lot of jerks in this town—but not by me, and I'd never muscle in on his girl."

"Neither would I."

His turn to laugh a little laugh. "So, what kind of food do you like?"

"Aren't you supposed to ask me to dinner first?"

"Not a chance, then you could say no. What am I, an idiot? So, favorite food?"

"Um, let's say, Chinese."

"Yeah, I like Chinese too. We don't have that here. What's your next favorite?"

"Say . . . Italian."

"Yeah, I sure could go for a good linguini right about now. We don't have that either."

"Well, what do you have?"

"We have amazing, out of this world barbecue, and . . . pretty good barbecue."

"Then I'll go with barbecue."

"That'd be my choice too," he said as he snapped shut his tool chest. "I'll pick you up at your place Saturday at eight."

"You still haven't asked me out."

"No, I haven't," he smiled as he started off. "Try to get my check sent out quickly because this whole place could blow any minute."

Her turn to laugh a little laugh.

Daddy material?

Don't get ahead of yourself, girl.

"Jack, wait up. There's something you should know about me."

He made an abrupt halt in the doorway and turned to her. "Please don't tell me you have a dick."

She laughed heartily on that one then stood, revealing her whopping belly to him for the first time. "I honestly don't know what I have in here, just that there's two of 'em."

"Oh. Um, oh. Um, yeah, um, oh . . . So, um, listen, about Saturday . . ."

"I know."

"I'm kind of an asshole, aren't I?"

"Little bit, yeah."

* * *

THEY'LL HAVE a good aunt and a good uncle, Myla reminded herself as she drove home that evening. They'll make friends of their own, and I'll make more. They'll be fine. A daddy would be nice but by no means necessary. They'll have a family. I'll see to it. They'll be fine.

She was about to turn onto the dirt road by the *How to Train Your Dragon* billboard when a terrifying image caught her eye. At some point during the day, they had swapped out the old movie ad for the next one, a star-studded little picture entitled *Molly Parker*.

"Oh for Pete's sake!" she shouted to no one as she pulled over to read the particulars. "You've got to be kidding me."

The film starred Jennifer Lawrence as Molly, Antonio Banderas as Francisco, a previously unknown African American bodybuilder named Latisha Johnson as Janine, and produced, ironically or not, by Audrey's father. (All would go on to receive Oscar nominations, young Miss Johnson being the only one to bring the statue home.)

"Let it go already, will ya?!" she shouted at the sign. "I mean, Jeez Louise!" She put the pickup back into gear when she spotted the broken glass and beer bottles that littered the road. "Dang teenagers." She avoided the glistening shards and drove into the park.

* * *

SATURDAY BREAKFAST BARBECUES with Naomi had become a weekly tradition by then. Sometimes Dim would join them, sometimes not; never would he cook. The meal had to be moved indoors that particular morning due to heavy rains, and the women were wrapping up another of their post-cleanup Scrabble games, which had also become part of the ritual. Naomi laid down the last of her four tiles to make "r-o-u-t-e," acquiring the points of Myla's unused "j," "u," and "c" to win the match with a monster four-hundred-and-fifty-point score.

"Had enough?" she taunted with a smile.

"Not even close," Myla defiantly smiled back.

"You must be some kind of glutton for punishment."

"I'm improving."

"Not by a lot," Naomi chuckled.

They proceeded to set the board for the next match as Myla happened to glance upon the photographs of the young boy that were scattered about, then decided to broach the topic of which she'd been so curious all these months. "Can I ask you a question?" she asked tentatively.

"Of course," Naomi replied with a sudden empathy. "I was just giving you your space till you're ready. I didn't want to press. We all respond differently to that shit. What would you like to know?"

"I was just wondering . . . is that boy your son?"

"Oh, that question." The expression on the woman's face shifted quickly to something sad and dark. "Pride and joy," she solemnly replied.

"Where is he?"

"Let it go, okay?" She held out the little silver bag for Myla to choose new tiles.

"Sorry."

Naomi took her own tiles, placed them on her block, swapped them around to try to find a word, then turned back to Myla. "He's in Oklahoma City. With my grandparents."

"Do you ever see him?"

"Just play, okay? You can go first."

"Sorry again." She placed down "l-i-l-a-c" for a meager fourteen points.

"His name's Lorne," said Naomi. "He's thirteen. Handsome boy, ain't he? Grandpa won't let me see him."

"What?"

"He doesn't approve of some of my life choices."

"He can't do that."

"Well, he's doing it."

"No. You're the mother. You have rights. Your job is not illegal, and you have legal rights. We have to get you a lawyer."

"I can't afford one. Now play."

"But you can find—"

"Enough! You wanted to know the story, now you know the story. Just play."

"It's your turn."

"Then I'll play," she huffed as she shifted her attention back to her letters.

The poor woman, thought Myla. Someone ought to help her . . . and I will.

* * *

IT WOULD TAKE Myla a little longer than intended to set her plan into motion because that night, the heavy rains having yet to subside, was the night she felt her first pang of labor. The arrangement had always been for Naomi to take her to the hospital unless she was at work, in which case Chester would do it—Dim not part of the equation only because the lawman had the same shift hours as the stripper.

Naomi was at the club and Chester wasn't answering his phone, so she walked through the pummeling showers to the trailer park office only to find the curmudgeon passed out drunk. She knew it unlikely for Naomi to have her phone on her person at that moment but called her for help anyway, left a voicemail, then texted. She knew Dim was on duty but called and texted him too. She waited a few minutes as the next contraction came and went, and it hurt bad.

If you're going to have to drive yourself, she told herself, better get to it now.

She made her way back through the storm but had to pause as the next contraction came, more intense than the one before, then she got into her truck. She powered through the next spasm, more intense still, as she rolled onto the highway. The next one had her slam on the brakes right in the middle of the road for fear of driving with eyes closed.

I can't do this, she told herself.

No, you have to do this! she countered back. You are not about to have these babies in a pickup truck! No way, José!

She put the car back in gear when the phone rang. She answered without hello. "Demetrius! It's time! I'm in labor! Naomi's at the club and Chester's out cold! I tried to drive but—" The next attack had her interrupt herself with a loud, drawn-out grunt.

"Shh. Don't worry. I'm on my way. Where are you?" She told him. "I'm on the opposite side of town but I'm on my way. Won't be long. Did you call Dr. Ruddick?"

"I forgot. Dang!"

"Don't worry. I'll take care of it. Just sit tight. I'm on my way."

By the time he arrived, the contractions were coming only minutes apart. He opened her door and helped her to his squad car.

"I don't think I'm going to make it!"

"Yes you will. Shh. I'm here for you, Myla. I'll always be here for you. But this time I'm blasting the siren and flashing the spinny lights whether you like it or not."

"Please!"

He made sure she was well fastened in and then tore off. He drove less than an eighth of a mile before running over a broken beer bottle and blew out his left front tire. The car spun on the wet pavement in uncontrollable circles until he could bring it to a stop. He calculated quickly which would be faster—change the tire or walk back to get her Dodge?

"Wait here. We'll take your truck."

"No!" she groaned. "It's too late! It's happening! Oh, holy moly, it's happening!"

"Don't panic. I'll deliver 'em." He grabbed his radio transmitter, called for an ambulance, then turned to her. "Lie back."

"Do you know what you're doing?!" she shouted. "Have you ever done this before?!"

"Not myself, no, but they taught me it before I got deputized. I passed the test and everything."

"Oh God."

"It's all right," he said. "Besides, you're the one who'll be the one doing all the hard work."

"Is that a joke?!"

"Uh-huh."

"It's not funny! Oh shoot, it hurts!"

"I see a head. Oh my God! I see the top of a head! It's beautiful! Push!"

"I can't! I'm scared! Not here!"

"Yes, here, Myla. Right here! Push! You have to push! It said so in the manual!"

And so she pushed, and she screamed and she yelled, the faint sound of the ambulance's sirens approaching from the distance being utterly irrelevant. There was no way they would arrive in time.

And so it came to pass that on a stormy, rainy night on a lonely, dark highway, a *Molly Parker* billboard looming large above them, Demetrius "Dim" Vinton helped Myla Callahan bring babies Lori and Francine into our world.

CHAPTER FORTY-SEVEN

MELLOW HAD SPENT THE night by Whimsy's bedside, forcing herself to stay awake in order to dab the cold, wet moss upon the new woman's burny face and forehead. She left the chamber only when her with-child'cy demanded that she go make pee, then returned to continue the dabbing and stressing. It wasn't till almost the luncheon when the little one began to stir awake, and Mellow breathed out a relief.

"Welcome back, my dearest chum," she smiled warmly.

It took Whimsy a moment to find her bearings, then looked at Mellow with an arctic glare. "You knew," she faulted. "You knew what he'd do to me, and you never warned me."

Mellow looked to the floor. "Yes."

"And my pupa? He knew as well?" Mellow nodded. "Then I hate you both," sombered the new woman as she rolled onto her side to give Mellow her back.

"Whimsy, your pupa went to comba—"

"Don't call me Whimsy. All the whimsy has been thrashed out of me and I'll never be whimsical again. I'll remain Daughter-of-Love till the end of my days because Love, my moma, my real moma, would've prepared me for this."

"We're not permitted to—"

"Just go. If I need tending, send Playful. She's not my chum either but at least with her I know my standing. You, you're nothing but a phony."

"Daughter-of-Love, I—"

"Go!!!"

The last thing Mellow wanted was for the girl to over-emote herself. She exhaled a sadness, nodded a defeat, and left. She headed to the yard where Playful grilled lion ribs and crickets over the firepit. "I'll take over," she said as she seized the bigfork. "You go tend Whimsy."

"Are you too weary for the task?" Playful asked. "You're eight moonths with-child, Mellow. If you need to rest—"

"No, tis not it. The new woman requests you to be her tender."

"Oh. Um, me?" Playful asked with severe fret and furrowed brows. "Um, why? Are you sure?"

"Go."

"Yes, First Moma."

* * *

AFT THE LUNCHEON, Mellow lugged the big basket of dirty dishes and soily-clothes to the lake for washing. She returned with them clean, put the dishes in their place, hung the clothes over the outstretched twines to dry, went to make pee by the proper berry bush, then returned to her bedchamber to lie down. Her back was slaying her, her inner chest burned, her legs cramped, her rectal gas offensive even to her, and she had to make pee again even though she just went. Normal for her stage of with-child, course—normal for grown men to wed children, normal for husbands to thrash wives, normal for those you love most to come to hate you or die, all normal. She was so sick of normal.

There came a light tapping from the outside. "Drop in," she called as she sat up.

Playful opened the door but remained in the archway. "The new woman sleeps," she informed. "We chitted nicely, she and I. I think she'll be fine."

"Boon," said Mellow. "Gratitude." Playful didn't budge. "Something else?"

"I'm not a bad person, you know."

Mellow sighed, in no mood for it to the very. "I never said you were."

"Not with your words, no, but with your tone and eyes always."

"Not today, Playful. Please? We can chit on this another."

"I had eleven-and-half calendars when Clearsky took me as bride," the second wife spoke on, granting no heed to the request. "A whole calendar younger than young Whimsy has now. I had been taught what was expected of me and so I did my best for my husband. He was pleased with me, so I was pleased with myself. But no one ever told me that in pleasing my husband I would draw the ire of his senior wife. Dour thrashed me senseless, and I learned my lesson well. The next time I was brought to my husband's bedchamber, I lied still. I let him do his business inside me but I efforted no more than that, and he thrashed me for it—with far more severe than Dour ever could. I efforted through my tears to explain him what the First Moma had instructed, and his thrashing grew more severe yet. 'Tis my cabin, not my wife's! You do as I bid, not as she!' I learned new lessons that night. Please him just enough so he won't thrash me, and just not-enough so Dour won't either; never explain myself and only ever utter what they want to hear, no matter the truth inside me. Twas a goal un-possible to fulfill, yet twas all I could effort to do. That was my young life for fourteen calendars."

"'Tis a sad to the very, Playful. Much condolence of it, but the morrow may be a—"

"And for those same fourteen calendars, my childhood-hopeful strove to win me. I learned this only from others for he and I weren't permitted to speak—I'd been whipped in the public for the trying. You see the scars of it every time I give you my back. But this man to which you and I are wed is not the boy I once loved, no more than I'm the girl he did. My darling Son-of-Heat grew up to be a man filled with rage—everyone saw it long before you joined our Community—a rage he now cherishes and enjoys with a sickness; and his little Daughter-of-Gentility, me, grew up to be a woman engulfed by fear.

"So, a war is waged on my behalf and I'm taken by this beast with whom I'm supposed to be still in love, so I act still in love. I'm supposed to be happy, so I act happy. But all I could curious is if Dour's thrashings were too much for me, what torture will Thunder's bring? And I lie awake at night and through my bedchamber walls I hear what he does to you, and all I can think is . . . " she began to cry, "and all I can think is . . . praise the gods it isn't me!"

"Playful, you don't have to—"

"No! Quiet!" she sobbed on. "I know you think I should've talked him away from his cruelty upon you, that he'd listen to his precious Daughter-of-Gentility, but he wouldn't've—and I was too affrighted even if he would. He'd only come to see what I really am, Playful the lying scaredy-hare, Clearsky's second-hand garbage, and he'd thrash me as he does you.

"You were so strong when you sought to protect little Whimsy, and you paid the price, and I did nothing. Worse than nothing, I encouraged him. Maybe if I'd helped you, he wouldn't have taken her, but I did what I always do. Tell 'em what they wanna hear. Tis my blame for what befell the new woman!!!"

Mellow stood. "C'mere."

"Why?"

"Your First Moma says come here."

Playful sucked in her tears as she crossed, stopped before Mellow, and scrunched up her face in anticipation of the blow she knew to come. Mellow hugged her. "Tis all right."

"You say a what?"

"I know fear, my sister-wife," Mellow soothed as she gently stroked the young woman's hair. "I know what tis like to feel a need to always pretend. Tis a terrible to have in one's heart. I get."

"You give me a forgiveness?" Playful sniffled with confusions as her sobbles returned. "Aft all my mean and disrespects to you, you give me a forgiveness just like that?"

"Course."

"How?"

"Because you asked me to."

* * *

"Odd'm and Even lived the rest of their days in harmony-with," began Sandy the Holy One. It was the first day of the moonth of technology in the calendar of the god of stars, the moonth when umanity is to begin the hunt-and-gather-of-excess to hoard for the wintertide like the squirrel and beaver; and twas time for the telling of the second of the Great Punishments. Of all the Gatherings through the four seasons, this night was considered one of the two most sacred.

"And they taught their children to do so too for twas what the gods wished of them, and their children taught their children, and they theirs, and they theirs, and so it went for calendars more than numbers can count; and the gods were pleased, and they answered umanity's prayers like they did for all the other perfect critters that they had conjured.

"But it came to pass there was born a woman named Jezebel who grew to be more beautiful than any woman before her, and all men yearned her as wife, and they combatted for her hand one against the other. But in her beauty, Jezebel had grown vain and full of thought, and she said unto the men that whilst the mightiest of them could *take* her, only the one she *chose* would receive all the love that one exquisite as she could offer. And so the men foraged the lands for Jezebel's favorite foods and flowers to bring to her as gift to win her heart, until all the fields went bare, and no man could rise above another.

"And it came to pass that a man named Satin, who would grow to be the devil, turned his back to the gods and used thought to teach himself to agricult; and he brought to Jezebel her favorite foods and flowers in abundance and with no end in sight for he could harvest all the produce and meats whenever he suited it; and Jezebel chose him as the one to wed, and together they lived in their sins for the rest of their days.

"And the other women saw what Jezebel had done and judged it wise and put forth the same decree, for they knew the dominion the gods had given them over men. And the men were weak against their wiles and the dominion they held over them, so they copied Satin on how to agricult so they too could win the women of their desires. And for generation upon the next did man learn to agricult until they all knew how, and then the skill impressed no more.

"And it came to pass that a man named Hitler was born who sought to rise above the agricutl-ing others, and he used thought to conjure a machine, the first machine, a stick that blasted fire, and he called it gun, and with it he could take whatever he wanted without toil for he could make all others toil on his behalf, and he became the man most desired by women.

"And every man saw that if he could be the one to conjure the next great thing then he would be the one most desired by the woman most desirable. And so came the mighty machines that rolled on grounds, that floated on waters, that soared through the skies and up to the stars; the towering structures of brick and steel and glass; the factories that forged invisible bacterium fatal to all; and the projectiles so powerful that even those who possessed them were affrighted to wield them.

"And the women were pleased, and they chose to wed only the men most full of thought to share in his comfort and wealth. And the men struck their women no more for the women forbade it; and they let their women toil by their side as if they too were men, and hand-in-hand they sought to conjure the next great thing. And the air grew brown with stink, and the waters muddy with germ, and the grounds desolate and barren.

"And the gods were saddened, and they knew they had to correct their mistake once and for boon. And the god of water offered to erase umanity from existence by flood, and the god of air said it would erase them by tornado, and the god of fire by fire, each god to the task in its own way. And the god of scorn put forth the method most cruel of all.

"And it said unto its brethren, 'Let us do nothing. Let us let our mistake correct our mistake. Let us let umanity erase itself. And when they come to us praying for our mercy and begging for our intervention, we will say nothing, as if we're not even here, as if we never were."

And the god of pity said it was a punishment too atrocious, but the others wouldn't sway, and a decision was forged, and the god of pity's voice was outvoiced.

"And so the gods allowed the waters to flood over the coasts to submerge their perfect coasts, and the men and women who lived there sought refuge inland where the grounds were already lived so there was no space for them to be. And those who lived there first sought to put into camps those who came second, but those who came second would not adhere and so began the combats bloody and heinous. And brother turned against brother, sister against sister, child against parent and parent against child. And the factories crumbled and released their deadly bacterium for all to breath. And the projectiles that umanity was too affrighted to wield got wielded.

"And umanity prayed the gods for mercy and intervention, and there came not a sound in reply.

"But the god of pity could stand it no more and reneged the decision and chose smatterings of men and women to live on forth. There was no rhyme or reason to its choices for all umanity was equally pitiful.

"Less than one in a thousand thousandths were left to live on in the fiery, smelly wreckage, only to pray that the gods would heed their prayers once more. And only if we, the children of those poor, wretched souls, stay steadfast and true to the laws we were given may the gods one day return to caring for us as they do for all their other perfect critters.

"So ends the telling of the second of the two Great Punishments."

"The Gathering is shut," said the Sorry.

At no point during telling of the tale did the Sorry or Holy One happen to look up to the mountaintops that protected them, nor did

THE GIRL WHO WOULDN'T DIE

the Two, the apprendix, the First Moma, or any of the congregants, but atop the plateau far above were three heathen men and two heathen women. They wore tattered poly cotton garments to their knees and decorative wool over their torsos—what the old world would've called skirts and ugly Christmas sweaters. One of the men lay flat on the ground staring downward through old-world military-grade binoculars. He whispered what he saw to one woman who sketched his words into pictures with crayons on cardboard, and to another who jotted down the precise numbers of men, women, children, and cabins onto a paper on a clipboard. One man sat on a rock as he assembled a plastic t-shirt launcher, while the third man stood to oversee them all.

As the backward folk below began their partying, the binocu-lared man removed the rifle strapped to his back and pointed it down at them. "Pshhht, pshhht," he quietly uttered to mimic the discharge of his weapon. "Pshhht."

The man in charge stifled his laugh, as did they all, then he motioned for the squad to pack up. They'd been there since morning and had acquired all the intelligence they needed. The young meat-scouts had done well, and well deserved their promotions. These tribes-folk will be no trouble, the taking of their valley no risk, and those that survived will make good slaves.

They strapped on their gear, clipped the tethers to their belts, and proceeded to scale down the far side of the hill.

CHAPTER FORTY-EIGHT

OKLAHOMA CITY, OKLAHOMA
JULY 2019
2 MONTHS SINCE DELIVERING

"SHE ABSOLUTELY HAS A CASE," said the well-groomed Oklahoma City lawyer from behind his oak desk in his elegant corner office. "Strong one. Unless there's more to this than you're telling me."

"I've told you everything I know," Myla assured him. "If there's more, Naomi will fill in the gaps when you meet her."

"Sounds fine. My fee is four-seventy-five an hour, and I'll need a five-thousand-dollar retainer to get started."

"I'll wire it over as soon as I get home, but here's the catch. She can't know I'm paying you."

"I'm sorry?"

"She can't afford you, and she's too proud to accept me footing the bill on her behalf. She'll think it's charity. So, as far as she's concerned, I just happened to mention her situation to you, and you were so moved you decided to take her on pro bono. You send all invoices directly to me. In fact . . . " she took a dollar bill from her purse and slapped it on his desk. "Now I have attorney-client privilege too. Nobody can know I'm paying for this."

"This is remarkably kind of you, Myla. You're a very good friend."

"So is she."

* * *

IT WAS ALREADY dark by the time Myla got home, and she felt absolutely fabulous about herself. She parked the pickup next to her RV and went inside. Lori was nestled soundly in her crib, excellent sleeper that she was, true to her namesake. Dim stood in the center of the cabin holding a listless Francine in his arms, softly singing *To All the Girls I've Loved Before*. Myla smiled at the sight of it. It was the first time she'd left the twins in the care of another, but she knew she could count on him—if he could deliver 'em, he could care for 'em. He noticed her, worriedly put his index finger to his mouth to hush her, then gently placed Francine into the crib next to Lori's. He tilted his head toward the door and led her outside.

"Boy oh boy, she was crying up a storm, that one," he told her. "Just like you warned it. Hard to believe so much sound can come out of a thing so little."

"But you calmed her down."

"I sure did," he beamed. "Took me all my Toby Keith and half my Willie Nelson, but I calmed her down."

"And how was Lori?"

"A doll that one, a breeze. You know, I almost made her laugh. Tickled and tickled and tickled and got her to smile, and she went, 'grgrgrgr.' Not quite a laugh but close."

"Laughing usually doesn't happen till the third month."

"Bet I can get it in two. So, how'd it go in the city? Accomplish what you needed?"

"Couldn't have gone better. Wait, you didn't tell Naomi anything, did you?"

"I don't know anything."

"Perfect. I just need another ten minutes to go talk to her. Can you hang a bit more?"

"Take as long as you want. I love this stuff. I hope one of them wakes up."

She smiled again. "Thank you, Uncle Demetrius."

"You know, I've been thinking, they'll never be able to say that. Why don't we stick with Uncle Dim, least till they're older?"

"All right, Demetrius, Uncle Dim it is. Be right back." She walked to Naomi's camper and knocked on the door. Naomi answered to find Myla grinning ear-to-ear. "Guess what?" she asked as she entered without invitation. "I found you an attorney!"

"I told you. I can't afford one."

"That's the beauty part. He's this big-time Oklahoma City family lawyer. He called the office the other day pertaining to something I'm not allowed to tell you, but then we got to talking—you know me—one thing led to another and I ended up telling him your story, without mentioning you by name, of course. He was so moved he offered to take you on pro bono. That means for free."

"I know what pro bono means," she bristled. "You shouldn't have done this, Myla."

"Hey, your grandfather's being an ogre and you have rights."

"My grandfather's not an ogre," she sighed. "He's . . . he is . . . he's a goddamn fucking saint is what he is. I'm the ogre."

"I don't understand."

"I lied to you, okay?! I can see Lorne any time I want. My grandparents want me to see him, urge me to. Grandpa's been telling the boy he won't permit it as if it's his decision so Lorne will hate him, not me. He's letting his own great-grandson hate him, for me."

"Now I understand even less. Then why not go see him?"

"Look at me! I'm a thirty-year-old stripper with bleached hair and fake tits up the wazoo! What if he's ashamed of me? What if he doesn't like me?"

"Oh Naomi, that's not possible, you're his mother."

"Now you're wondering why the fuck I got into this business in the first place, aren't you?"

"I never asked that."

"I don't know anymore, okay? Because I was mad . . . because I got knocked up by a bad guy when I was sixteen who left me flat and dry, and then hooked up with men even worse after him . . . because I was young . . . because I was high . . . because flaunting my boobs and ass pays better than anything else I can do . . . because it was wrong and I wanted to be wrong. How many more reasons do you need?"

"I didn't ask for any. Go see your son, Naomi."

"What do you care anyway?"

"Because once upon a time I didn't step up when a teenage boy needed me, and it remains the single greatest regret of my life. I wouldn't wish that feeling on anyone, least of all you. You reached out to help me before you even knew me, and that was amazing. You're a good soul, Naomi, and now you just need a gentle, loving shove to do what you already want to do."

"I can't," she sniffled. "It's too late."

"It's never too late," said the old lady as she took her young benefactor's hands into hers. "When did you last see him?"

"I dunno. I'd pop in every once in a while, back when he was younger, when I was younger, spend a few days before running off to hook up with the next wrong guy. So yeah, it's been some years. So, you see . . . " Her eyes grew moist and her voice began to crack. "Even if my boy doesn't care that his mama's a ho, a professional sleaze, he has to be crazy pissed at me for not having been around. I never forgave my mother for it, why should he forgive me? No, it's too late. I blew it," she wept. "I blew it long ago, but I made my peace with it. Why do you have to show up and drudge it all back to me?!"

"Do you want me to come with you?"

"I never said I was going!"

"You're going. You are. C'mon, what if you're wrong? What if it's to be this big, happy, sappy reunion? And even if your worst fears are realized, wouldn't it be better to know for sure?"

"No," Naomi decisively answered. Myla laughed, and then so did she, then her laugh turned somber. "I'm scared, Myla. I can't do it. I'm scared."

"I know, dear," she said with a hug. "I know."

* * *

A FEW WEEKS LATER, Myla went to see the *Molly Parker* movie with Charlene, Dim's kid sister, who she'd come to admire as a kind, pleasant, albeit sometimes overly serious woman with little sense of humor. No biggie. Kind and pleasant trumps the rest.

She found the film to be quite good actually, despite it having nothing to do with what really happened. Even if one were to ignore the unsterblich aspect, the story they made up could have been about anybody, the characters had nothing to do with those they were based on, and the relationships between them a total fabrication, most evidenced by the super-charged scene when Janine goes to confront and threaten Francisco in a crowded Beverly Hills restaurant, even though the two never once spoke outside of class. Still, Myla was on the edge of her seat.

Overall, the performances were strong, the dialogue snappy and clever, the cinematography stunning, and the filmmakers did an excellent job of walking that fine line as to whether Molly was a victim or a psychopath. As long as she could divorce herself from the real story, she found it all very moving and sad. The word "relatable" even popped into her head at one point during a particularly heart-wrenching scene and she had to stifle her laugh so no one would think she was a psycho too.

She could envision the picture doing well. Dang it.

* * *

IT WOULD TAKE two months more, not until late September, for Naomi to muster up the courage to do what she'd wanted to do for years, but she had come to see that Myla made sense. This could be a glorious afternoon. Little Cuz's annoying meddling may turn out to be a blessing in disguise.

Newcastle was a nice, quiet suburb on the South side of Oklahoma City. The leaves on the trees were just starting to change, kids threw footballs on lawns, played basketball on driveways, bicycled and tricycled on roads and sidewalks, while husbands and wives lounged on their front porches sipping their whatevers.

Naomi sat in her pickup truck parked a half block down from her grandparents' house, her house, the home in which she'd been raised. Her vehicle was clean inside and out for she had it washed immediately upon rolling into town. She wore a conservative blue cotton dress that fell down to her shins, a patterned pink sweater with matching scarf, low heels, her hair dyed back to its original brown, and a tight sports bra compressing her triple-D's into something akin to normal. She'd been there for more than half an hour, convincing herself to get out of the car and ring the doorbell, but not listening to a damn thing she was saying.

She saw the front door open and she hunched down in her seat so as not to be seen. Grammy stepped onto the porch—aw, I miss her so much—followed by Lorne who carried a gym bag. So beautiful, so handsome, just like his asshole father. She slid further into her seat.

Grammy began to laugh and playfully slapped Lorne's arm as they headed toward the Ultima parked on the driveway. He must have said something funny. He's so smart.

They got in the car and drove away. Naomi waited just a few minutes, sniffled briefly, then turned the Dodge around and went home.

* * *

THE SATURDAY BREAKFAST barbecues had since grown to include Charlene, Tammy who worked at the daycare center, Tammy's older sister Leslie, of course Dim, and even Jack. Despite their dubious start, Myla still found him to be smart, kind, and hilarious—you can't really blame a guy for not wanting an instant family on a first date. He was good with the girls, albeit in short bursts, as was Charlene and Leslie who applied no time restrictions, and naturally Tammy who was an absolute pro. Three more aunties and a second uncle. Everything was falling into place.

On weekend afternoons, she liked to put her daughters in the double stroller and take long aimless walks through the town, letting her mind wander just as aimlessly. There was a quiet to the place, an ease, especially compared to the fast-moving hustle and bustle of New York and LA. True, opioid and crystal meth addictions ran rampant within certain crowds, but it wasn't as if big cities weren't plagued with the same troubles, just a little more obvious when there's less people around.

As she initially feared, the *Molly Parker* movie did very well, the highest grossing film of the year not counting comic books, sequels, and reboots. The irony—that lovely, beautiful irony—was that now the whole world thought that Molly Parker looked like Jennifer Lawrence. Even on the rare occasion that cable news or podcasts would run a segment on the deranged killer, they'd show clips from the movie and not Josh's video. She was free, free of her, free of Molly at last, free to take her babies and move on to wherever she wanted to go.

Yet she chose to remain. She liked Dukane, and the thought of starting over again seemed exhausting, as well as possibly leading her to make new mistakes. It'd been almost a year since she arrived and there was no sign of anyone coming after her. Staying was clearly the safer way to go.

Every now and then in life, not often but sometimes, the thing you want to do coincides with the smart thing to do.

Still, just in case, she had a Volkswagen Bug waiting for her in storage in Lawton, vehicle and unit both registered to next-girl, walking distance from her reconfigured batcave where she kept her next-girl documents and her daughters' next-people birth certificates.

She strolled on as she planned out Myla's small town country future. She'd continue working for the county until it seemed plausible for her to have saved enough money to start a little business of her own, making patio furniture or kitchen thingies or something; she'd figure out the specifics later. But in addition to selling her product from her little shop on Main Street, she'd fabricate customers in Lawton and Tulsa and Oklahoma City who'd buy her product in droves so she could launder in some of the cash she had hidden in Switzerland and the Caymans. She'd buy a little house to raise the girls, and oh what a wonderful life it will be.

Making Naomi a junior partner in the venture was her initial impulse, but that would give her access to the books so, no, can't have that. Instead, she'd hire her as a grossly overpaid employee. Her dear friend, her benefactor, could quit her job at the nightclub, buy a house of her own, and finally have the cover she'd need to garner the nerve to reconcile with her son.

And just as Myla was thinking that things couldn't get any better, little Lori sneezed. Myla put her hand to her baby's forehead, and she was indeed warm. Then Francine sniffled. Her forehead was warm too. Then they both coughed.

They have a cold! Myla screamed joyously in her head. "They're normals," she exhaled with a giggle. "Normals," she whispered with a tear. She looked up to the clouds and nodded forgivingly. "Okay."

She headed back to her truck to get her babies home and out of the chill, stopping only briefly at the UPS Store to pick up her mail and send in the check and registration form to renew her RV before the deadline.

CHAPTER FORTY-NINE

I T WAS A LOVELY AUTUMNAL after-lunch. Warmer than usual for the moonth of technology, the sky was at its bluest blue and the sun shone strong. Mellow struggled with the basket of dishes and yesterday's soily-clothes as she trudged to the lake for it was her turn for the cleaning once again, her swelling belly rendering her no validity to bow out. Twas their way.

She hadn't seen Whimsy since that first morn aft her wedding night, so she was a tad surprised when the new woman approached to offer help with the lugging.

"Gratitude," she said as she handed over the basket.

"Course."

An awkward silence followed as they plodded onward. Mellow could tell the girl had a thing she wanted off her heart, but she felt it best to wait for it. Also, her feelings were still a little smarting from the girl's brush-off. She knew she shouldn't let it bother her, knew the new woman was really but a child, knew she should be the adult one, but twas a hard. She'd felt a kinship to the girl, and the girl broke it. Yes, let her speak first.

She looked well though, Mellow noted. Still a titty-bit banged up but nothing that wouldn't heal all the way in time. "You appear close to a fine," she said. "How you feel?"

"I'll live."

"Praise."

The silence returned, and nothing more was said till they arrived at the beach. Many of the wives and girls were already at toil, including Whisper, Steady, who was previously called Daughter-of-Kindness, and two of their chums who sat at the far end sneakily sharing a mini-jug of hooch. Upon seeing Mellow, they quickly hid the naughty substance in a basket of laundry and proceeded to act the innocent. The First Moma knew it her duty to reprimand the young women, but her priority was to Whimsy so she opted to play dunce.

She stopped by the shoreline edge near the jaggy rocks at distance to the others—if a chit was to be had, let it be with a privacy. "Here," she said.

Whimsy planted the basket on the sand and clumsily began what she'd come to begin. "So . . . Playful tells that you efforted to sway Thunder to change his brain re me."

"That's correct," Mellow answered as she began the wash.

"And that you received a thrashing for the trying."

"That, as well, is correct."

"Why didn't you tell me?"

"When? Before you were of our cabin and I wasn't permitted to speak of it? Or after you said you hate me and that I should leave you be?"

Whimsy looked away for she had no boon in reply. She joined in the wash, then tried again. "Pupa tells that you urged him to cheat the gods on behalf of Dachshund Dog, for me."

"Tis a praise that you and your pupa speak again. He went to combat to protect you."

"I know. I finally came to get such. Tis why he and I speak."

"Yes, a praise to the very. But he shouldn't have spoken to you of what I did."

"He doesn't want me to hate you anymore than you want me to hate him."

"He's a good man, yet still, I wish he'd kept it unknown."

"I don't wish it so."

"Well, anyway, tis done."

They worked in silence more moments still until Whimsy just whined it out. "I shouldn't have doubted you, Mellow! You've always been my chum. I don't know why I did!"

Mellow softened—it was all she needed. "You were in pain," she empathized. "You felt betrayed and confused and you needed someone to hate for it, so you chose me."

"And my pupa," Whimsy corrected with a smile. "I chose my pupa to hate too."

"And your pupa," Mellow responded with a small titter.

"So, you give me a forgiveness?"

"No."

"No?" the new woman exclaimed with wide eyes. "Why in fuckety-fuck not?"

"Because," chortled Mellow, "you have yet to offer apology."

"Apology!" Whimsy shouted merrily as she wrapped her arms around Mellow and showered her face with kisses. "Apology! Apology! Apology!"

"All right, all right," Mellow laughed as she pushed the girl away. "Enough. Back to work, my sister."

"'My sister,'" Whimsy repeated with a gush. "I like the sound of that from you."

"Me too, yet still, I wish tweren't so."

"Me too."

"You too?!" kidded Mellow. "You wish not to be my sister? How dare you!" and she rolled the girl over and began to tickle. Whimsy laughed and laughed as she writhed on the sand. "Okie! Okie! I tap out! Mercy! I tap out!"

BANG! went something in the distance. BANG! BANG! BANG!

The wives and girls ceased their chores and looked up to the skies with confusions. How could it thunder when not a cloud was up above? But Mellow knew well the sounds and knew they weren't of thunders. They were gunshots! Except, from where? Who? How?

"Look!" shouted Daughter-of-Playful-1 as she pointed out to the waters. "Everybody, look!"

They all turned to see it. Emerging from round the bouldery ridge where their lake curved to the out of sight came a ship. It was long as a Sorry's cabin and tall as two, with grand sails bowing majestically in the winds.

None had ever seen such a thing—heard about them in the tales of their lore, but never with their eyes—yet they all knew that even the most heathen of heathens wouldn't dare violate one of the gods' most basic laws. It could only mean one thing.

"The gods have returned to us!" shouted Whisper.

"Praise the gods for their resume!" shouted another, and then another, then another, and they all dropped to their knees and waved their arms to the horizon in exultation.

"No!" shouted Mellow. "Tis not the gods! We're under siege! Tis heathen others!"

"Can't be," cried Steady from across the beach. "Even the most heathen of—"

"Tis an attack!" Mellow insisted without a trace of doubt. "Momas, garner your children and sprint them to your cabins! The rest, get yourselves inside! Inform the men!"

"But Auntie Mellow," Daughter-of-Playful-1 began with a fright, "how could you know such a thing?"

"Because I, um, um . . . Because I'm First Moma. We know things. Run!"

They obeyed with a jiff. Whimsy wrapped her arm round Mellow's waist to aid her in the flee, when the first cannon shell was fired from the ship.

BOOM! it exploded, igniting a pine tree into fire and smoke, the shockwave knocking many off their feet, Mellow and Whimsy among them.

"Get up! Get up!" Mellow shouted to those on the ground as she rose, then looked out to see the others running together in a cluster. "No! Spread out! Separate!"

BOOM! exploded the next, landing in the center of the clump, wounding many, slaying others, Daughter-of-Playful-1 among them.

"Awww fuckety-fuck," Mellow groaned with a sad. "Spread out!" she shouted with a mad. "Now!"

"Owww!" shouted Whimsy. "I can't stand!"

Mellow turned to see the new woman lying atop one of the jaggy rocks, her thigh ripped open and oozing blood. Mellow moved to her fast, gave her back to her and crouched. "Hop on!"

BOOM!

"No, tis too much for you! You're with-child!"

"Do it!"

Whimsy jumped on her back and off Mellow raced, off as fast as her with-child'cy permitted, baskets and bushes and trees flaming all round them.

BOOM, went the next, decimating a cabin to smithereens. BOOM!

By the time they got home, it was evident that the men needed no informing for they were outside and ready for battle, crotch-covers on, spears and shields in hand, cutters and slings by hips. Thunder stood on his porch, barking tactics to his warriors as they stood beyond the cannon's reach. Upon seeing his two wives, he exhaled a relief. "Praise. Get inside."

BOOM! BOOM!

Mellow headed toward the door where a distraught Playful awaited, her mouth in a pout, eyes red and moist. She had seen it all.

"Playful," Mellow mournfully began, "I present my deepest regrets to you. Your daughter was a good girl, she was."

The second wife merely nodded back in stoic acknowledgement when Mellow came to register the commands Thunder was roaring to his men. His entire strategy was predicated on the notion that the enemy's only way in was by water, and it instantly struck her as to what those initial gunshots were about. She passed Whimsy off to Playful then returned to Thunder.

"Husband! You're wrong!" she shouted over the cannon fire. "Our enemy can enter from the tunnel! Your sentries are dead!"

"How could you know such a thing?!"

"The gods put it in my brain!" she answered quickly, but he only glared at her. "Trust me," she pled.

He considered but a moment for he saw that the look on her face was strong. "Get inside," he said, then assigned Sunburst to take three men to guard the tunnel opening.

Mellow went in to find Playful's little ones secured in their playpen, Whimsy on the sofa, Playful applying hooch to the girl's open wound, maple leaves and honey jar beside them.

Boon, she thought, but suddenly something didn't sit right. The cannon fire had stopped! Why? She looked out the window to see a barrage of glass cannisters raining down from the mountaintop, cracking open upon contact with the ground to release a brownish-purple smoke. Tear gas! "Whimsy! Can you tend your own wound?"

"I—I think so."

"Then do so! Playful, we must close all doors and windows, then seal any cracks that remain with honey. No air must flow in!"

Out on the lake, titty-bitty yellow boats, what the Old World called life rafts, were being lowered from the main ship. Critters with human bodies and demonic faces with elephant noses that hung below their chins, what the Old World called gas masks, rowed toward the shore.

Sunburst and his men arrived at the tunnel entrance. He set two of them to kneel on opposite sides of the opening with spears drawn, ready to strike low to the legs of any who dared enter. He and another stood tall behind the kneelers, axes raised high to cleave through heathen skull. They waited in disciplined stillness till they heard footsteps. They readied for the slay when they heard an odd rolly sound, then two cylinder-y-looking things bowled out the cave steaming brownish-purple smoke. It burned at their eyes and put them to crying even though they had no sadness, but the brave men held steadfast and true to guard their post. It ripped at their throats and put them to coughing till they could barely breath, and then it dropped them to the ground in futile search of air they couldn't find.

Through the slits of his scorching eyes, Sunburst saw the demonic critters emerge from the opening. Most jogged onward yet two remained by the tunnel. Despite his weakness and lack of breath, the mighty warrior sought to fight them—only to receive an unnaturally smooth and rounded wooden club, what the Old World called a baseball bat, bashed to his head. He lay on the ground bleeding from his temple, then heard a ripping sound, then felt something sticky wrap round his wrists behind him to bind them inescapably together. He saw his comrades being bound in the same manner with a wide yet skinny gray fabric that the heathens tore from a thick roll, what the Old World called duct tape, and there was nothing he could do to stop them.

Mellow and Playful were more than halfway through their task but still too slow at it for Mellow's liking. As she toiled, she studied her new enemy. Without an actual count, she guesstimated about thirty of them storming the beach, another twenty who'd entered from the tunnel, fiftyish in all. Their garments were ragtag and from different eras. Some had weapons, most not, but they had no uniformity, their firearms ranging from semi-automatics to muskets; some held baseball bats or hockey sticks, some foils or scimitars; one giant brute of a man wielded a rusty helicopter tail rotor blade.

This was not a band of men who'd rediscovered industry, she easily determined, but one of scavengers who'd stumbled upon Old World stuff with which to conquer at advantage. They were a "look-at-what-it-does" people, not a "this-is-why-it-works" one. Stealers not builders, takers not makers. Of little matter, course, her Community was outmatched to its death.

"How can I help?" Whimsy asked, bandaged and hobbling toward them. "I can help."

"Boon," answered Mellow as she gave the girl her brush and honey jar. "Fill my spot. But take heed, little chum, what you see out our windows may turn your insides sour."

"I'm strong of heart."

"I know you are," she smiled, then tore off in search of the tools she'd next need.

Where would he have put it? Mellow asked herself as she frantically checked one cupboard aft the other, one chamber into the next.

He wouldn't have garbaged it away, no, not him, not Thunder. It's somewhere in here. It has to be, has to be.

As forewarned, Whimsy was aghast at what she saw. The world outside was full of colored smoke. The elephant-faced heathens moved about as if they owned the dwelling. The strong and brave men that she had admired since her infancy lay choking on the ground as the heathens bound them with unholy materials—her husband, her Sorry, the strongest and bravest of them all, helpless as any.

Her beloved Dachshund Dog lay coughing among them, gloomily awaiting his turn to be bound. She knew she wasn't permitted to love him anymore, had always assumed the gods would lift away her feelings for him if she'd ever wed another, but they didn't—and what with her new husband turning out to be a horror, she didn't want them to. She'd love her darling Dachshund Dog till time was a thing no more, even while knowing she could never show it.

One of the heathens approached to bind him when her love suddenly spun round and bit into its calf hard with all his teeth. The heathen screamed.

Yes, Whimsy smiled proudly, that's my love, my Dachshund Dog! Tough and low-to-the-ground and surprising to everyone always! What a mighty warrior he'll be!

Another heathen moved in with haste, bashed the un-pointy end of its odd-looking club, what the Old World called a tommy gun, to bloody Dachshund Dog's head. He turned the odd club round and riddled a million blasts of BANG into her true love's face and body in less than a moment, and the little man lived no more.

Her mouth gaped open and her eyes grew wide and filled with tears. Playful put her arms round her little sister with condolence and stroked her hair. "Shhh, shhh."

"No!" Whimsy sniffled the sad inside her. "We must toil! The First Moma said we must do this!"

Twas then that Mellow returned. Her hair was tied back in a tail, Thunder's bow from before the temporary ban six calendars ago slung over her shoulder, his quiver filled with his arrows strapped to her back, one of his crotch-covers tied round her waist, his back-up cutter and sling tucked by her hips. Before either of the sisters could remark on the sinful sight, she assessed the situation and spoke.

"You're close to done. Praise. Whimsy, finish it up on your own then stay here to tend Playful's little ones. Playful, go instruct the other women to seal their cabins as we have done. Put a rag to your mouth and breath little as you're able while you run. Squint your eyes closed as a possible while still being able to see, and know twill still hurt. Go."

"Me?" gulped Playful. "Go out there? Are you of madness?"

"I'll do it," Whimsy braved with arctic eyes. "Just help me find a thing to crutch me, and I'll do it."

"Nooo," Playful moaned with reluctant fright. "You can barely walk, Whimsy, for certain cannot run." She took a deep, anxious, terrified breath. "I'll do it."

"Boon. Start with the cabins with little ones. Whimsy, re-seal the door behind us."

"Where are you going?"

"I despise this place, and our husband even extra on top. But I've lived here six calendars and more, and tis my home. You two both and everyone else in it my family. Someone's got to protect," and off she went.

CHAPTER FIFTY

QUEENS, NEW YORK
NOVEMBER 2019
10 MONTHS SINCE MEETING THE ELDARS

P ETE HAD ALMOST GIVEN up hope. What if she pushed the RV off a cliff or set it on fire? There'd be no record of it. What if she drove it to Mexico and sold it or abandoned it there, hopped on a plane to Europe or Australia or anywhere? He'd never find her. Gone forever.

These were the thoughts he tried not to think every day for close to a year, so when his former NYPD colleague called that morning to say that his search had at last pinged Myla's RV registration renewal, the first thing Pete wondered was why she hadn't done any of those things?

Because she feels safe, his answer came quickly. She got where she got, nobody recognized her, so she stayed put. No one came after her in all this time so she figures she's home free. Not dumb. I'd think the same in her shoes. "How long ago?" he asked the colleague.

"Let's see . . . got it right here . . . three weeks."

"Three weeks?! You said you'd tell me ASAP! That was the deal, you son of a bitch!"

"I got shit going on too, you know. Now do you want her address or not?"

"Give it."

"Say 'thank you.'"

"Thank you," he grunted the most ungrateful 'thank you' ever uttered by man.

"Are we even?"

"Sure."

The colleague gave him the address, Pete hung up without good-bye, then booked the next flight to Oklahoma City.

* * *

HE TOUCHED DOWN AT FIVE, rented a midsize Subaru, and made his way to Dukane. He arrived at the stated address well past seven only to find it to be a UPS Store—unit 145, a mailbox number not an apartment. Shit. He checked the door to find it closed for the day, then paused to look around the very unimpressive Main Street.

Small, he observed, a shithole, she shouldn't be too hard to find. He noticed the shabby hotel across the street, pulled his car around, and parked in its lot. Only two other cars were there, one of them from the County Sheriff's department.

Shit. Okay, tread lightly. Last thing you want is law enforcement getting involved and mucking this up for you.

He got his bags from the trunk and went inside. The man behind the counter was mid-thirties, paunchy, of average height, sporting a big mustache and a retardedly cheerful smile.

"Welcome to the Old Vinton. How may we help you, sir?"

"I need a room, thanks."

"We got plenty of those," the clerk chipperly answered. "Pasture view or street?"

"Street."

"Most prefer pasture. It's all right. Credit card and ID please."

Pete handed them over. Dim made a photocopy of the license and ran the credit card as Pete decided there was no reason not to get started. "I'm looking to track down an old family friend while I'm here, daughter of one of my best buddies. Heard she moved out this way. Her name's Myla Callahan."

The clerk's jolly demeanor vanished in a flash. "Never heard of her."

Worst liar ever, noted Pete. "Maybe you've seen her around." He removed a printout of redheaded Myla from his jacket pocket and showed it. The bumpkin actually gulped.

"Nope, never seen her. But Oklahoma's a big state. She must've gone to another county. Sign here and here. You'll be in room 203, just up the stairs and to the left. Need help with the bags?"

"Nah, I got it, thank you muchly," said Pete as he signed, took his key and cards, picked up his two suitcases, and headed up the stairs.

Dim waited until he heard the guest's door open then some seconds later close, then hollered, "Charlene! Man the counter! I got to go!"

IT WAS Myla's intention to stay in for the night—play with the girls till their bedtime, do a little laundry, enjoy a little reading. It was a warm evening, particularly for October. She wore a pair of ripped jean cutoffs and a pink t-shirt—the same top in which Molly Parker had made her daring escape, although far more daring in the movie than in real life. It was a look that churchgoing Myla would never don in public so perfectly perfect to waste on laundry night.

She had just put in her second load when she heard the sirens approaching, and was already nestled deep into the couch re-reading her favorite Jeff Abugov sci-fi when came the banging on her door. She opened it to find Dim drenched in nervous sweat.

"You got to go," he said as he hurried inside. "Grab what you need. Pack up the girls. Let's move!"

"What're you talking about? Demetrius, what's going on?"

"A man came looking for you. He had your name, your picture, everything. They're onto you."

Dang it, she thought. How? Then something didn't make sense. "What do you mean, 'onto me'?" she asked. "Who's onto what?"

He took her hands. "I know who you are, Myla. I know you're Molly Parker. Knew it from that first day I saw you in daylight, and I don't care. You want me to kill him for you?"

"What? No."

"I've done it before, you know. It was in the line of duty, but still. I can bury his body so no one'll ever find it. No one will ever know. I can do this for you."

"Nobody's killing anyone, Demetrius, now slow down. First of all, I'm not—"

"I love you, Myla," he said as he dropped to a knee. "I don't believe what they said about you in that movie. I love you." He removed a small, purple, velvet box, a Tiffany box, from his jacket pocket and opened it to reveal a two-carat diamond ring. "Will you marry me?"

Shoot, she thought. Now? I don't have time for this now! "Demetrius . . . "

"I know you don't love me back, but you like me and that's enough. I may not be the brightest lightbulb in the room, but I'm a good man, and I'll be a good husband."

He would, she acknowledged inside, for someone, but I've got to get out of here!

"And you won't have to work for Sheriff Billy no more. Between my county job and the hotel, I do all right, better than all right. And I'll be a good daddy to Lori and Francine. I'll love them even more than I love you, and that's a lot. I'll make for a fine daddy."

Yes, he would, poor guy. His eyes were so big and wide and puppy dog, she just didn't have the heart to give him a flat-out no, at least not yet. "Can I think about it?"

"Sure," he smiled, then looked to the floor with a blush and said nothing further.

"What?"

"It's already a better answer than I expected," he giggled, then shifted gears. "Now, c'mon, pack up. We gotta move before this Mailor character figures out where you are."

"Who?"

"The man who was asking about you, goes by the name Pete Mailor."

"Peter Mailor?"

"Yeah, why?"

"Oh my God."

* * *

"Nah, I got it, thank you muchly," Pete told Dim as he signed, took his key and cards, picked up his two suitcases, and headed up the stairs and into his room. He threw the luggage onto the bed, quickly opened one, removed his Glock which he holstered and his stun gun which he pocketed, walked back out, slammed the door loudly behind him, then stood quietly against the wall.

"Charlene!" he heard the hayseed shout. "Man the desk! I gotta go!"

He waited till he heard the front door close, then made a beeline back down the stairs. "Forgot to buy me some smokes," he explained to the ugly woman behind the counter, then exited the hotel in time to see Dim backing out in the squad car.

Shit, he's the cop? Him? How dense are these fucking people? Okay, Pete, full vigilance.

The squad car zoomed off on all cylinders. Pete got into the Subaru but knew better than to match speeds for it would bring too much attention upon himself—the yahoo would realize he's being followed and wouldn't lead him where he wanted to be led. In fact, had the rube not flashed his lights and siren, Pete would've lost him entirely.

He saw the car turn onto a little dirt road by a *Zombieland Double Tap* billboard, then saw the sign directing passersby to the Dukane County Trailer Park. Got you, bitch. He drove a quarter mile past it, turned around, parked in the shoulder, shut the engine, and waited.

Twenty minutes later, the squad car pulled out, the yokel driving with no one beside him. Perfect. Except, what if she's hiding in the trunk or on the floor? Do I follow him, or go in to get her? Unlikely

423

she's hiding—hick-boy never caught on that he was being followed. If he had, he'd never have led me to her in the first place. Eighty-twenty she's not in that car.

He waited till the squad car was out of sight then drove on. He parked in the lot by the office and went inside where a fat old drunk sat at the desk. "Boy oh boy," he exclaimed in friendly exasperation. "A three-hour flight to Oklahoma City, then a two-hour-plus drive to here; and finding this place in the dark ain't no easy task, let me tell you. But here I am."

"You looking to rent a spot?" asked Chester. "We don't normally get car-ers."

"No, I'm sorry. I'm here to visit with an old friend. The daughter of my best buddy, actually. Myla Callahan. You must know her. Perky little redhead. She gave me the address here, but I can't for the life of me remember where I put the piece of paper where I wrote her lot number. What was it again?"

Chester studied him. "I'm not usually in the habit of giving out such confidentials, but I'll let her know you're here." He picked up the landline. "What's your name?"

"Ben Franklin," Pete said as he slammed a hundred-dollar bill on the desk with one hand and hung up the phone with the other. "I want to surprise her. She likes surprises."

"Ben Franklin, eh?" Chester considered, pocketed the cash, told Pete what he wanted to be told, and sent him on his merry way.

He got to her RV, which he recognized from the Eldar's photo. He tapped on the door. No answer. He tried the handle. Locked. He got out his trusty half diamond pick and unlatched it open with ease. He slid his hand into his jacket for quick and easy access to his weapon then barged inside, wondering what he'd say to her. Play it cool, kiddo. This is your moment.

No one was there.

Shit. She must've been hiding in the car after all. Or, shit-shit, there must be a ton of other exits out of this place. How'd I miss that? Okay, don't panic, think this through. She might not have even been here when Farmer John arrived. She might not even know about me yet, might be coming back—and if she did run, she would've run fast, would've had to leave a clue or two behind as to where she's heading next. Get to work.

He proceeded to scour the place, not trying to draw any conclusions just yet but only to collect as much info as possible that he could piece together later. He didn't get very far before he heard a child crying and then a woman's voice.

"Hey you! I thought you'd already—" A big-titted broad swaddling a baby walked in, then stopped abruptly upon seeing him. "Oh."

"Hey, hi," he said good-naturedly. "I'm Pete, an old family friend of Myla's. Went to high school with her daddy. Known her since she was a pup. So, you must be, um, um, oh she spoke about you a bunch of times. What's your name again?"

"Naomi."

"That's right. Naomi. Pleasure to finally meet you, Naomi."

"Yeah, uh, likewise," she said as she opened the fridge and took out a fresh bottle of breast milk. "Let her know Francine's been having a little trouble going down again."

"Will do."

Naomi left, Pete returned to his search, then Naomi returned with her shotgun.

"I don't know who the fuck you are, mister, but if Myla had any friends coming to visit, I'd have known about it. So, git."

"No, you don't understand. I was supposed to be arriving next month but—"

She pumped it. "Better git while the gittin's good, boy. My finger's growin' awful itchy."

"Yes ma'am."

He stepped out of the camper and made his way along the dirt road to the parking lot, well aware that jugs-lady's gun remained pointed at his back. He got into the Subaru and started back to the hotel.

Okay, Pete, what did you see? Wasn't much but could be enough. Piece it together. You haven't lost the bitch yet.

It was past nine by the time he entered the lobby, and he still hadn't come up with a theory. He headed up the stairs and into his room with the singular intention of jotting down every detail he'd garnered from the camper, and there she was. Sitting on the little chair by the little table by the draped window wearing a pair of jean shorts and a tight pink t-shirt so sheer he could almost see through to her nipples, her lovely red hair tied back in a ponytail, her glorious legs daintily crossed with a little throw cushion upon her lap.

She looked good.

"Hello, Peter," she said. "It's been a long time."

CHAPTER FIFTY-ONE

The Dwelling
While She Was Searching For The Bow

THE BARRAGE OF TEAR gas continued as the warriors lay bound and gagging on the ground, masked and weaponized heathens hovering round them. Two new heathens approached, marching forth Sunburst and his men minus one at gunpoint, shoving them to the ground and proceeding to bind their feet. One of the two turned to the heathen who seemed to be in charge and addressed him with strange words in a dialect even stranger.

"We had to snuff uno of the dudes but here's tres more."

"Fifty-dos," said a heathen by the leader's side. "That's the last by the clipboard."

"Groovy," replied the one in charge, then turned to others. "Time to round up the chicks and kids, get going." He turned to the bound warriors. "I know this's freaking y'all out, but youse belong to us now. The sooner youse accept that factazoid, the less of youse we'll hafta snuff." He turned to another of his own. "They don't copy a damn thing I'm saying, do they?" The other shook his head and the one in charge turned back to the warriors. "You will, just sit tight."

He looked out to the ship on the lake, took a rectangular block from his belt and spoke to it. "Come in. Over." To the horror of the warriors, the rectangle spoke back.

"I read. How'd it go? Over."

"Easy-peezy, boss-man, just as you planned it. We got all the dudes duct'd up and—"

No one at first noticed, and then couldn't believe it when they saw it, but this naked pregnant lady came barreling out of nowhere plucking one arrow after another from her bow into their chests, throats and eyes. By the time they had the wherewithal to draw their firearms, she was already atop the man closest to her, strangling him as she rolled him over so that he was on top, their bullets flying into his back like a pin cushion. She yanked his gas mask off his face, put it on her own, grabbed the Colt .45 from his holster, and fired. She leapt to her feet while keeping the corpse in front of her like a shield as she backed away, gunning down one heathen aft the next till she ran out of bullets.

She thrust the dead man forward into two others, threw the empty pistol into another's eye, then serpentined away. Bullets sprayed all round her but not a one connected, and she dove behind the Condemnation Rock for cover, stone fragments chipping off the holy boulder with BANGs.

"What's going on?" screamed the walkie. "Come in! Come in! Over!"

"Only an issue, boss-man," asserted the ground leader. "I own it." He pointed to a batch of his soldiers and ordered them to go after her.

Mellow panted behind the Rock as she efforted to slow her breath, and heard the footsteps approach. She could tell from the shadows cast by the after-lunch sun that there were four of them— too many if more than one had a gun, and she only had four arrows left. No margin for missing.

She rolled right, popped up to her knees with arrow drawn, observed in a flash two with swords, one with a Smith & Wesson, one with an Uzi. I want that Uzi, she thought, but her best shot was at Smith & Wesson man so she took it. Woosh-thwack! Right through his heart before he could pull the trigger. She dropped back to the dirt, rolled behind the big oak tree as the enemies' blasts whizzed beside her close enough to feel its wind.

The three that remained looked to each other and smiled. They had her. They formed a wide circle to approach from differing sides of the tree, one of the sword-men dropping his foil in exchange for the revolver. They arrived at the far side of the oak only to be astounded for no one was there. They saw the imprints in the grass showing it was where she'd gone, but nothing showing she went away, as if she disappeared into thin air.

"Hello, boys," they heard a motherly voice from above. They looked up to see the naked pregnant lady perched on a branch smiling down at them. Woosh-thwack! Dead. Woosh-thwack! Dead. Revolver-man aimed and pulled his trigger before she could fire her last arrow. Click. Out of bullets. Woosh-thwack! Dead.

She leapt out of the tree, landed in a perfect drop'n'roll, grabbing the Uzi mid-somersault. She popped back to her feet and fired, slaying some, injuring others, but the enemy artillery kept coming, and more than she could handle. She ducked back behind the oak and could sense the bark on the front side exploding off its trunk, and the heathens in turn took cover behind wood piles and over-turned picnic tables.

She waited but a moment, then popped back out and fired again, nailing one, missing two, then back behind the tree as the bullets abounded. Another moment and back out blasting, but this time mainly to confirm a hunch, then behind the tree again.

Yes, several of the ones who'd had guns had traded them in for swords, meaning they were running out of ammo too; better still, the only semi-automatics left in play were the Uzi in her hands and the tommy gun held by the one who killed Dachshund Dog. If she could just take him out . . .

She popped out again, aiming exclusively at tommy-gun man as he and everyone else fired back at her. All missed, her included, and she ducked behind the tree once more, then took a moment to squat down to make pee.

It occurred to her that the barrage of tear gas cannisters had stopped barraging, and she wondered why. Maybe they ran out. Maybe they figured they didn't need it since all the warriors were tied up. Maybe they'd been ordered down to the dwelling as reinforcements against her. Running out made the most sense—they were running out of everything else.

She popped back out from behind the tree and nailed tommy-gun man between the eyes. Yes! She turned her attention to the last two with revolvers. Slayed the first, slayed the second, aimed on their leader and fired! Click. Out of bullets!

"Get her!" he shouted.

The heathens raced toward her wielding sabers, scimitars, baseball bats, and hockey sticks, the goliath helicopter-rotor-blade man leading the charge, a musket man loading his weapon steps behind. She reached to her quiver only to remember she had shot her last arrow, and she knew she couldn't outrun them in her condition. She bent over and picked up two stones as she whisked her sling from her hip. Musket man was already taking aim and rotor-blade man only steps away, his rusty steel perched and ready to slice, but she'd taken out two men with one shot plenty'a times. She put the stones in the sling and swung.

Woosh, woosh, BANG! The sling exploded into threads in her hand before she could release as musket man's weapon smoked. A miss for him but bad news for her still. Rotor-blade man was now upon her, swinging the propellor viciously at her head. She dropped to her back as she pulled the cutter from her hip, his blade trimming off a waft of her hair on the descent, then she thrust the cutter up into his stones. BAM! The brute stopped cold, his eyes bulged out, blood dripped out his mouth, and he fell forward. She held her cutter up for him to land upon with his heart, yanked it back, squirmed out from under him, and grabbed hold the propellor as the others converged. She swung it swiftly and evenly, chopping off the knees of the first, popped to her feet, swung, and removed an arm from the next. And so she slayed as she moved forward, ever forward, taking down one heathen aft the other.

The heathen leader yanked the tommy gun from his compatriot's dead hands and took aim. "I got her!" he yelled to his men. "Gimme a clear shot!" The heathens backed off.

She knew she was too far to charge him before he'd start firing, and the rotor blade would in no way be an effective shield against such a machine. She gripped onto one edge with both hands, spun herself round in a circle three times and released it like a discus (a category for which she had won a bronze medal in the 2076 Summer Olympics.) The heathen leader opened fire as the thrust from her throw felled her to the ground. Bullets whizzed inches above her as the blade spun through the air with barely a wobble and soared into the leader's neck, pinning him to a tree for but a moment until head tipped off body and both plopped to the ground, the rusty blade remaining fixed in the trunk. She seized a scimitar from the hands of one of the fallen beside her, stood, and faked herself into an impressive position even though she'd had no actual experience with such a weapon.

The remaining heathens watched her with pause as they came to realize that their petty swords and sticks were no match for this mighty warrior. "Retreat!" shouted the presumptive next in charge, and then they ran to the beachfront in terror.

The wind off the lake had grown strong as it so often did in the late after-lunch in the moonth of technology, and the smoke from the tear gas had begun to dissipate. The warriors' eyes still burned but not so much that they hadn't been able to open them a slit to watch Mellow go. They gaped dumbfounded at the sight, unable to determine what perplexed them more—that any person could fight like that, that it was a woman, or that she was eight moonths with-child.

She made her way to the heathen leader's corpse, picked up the tommy gun, and checked its ammo. Still pretty good. She slung it over her shoulder, then yanked out the arrows from the nearby corpses and replaced them to her quiver. She moved to Thunder on the ground, removed her cutter, which was really his cutter, and sliced the duct tape from his wrists. She handed his cutter back to him and said, "Free the others," then moved on.

"Where are you going?"

"We don't want any of them coming back, now, do we?"

She pulled the walkie-talkie from the dead leader's belt, looked at it only long enough to find the "talk" button, then pressed it and said, "Come in. Come in. Over."

She waited but a moment then heard the static and then a voice. "I read you. What's going on? Over."

"Is this the person in charge? Are you 'boss-man'?"

"Who's this?"

"Are you the one in charge?"

"Yes."

"Fuck you."

She dropped the walkie to the ground, moved the tommy gun off her shoulder and to her arms, then strolled casually to the beach as she opened fire, gunning down one fleeing heathen aft the other like an old-world gangster from those old-world movies she so adored during her Baton Rouge solitude.

"Say hello to my little friend!" she quoted as she blasted away. "You think I'm a clown?! Like I'm here to amuse you?! You think I'm funny?! Say 'what' again, motherfucker! I got your Jim Crow right here, pal! Tis business not personal!"

She arrived at the beach to find the bushes and plants still aflame. Eight of the heathens had gotten away, or so they thought, floating in their little yellow life rafts halfway back to their ship atop waters deep and cold. She rechecked her ammo and saw she only had enough to slay them all if she didn't miss once, but they were too far out for such confidences. Instead, she aimed for the rafts, nailed the first with her first shot, the second with her second, watched the boats deflate, watched the heathens submerge, and watched them not come back up. She let the gun drop to the sand and removed her gas mask.

BOOM! came a cannon shell. From this distance, and with no one to worry about but herself, she could tell it wasn't going to land anywhere near her, so she remained standing calmly. "Praise, I was hoping you fellas still had some explosives left on there."

She crossed to the basket where Whisper, Steady, and their chums had hidden their hooch—gods bless their innocent little souls. She took an arrow from her quiver, doused its tip with the liquid, then held it to one of the burning bushes till it caught.

BOOM, another shell soared over her head. BOOM, another crashed ten steps to her left.

She removed the bow from her shoulder, pulled the flaming arrow back, and let 'er rip. The arrow soared up, up and away to land smack-dab in the center of the ship. She waited as a moment passed, then another, then KAPOW! The heathen craft erupted in the biggest ball of flames she'd seen since the old world died. KAPOW it erupted again, and KAPOW it erupted again, and again, and again.

She took a deep breath, let her bow drop to the sand, and sat. She looked to her tummy and smiled. "You okie?" she asked in a panting, googy-ga voice, waited as if listening to the response, then replied. "Praise." Waited again. "Oh, twas nothing, little you, just a titty-bit of a brawl, but your moma won. Yes, sweet baby, your moma saved our people."

"Demon!" she heard Thunder shout. She looked up to see her husband amid a horde of his youngest warriors who surrounded her with spears and slings drawn. "No mortal can fight how you fought!" accused her husband. "Specially not a woman!"

"Demon!" shouted the warriors. "Demon! Devil! Woman!"

Oh fuckety-fuck, she groaned. "Seriously?"

Thunder nodded to one of his men who slung a stone at her head, and all went black.

* * *

BY THE TIME she came to she was already bound at the feet with their strongest twine, her hands tied behind her back, two of Thunder's men carrying her by the legs and pits. They arrived at the base of the fishing dock where Thunder, Sandy, Leaf, and Raven the apprendix awaited, the rest of the Community standing in two long queues before them, one for men, the other women. The men carrying her placed her upright in the center of a long runner of moose and antelope hide that was twice the length of her height, hefty rolls of twine beside it. The men placed fist-sized rocks on the hide in a circle round her feet.

"Don't be dunces," she told the authorities. "I'm not a demon."

"Exactly what a demon would say," smirked Thunder. "Yet your dark magic duped my predecessor to embrace you, our Holy One to befriend you, and me to marry you."

Yeah, that last one was real hard, she sarcastically noted but said instead, "If I were a demon, wouldn't I use that same dark magic to save myself right now? So then why aren't I?"

"Nice try, demon," said Leaf. "But everyone knows that once a demon is outed its dark magic can defeat man no more." He turned to the Holy One. "Tell her."

"Tis a truth," said Sandy as he glared at her with revulsion. All her warm words of comfort to him over the calendars had been but the devil's lies. He was the sinner he'd always thought he was, and her effort to get him to accept his bad as the gods' will just more example of her evil.

But what if she speaks of my bad to the others as she'd once threatened? it occurred to him with a fright. I'll be the one to be bagged and drowned!

He spat on her feet. "Your wickedness is known, demon, your power over umanity gone. So, make your slanders against me. Your lies will be believed no longer."

A perfect circular argument, she saw, the likes of which she'd seen so many times before. But accused then guilty as charged. No room for reason to enter into it. How many versions of it over how many lifetimes had she witnessed?

"I have no slanders against you, Sandy," she sighed. "Do what you must. I get."

Interesting, he thought. "I don't need your permission, demon," he growled.

He turned to Thunder who nodded his consent to proceed, then he turned to Raven. The apprendix presented a sleek wooden box before his master then opened it to reveal two shiny, pointy stones with holes in their middles. The Holy One took one in each hand, kissed them, then looked up and whined a prayer condemning

Mellow to her unholy death. Leaf and Raven moved off in opposite directions, picked up the edges of the hide runner and carried them back to hold to Mellow's head, blanketing her from front and back.

The Holy One ended his song, and the only sounds left to be heard were the waves of the lake caressing the shore. The Sorry nodded to the first man and woman in the queue. They stepped forth and took the stones from the Holy One's hands, then kneeled by Mellow's sides, man to her right, woman to her left. They threaded the twine through the stones and began to sew the two sides of the hide together. They made nine stitches each till Mellow was bagged to the ankles, rose to take their place at the back of the line as the next couple came forth to make nine stitches more, returned to the line as the next took their place, and on and on, so that every adult of the Community could be part of the blessed event.

Few could look Mellow in her eyes while they fulfilled their solemn duty for most had liked her, had fallen for her ruse, and were ashamed because of it. Sunburst was able to throw her but a momentary glare of derision for she had almost convinced him to cheat the gods, and then he too spat on her feet; Playful, barely a confused sigh. Only young Whimsy was able to hold face for any length of time, her eyes abundant with moisture all the while. Mellow couldn't read if the new woman held sadness for participating in the execution, or if she too felt betrayed.

"Tis not true, dearest chum," said Mellow. "I'm not what they accuse."

"Don't talk," ordered the Holy One.

"What're you going to do? Slay me?"

Thunder punched her in the nose.

She was already bagged to the waist when she decided to take one final stamp at it. "You're making a terrible blunder. I saved you all from the heathen others. Me'n'me alone."

"And for what evil purpose we'll never know," said Thunder.

"Nor do we wish to," added Sandy.

"Nor do we wish to," repeated Thunder.

She sighed her final acceptance—perhaps tis for the best after all.

She'd never been able to take her own life and twas long since passed her time to go. Nothing left for her to see, nothing left for her to do; she'd seen and done it all. Her only regret was that the child inside her would never know daylight, and that she never got to fulfill this lifetime's purpose.

She was bagged to the chin as the sun began to set, and time for the Sorry and Holy One to take their honors to sew her shut for good.

"Now's your moment to speak," said Thunder. "Any final words, demon?"

"There were enemy soldiers up on the mountaintop," she advised, "the ones hurling the crying gas. You should send out a team to find them. They're likely un-weaponed."

"I already have," sneered Thunder. "Strangest demon I've ever seen. Let's close her."

Sorry and Holy One sewed the hides together over her face and atop her head. All went dark for her, and the smell stunk. She felt herself lifted from legs and pits then carried to the far end of the dock. She heard Sandy whine a new prayer that condemned her to the hellish, fiery depths of the Earth's center till time was a thing no more, felt herself swung to the left and to the right and back again, felt herself airborne, then falling, then the arctic chill of the autumnal waters.

Tis time, she said inside as she descended to the lake bottom, embracing herself for the sweet, sweet nothingness that she'd craved for so long. I'm ready.

Many moments passed before she felt the excruciating pain of the life within her tummy diminish away, and the sorrow made her cry —at least she thought it did, hard to distinguish the lake water from the tears.

Now my turn, she said inside. Tis time. I'm ready. Stop trying to hold your breath. Let the sweet nothingness take you. There's nothing left to see. Nothing new to do. You've seen and done it all, over and over and over again. Let it go. Stop holding your breath. STOP HOLDING YOUR BREATH!!!!!!

CHAPTER FIFTY-TWO

A LTHOUGH AL FOREVER DENIED it, Millie always had a sneaking suspicion that he was the one who killed Christoph. She held little remorse over the fiend's passing, but her husband's lying about it gnawed at her. *If* he was lying—he was the one who taught her so he was clearly too good at it to be certain either way. She knew he'd consider it to be for her own good, as everything he'd done over the years had been, yet there was no point in asking how deceiving her could be for her own good since any reason he'd give would be tantamount to a confession, which he wouldn't do, so she let it gnaw.

Like every morning that morning, she made him a hearty break-fast—most important meal of the day—helped him pick out his suit and tie, kissed him off to work, then lounged back on the living room couch in their swanky Manhattan co-op to enjoy the paper and her steaming cup of joe before getting ready for her improv class.

Carter, Soviets, the Cold War, rising crime, nuclear proliferation, end of the world as we know it—life as usual. She skimmed on, scanning the headlines for something new in the news when a name in a tiny article on the bottom of page nine jumped out at her. Dieter Mueller.

Mueller was a name she would never forget, but wasn't Dieter the name of the baby? She read on to confirm that it was.

The fifteen-year-old boy had been apprehended stealing a car, nothing newsworthy in itself, except that his father had been a Nazi war criminal assassinated by Israeli Mossad agents in the 1960s, said the article, referencing earlier articles. His alcoholic mother committed suicide two years later, her note citing the cause as her inability to cope with the ostracization and ridicule that befell her after her husband's evil past became known.

Millie paused to feel the sadness. She had only met Clara that one time, and she seemed a nice woman. Did she know her husband was a monster? Had she been a part of his diabolical scheme? Didn't seem likely, but then again, how do Nazi women act off duty?

She read on. After the suicide, the child spent the subsequent eleven years bouncing from one foster home to the next. His most recent family wanted nothing more to do with him, and no other would take him in under the circumstances. He was all alone.

It almost made her cry. Whether Clara was accomplice or not, the boy couldn't have been; he was just a baby at the time. Had Clara not taken her life, in what direction may her son's had gone? Would the mother have lived had the father not been murdered? Was it her own husband's doing that put this innocent child on his tragic path? Was this all somehow because of her?

She washed the gray out of her hair to return it to its natural blonde, threw on a pair of corduroy slacks, wool sweater, gaudy hoop earrings, and tinted glasses, then for the first time since she'd learned what she was, she left her home with no aging makeup applied. She snuck out the back door into the alley, crossed back to the street, and hailed a taxi to take her to the station where Dieter was being held. She signed in as his foster mother and was eventually led into a small room where he awaited.

He was short for his age, scrawny as if he hadn't had a decent meal in a year. He had shaggy brown hair and bad acne that concealed any similarity he may have otherwise had with his father. "Who the hell are you?" he contemptuously asked.

"An old friend of your mother's. Janice Foley."

"Okay, fine, whatever. What do you want?"

"Well, I read about you in the paper and—"

"I'm in the newspaper?" he brightened. "Like, I'm important?"

"Of course you're important, Dieter. Everyone's important."

"That's not the same thing," he frowned. "Come to think of it, it's not even because of me, is it? It's because of Christoph. Don't answer, I'm right. So, what do you want from me?"

"I just thought you might need a friend."

"I don't," he blustered. "By the way, nice rack."

"Don't be coarse."

"It was a compliment. Next?"

"Look, I can go if you want," she said as she rose. "Sorry to have wasted your time."

"No, wait," he squeaked with a tiny tremor in his voice, a chink in his armor exposed, just a frightened little boy. "You can stay if you want. I got nothing better to do."

"I *have* nothing better to do," she corrected.

He glared at her, but then conceded. "I *have* nothing better to do."

She sat back down, and then let him do most of the talking. It didn't take much to get him going, and it didn't take a rocket scientist to see that he had a sharp mind with much to say and no one to listen, so she listened. He never spoke of his parents, didn't dare to speak of his own difficulties or pain, but he took great pride in espousing his opinions on topics ranging from politics to TV shows to classic literature, crime stories being his favorite.

"Agatha Christie sucks," he decried. "She cheats. Like, she gives every character a motive and clues pointing their way so by the end, okay, it's that guy, could've just as easily been the other guy. Sometimes it's all of them. One time, the dead guy wasn't even dead.

"Now, Sir Arthur Conan Doyle, there's a challenge for you. He gives you just enough to figure it out, but only if you're really, really smart. So how long you been divorced?"

She laughed. "What makes you think I'm divorced?"

"That white circle thingie around your finger," he boasted. "Pretty astute of me, huh?"

"Yes, it is." Observant kid. "But no, still married, I brought the ring in for polishing."

"Oh. That was my second theory. I would've gotten it next if you hadn't told me."

Their chat was interrupted when the boy's public defender arrived. He had bags under his eyes, seemed harried, and addressed Dieter by the wrong name. Millie insisted on staying and the lawyer consented, too much on his plate to waste time arguing.

Her instincts were quickly proven right as she listened to the exhausted man lay out his plan, which was, in a nutshell, to accept the prosecution's first offer in which the boy would serve a year of detention. "I think we'll go with private counsel," Millie told him.

Dieter whispered sharply, "I don't have money for that!"

She whispered back with a wink, "I got you covered, kiddo."

The boy smiled, then turned to the lawyer and proudly said, "You're fired, asshole."

"Language," Millie admonished.

Dieter re-addressed the man. "You're fired . . . sir."

"Something in between would've sufficed," Millie tittered, "but better."

"Okie-doke by me," said the defender as he gathered up his papers, "one less case." He banged on the door. A policeman opened it, the lawyer left, and the cop turned to Millie.

"Your time's up too, ma'am."

"Guess that's all for today, kiddo," she told the boy. "I'll be back tomorrow with your new attorney." She got up and started out.

"Hey, Janice?" he blurted. She stopped by the door, whereupon Dieter made his humble, heartfelt apology. "I didn't mean it when I said you have a nice rack."

She stifled her laugh. "I'll see you tomorrow."

And thus began their friendship.

That night over dinner, she told Al that she decided not to wear her wedding ring anymore except when they went out to socialize due to the tan line that had developed over the years. "The girl I'm going to be next shouldn't look like she'd been married."

"Good thinking," he responded without giving it much thought.

She didn't, however, mention what brought her to that conclusion, nor who she met with that day. She knew what her husband would say about it, and she didn't need to hear it.

The next afternoon, she returned to Dieter with the high-priced attorney she'd hired that morning. The day after, she attended his hearing where he pled guilty to receive six months' probation and community service, no time served. After that, she had the lawyer convince the court to let her take the boy out for ice cream before being whisked off to his next family.

"So, why'd you steal a car of all things?" she asked mid-slurp. "You don't even drive."

"I dunno," he mumbled ashamedly and looked to the floor.

"Hey," she said as she put two fingers under his chin to lift up his face. "Don't do that. If you don't want to tell me, say so, that's fine, but none of this 'I dunno' business."

He took a deep breath. "I get blamed for everything anyway. A foster parent's real kid does something, they get caught, say it was me, and everyone believes them. As long as I gotta do the time I may as well enjoy the crime, to paraphrase the best show on TV ever."

"You're better than this, Dieter."

"How do you know? My father was a Nazi. I'm probably not better than anything."

"You're not your father. Your father was a—"

"Can we change the subject please? I don't like talking about him."

"Of course. What would you prefer to talk about?"

"Um . . . well . . . am I . . . you know . . . um . . . am I ever going to see you after this? Or are you just like everyone else? Pop into my life, pretend to care, then, so long, kid, nice knowin' ya."

"I'm not going anywhere," she assured him as she took a pen from her purse and wrote on a napkin. "Here's my number. Oh, but hang up if anyone other than me answers."

"You mean, your husband."

"Yes, my husband."

"So then . . . " he smiled and put his hands on hers, "we're, like, having an affair?"

"No," she smiled back as she removed them. "I'm your friend. Okay?"

"Okay."

"Come to think of it, only call in an emergency. Let's set up now to meet next Thursday, say four o'clock? Can you make your way to Greenwich Park?"

"By hook or by crook."

She returned him to the courthouse whereupon he was shipped off to his new family. He arrived at his new home, threw his stuff on his new bed, then went to his new bathroom where he and Janice made mad, passionate love in his hand.

They met the following Thursday as planned, and the one after that, and after that, and on and on. Roughly forty years before Francisco would tell her that she needed to find a purpose in her lives, she had found one, and it was him, this troubled young boy.

"How are you doing in your new school?" she asked on one occasion.

"Well, the good part is that they haven't figured out who my father was. Once they do, the beatings start."

"That's terrible." He shrugged as if business as usual. "How are your grades?"

"I'm passing."

"Dieter! You should be doing a lot better than just passing."

"Why? I could work hard to get A's, or just breeze it and take the C's. What's the diff?"

"The diff is you're too smart for C's. You're a smart boy. Are you doing your homework? Don't answer, of course you're not. I want you to start doing your homework. Better still, I want to check it."

"You kidding me?" he laughed at her. "No one's ever asked to check my homework."

"Maybe that's why you're only getting C's. Next Thursday, I want to see the whole week's worth, done thoroughly and neatly."

He stared at her in disbelief, then muttered, "Okay."

The following week, they met at the same picnic table in the park and she went through his notebooks. "This is very good, Dieter," she said. "Very good indeed. Nice job."

"Well thank God that's over with."

"Nothing's over with. I want to see the same due diligence next week."

"Sheez, how long are you going to keep this up?"

"Until I'm satisfied that you're getting your work done without me. Let's go walking."

"Sheez," he repeated as he shoved his books into his backpack and followed.

"So, what do you want to be when you grow up?" she asked.

"Dead."

"Stop that. If you could have any career you want, what would it be?"

"I don't know. What does your husband do?"

"Let's keep our focus on you."

"Just tell me. What's his job?"

"He's done many different things over the years."

"What was he when you married him?"

"He was a policeman."

"Then that's what I'll be."

She smiled. "Yes, I think you'd be very good at that."

He smiled back, but by the following week, he had a change of heart.

"I can't be a cop, Janice. I don't want to work with other people. They'll hear my name, connect me to Christoph, and it'll be the same shi—stuff all over again."

"If that's the only reason, you can change your name, you know."

"I can?"

"Legally not till you turn eighteen, but absolutely."

He smiled, then frowned as he reconsidered once more. "No, then I won't have anything. I mean, I know my father was a terrible man and my mom a sick woman, but they're my only family. Changing my name away from them just feels, I don't know, lonely."

"I can see that," she sighed, relating in a way that only she could.

"Hey, I know. Make it similar so you'll always remember who you are, but different enough so that no one else can. Let's see. Dieter, beeter, keeter, leeter, meter, peter—Peter! You can be Peter."

"I like that. And for my last name . . . Bueller, Cueller, Grueller, no, it won't work! No matter what, it still sounds German. Wait! Wait, wait. Mueller, m-m-m, Mailor. I'll be Peter Mailor."

She smiled and held out her hand to shake. "A privilege to meet you, Peter Mailor."

As winter turned to spring, spring to summer, summer to fall, and fall back to winter, the boy grew ever more open, ever more trusting. When she said she no longer needed to check his home-work since he was by then getting straight A's, he said he wanted her to anyway. On one encounter, he even asked her about his mother and why she abandoned him the way she did, but then quickly changed the subject before Millie could get a word out. Still, it was progress.

"You know, I never kissed a girl," he confessed one afternoon.

"You will," she smiled encouragingly.

"No, I won't. Look at me. I'm ugly. What girl worth kissing would want to kiss me?"

"You're not ugly; and girls don't care about that. We care about what's inside."

"Can I kiss you?"

She sighed. "No, Peter, you can't. That's not the kind of friend-ship we have."

"Then can I . . . you know . . . um, can I . . . Janice, may I . . . touch your chest?"

"Peter . . ."

"Just once? Just for a sec? Just so I know what it's like. No one else will ever let me."

She took his hands and looked into his eyes. "Some girl will, I promise."

"I love you."

"I love you too, kiddo, but what you're asking is not appropriate. Tell you what. You want a kiss? Here." She leaned in and kissed him on the cheek.

"That's not what I meant," he brooded.

"I know," she smiled, "but it's all you're going to get, mister, so you may as well cherish it." He laughed a little laugh, and that's when she saw Al strolling through the park with some colleagues. Their eyes caught briefly, then they turned away quickly, both well aware that the fifty-six-year-old banker had no earthly reason to know hot, young Janice.

But that night . . .

"Are you out of your friggin' mind?!" Al shouted after hearing the full story. "Do you not grasp the danger you're putting yourself in?"

"Al, you have no idea what this boy's been through," she countered as she launched into the argument she never wanted to have. "And no idea how far he's come."

"That doesn't matter. It's a crazy, unnecessary risk. No! It's too dangerous for you."

"How could it be a risk? No one's come after me for fourteen years."

"That doesn't mean they're not watching you. Or maybe they're watching *him* for some reason and stumble upon you by accident, still forever young, and there's their absolute proof. Or something else entirely. We don't know anything, honey. In fact, what the heck, you should've at least aged yourself! Goddammit, if someone out there's already wondering about you, going out all youthful and blonde, that's the ballgame."

She sighed, seeing the folly of that particular tactic. "It was in case I ran into one of our friends," she muttered. "I didn't want to look like the Millie they know. I didn't want to have to explain my connection to the boy."

"Well, it was a mistake. I love you so much, baby, you know I do, but unlike you, I'm not going to be around forever. You've got to stop making mistakes."

"Got to stop making mistakes, got it. But I have to see this through, Al. You murdered this child's father for me—for me! I know you did. I'm the reason his life turned out so miserably. If I don't reach out to help him . . . "

"Honey," he began softly, "I told you, I had nothing to do with Christoph's death, so it had nothing to do with you. Nothing. You're no more responsible for this kid's plight than you are for any of the other suffering children in the world, and you can't save the world. The only question is, do you really want to chance being captured by the next Christoph?"

"Sweetie, after all this time, the odds of the scenarios you describe are so—"

"What if they're one in a hundred? In a thousand? Is there any number that would make this a smart bet? A million? Tell me the number that makes being kidnapped and tortured and raped again a gamble worth taking."

She paused, reflected quietly, then sighed. As usual, her big idiot was right. But shoot, you know? "Fine. I'll end it when I see him next Thursday. I don't know how I'm—"

"No. You can't see him next Thursday, not ever. If bad guys have been watching him and haven't spotted you yet, let's just chalk that up to dumb luck and not push it."

"I can't just disappear on him!"

"You have to."

She buried her head helplessly on his shoulder. "I don't want to."

He hugged her and answered tenderly, "I know."

The following Thursday, Dieter arrived at the park to find Janice a no-show. He considered phoning her, but she had said only in emergencies. She'd like that he honored her request, how very mature of him. He'll find out what's what next week. But she was a no-show that Thursday too, and the one after that, and his greatest fears flooded his mind. No, he told himself, she wouldn't, not her, not Janice, not my Janice. He took the train home and made the call. A man answered.

"May I speak to Janice please?"

Al stood by the phone on the kitchen wall while Millie did the Times crossword puzzle at the table. He took a breath as he pondered the best way to proceed. She needs this, he told himself, she needs the closure. He held out the receiver. "It's for Janice."

Millie clenched her eyes in dread, then stood and took the phone. "Hello."

"Janice! What's going on?" She could hear his tears. "Why aren't you coming?!"

"I'm sorry, Peter," she began, the lump in her throat feeling bigger than the neck that contained it. "We can't see each other anymore. I'm so sorry."

"No! Don't! Not you! Please?! It's because I asked to touch your chest, isn't it? I didn't mean it!"

"No, Peter, it's not that, you did nothing wrong."

"Then why?!"

"I'm sorry, good-bye, good luck," and she hung up. She could see Al moving toward her to hug her his empathy. "Don't talk to me!" was all she said to him and then stomped off.

For young Dieter, the depth of the loss was too much to bear so he reshaped his sorrow into the far more comfortable anger and hate. "Fuck you!" he scolded the phone as if it were Janice herself. "No, you did me a favor, bitch. You taught me a lesson. Never trust nobody. Many others taught me it before but never good as you, so fuck off. Suffer and die."

* * *

BACK TO NOW.

"Hello, Peter," said Myla as she sat on the hotel room chair in her pink t-shirt and jean cutoffs, her glorious legs daintily crossed with a little throw cushion upon her lap. "It's been a long time."

The fifty-six-year-old man was thrown by her presence but had no intention of letting her see it. "Only about two years since the pool hall," he dispassionately corrected.

"Pool hall?" She tried to decode what he was talking about, and then it hit her. Pool hall. Queens. The hustler, Lucas. Him, the mark. "That was you. Yeah. You thought I looked familiar."

"And you didn't recognize me at all."

"You've changed a lot more than I have."

"Okay, let's get this over with," he said as he reached to his holster.

"Ah, ah, ah," she said as she revealed her own pistol that she held pointed at him from under the cushion. "Now, slowly and with two fingers only, take your gun and place it on that table." He did. "Good boy. So, before we get to business, it's important to me that you know . . . Peter, of all the mistakes I've made in my life, and I've made plenty, abandoning you how I did is the one I most regret. Truly. You were a good kid. Troubled, yes, but sweet. You deserved better, so much better. I am so sorry."

"Why are you here? You got away. You could've run."

"I need to know who's after me, Peter. Who do you work for? Is it Treasury again, or another department this time?" He laughed. "I said something funny?"

"I don't work for anyone, bitch. I work only for me. This whole thing came about because of how stupid you are. You always thought you were so smart, but you're a fucking idiot."

"You're still angry with me. That's fair. I understand. How am I an idiot?"

He gestured toward the suitcases on the bed. "May I?"

"Slowly." She kept her gun on him as he opened the valise and removed the 1954 Polaroid of her and Al. Her mouth gaped open in shock upon the sight of it, which he enjoyed.

He went on to boast how he came to find it, of the photo he had taken of her at the pool hall, his father's dossier, Szabo, the tobacco barons, the new lab and all its terrors; and he took great delight from the horror on her face as he bragged how it was he who had convinced Szabo to resurrect the unsterblich project, he who had convinced the man to keep the project going even after all the backing had dried up, his promise that he alone would find her, and his sheer brilliance in doing so.

"I always said you were smart," she replied in earnest.

"Yeah, but you never knew how smart, did you? Who'd have ever thunk it'd be the mad Nazi's fucked-up son who'd bring you back in and get it started all over again?"

"Except I'm the one holding the gun."

"You're not going to shoot me, Janice. You wouldn't destroy me a second time. You don't have it in you. You'll beat me up or something, maybe—seems you're pretty good at that—but if you get away, I'll find you. If you get away again, I'll find you again. I got no wife, no girl, my life is forever dedicated to sticking you in Szabo's cage like the pathetic lab rat you are to watch you suffer . . . then immortality for all! Yay! Hell, maybe the good doctor will even let me do some of the torturing myself."

He's obsessed with me, she realized, and I'll be running from him till he's too old to chase me. But how can I run with two babies on my back? We'll never be safe. *They'll* never be safe as long as they're with me. Except I can't leave them behind, I have no one to leave them with. My friends are wonderful, but I've only known them a year, they can't be expected to raise my children for me.

I can't take my babies with me and I can't leave them behind. How did I miss this? Stupid!

Got to stop making mistakes, Myla.

She could see only one way out, and it was unacceptable. Unless . . . unless . . . and a new idea began to take form. Far better than the alternative, and she owed him at least that. It was fair. Yes, there's always another way.

"Let's end this," she said. She slid the tie off her ponytail, shook her head so her luscious red locks went wild, then she put down her gun on the table beside her. She rose and glided enticingly toward him. "Let me take care of you, Peter," she purred. He froze for a moment, confused or mesmerized he couldn't be sure, then he lunged for his Glock. "Shh," she whispered as she took his hands, removed the pistol, and put it back on the table. He didn't know why he let her, but he did.

"What are you doing?" he gulped, all his bluster gone.

"Let me make it up to you, Peter," she soothed as she moved his hands to the small of her back and put her arms around his neck. "I don't want to spend my life on the run, and you won't have to waste any more of yours chasing me, because you already have me."

"Stop it."

"I have money, lots of money. We can go anywhere, French

Riviera, Bora Bora, anywhere you want; and wherever we go, everyone will be wondering what that old dude's got going on that he can score this hot, young chick."

"You're only doing this so you can get close enough to take me out."

"Could've done that already, kiddo. No, I wronged you, Peter. I was afraid that contact with you would lead to me being outed." She ran her fingers through his hair. "But I have been outed, by you, my clever boy. Let me right my wrong. Let me make you happy."

"I hate you!"

"No, you're just angry with me. Seems you've been so for a very long time, but I have a feeling you've wanted me all that time still; and now you can have me."

"You—you have kids. I saw their cribs."

"You can be their daddy if you want, or Uncle Peter, or just a friend of their mom's. Whatever you want, I'll make it work. I've become very good at making things work."

"No. Stop. I don't know!"

"It's everything you've ever wanted, Peter, just take it. Just take me."

"Stop!"

"Can I kiss you?" she asked him as he had asked her so long ago, only she didn't wait for his answer, merely pressed her luscious lips to his, and put his hand to her breast.

He melted like ice cream on a hot summer day. He had dreamed this dream for so long, except this time it wasn't a dream. She was his boyhood crush unchanged after decades, his movie star pinup girl come to life, the only mother he'd ever known, his masturbatory fantasy queen. I love you! his head screamed; I hate you! Her tongue slid into his mouth. His cock throbbed and a tear rolled down his cheek, and he removed the stun gun from his jacket pocket and zapped her with twelve-hundred volts of electricity. She writhed and quaked and fell to the ground immobilized by the pain. He dropped to his knees and handcuffed her hands behind her back, zapped her again to keep her still, then cuffed her feet at the ankles.

By the time her world came back into focus, he was seated on the chair by the window as she had been earlier, smiling down at her in gloating triumph, all his bluster back.

"Seems my desire to fuck you supersedes my desire to fuck you," he chuckled.

"Don't do this, Peter. I beg you."

"I like that. I've often imagined you begging me. Keep it up." He stood, put his hands under her armpits, and yanked her up to her feet. "Let's go, Mildred. It's a long drive to Virginia."

"You don't understand. Don't make me do this, Peter. Please! Let me make you happy."

"This is making me happy," he laughed. "Thank you. Can't wait to hear your screams."

"This isn't who you are, Peter. Please don't make me do this!"

He spun her around to face him. "This is exactly who I am, bitch," he seethed. "This is who you made me to be, so fuck you. Fuck you Janice, Mildred, Molly, Myla. Fuck you, cunt."

"I know," she mourned with tearful acceptance, then bashed her forehead into his nose. He stumbled back, blood spurting. She pivoted hard and rammed her shoulder up into his jaw to send the back of his head crashing into the wall behind him, and he dropped to the ground unconscious. She squatted down upon his chest, removed the keys from his pocket, unlocked the cuffs from her hands and feet, and then looked into his closed eyes as she began to cry.

"Why couldn't you just let me take care of you?!" she wept as she reached for the cushion on the chair and placed it on his face. "Why couldn't you let me make you happy? Why'd you make me do this?!" She pushed the cushion down hard and the unconscious man, her precious little Dieter, wasn't even aware that he was dying as he died. "I could've made you happy!" she wailed. "I wanted to! I told you so! Why wouldn't you let me?! Why'd you make me do this?!!!"

She could feel his life slowly drift away. She removed the cushion and checked his vitals to confirm it. She lied down next to him and rested her head upon his chest. "You were a good kid, Peter," she sobbed. "Troubled, yes, but sweet. You didn't deserve this. I am so sorry!"

And that is how it came to pass that the ninety-six-year-old woman made her first slay.

She remained weeping on his chest for minutes or hours, she couldn't tell, then pulled herself together. The girls. Lori and Francine. They're all that matter now. No more mistakes.

She stood, got a washcloth from the bathroom, brushed her fingerprints off everything she had touched, picked up her purse, and headed to the door. She stopped, returned, retrieved the Polaroid, then walked out of the room to go plan her wedding.

CHAPTER FIFTY-THREE

The Dwelling
The Night Of The Day The Demon Was Drowned

THE DRUMS POUNDED AND the whistle bones crooned, and the hooch was cold and plentiful. The honkytonk that night was among the rowdiest they could remember for they knew it a day that would live in their lore till time was a thing no more. They had defeated the wicked techno-heathens, had discovered the traitorous demon who had lived amongst them, and destroyed her. Songs of Thunder's glory were already being crafted, history re-written in real time.

Son-of-Moon, a manling of fourteen calendars, and Daughter-of-Sharey, just shy of thirteen, smooched under a tree near the dock of the lake. The young hopefuls knew it not permitted, but they also knew that unless Son-of-Moon hurried up and made first slay soon their time together was running out.

"What is that?" Daughter-of-Sharey asked out of the bloom as she noticed a movement in the waters. "Is that a, a person? Is that—"

The manling turned to where she pointed, and his jaw dropped open. "Oh my gods."

"Then I'm right?" the girl asked affrighted. "It's, it's—"

"We—we have to tell the Sorry," the boy answered affrighted "We have to tell all!"

"No, we'll find in trouble."

"We'll find in trouble more if we don't tell of it. Come!" He took her hand and together they raced to the honkytonk. "She's back! Back from the lake! Mellow has risen from the dead!"

The music stopped and all turned to him. "Of what you speak, manling?" snapped the Sorry, but before his ask needed answer, they all saw it. Mellow, clear as clear, dazedly walking toward them, ripped shards of animal hide draped upon her like a pauper's rags.

She stopped and looked at them awkwardly as they stared back in shock. She knew she had to say something, anything, but nothing close to reasonable came to her brain.

"I . . . I . . . I am the god Mellow," she said because she couldn't think of anything better. They gawked at her wide-eyed, confused, affrighted, bewildered. She couldn't tell if they were buying it, but they weren't *not* buying it, so she went with it. "I am the god Mellow!" she repeated with gusto. "I was here when the old world died and here when the old world thrived! I live forever and I know all that can be known!"

"Liar!" shouted Thunder as he pulled his cutter from his hip and charged.

She captured his arm with ease, jutted out her hip, flipped him over her side and down to the ground, his arm twisting in mid-flight causing the cutter to drop from his hand. With his weapon on the dirt, his elbow locked and ready to crack in her inescapable hold, her foot pressed firmly into his larynx, she stared icily down into his eyes. "I am the god Mellow, and we are very disappointed with your leadership."

"Off of me!" he shouted as he struggled to free himself. "Turn me loose, demon!"

"Nuh-uh-uh," she began. "Everyone knows that once a demon is outed its magic can defeat man no more, so then how could I be demon?" She turned to Sandy. "Tell him."

It all made sense, thought Sunburst. He remembered wondering how she could lay a moral test upon him when only a god could do so, and now it made sense. He remembered pondering so many calendars ago if she were an angel come to save his darling Love, and he remembered his precious wife healthing so long as Mellow lived within his cabin. Yes, it all made sense.

"Praise the god Mellow!" he shouted as he dropped to his knees and put his face to the dirt and flailed his arms in exultation. "Hail her goodness and glory!"

Yes, it all made sense, thought Sandy. From her very first night amongst them, she knew of his wickedness without being told, and she came to him to offer comfort. She could've spilled the beanery on him as he officiated her execution, yet she didn't—he couldn't make logic of that, till now. And all her questionable antics over the calendars had been only on behalf of others—for Whimsy, for 3, for so many, but never for herself. And she knew things a woman couldn't know—that Horizon himself didn't know—that no mortal could know. Only one ancient as a god could know all the things she knew. Yes, it all made sense.

"Hail the god Mellow!" he shouted as he too dropped to the ground in veneration. "Pity your lowly critters, pity your mistake!"

She's my chum, thought Whimsy. "Yippee the god Mellow!" she shouted as she fell.

"Don't be dunces!" Thunder shouted as he continued the struggle. "She's a demon!"

She gave me a forgiveness, thought Playful. I never got the how of it aft I'd been so cruel to her and weak, but yes, only a god could grant such a forgiveness. "Praise'd be her holy name!" she shouted and dropped, and her betrayal brought a tear to Thunder's eye.

One by one, each, having been touched by Mellow in one way or another over the six calendars she'd been amongst them, dropped to the ground to praise her glory, and Mellow's new plan began to take shape. It was dastardly, it was vicious, and it was perfect. Her lifetime's purpose would soon be complete.

On and on they dropped and on and on they worshipped until only Leaf remained standing. She turned to him with a patient, friendly, all-knowing smile, and his lips quivered. He looked to his brethren on the ground round him, and at last he too kneeled. "Hail the god Mellow."

"Boon," said Mellow, "that's everyone." She released Thunder and stood, looked down upon him and said, "Get up. Don't forget your cutter, you're going to need it."

Thunder picked up the cutter and stood, then quickly raised it to the heavens and charged her once more. "Demon!" he shouted and was once more felled to the ground and pinned.

"Had enough?" she asked good-naturedly. "Let's try this again, shall we?" She stood and held out her hand. With confusions that bordered on paralysis, Thunder put his palm in hers and let her help him up. "The cutter," she reminded. He picked it up and tucked it by his hip, and she moved in close. "You won your position on a cheat and lie, Thunder. You slay your own children, and you give cruelty to their momas."

Then she turned to the rest, pacing before them like an army drill sergeant of old. "And you, you honor him for his wickedness and sing songs of his praises. You know nothing of the laws of harmony-with. A god lived amongst you, and you couldn't feel her presence. A god lived amongst you, and you sought to slay her. Tsk-task, for shame.

"Vengeance is mine! sayeth the god Mellow, and so I banish you all to the hellish, fiery depths of the Earth's center to burn till time is a thing no more." The men gulped and gasped, the women began to cry. "BUT," she added with a forgiving pout, "perhaps tis not your fault entirely, perhaps you'd been led astray. With a selfless act, perhaps we'll allow your Sorry to save your souls, if he so desires, if he has the stones." She turned to Thunder, swiftly snatched the cutter from his hip then calmly presented it to him. "Save your people, Thunder. Take your life."

He looked at her in wide-eyed disbelief. He took the cutter as if to comply, raised and thrust, "Demon!" only to find himself once again pinned to the dirt.

"I can do this all night, you know," she smiled. "Get up." She released him, picked up the cutter, then turned back to the others as she twirled the cutter round and round in her hand like a magic

456

prop. "The great Satin, the devil himself awaits, and he deserves his just desserts. The question is, for whom does he wait? What say you, Leaf? Who shall burn till time is a thing no more? You and everyone, or your Sorry alone?"

Leaf looked to her as his eyes began to water. He looked to his best chum to whom he owed so much, yet he couldn't hold his gaze. He looked to the dirt and shamefully muttered, "The Sorry should burn."

For Thunder, that betrayal was the greatest cut of all.

"You were named well, Leaf," said the god, "for you sway easily with the wind. But why tell me? To all of you, it's your Sorry who needs the convincing, not me. So, convince."

"Take your life, Thunder, my Sorry, my bestest chum," Leaf uttered with his greatest sadness. "Save us. Save your people."

"Protect your people, Thunder!" shouted Sunburst. "Prove your worthiness at last!"

"Accept your fate, Thunder!" shouted Sandy. "Die!"

"Die, Thunder!" screamed Playful. "Slay yourself and die! Save us!"

Each and every joined in with words of their own, but all to the same effect. "Die!"

Mellow turned back to him with a smile and held out the cutter. "Your people have spoken, husband."

He took the cutter slowly from her hand then raised it fast and high to strike. She didn't flinch, and he stopped as he realized its futility. He passed it back to her. "You do it. You slay me."

"If the gods take one life, we take them all. No, you must give it, or your people burn forever."

"Don't be a coward, Thunder!" "Make this sacrifice!" "Show your stones!" "Die!"

"If I commit this selfless act," the Sorry sniffled, "if I do this on behalf of my people of my own accord, will the gods see my atonement? Will I ascend to their warm embrace?"

"No," she answered coldly. "You will descend to the centerest center of the Earth's center where it burns the hottest, where the devil Satin himself will love you up the asshole with his stick large as oak tree every morn and every eve till time is a thing no more."

"P-p-please?" he sobbed.

"No."

"Die, Thunder!" "Don't be a scaredy-hare!" "Save us!" "Slay yourself!" "Die!"

"Thrust deep in below the belly button," Mellow explained as she pantomimed the motion, "then hard and fast up till you hit bone."

"Please!" he wailed. "Grant me but one calendar to atone my wickedness. Pleeease!!"

"Die, you coward!" "Die, crying baby!" "Die, little girl!" "Do it! Do it!" "Die, coward!"

"Deep in below the belly button, then hard and fast up till bone."

"I beg your mercy, god Mellow wise and mighty. Pleeeeeeease."

"Deep below the belly button, then hard and fast up till bone."

He looked to his people screaming their contempt for him and he could stand it no longer. With tears raining down his face, he stabbed the cutter in below his belly button then fast up till he hit bone, then he plopped to the dirt with his insides gushing out, the last image in his brain being the devil's rape, his last thought that it would be his eternity.

For the first time in her many lifetimes, Mellow had failed to fulfill the vow she had made on the souls of her progeny. Yes, she had Thunder disgraced before his people, yes, he had felt the tortuous torment of spirit and body both, and yes, he had sobbed like a little baby girl before them, but no, she hadn't laughed in his face for t'would be out of character for a god to do so, and no, he hadn't died by her hands . . . for this was far more satisfying.

The others remained on their knees as they crawled to her, encircled her, groping at the rags of hide that draped over her body yet not daring to touch the actual skin of a god.

"Praise the god Mellow!" "Yippee Mellow!" "Grant us your pity, oh god Mellow!"

She looked down upon her people with a new curiosity.

I've never been a god before, she mused. This could be interesting.

Thank You!

Indie books and authors rely on support from their readers. If you enjoyed this book, please take a moment to leave a review. Thank you!

GRATITUDES

The worst advice anyone can give to a young writer, to any writer for that matter, is "write what you know." Can you imagine a world in which all writers of fiction only wrote what they knew? Every book, movie, TV show or play would be about writers! How ridiculously boring. Granted, *Fools Die* by Mario Puzo was a terrific book, *Adaptation* a tremendous movie, and *The Dick Van Dyke Show* a classic sitcom for good reason—but every single work of fiction? Count me out.

Besides, why would any bona fide storyteller want to focus only on him or herself? The most fun part of creating fiction is to escape your own reality, just as it's the most fun part for the reader/audience to absorb it.

That said, the writer still has to get things right. If you're going to talk about concepts and worlds unknown to you, you're going to have to do a little digging to keep it feeling real, especially if your main premise so very much isn't.

In my case, that part's fun too. Only because I know so little about so much did I get to meet some truly brilliant and inspiring people who I would have had no reason to otherwise contact.

Several have become good friends. (Some were good friends already —all my friends are smarter than me. I'm not threatened by it.)

As you read on, you may notice that, in some instances, I used more than one expert in a given field. That's because I do my research backwards. The forward, normal way to do research, as I'm sure you know, is to learn everything you need to know about a topic and only once on solid ground do you begin to write about it. Me, I just make it up best I can and then seek out the proper experts to correct me after it's done. So, it would happen from time to time that an expert I began with would become too busy to continue helping when I'd return with additional needs, and so I would seek out a new expert in the field.

Since biology and genetics lie at the very foundation of this story, I'll begin there. Caltech Professors Christina Su, Sara Cohen, and Prashant Bhat not only corrected my mistakes, but added cool and nifty scientific tidbits that I never would have thought of. I thank each of you for your time and generosity.

Did I mention that I began this project knowing hardly anything about genetics? Well, I knew even less about herbology, but thanks to Talal Al Hamad and "Doc" Rob Streisfeld you'd never know it. Gratitude to you both.

For the fighting sequences, my full appreciation goes out to Kevin Kelton, Jay Lindhom and Bobby Schaul; for UCLA-law-school-living in the 2010s, Ashley Phillips, Nancy Nam, and Arian Zadech; for the gumshoe section, fire inspection section, and Oklahoma details, to my dear friend and favorite jack-of-all-trades, J. Craig Stiles; for the official police work, to NJPD Detective Julia Torres (who also has the unique distinction of offering her expertise on all my books to date); for skydiving, to George Calder (who has the distinction of trying to convince me to do it); for sailing, to Roger West; for NYC details, to Tyler Abugov; for women's apparel, to Maureen Weigen-Liebovitz; for the ins and outs of trailer park living, to Barry Burko; and to my wonderfully anal copy-editor, Charles Horn.

Last but absolutely not least, my greatest thanks must go to my dear friends who gave their time to read this story and provide their honest, sometimes brutal feedback. Some read it as a completed

THE GIRL WHO WOULDN'T DIE

whole, others in the three different sections months and months apart. Only because they would sometimes say the pages were confusing, or stupid, or dull, hurting my feelings terribly, was I able to believe them when they finally told me they loved it, giving me the inner confidence to reveal my insanity to the world. Without being able to quantify their invaluable help, I can only think to list them alphabetically. My heartfelt gratitude to Aria McKenna, Dave Zobel, Don Foster, Gary Loder, J. Craig Stiles, Julie Kenner, Maureen Weigen-Liebovitz, and Nancy Quinn. You guys are amazing!

Lastly, I want to thank you, dear readers, for getting this far. I take that to mean that you enjoyed this tale (because hardly anyone reads the acknowledgements part of a book), and I hope you will continue to enjoy Millie's ongoing saga. I'll do my best on my end.

Thank you, all.

ABOUT THE AUTHOR

 JEFF ABUGOV began his professional career writing freelance for the NBC hit *Cheers* for which he eventually became a staff writer and then story editor. He served as executive story editor on *The Golden Girls*, then went on to write and produce such hit shows as *Roseanne* and *Two and a Half Men*. He served as executive producer of *Roc, Grace Under Fire*, and the animated series *Fugget About It*. He also wrote and directed the feature film *The Mating Habits of the Earthbound Human*, starring David Hyde Pierce, Carmen Electra, and Lucy Liu. He has received a Golden Globe Award, a Peabody Award, and three People's Choice Awards, as well as being nominated for a Humanitas Prize, a Canadian Screen Award, and a second Golden Globe.

Join Jeff Abugov on the internet at www.jeffabugov.com.

You can sign up for Jeff's newsletter or email him at: www.jeffabugov.com/contact.

ALSO BY JEFF ABUGOV

Novels

Time Travel for Love and Profit

Zombies vs. Aliens vs. Vampires vs. Dinosaurs

Short Stories

The Autobiography of @

Visit Jeff at WWW.JEFFABUGOV.COM. He'd love to hear from you.